The Christmas Eve Secret

Book 3

Book 3

A Time Travel Novel by

Elyse Douglas

COPYRIGHT

The Christmas Eve Secret
Copyright © 2019 by Elyse Douglas
All rights reserved

ISBN: 9781089876564

All the days and all the nights have led me here with you, and there are more mysteries to come.

—Louisa Chapman

Time is really the only capital that any human being has, and the only thing he can't afford to lose.

—Thomas A. Edison

To our readers, who have faithfully and, we trust, happily, journeyed with us to times past with Eve and Patrick Gantly.

The Christmas Eve Letter - Book 1

The Christmas Eve Daughter - Book 2

The Christmas Eve Secret - Book 3

THE CHRISTMAS EVE SECRET

CHAPTER 1

Early in the night, fine, glittering snowflakes began to fall, blurring the gleaming towers of Manhattan, slowing traffic and dusting the sidewalks. Soon, the snow was swarming the amber streetlights and sugar-coating dark, bare trees in Central Park.

Dog-walkers emerged from lighted doorways, searching the sky, breath smoking. In the Park, they strolled along white-ribbon paths as their dogs barked and romped, as children reached for snow with outstretched fingers and licking tongues.

As the night lengthened, snow flew down on swift, whispering currents of wind, in misty clouds, glazing cars and wrought-iron gates, accumulating on roofs, balconies and windowsills.

Deeper into the night, fat flakes sailed on the wind circling the cathedrals, the shops and the brownstones, making a pleading moan as if the night were troubled and calling out for help.

Eve Gantly sat up with a start, searching the darkness. "Patrick... Patrick are you there?"

Patrick stirred slowly, a ragged snore fading into the silence. "Yes..."

He rolled over, his eyes flickering open, and he saw Eve sitting up in silhouette. "What's the matter? Bad dream?"

Eve's voice sounded strange and far away. "Yes."

Patrick lifted on an elbow. "Need to talk?"

He reached, switched on the three-way bedside lamp to dim, and then sat up, looking at her, concerned. When their eyes met, Patrick saw a strangeness in Eve's.

"What is it?"

Eve shivered. "I just feel weird, like I'm not quite in my body or something. It's the way I feel after I've just time traveled and part of me is still swirling around out there."

She touched her stomach.

"Is it the baby?" Patrick asked.

"Yeah, that's some of it, I think."

"Any pain?"

"No... Nothing like that. The baby's fine. I just feel this kind of foreboding."

"Describe foreboding."

"I don't know... like a premonition or something. I feel like I'm half asleep and half awake. Part of me in one world, part in another."

"Like a lucid dream?" Patrick asked.

Eve looked at him soberly and ran a hand through her hair. "Patrick, ever since I got pregnant, I just haven't felt right. I can't quite explain it."

"Women often feel different when they get pregnant, don't they? Especially when it's the first?"

"Yes, but I just can't shake this feeling… that something just isn't right or that something, I don't know what, but that something bizarre is going to happen. I try to push it away, but it always comes back, like now, in the middle of the night."

Patrick reached and stroked her hair, listening to the squeal of the wind outside.

"I know you, Eve. You're not telling me everything because you don't want to upset me. So don't worry about upsetting me and tell me everything."

Her stare was honest and sharp. "Patrick, I want to get rid of the lantern. Once and for all. I just want to get rid of it. I don't want it around anymore."

They locked gazes. He nodded. "I had the feeling it was something like that."

"Now that we're going to have a baby, we don't need it. We don't need to keep it or hide it. I don't want it in our apartment anymore. I don't want it in my thoughts. I don't want it in my closet, tucked away in that little safe, waiting, like some hibernating thing that's waiting to be awakened. We don't need it and there's no reason to keep it."

"All right. What do you want to do with it?"

"Take it down to the Hudson River, bash it to pieces with a hammer and toss it into the river."

Patrick ran a thoughtful hand over his stubble of a beard.

"Can you think of any reason to keep it?" Eve asked.

"Reason? No, I guess not."

"But…?" Eve said, lifting a curious eyebrow.

"Okay, I have two questions. First, I've always wanted to know where the lantern came from. I know we've talked about this, but how is it that an old lantern, when lighted, glows with a light that somehow transports us to another time? It just boggles my mind. It makes no logical or reasonable sense. That lantern had to have a beginning. Something or someone had to, I don't know, program it or something."

As he left the bed, wearing only dark blue pajama bottoms, he turned back to her with a question.

"So I'd like to know: where did that lantern come from?"

"We're not going to know, Patrick. It's a secret, and it's always going to remain a secret."

Eve studied her handsome husband: his thick curly hair, the steady blue eyes, prominent nose, and solid, determined jaw. She never grew tired of looking at his body: the broad, hairy chest, muscular neck and good shoulders.

"Where are you going?" Eve asked.

"To the boy's room and for some bottled water. Be right back."

Eve rested her head into the pillow, still unable to shake that uneasy feeling of dread.

Patrick returned and handed the half-drunk bottle to Eve. She took a swallow.

"What time is it?" she asked.

"After three."

"How much snow do you think we have?"

"Five or six inches."

"It doesn't usually snow this much in early November," Eve said, handing the bottle back to Patrick. He tipped it back and drained it.

"Okay, my second question. Why should we destroy the lantern?"

"It's not like it's a person or anything, Patrick. It's a thing. It's not really alive."

"It certainly seems alive to me and, anyway, it's not like it has ever harmed us. If anything, it's helped us. It brought us together, and it helped save my daughter, Maggie, from a terrible fate. And we don't know what might happen in the future. We might need it again."

Eve stared at the ceiling, not meeting his gaze. "We're never going to know where it came from, Patrick. That's going to stay a mystery. And as for it being harmful, I feel like the longer we keep the thing, the more it has the potential to hurt us."

"But why? That's what I don't get."

Eve sat up again. "I don't know. I just feel it. In the last few weeks, I feel threatened by it. I know that's not rational, but there it is. And we'll never use the thing again. Why would we? And we certainly can't hand it over to anyone else, and we can't leave it to anyone in our will. So why not destroy it now and be done with it?"

Patrick looked at his pretty wife, her heart-shaped face, broad forehead, strong cheekbones and blueberry-colored eyes that stared back at him with direct intelligence. He loved her steadfast manner—the determined energy she used to confront and overcome any problem. She was smart, unswerving and warm, often all at the same time. Her honey-blonde hair fell around her shoulders in a sexy, careless way, and he often found it difficult to keep his hands from reaching for her, even at times like this.

He dropped the empty bottle into the wicker waste basket and climbed back into bed, sitting up, pulling the sheet up to his waist. His eyes shifted in thought.

"So I think we should name our boy Sean," he said.

"That was a quick change of subject."

"Yes, well, I've been giving his name a lot of thought lately.

"What makes you think our baby will be a boy?"

"I feel it."

"Well, I'm feeling like it's going to be a girl and I think we should name her Anjelica."

Patrick tried the name out. "Anjelica. Nice name. Very nice name, but I was thinking more like Colleen."

Eve tried that one out. "Colleen... Not bad. Not bad at all."

"But I'm sure it will be a boy," Patrick said, folding his arms, giving a definite nod of his chin.

"Well, don't be so sure."

"So, again, I say don't go for that test, whatever it's called and..."

Eve broke in... "It's called amniocentesis."

"All right, if you say so. I say, let's allow nature to take its course, like in the good old days..."

"You mean like the good old days back in 1885?" Eve asked with a grin.

"Yes, in 1885, you couldn't learn the sex of your child until the little tyke made its grand appearance into the world. I say that is much more fun, and entirely more romantic."

Eve reached, wrapped a hand around his neck and pulled him down for a deep, warm kiss.

Eve smiled into her husband's eyes. "All right, Mr. Gantly, if that's what you want. We'll do it the 1885 way and I'll just have to be patient."

"It will be fun, Eve, you'll see."

"Okay, but I'm exhausted. I've got to get some sleep."

Patrick rolled over and switched off the light. "Good night, my love."

Eve had nearly returned to sleep when Patrick's small voice woke her.

"Can we sleep on the other thing? The lantern, I mean? Can we give it a few more days?"

Eve sighed audibly, her voice slurring and sleepy. "All right... Whatever. Anyway, it's not going to be easy bashing the thing."

She yawned. "I'm going to feel like I'm killing an old friend."

A minute later, Patrick said, "The next question is, *can* we destroy it? Will it allow us to destroy it?"

That question stayed hanging in the air as they drifted off into a restless sleep.

CHAPTER 2

Three days later, on a Friday afternoon, Eve returned home a little after 3 p.m., having left the doctor's office early. As a nurse practitioner, she'd spent most of her day giving routine health exams, issuing some meds, doing Pap smears and HPV testing.

Eve loved her work and her interaction with her patients and the staff. They were a friendly and caring group of health professionals, who were constantly striving to be helpful and make a positive difference in people's lives.

Eve liked the science of her job, with its discipline, procedures and documentation. She was comfortable with the day-to-day routines of her life, both at work and with Patrick. But ever since the fall of 2016, when she'd found that antique lantern in the *Time Past Antique Shop* in Pennsylvania, there were times when her life had been chaotic and stressful. And that was an understatement.

Twice she'd time traveled, something that often still struck her as absurd, even though the proof of it was her marriage to Patrick Gantly, her pregnancy and her clear memories of past events.

She'd time traveled to 1885 and saved the life of a distant relative from certain death, and then somehow managed a fateful meeting with the man she loved. They'd married and lived, as the fairytales say, happily ever after.

During their second time travel journey, she and Patrick had landed in 1914 and helped to save his daughter, Maggie Lott Gantly, from being brutally murdered by her gangster boyfriend.

In both instances, they had made it back to their own time by strategy, hard work and great good fortune.

Now Eve was pregnant, thank God. She and Patrick were about to begin a family and an entirely new way of life, a life she'd hoped for ever since she and Patrick had fallen in love back in 1885. They'd been through so much together; so much drama; so much danger. Now, all she wanted was to live a simple, normal life and leave the past far behind them. So why not destroy the lantern? Why wait?

Eve was standing at the kitchen counter, chewing a raisin bagel while spooning dog food into Georgy Boy's yellow plastic dog dish. He swam her ankles, not letting her out of his sight, his brown liquid eyes filled with happy anticipation, his tail wagging in a circular motion.

She looked at her dog with love and pleasure. He was half-beagle, half-springer spaniel, with large chocolaty spots and floppy, solid brown ears.

"You, Georgy Boy, have to go on a diet. You're getting too pudgy. Patrick is feeding you too many treats."

Eve set Georgy Boy's dish on the floor next to the fridge and he nosed into it, eating with zest and zeal.

When a text "dinged" in, Eve was inserting the remaining dog food into the refrigerator. She glanced left at her phone and saw it was from her good friend, Joni Kosarin.

Where are you?
Home.
So early?
Yeah. Tired, and I'm only three months pregnant. Where are you?
Just finished for the day. Can I come over? Would love to chat about something.
Yes, I'm here for the night.
Is Patrick there?
No, still at school.
See you in a half hour.

In the bedroom, Eve changed clothes, pulling on sweatpants, a long sleeve red and black flannel shirt, and house slippers. As she glanced over at her walk-in closet, where the lantern was hidden in a safe, she again recalled how the lantern had completely changed her life.

When Eve and Patrick returned from their last time travel journey, Joni had physically changed. Something they'd done or not done in the past had changed history in small ways—or perhaps in dramatic ways they still hadn't discovered.

The shock of seeing Joni transformed had shaken Eve and Patrick. They could only stare in shock. Joni had insisted they were crazy. She said she was the same as she'd always been.

The old Joni had been tall, with a jet-black Cleopatra hairstyle, snow-white skin and dark blue eyes that held wonder and suspicion. She was an actress, dancer and singer, who often worked out-of-town in regional theater. When she was not performing, she supplemented her income working in sales at a camera rental house, renting cameras and lenses to Indie filmmakers and companies like *Netflix* and *Hulu* for their movie production streaming service.

The changed Joni was shorter, with wide hips and long, shockingly beautiful red hair, styled in a flip. She had sharp green eyes and a swirl of freckles. Joni's new voice was rather high in pitch, a soprano, and not the contralto the old Joni had been. She was not an actress or dancer but worked as a massage therapist.

But after weeks of adjustment for all three of them, Joni had remained a good, trusted friend, and she was the only person who knew about the lantern and the time travel adventures Eve and Patrick had experienced.

Joni swept into the apartment, breathless and talkative.

"I broke it off," she said, with a flick of her hand.

"With Jake?"

"Yes."

"Why?"

Joni frowned and then peeled off her hat and gloves and shouldered out of her coat.

"Can I have some tea or coffee? Whatever is easy. And some bread and butter, and maybe some ice cream. No, forget the ice cream, just the bread and butter. I need comfort food."

After Eve made a pot of black tea and toasted bread with butter, Joni searched the cupboard and found some chocolate chip cookies.

"Do you mind?" Joni asked, pulling the package down.

"Go for it," Eve said.

Joni carried the plate of buttered toast and cookies into the living room, with Eve behind managing the teapot and two mugs. They arranged their snacks on the coffee table and Eve poured the steaming tea into the mugs.

Joni snatched a half piece of the toast and jammed it into her mouth. "Oh my God, this is so good," she mumbled, her mouth working to form the words. "It's so perfect, Eve. Thank you. I almost busted my ass on a patch of ice coming over here. If it's already this cold with snow now, what will December and January be like?"

They sat near the gleaming, glassed-in fireplace, Eve in the recliner and Joni on the couch. A log shifted, and the fire hissed and popped. Patrick had made the once unworkable fireplace, workable, and Eve loved it.

"So talk to me," Eve said. "What happened?"

Joni's face wadded up with distress. "It's the old, old story, Eve. Boyfriend Joni likes, but doesn't love, but thinks she may grow to love someday way off in the future is, after all, a jerk. Joni finds boyfriend's cellphone, left right out there in plain view where Joni can see it. Joni does see it, because Joni is nosey and, anyway, boyfriend probably wanted her to see it. Anyway, Joni sees texts from another girlfriend, not me. Now get this—the other girlfriend's name is Caprice. Caprice? Who names their daughter Caprice? What the hell kind of name is that, anyway? Did her parents take the time to look up that name in the dictionary? Did they check out the synonyms? Well, I did, and caprice means fad, fancy and fickle. It also means freak and jerk."

Eve loved Joni's drama. That's the one thing that hadn't changed. Both the old Joni and the new Joni were drama queens.

"Okay, so I told Jake to go to hell. I told him to go to hell with Caprice, the fad, the fancy and the fickle Caprice."

Eve sipped her tea. "Didn't you even discuss it with him?"

"What was there to discuss? What?"

"Well, I don't know. Maybe Caprice was just a friend or something. Maybe…"

Joni cut her off. "… No, Eve, Caprice is just who you think she is…"

"And that would be?"

"A computer programmer."

Eve scratched her nose. "Okay, well computer programmer didn't come to mind. I was thinking more like restaurant hostess or administrative assistant."

"Well, whatever. Anyway, Jake said he was going to tell me next week. I don't know why it was going to be next week, but I told him to get out. So he got out. Fine and good. Chalk up another guy who didn't work out. How many is that now?"

"I don't know. Three… four?"

"Four?" Joni exclaimed, almost choking on the toast she was chewing. "Not four. Six, Eve, okay? No, wait a minute. Seven. There was that guy from Boston, Payton."

"I was never wild about him, and speaking of names, I never cared much for his name either."

"Well I was wild about his big wallet. And he was an excellent kisser. Unfortunately, I wasn't the only woman who thought so. He liked to spread his kisses around, uptown and downtown, and all over Brooklyn."

Joni reached for her mug of tea and washed down the toast. She started to speak, stopped, and grabbed a chocolate chip cookie.

"I think I've exhausted all the men in this time. I think I should use that lantern and time travel back somewhere and see if I can find a guy there."

"Don't even think about it, Joni."

Joni turned serious. "So, have you discussed it with Patrick? I mean, bashing the lantern and throwing it into the Hudson?"

"Yes…"

"And?"

"He wants to think about it a little while longer. He's not as impulsive as I am, at least not about this."

Joni turned reflective. "You were lucky, Eve, to find Patrick."

"Yes, I was lucky, and I want to keep it that way. That's why I don't want that lantern tempting us. Anything could happen, or Patrick could discover some other thing that happened in the past that he wants to change. Something like what happened to his surprise daughter, Maggie. I want to eliminate that possibility once and for all."

When they heard the downstairs buzzer, Eve pushed up. "Must be a package."

Georgy Boy's ears lifted, and his nose sniffed at the air.

In the hallway, Eve pressed the speaker button. "Who is it?"

A scratchy male voice responded. "Mrs. Gantly?"

"Yes. Who is it?"

"UPS."

Eve could have walked to the bay windows and peered out from the blue draperies down to the front door to confirm the voice, but she didn't. She buzzed him in.

She heard footsteps on the marble stairs as they climbed to the third floor. Eve said something to Joni as she released the metallic lock and opened the door.

To her utter shock, she saw a sinister-looking man dressed in a black overcoat and dark fedora pulled low over his forehead. He was pointing a handgun at her chest.

He spoke at a threatening whisper. "Don't scream. Don't talk. Let me in."

Eve was frozen in place.

"I'll shoot. Let me in. Now!"

CHAPTER 3

Eve and Joni stood close, near the fireplace, feeling its heat. The medium-built man with bony features, tight build and hard, menacing eyes kept the gun pointed at them.

Joni's hands trembled. Eve's heart pounded, and she instinctively touched her stomach as if to protect her baby.

"What do you want?" was all Eve could say.

"Where is it?"

"Where is what? Money?"

"I don't give a damn about your money," the man said, his voice low and breathy. "Where's the lantern?"

Eve was so startled that, for a few seconds, she thought maybe this was some kind of joke. Maybe Patrick had sent the man. Maybe Joni. They were the only two people on the Earth who knew the lantern existed.

"What lantern?" Eve forced out, searching the man's face and eyes for signs of a grin. There was no grin. His

16

dark eyes hardened, and they were pointed at her, just like the barrel of the gun was pointed at her.

"Okay, hotsy-totsy, stop with the doe-dumb eyes. I'm no sap. I know you've got it, so go get it. There are real bullets in this gun, and I'll use them on the both of you if I have to."

Eve and Joni exchanged frightened glances. His voice was strange. His inflection odd, his use of slang cartoonish. But the man before them was no cartoon. His evil intent was evident and palpable.

Georgy Boy, sensing something was wrong, left the comfort of the fireplace and retreated to the bedroom, where he wriggled under the bed.

When the truth struck, Eve felt the cold fill her up, a cold that the heated fire couldn't touch. Her legs went rubbery, and she fought to stay on her feet and not faint.

This guy was from the past: his look, his gestures, his slang. There was no doubt about it. But what past? What year? What date, and how did he know about the lantern?

"Who are you?" Eve said, her voice a little whisper.

"It don't matter who I am, doll. You just go get the lantern," he snapped, waving the gun around. "I don't plan to stay here all day until your big boy husband shows up. Get the lantern. Now!"

Eve's breath sped up. Her only thoughts were of her baby. Protect her baby. Give this man anything he wants but protect her baby. Eve took a couple of steps forward, gathering strength. Joni stared, her eyes two terrified circles.

Eve moved past the man, down the short, carpeted hallway toward the bedroom. Patrick had texted that he'd be home about 5 p.m. What time was it? She'd taken off her watch. Her phone was on the coffee table in the living room.

The man followed her close, the barrel of the gun pointed only four feet from her back. Inside the bedroom, Eve glanced at the digital clock near the queen-sized bed. It was 4:23 p.m. Maybe Patrick would be early. On the other hand, Eve didn't want him coming through the front door. The man looked determined to get what he wanted, and he might shoot Patrick.

Eve paused at the bedroom closet, her mind suddenly running through speculation. If this man knew about the lantern, then it was reasonable to assume that he knew how it worked and what it was capable of. She breathed out a jet of air. Her worst nightmare had come true. For days she'd had the premonition that something concerning the lantern was about to happen. Why hadn't she just tossed the thing into the river when she had the chance?

"Hurry up," the man demanded. "I don't have all day."

Eve glanced back at him. His expression was ugly. His tight mouth twitched. His eyes held resolve.

"It may not work for you," Eve said, in a small voice.

"Don't you worry your head about that, doll face. Get it! And don't try anything. I'm sure you have a gun hidden back there someplace, just in case something like this happened. But don't even think about it. You'll be dead before you can reach for it."

Actually, there was no gun hidden away. She and Patrick never thought they'd need to protect the lantern, other than to put it in a safe. Except for Joni, no one knew about it.

Inside the closet, Eve crouched down. To her left stood the three and a half foot safe. Patrick had found it online. It was constructed of steel, was pry-resistant and seamlessly welded with a military, scratch-resistant finish. The inside was carpeted and integrated with an LED light. It was accessed by a six-digit PIN that was easy to remember because it was her mother's birthday.

"Hurry up in there," the man growled.

Eve nervously punched in the PIN, tugged on the handle and opened the safe door. In the glow of the LED light, the old lantern looked eerie and ominous. Her temples pounded as she reached for it, feeling sad, confused and angry. Of all the people to get the lantern, this man was surely not worthy. Who knew what he'd do with it, or what he'd already done?

"I said, hurry. Have you got it?" he barked, pushing in, glaring down at her, gun poised.

Eve carefully wrapped both hands around the lantern and removed it from the safe. As she was about to stand, the man seized it by the wire handle, yanked it out of Eve's hands, and with his booted foot on her forehead, he shoved her away. She toppled over under a rack of winter slacks, coats and tops. Clumsily slapping the clothes away, she scrambled to her feet.

Before she could clamber out of the closet, she heard his heavy footsteps in the hallway, moving toward the living room. Just as Eve darted into the living room, the front door slammed shut. Eve heard his footfalls skipping down the stairs. The lobby door burst open, and he was away. Joni hadn't budged, terror etched on her face.

Eve rushed to the bay windows, shoved aside the draperies and observed him dashing off toward West End Avenue, the lantern tucked under his coat.

Eve's blood ran cold. She folded her arms tightly against her chest, unable to process what had happened and what it would mean.

"Who the hell was that?" Joni asked, in a trembling voice. "I mean, what was that? What just happened?"

Eve didn't turn around. She stood as still as a stone pillar for long minutes, staring out the window, her thoughts galloping. She wasn't aware that Georgy Boy had returned and was nudging her leg.

When she saw Patrick striding along the sidewalk in his usual casual way, approaching the brownstone, her eyes misted up. Touching her stomach, she couldn't shake the terrible feeling that whatever had just happened was only a beginning. She knew in her heart of hearts that this was just the beginning of something dark and sinister, something that could threaten her and Patrick's lives, and something she didn't understand.

CHAPTER 4

That night neither Eve nor Patrick felt like eating. They ordered Chinese takeout and sat in the living room, paper plates in their laps, the food half eaten. Patrick was in a dark mood and Eve fought depression. Now that the lantern was gone, she should have felt lighter, but she didn't. There was nothing pleasant or light about what had happened.

"Did he leave any clues at all?" Patrick said, knowing he was repeating himself.

"No, Patrick. I told you. Except for the slang and his vintage coat and hat, he didn't say anything or do anything that suggested who he was, or where he came from.

Patrick laid his plate aside and stood up, facing the fire, his hands clasped behind his back.

"Well, he obviously knew who you were and that you had the lantern. How? You're sure Joni hasn't told anybody?"

"No, I told you. Joni has never told anyone. She had no idea who the man was. She was scared to death, so scared that she's going to stay with a girlfriend tonight."

Patrick turned to Eve; his eyes warm on her. "You did the right thing. I'm so glad you gave it to him without resisting in any way."

"What could I do? He had a gun pointed at me."

Patrick went to her, stooped, and kissed her on the forehead. "I'm sorry you had to go through that. He obviously waited until I wasn't around. No telling how long he's been watching us."

Patrick turned to Georgy Boy, who was lying asleep near the fireplace. "Too bad we don't have an attack dog."

"It's not his fault. Georgy Boy's an orphan. He had a bad puppy-hood until I rescued him."

"How's the baby?"

"The baby is fine. I kept as calm as I could, taking a lot of deep breaths."

"I'm sorry, Eve. I'm sorry we didn't get rid of the lantern the other day when you wanted to."

"Yes, well, I've been thinking about that. What would that man have done if I told him we'd bashed it up and tossed it into the river? He probably wouldn't have believed me, and then who knows what he might have done."

"Good point. I hate to say it but a proverb from my old Da comes to mind."

Eve tilted her head, giving him a faint smile. "I figured it was about time for one of your Da's proverbs. Okay, out with it."

Patrick arched an eyebrow. "There is misfortune only where there is wealth."

"And what does that mean with regard to us, and about what just happened?"

"It means that the lantern made us wealthy in many ways. Remember, not only did it bring us together and save my daughter, Maggie, but it also brought you over five million dollars from John Allister Harringshaw."

Eve looked away into the fire, watching the play of the orange flames. "So maybe it's all over now. Maybe now we can finally get on with our lives and forget the whole thing. Most of me is relieved."

Patrick stepped behind her and began massaging her shoulders. She shut her eyes and hummed out pleasure.

"That feels so good."

"You're as tight as a drum, Mrs. Gantly. Where do you want my hands to go?"

"Everywhere... I hope I can sleep tonight."

"Let me give you a massage."

They were silent for a time, as Patrick worked her neck and shoulder muscles. She began to relax, her eyes growing heavy.

"Eve..."

She mumbled out a "What?" And then "Oh, yes, right there. Stay there for a while."

Patrick was thinking aloud. "If that rogue time traveled from the past to 2019, then he must have used the lantern from the past, right? Because we both know that the lantern never travels back in time, it stays in the time it's in. The lantern in the present, stays in the present. The lantern in the past, stays in the past. So, where did our scoundrel find the lantern in the past, and how did he know he could time travel with it? And how did he know who we are, where we live and that we had the lantern that he needed in order to return to his own time?"

Eve leaned her head back to look at her husband. "So many questions."

"I know. I wish I could stop them from crowding into my head."

"I've been thinking about that too. We know what happened to the lantern in 1885, the lantern that brought us back to 2016. Daniel Fallow and Jacob Jackson got it. Just before Jacob Jackson died in 1908, he gave that same lantern to Dr. Ann Long. She gave it to her son, Logan, and in 1914, we used that lantern to return to 2018."

Patrick gave Eve's neck a final squeeze and then returned to his chair, his mind lost in thought.

Eve continued. "According to Maggie, Logan gave the lantern to her in 1914, after we used it to return to 2018. In Maggie's letter, she said that she lost the lantern. I re-read the letter a couple of hours ago. Maggie said that in 1924, at a wild party in St. Paul, Minnesota, the lantern was taken from her. She thinks the woman who took it was a famous actress at the time, named Lilly Hart. I'm just thinking out loud here. I know you know all this. But I'm thinking that Maggie, when she was drunk, probably told Lilly all about the lantern and its powers and then, unfortunately, Maggie also probably told Lilly about us."

Patrick sighed. "It's possible. I mean, anything is possible. We just don't know what happened after Maggie lost the lantern in 1924. You know how many times we've *Googled* Lilly Hart and read her history on various sites. Of course, there was never any mention of the lantern, so we don't know where that lantern ended up. Did Ms. Hart lose it? Give it away? Was it stolen from her? We just don't know."

Eve resumed eating, mixing white rice with a dumpling. She took a thoughtful bite and chewed.

"But we know Lilly Hart had a number of, shall we say, boyfriends? And we know she died somewhat mysteriously, at least according to some movie historians."

"It's all speculation, Eve."

"Okay, but I think we both suspect that the man who took our lantern was from the 1920s. Logically, he either knew Lilly Hart, or he knew someone who knew about the lantern. From there, we have to speculate that he time traveled to 2019."

Patrick closed his eyes and massaged them. "The whole thing is giving me a headache."

Eve stared down at the floor. "Somehow, I'm going to have to forget about the whole thing. I've got to move on. It's lost to us now. It's gone, and wherever it ends up, we're never going to know."

Patrick nodded. "Yes, I know. But our lantern, the one that man stole from you, will remain in this time, someplace. Somebody is going to find it and then..."

Eve interrupted. "... And that somebody else will have to deal with it."

Patrick lowered his voice. "Well, then, God help them."

Eve took another bite of rice. "Yes. Whoever finds the lantern, I hope they know the power of it, and they use that power wisely."

CHAPTER 5

Two days later, on Sunday evening, Eve returned from Riverside Park with Georgy Boy after a walk. She unfastened his leash, and he frolicked off toward the kitchen to drink some water. While Eve removed her coat and hat, she noticed Patrick standing by the bay windows, gazing out of slightly parted draperies.

"Did you notice anyone when you came from the park?" he asked.

"What do you mean, notice anyone?"

Patrick faced her. "I've seen this woman hanging around outside for the last day or so."

"Are you getting tired of me, Mr. Gantly? You seem to be spending all your free time watching women come and go."

"I'm serious, Eve. Twice when I've made a run to the wine shop or market, I've felt someone following me. It's the old detective in me. Early this afternoon, I saw that same woman outside, two doors up, looking at our brownstone. Yesterday she was across the street near that pin oak tree."

Eve stepped to the fireplace to warm her hands. "How old is she?"

"I'd say late twenties, with a thin build, small nose, oval face, wearing a black ski cap, dark hair sticking out, a long royal woolen coat and sheepskin boots. She moves about nervously, frequently glancing up and down the street."

Eve started over to him. "I didn't notice anybody in the park or walking up the street, but then, I'm not a former police detective and I'm not studying forensic psychology like you are. Is she there now?"

Patrick turned back to the windows. "No... I don't see her."

"It's cold out there. You can't stay out long in that sharp wind. Even Georgy Boy was happy to get back."

Patrick moved from the windows to the fireplace, turning his back to it, feeling its warmth, watching the dance of shadows on the walls from the firelight.

"The girl is not my imagination. I've seen her four times now, and I've never seen her around here before. Her coat and hat do not look especially prosperous, and I get the feeling she's scared."

Eve shook off a shiver. "I don't like it when your voice gets all low and serious. You sound like the detective I first met back in 1885."

Patrick abruptly left the fire, went to the closet and removed his hooded black parka. He slipped on a pair of gloves and passed Eve a glance.

"I'm going to see if I can find her."

Eve crossed to him. "Are you that sure?"

He nodded.

"Want me to come?"

"No. I'll text you if I see anything. Meanwhile, you know where the .38 is?"

Eve dropped her gaze. "I don't like it, Patrick. You know I don't like guns."

Patrick gently took her shoulders. "If that guy comes back, you might need it."

"Why would he come back? He's got the lantern."

"Eve, I'm not going to stand here arguing. I won't be gone long, and I'll be watching the building, but don't let anyone in unless it's me, okay?"

"Of course I won't let anybody in."

"All right."

He leaned, giving her a peck on the lips. "See you soon."

Eve reached and tugged the hood up over his head. "Be careful out there, Detective Sergeant Gantly."

After he was gone, Eve returned to the windows, parted the drapes and cast her eyes about the quiet street. The light was leaving the day, and two amber streetlights blinked on, their light gleaming off the two-day-old snow. She watched Patrick retreat left and walk down the street toward Riverside Park. When he left her line of vision, she felt a small twist of fear.

His senses on alert, Patrick edged along the street, entered the carriage path of Riverside Park and turned south. Above the river, clouds were purple and gray, fringed with orange light from the setting sun. Bursts of cold wind rattled the bare limbs of trees as he wandered along the carriage path, joggers and dog-walkers occasionally drifting by.

His furtive glances found shadowy areas near the stone wall and trees and park benches, but he saw nothing unusual. After checking his cellphone to ensure

Eve hadn't texted, he crossed Riverside Drive at 103rd Street and walked to West End Avenue, where he turned left. At 107th Street and Broadway, he paused, hood still up, eyes peeled, as people passed, as passengers disembarked yellow taxis, and as customers wandered in and out of the wine shop and Mexican restaurant.

Darkness had settled in when he saw her emerge from the West End Magazine and Tobacco House two doors down, rubbing her hands together. She must have ducked in to warm herself. Patrick shrank away from a pool of light spilling out from the wine shop and crept toward the display window, pretending to look at a rack of red wines that were on sale.

From a side glance, he saw the young woman turn left on West 107th, puffing out white clouds of vapor, her shoulders hunched against the wind. Patrick deftly stepped back, keeping her in sight as she retreated west. He turned onto West 107th and followed a safe distance behind, on the other side of the street.

The amber streetlights cast pools of light on the sidewalk and on the snow-covered cars. Patrick heard her footsteps crunch the snow as she moved past brownstone row houses and approached his. She hesitated, glanced up, spotted something, then hurried off.

Patrick hid behind a tree and a parked car. He glimpsed a sliver of yellow light leaking out from the third-floor bay windows. He grimaced. Eve was peering out.

The girl went to the end of the street, turned and started back. Patrick decided to move in gingerly, so as not to frighten her. He was afraid she might spook easily, run away and then never return.

As she came back up the street, east, he passed her on the other side heading west. She glanced his way, but he was already in the shadows moving away.

He quickly crossed the salted street about 30 feet from her. Fortunately, the street was always quiet, but especially so on a cold Sunday night.

Patrick saw her pause near the right base of the brownstone stoop and then hide away in a place beneath the main stair, where there was a second entrance. In the old days that entrance had been used by servants and delivery people. It was a great place to linger in the shadows and that's just what the woman was doing.

Patrick planned his strategy and then moved into action. He was not going to be coy and clever. Walking purposefully across the sidewalk, with his eyes straight ahead, he pretended not to see the woman. At the last minute, he darted to his right, grabbed her, spun her around so her back was against his chest, and then he clapped his gloved hand over her mouth.

"Don't scream."

He felt her tremble against him; felt her chest heaving, terrified.

"I'm not going to hurt you. I just want to ask you a couple of questions. If I release you, will you promise not to scream? A nod will do."

It took a few seconds before she did, a quick, frightened jerk of a nod.

"I'm going to drop my hand now."

Patrick did so, in measured increments. Her breath smoked. Her teeth chattered. She was nearly scared to death.

"Please don't hurt me," she forced out between chattering teeth.

"I'm not going to hurt you. Tell me, who are you and why do you keep hanging around out here?"

She stammered out her name. "...Lu...cy. I'm Lucy Rose."

"What do you want?"

"I'm.... I'm so cold. So... cold."

"Why are you out here? What do you want?"

Patrick slowly turned her around to face him. Her eyes bulged in raw terror and she was shaking uncontrollably.

"Please don't hurt me," she pleaded, her eyes scrunched together as if she were expecting a slap.

"I'm not going to hurt you. What do you want? Why do you keep hanging around out here?"

"I'm... so cold."

The girl was petrified and freezing. Against his better judgment, he felt compassion for her, but he wasn't going to take any chances. "Are you carrying a gun or a knife?"

"No..."

Swiftly, before the girl could respond, he patted her down.

"Hey, you're a rough one..."

"I'll be a lot rougher if you're hiding a gun."

"I don't have a gun. I'm freezing to death. I'm cold."

Satisfied, he removed his hood and leveled his stern eyes on her. "What do you want?"

"It's not what I want," she said. "It's what do you want?"

Patrick didn't budge. "Is it about the lantern?"

Lucy hesitated.

"Tell me. Do you know the man who broke into our apartment and took the lantern?"

Lucy wiped her runny nose with her gloved hand. "Yeah... I know him."

Patrick grabbed her arm and yanked her toward the stairs. "All right, let's go inside."

She resisted. "Please don't hurt me. I don't mean nothing."

"I told you, I'm not going to hurt you. I'll take you upstairs. My wife is up there and it's warm. Come on."

She stared, eyes shifting, finally following him through the heavy, wrought-iron gate that led up the six steps to the heavy oak front door. Patrick found his key, inserted it into the lock and opened the door. In the lobby, Lucy Rose felt the warm breath of heat, and she sighed in relief.

"This feels like heaven."

Patrick lowered his eyes on her. "You know where the apartment is, don't you?"

She avoided his eyes. "Yes... the third floor."

"Let's go."

CHAPTER 6

It was Eve who had to coax Lucy inside the apartment, while Patrick waited out in the hallway, his watchful eyes on the girl. Lucy finally entered, like a frightened puppy. Georgy Boy took one look at her, sniffed her boots, lowered his head and bounded off toward the bedroom.

When Patrick shut the door behind him, Lucy trembled, feeling trapped.

"I didn't do nothing. Please don't hurt me."

Eve said, "We're not going to hurt you. Step over to the fire and warm up. Your face is beet-red and you're shaking all over."

"Her name is Lucy Rose," Patrick said, sliding out of his coat.

Lucy trudged gratefully to the fireplace, shutting her eyes, feeling the immediate warmth.

"I'm Eve. My husband's name is Patrick."

Lucy shot Patrick a pouting glance. "He man-handled me."

Eve gave Patrick a mock scolding glance. "Yeah, well, he does that sometimes. Do you want something hot to drink? Coffee or tea?"

Lucy's attention was taken by the cozy, lovely room; the polished parquet floor and throw rugs; an open brick wall above the fireplace; comfy-looking chocolate brown leather couch and chairs; a ceiling-to-floor ornate antique mirror and two polished mahogany bookshelves filled with books and CDs and DVDs. Her eyes circled the room twice, finally resting on the large, flat screen TV.

"It's so homey," Lucy said. "Such a nice place."

"Thank you," Eve said. "So, something hot to drink?"

"Oh, yes, please. Coffee, if you have it. Some gin in it, too, if you don't mind."

Patrick arched an eyebrow, and Eve gave him a humorous wink as she left for the kitchen.

Patrick studied the mysterious girl who, in the better light, appeared to be in her early 20s.

"Where are you from?" Patrick asked.

Lucy peeled off her black ski cap, revealing a 1920s-style bob haircut. He could imagine the hairstyle, when not flattened and distorted by a hat, to be sleek and straight, like a black helmet.

"Originally... Baltimore. Then to Hollywood and then... other places. I danced around."

"And now?"

Lucy looked Patrick over for the first time, and he saw that she liked what she saw.

She shrugged. "New York."

"You mean, right here, in New York?"

"Yeah, sure, but it certainly ain't the same town that I knew, or we knew."

"Who's we?"

She looked away. "I didn't do anything bad, you know."

"I didn't say you did, but I suspect you know the guy who broke in here and took our lantern. Who is he?"

"A killjoy. A backstabber. You know the type."

"What's his name? Why are you with him? Where is he?"

She shrugged again. "You sound like a Mulligan, with all the sixty-six questions."

Patrick knew what the slang word Mulligan meant. Even in his day, in 1885, Mulligan meant policeman.

"And you sound like you don't belong around here. And where did you get the hairstyle?"

Lucy finger-combed it self-consciously. "It must look a mess now. It looked real good a few days ago."

Lucy looked him up and down again, and Patrick noticed a slight change in her demeanor. As the warmth of the fire thawed her out, she began to relax and grow sassier and bold.

"You're a big one." She made a motion with her head toward the kitchen. "You married to the blonde?"

"I am. Are you and the killjoy married?"

She barked out a laugh. "Are you kidding? He's all big mouth and mumbles, that one. He mumbles about how bad the world treated him. How bad his boss treated him. How bad I treated him. Hell, the only reason I hanged with him was because of his dancing. He's a real Oliver Twist."

"A what?" Patrick asked, having never heard the slang.

"A good dancer."

Eve entered with a mug of coffee. She crossed to Lucy and handed it to her, her eyes quickly scanning her new guest.

Lucy studied Eve, as if she were competition.

"I put a shot of whiskey in it."

"Just one shot?" Lucy asked, disappointed.

"Yes," Eve said, firmly.

Eve had time traveled enough to know that Lucy Rose was not from this time. It was written all over her: her attitude, her posture, her slang. Eve had heard most of Patrick's and Lucy's conversation from the kitchen and now, as Eve sized up the girl and Patrick's tight, concerned face, she was worried. What did this girl want?

"Do you want to sit down?" Eve asked.

"No, it feels good here," Lucy said, moving closer to the fire.

"Are you warm enough to take off your coat?"

Lucy set her mug on the mantel, unbuttoned her retro-looking wool coat and artfully slipped out of it, almost as if the movements were part of a dance. Lucy handed it to Eve, while Patrick appraised the girl's clothing. The jeans and white wool sweater revealed a slim figure, with long legs, thin neck and modest bust. Patrick calculated her measurements: bust 34 inches, waist 26, hips 36.

After Eve returned from the closet, she sat down in the chair to Lucy's right. Patrick remained standing near the couch. Lucy sipped the hot coffee, blowing off the steam.

"It's good," she said. "But I prefer gin."

"Don't have any," Eve said.

Patrick went to work. "Let's talk about the lantern, Lucy. Tell me everything you know. And then tell me what you want."

Lucy looked at him dubiously. "Like I said, he's a backstabber."

"So you know for sure that the backstabber broke into our apartment, threatened my wife with a gun and then took the lantern?"

"Of course I know. I was with him. I was downstairs. I didn't want to be. He made me. He said I had to be the lookout in case you came," she said, nodding at Patrick. "He said you were big, and you'd break him into pieces if you caught him."

Eve felt the start of a headache. "I didn't see anybody with him when he ran up the street."

Lucy turned petulant, throwing a fist on her hip. "Because I was already up the street. I'm not stupid, you know. I wasn't going to hang around so Mulligan here could grab me."

"Okay, so what's his name and where is he?" Patrick asked.

"His name is Mickey Blaine. He's gone."

"Gone where?"

Lucy flashed him a sassy grin. "Come on, Mulligan, you've got to be smart enough to put it all together by now. Mickey Blaine steals lantern. Why? Time travel. Got it?"

Patrick had assumed Mickey Blaine was gone, but he wanted to hear it from her.

"Did you time travel here with him?" Patrick asked.

Lucy looked at Eve, who stared back at her with clear, piercing eyes.

"Yes. We came together."

Eve said, "What year did you come from?"

"…1925."

Patrick and Eve traded meaningful glances.

"If Mickey is gone, if he has time traveled back to 1925, why didn't you go with him?" Patrick asked.

Lucy's grin was tired, but her eyes held cunning. "I was sick of him slapping me around every time something bothered him, or he was drunk. I was tired of dancing in that night club for peanuts. I was tired of being called 'doll face' and 'my dancin' rag doll' and 'come here, baby toes, let me kiss away some of that lipstick,' because that's what the mugs in nightclubs shout out when you're on stage dancing under those hot spotlights. Well, I had had it up to my eyeballs with all that, see?"

Lucy shook her head with disgust. "Anyway, I like it here. I like it here a lot. There's so much life in this time. So much going on and I'm just wild about those cellphones and laptops and movies and TVs, like that one over there. I'm crazy about it all, including the texting and social media. It all makes me a little crazy and dizzy and I love it—that high-in-the-sky feeling, you know? And then those big airplanes flying over. Well, it scared the living hell out of me the first time I saw that. You should have seen Mickey's face the first time he saw one of those big, roaring planes fly over: he looked like a hooked fish. You know what else I think? I think men are better lookin' in this time. They're bigger and they're not so in your face all the time, makin' with the come-ons and the wise-guy cracks."

"How long have you been here? When did you time travel?" Eve asked.

"Two weeks ago. Something like that. I've lost track of time. Late October."

"Why did Mickey bring you along?" Patrick asked. "Why didn't he come alone?"

Lucy sneered at him. "Because I was his doll face, Mulligan. And his doll face always goes where Mickey goes, see? Wouldn't you take your doll face with you if you went off time traveling?"

Eve pushed the tip of her tongue against her inside cheek and winked at Patrick.

Lucy drained the last of the coffee. "Can I have another, and with a little more whiskey?"

"I'll get it," Patrick said.

Lucy looked on with surprise. "Mulligan's going to wait on me, a woman? Well, did you ever? Hey, keep this one, Blondie, he's a Sheik."

Eve blanched. "First of all, my name is Eve, not Blondie, and second, what does Sheik mean?"

Lucy presented a lopsided grin. "Oh, yeah, that's right. I still sometimes forget what time I'm living in. A Sheik means, your Mulligan here, your man, is nice to look at, you know like Rudolph Valentino, the actor."

Patrick gave Eve a side-glance grin, took Lucy's cup and made for the kitchen.

Finally warm, Lucy left the fireplace and eased down on the couch, sliding her hands along the leather. "Nice couch. Everything's better in this time. More comfortable, faster, easier, and..." she paused for emphasis, "everything costs a fortune. Mickey and me were knocked off our feet by the prices here."

Eve lowered her voice to deep authority. "Lucy, where did Mickey get the lantern to time travel here?"

Lucy folded her arms. "From that woman."

"Which woman?"

"From the drunken movie star face stretcher."

"Can you please translate that for me?"

"Mickey was two-timing me. He thought I didn't know what was going on, but I'm not a stupid floosy."

Eve fought impatience. "What was her name?"

"Lilly Hart."

Patrick returned just in time to hear the name. "What's a face stretcher?" Patrick asked, always curious.

"Oh, you know. An old woman trying to look young. Mickey only hung around her because she spent money and brought high brows and high rollers into the speakeasy. So he was bedding her down, and he thinks I don't know. Then later, he tells me she has this lantern that she says is magic. Well, anyway, that was sometime in 1924. A few months later, she dies in a car crash. She was drunk or something and ran her car into a big tree."

Patrick handed Lucy the coffee with whiskey. She nearly snatched it from his hands and took a careful drink.

"Good, much better with the extra whiskey." She grinned up at him. "Thanks, Mulligan."

Patrick moved to Lucy's left, near the fire, where he could see her face. "Did Lilly give Mickey the lantern?"

"No. He stole it from her. He told me that she kept it around as a joke, like it was a novelty or something. She told him she could never get the thing to light. Mickey said she was a dumb, boozed-up broad. He said the lantern didn't light because the wick had been damaged. It was an easy fix."

Eve thought about that. "Lucy, when did Mickey learn that the lantern had power?"

"I don't know. He never said. He just came charging into my bedroom one morning and said he was going to take me on the trip of a lifetime. When he first lit that thing and hugged me into him, I thought he'd flipped his lid. But then, when we ended up in this time, in 2019, wandering around Central Park like lost kids, I flipped my lid. It took us both two or three days before we could believe it, and we were pretty shook up, I can tell you. I felt like I'd been put through the ringer. Mickey said he felt like he was punch drunk on bad gin."

"Where did you get money?" Patrick asked.

Lucy beamed with pride. "Easy. Mickey stole it. He's a great pickpocket. He grew up on the Lower East Side of New York, and for years made his living as a pickpocket. We had plenty of money. We stayed at the Sheraton Hotel on Seventh Avenue. That place is tops."

When Patrick fixed his eyes on Lucy, there was force in them. "How did Mickey know about Eve and me? How did he know where we live and that we had the lantern he needed to return to his time?"

"Easy. A woman named Maggie Gantly."

Eve and Patrick looked stricken.

CHAPTER 7

Patrick had joined Lucy on the couch, sitting on the opposite side, head in his hands.

Eve sat glumly, staring into the fire.

"What did I say?" Lucy asked.

Patrick lifted his head. "Lucy, did you meet Maggie Gantly? Did you know her?"

"Yeah, sure. She and Lilly were friends. Lilly was a boozehound, but Maggie was a right broad. Everybody liked Maggie. Hey, she liked champagne, but you know what? She shared it with people. She was all right that way."

Eve sat up on the edge of her seat. "Lucy, did Maggie tell Mickey about us?"

Lucy stared down at the floor. "No. Maggie told me. She was really proud of you two. She said you saved her life. She told me the whole story. We were kind of friends. We both liked gin and champagne. We even dreamed up this crazy cocktail with gin and honey, lemon juice, and orange juice, topped with champagne. We called it the Bees Knees. Maggie loved them. She said we should patent it or something. She showed a couple of bartenders how to make them and all the girls went wild for it. That cocktail was tops. Everybody was drinking them."

"Then it was you who told Mickey about us?" Patrick asked.

The room plunged deeper into unease.

"Yeah, so what?" Lucy said, defensively. "What was wrong with that? We were together, and he had the lantern and didn't know nothing. So I told him what Maggie told me."

"Why did Mickey want to time travel, Lucy?" Eve asked.

"Come on, Blondie, you can figure that one out."

Eve ignored "Blondie," fully engaged in Lucy's story.

"It was about money. Ain't it always? When Mickey got here, he learned all he needed to know about the stock market in the 1920s, and about the crash in 1929. He's gonna be a big millionaire, buy his own club and live on Easy Street for the rest of his life."

Patrick sighed through his nose. "What does he plan to do with the lantern when he returns to his own time?"

Lucy shrugged a shoulder. "He's gonna sell it to the highest bidder."

"Of course," Eve said, sadly. "Of course he will."

Patrick looked at Lucy with frank appraisal. "And you, Lucy? If you didn't go with Mickey, then you must have the lantern that Mickey stole from us, right?"

Lucy's grin started small, then slowly grew in size. She lifted her chin as if to bolster her courage. "I was sitting next to Mickey on a park bench in Central Park, just like Maggie told us you two had done when you time traveled. At the last minute, just when that round swirling orange and blue light circled us, I jumped up and ran away from it. Mickey cursed me and threatened me and said he'd kill me, but it was too late. Within seconds he just..." Lucy snapped her fingers. "Poof! He was gone. Gone from my life forever. Like my mother used to say, good riddance to bad baggage."

Eve silently willed herself to relax. "Where is the lantern now, Lucy?"

Lucy looked first at Eve, and then at Patrick, her eyes glowing in the firelight, her expression expectant. "Yes, I have it."

Patrick rose, turned to her and folded his arms, waiting. "How much money do you want, Lucy?"

Her voice took on an edge. "Well, why shouldn't I get something for it?"

"Because it's not yours," Eve said.

"I want to stay here. Like I said, I want to stay in this time. Hey, if I hadn't taken it, who knows who would have grabbed it? It could have been anyone. Maybe a cop would have taken it and tossed it into the park trash. Then what?"

"Then we'd all be a whole lot better off," Eve said, at a whisper.

"How much, Lucy?" Patrick repeated, arms still folded.

"I'm not asking for that much. I need something to live on, don't I? It costs a fortune to live in this time and all I have in my purse is a lousy forty-four bucks. I've only got one more night in that hotel before they kick me out. Mickey took all the money, that rat. And I see that most people use those credit cards. I want one of those, too. I have to have money to get one of those. And I want to buy a cellphone and a computer. I want to live in a nice place, like this."

"How much, Lucy?" Patrick persisted, eyes narrowing on her.

She swallowed. "A million bucks."

Eve looked away, with a shake of her head.

Patrick glared at the girl. "Impossible."

"Maggie told me that when you two returned from 1885, some rich guy left you over five million bucks. I'm just asking for a million. Just a lousy million bucks. I think the lantern is worth it."

Exasperated, Eve shot up and walked off into the kitchen. Lucy watched her go, confused. She turned her full attention to Patrick, straining to read his face, nerves gnawing at her gut.

"Okay, if that's too much, how about eight hundred thousand? I know you can afford that."

Patrick ambled over to the windows, opened the drapes and stared out. He allowed his mind to sift, weigh and consider all the possibilities. Snow flurries drifted, and he saw a kid pulling a sled down the center of the street on his way to the park.

Eve returned with a mug of coffee. She didn't mention that she'd poured two shots of whiskey in it. How she wanted and needed that coffee and that booze, but she was pregnant, so she took it to Patrick.

He smiled his thanks. After a sip, he glanced up with happy approval. "Thank you, Eve. Your coffee is always good, but this one is perfect and right for the moment."

Eve moved to the center of the room, letting the silence lengthen, observing Lucy grow increasingly uneasy.

"I need some money to get started," Lucy said, her voice almost pleading. "I don't want to go back there. I want a new life... a better life. Hell, do you know it's against the law to drink hooch back there? They call it prohibition, and they put you in the slammer if they catch you. They have these clubs called speakeasies, and you have to know somebody, or know a password, or know a cop to even get in. Everybody, even the cops and politicians, get their palms greased. Even then, the Feds sometimes bust the place. When I got here and learned that prohibition wouldn't be over until 1933, I said to Mickey, 'Why the hell do you want to go back there? It's nowheresville.'"

Patrick turned to her. "What will you do with your new life? How will you make a living? Where will you go?"

Lucy got up and turned to them, twisting her hands, her eyes wide and vulnerable. "I don't know, but I'm a fighter. I've been through thick and thin and I've had plenty of knocks, but I always buck up and keep on going. And that's what I'll do. I'll find a job, and a good man with a good job, and then maybe I'll marry him and move somewhere nice and pretty, where I can raise babies. I just want a better life, where guys aren't pawing at me, throwing money at me, and where I'm not waking up in the morning sick at myself for what I did the night before."

Eve softened. Patrick turned back to watch the lazy glide of the snow. For a long, chilly silence, no one said anything. Finally, Patrick closed the drapes and looked at Eve. Eve looked at Lucy, who was standing stiffly, measuring the scene.

Eve said, "Lucy, Mickey has the old 1925 lantern. He could come for you."

"No, he won't. Oh, he loves me in his own doped-up way, but he loves money more than me or anything else. He'll never come back for me."

Eve studied Lucy in a frown of concentration, feeling conflicted.

"Lucy, Patrick and I need time to think about this."

Lucy's lips formed a pout. "No. No more time. You either want the lantern or you don't want it. I'll find somebody else, and don't you think I can't find somebody else. There are rich people and powerful people all over this town. I've seen them on TV. I'm sure I can find one of those who'll give me millions."

Patrick lowered his voice. "Lucy, you're not stupid. You're right. There are plenty of people out there who will want the lantern. But will they pay you for it? They have ways of getting what they want. And then what will they need with you? They will kill you and take the lantern, and not give you a minute's thought."

Lucy scratched the side of her face, her eyes suddenly fearful. "Oh, so now are you trying to scare me?"

Patrick's expression was firm. "Yes, Lucy, I am."

Her expression changed into a facade of bravery. "Well, then, maybe I'll light the thing and time travel to another time."

"Lucy," Eve said, "the lantern often acts like a kind of boomerang. It would most likely take you right back to 1925."

Lucy was flustered. "Well, why don't you want it? I don't get it. I thought you'd want it. It's yours, isn't it? So why don't you want it?"

Eve and Patrick exchanged looks, each calculating the others' response.

The truth was, Eve wanted the lantern back, but only to keep others from getting their hands on it. She wanted to destroy the lantern and be done with it, so nothing like this could ever happen again.

Patrick knew what Eve was thinking and, at this point, he had to agree with her. With a baby on the way, and with their entire future and their child's future hanging in the balance, they needed to get that lantern back and destroy it.

"All right, then," Lucy said. "I'll give it to you for five hundred thousand, but I'm not going any lower than that."

Eve and Patrick had plenty of money, thanks to the trust they'd received from John Allister Harringshaw, who had invested the money in 1930. It had accrued interest over a period of eighty-six years. The total amount they'd received in 2016 was more than five million dollars. In the last three years, the money had been well invested, and they were comfortably well off.

Eve felt sympathy for Lucy Rose. There was no doubt the young woman had had a difficult life, filled with hardship, poverty and abuse. Eve's fear was that Lucy would spend the money on clothes, travel, clubs and alcohol. It was obvious that Lucy already had a drinking problem. But what could Eve do? She and Patrick wanted the lantern.

"Lucy, have you made any friends since you've been here?"

Lucy seemed puzzled by the question. "I don't know. I've met some girls. A boy. Seems like a nice boy."

Patrick had only misgivings but, like Eve, he wanted the lantern.

Eve looked at Lucy, and her eyes filled with tenderness and a gentle sorrow. "Lucy... we'll give you the money, but please promise me you'll put most of it in the bank and not spend it foolishly. Promise me, you'll use the money to go to school or learn a trade and make something of your life. Will you promise me that?"

Lucy's features brightened; her eyes filled with hope. "Yes... Sure, I will. Does this mean you'll give me the money?"

Eve whispered a silent prayer of support for Lucy. The young girl from the past would need it.

CHAPTER 8

On the afternoon of Monday, December 9, $500,000 was transferred into Lucy Rose's new bank account, and she was ready to begin her new life. During the time it had taken to complete all the transactions, Eve and Patrick had found and paid for a Greenwich Village Airbnb for her. They also provided her with cash. She was grateful but suspicious, obviously not used to kindness or generosity.

As per their agreement, the money would be transferred only after Lucy delivered the lantern to them. She brought it on Sunday, December 8. When Lucy entered their apartment, Eve and Patrick saw a change in the girl. She was perky, confident and impatient to jump into her new life. However, they were disappointed to smell booze on her breath.

Lucy tugged the lantern from her backpack and held it up for them to examine. As Eve took possession of it, she and Patrick couldn't help but smile. Despite what they knew had to be done—the lantern had to be destroyed—the lantern seemed like an old, lost friend and they were happy to have it back.

Lucy had remained distrustful. "If I give this to you now, you've got to promise me that you'll still transfer the money," she said, her eyes shifting nervously.

"Relax, Lucy. You'll receive the money next week," Eve said.

Lucy was all nerves and talking, in a hurry to leave, so there wasn't much of a goodbye; she was anxious to leave everything and everyone behind and begin her new life in 2019.

Eve asked if she'd stay in touch, but from Lucy's bland expression and noncommittal answer, Eve was sure Lucy had no intention of doing so. She had signed an agreement that she would never again ask them for money.

When she was gone, Patrick stepped to the window and watched her walk jauntily up the street, head up and shoulders back. He sent her a silent wish of success.

"I hope she makes it," Patrick said. "But I have my doubts. I've seen that type, both in 1885 and in 2019. Perhaps Maggie had a little of that in her. Thank God Maggie found that husband of hers."

Eve was standing before the fireplace, examining the lantern. She'd placed it on the green enameled hearth, and the poor thing looked the worse for wear. In the short time Mickey Blaine and Lucy had had it, they'd dinged it up, cracked one of the glass panes, and even bent one of the wire guards.

Memories flooded in as Eve reminisced, as faces and movie-like scenes flitted across the screen of her mind, both past and present. Thanks to it, she'd traveled to distant places that others could only imagine. She'd met fascinating and wonderful people, and some not so wonderful people. But what adventures she'd had, and all thanks to the lantern.

She smiled, recalling the first time she saw the lantern on the shelf next to the ancient typewriter in *The Time Past Antique Shop* back in 2016.

Patrick came over. "When do you want to do it? I mean, get rid of the lantern?"

Eve didn't pull her eyes from it. "I guess the sooner the better."

She took his hand. "Do you want to do it?"

"Nope. It's your lantern. You found it and I think you should be the one to..." He let the rest of the words drop.

Early Wednesday night, December 11, the lantern remained on the hearth, and a sleeping Georgy Boy was curled up beside it, near the gleaming, crackling fire.

Eve sat on the couch, staring at the lantern, arms folded tightly across her chest, while Patrick stood stoically behind her.

"Ready?" Patrick asked.

Eve looked right and left, as if seeking a way out of what felt like an execution.

"I'm never going to be ready."

"Okay, then, shall I put it back in the safe?"

"No," Eve said, abruptly.

They remained for a time in an uncomfortable silence.

"When should we get a Christmas tree?" Eve asked, stalling.

"Not yet. It'll dry out."

"Not if we keep water in the basin."

"We could go after we finish with the lantern."

Eve dropped her arms and reached for his hand, pulling it down and kissing it.

"Yeah, why don't we? It will help cheer me up."

Still, Eve didn't make a move.

Patrick left for the bathroom. When he returned to the living room, Eve was wearing her winter coat, scarf and white cap. She held the lantern by the ring handle.

"So, I guess you're ready."

She nodded.

Under an overcast sky and in a quick winter wind, they caught a cab on Riverside Drive, instructing the driver to drop them at West 72nd Street. Once there, they left the cab, Eve carrying the lantern and Patrick the hammer tucked in his parka pocket. They rambled off along a deserted asphalt path that led west, toward the Hudson River.

The moody amber light from the park lamps lit the way as they trudged along south, in silence, down a flight of stairs to the bike and pedestrian walkway that paralleled the wide Hudson River. When they arrived at the outdoor Pier 1 Café, closed and quiet for the winter, they turned right onto a wide jetty that stretched out over the Hudson River.

"I feel like a mobster about to do a hit, and then throw the body into the river," Eve said.

"It will be over soon enough," Patrick said, having second thoughts, but keeping them to himself.

The distant, glittering lights of Manhattan were on their left and the George Washington Bridge, with its necklace of jeweled lights and glowing towers, was upriver to their right. A Circle Line Tour boat was chugging along down river, the silhouetted passengers inside animated, Christmas lights strung on the stern and upper deck, suggesting celebration. Eve flinched at the loud, low moan of a cruise ship whistle. It seemed to fill the night with a foreboding as it pushed back from Pier 88, about to journey south, to Bermuda and the Caribbean.

The night wind blew cold off the water and snapped at Eve's and Patrick's dimly lit faces, the meager overhead lights casting eerie shadows. They were the only people around, not even dog-walkers or young lovers braving the aggressive gusts of wind and the promise of more snow.

They drew up to the railing that looked across the river to the shimmering lights of New Jersey and its dark rambling hills.

Patrick pulled up Eve's coat collar and set his soft eyes on her. "Ready?"

Eve stared hard at the river that seemed close, the current swift, a gray swirling mass passing underneath. Up the river, she spotted a little boat battling the current, ramping and driving toward the New Jersey shore.

She lifted the lantern, resting it on the top chrome railing. "I've got to thank it, Patrick. I've got to thank it for bringing us together. I know it seems silly, but I don't care."

Patrick nodded, waiting as Eve's eyes closed and her lips moved in a silent prayer. When she was finished, she looked to Patrick for support.

"Want the hammer?" Patrick asked.

"No. No, I'm not going to bash the thing. I can't do it. I'm just going to drop it into the river. The current will carry it away, and it will eventually sink to the bottom."

Patrick lifted his shoulders then let them settle. "I still wish it could tell us the secret of where it came from. I wish I could understand the thing."

Eve said, "As one of my college professors once said, 'Understanding makes the mind lazy.' And that's what I remember whenever I think about this lantern and where it came from."

Snow began to fall, riding the currents of a sudden quick, wet wind. Eve looked up to see clumps of dark, rolling clouds sliding ominously across the sky. Soon, the snow thickened into a flurry of disorder, slinging cold flakes into their faces.

Patrick heaved out a breath, white vapor trailing from his mouth. "Time to let it go, Mrs. Gantly."

She looked at him, her face filled with love. "I love you, Patrick."

Eve inhaled a bracing breath, enclosing the lantern gently in both hands. She held it up, and then extended it out, over the water. As it hovered, suspended over the churning river, she finally exhaled and released it.

The lantern dropped like a stone, striking the water in a white splash. As it disappeared under a leaping wave, a flash of golden light rocketed up like a Roman candle, illuminating Eve's and Patrick's startled faces, shooting up into the infinite dark sky and piercing the clouds in an explosion of bluish white light.

When the light faded and darkness returned, Eve stood cold and shivering, staring in disbelief. Patrick gazed skyward, worried. The night was now a fury of chaotic snow and biting wind.

"Let's get out of here," Patrick said. "Let's get that Christmas tree and go home. We're finished here."

Patrick wrapped an arm around Eve, and they turned, ducked their heads against the driving snow and started for home. Eve paused, glancing back over her shoulder.

"What was that light, Patrick? What happened?"

"I don't know. It's over and done with. It's time to move on."

They walked on in a blurring of snow, cold, perplexed and troubled.

CHAPTER 9

For most of the night, Eve skimmed the edge of sleep. Nightmares about the lantern bullied her; dreams about the rapid, swirling current of the Hudson River washed over her and, in one terrifying dream, she was plunged into the river, flailing, screaming as she was swept along, sinking down into the black, freezing water.

Finally, near dawn, she fell into a deep sleep, awakening hours later, feeling heavy and sluggish. Her eyes felt sealed shut, but she forced them open, squinting into the sunlight that streamed in from the bedroom window. Putting a hand to a yawn, she looked left, as she always did, to whisper a "Good morning" to Patrick.

He wasn't there. *He's probably gone for fresh bagels*, Eve thought. Patrick loved the bagels and spreads from the Absolute Bagel shop on Broadway. She sighed and snuggled back under the blankets, lying on her back, thinking about her upcoming day.

It was the light coming through the window and the odd feeling in her body that woke her fully. She sat up, glancing about the room. Something was wrong. Yes, the light was wrong. Her phone-check of the weather the previous night had said the City would get another five inches of snow. It was to be cloudy and snowy till late afternoon. Then snow flurries. Why was a plank of sparkling sunlight lying on the floor?

And the curtains were wrong. They were parted. Of course, that's why the sun was pouring in. Patrick liked the curtains drawn when they slept. It hadn't mattered to her.

Her eyes narrowed, then focused on the curtains. Yellow curtains, with a top white fringe. But no, that wasn't right. They should be blue. Blue curtains, with a lovely burgundy flower print. She'd changed them. When? Five months ago.

Her body felt weird. Good, but weird. Yes, she felt fine, but different. Instinctively, she lay a hand on her breasts. They were normal, not swollen due to her pregnancy. She froze. Her hand moved, touched, patted, searched and then, in a flash of panic, Eve tugged up her flannel top, pulled down her bottoms and looked at her stomach. What? Flat! A totally flat stomach! The last time she'd weighed herself, she'd gained five pounds.

Eve hurled back the white comforter, swung her feet to the floor and shot up, feeling, inspecting her body, hot terror boiling in her chest, rising to her face. Heart pounding, her mind struggled for a thought. Each one tumbled over the next.

"Patrick!" she shouted.

No response. Of course not. He was out. She searched for her cellphone and found it on the night table. She stared at it dumbly. What? It was her old phone. She'd upgraded only two weeks before. She'd exchanged it. No, this phone was even older. Two years? Yes, it was. Her thoughts tangled again, and her mind locked up, a wild panic bulging her eyes as she searched the room, seeking answers.

She snatched up the phone, ready to shoot off a text to Patrick. She tapped, scrolled, searched, and cursed when she couldn't find his name. Of course he was on her contact list.

An impossible thought struck, loud like a gong. She pushed it away, tossed her phone down on the bed and hurried to Patrick's closet. Grabbing hold of the handle, she yanked the hinged door open.

Her heart kicked against her ribs, pushing out puffing breaths. She saw her summer clothes, fall clothes, old slacks and jeans. She picked through them, slinging them aside, searching. Where were Patrick's clothes? His shoes? His boots? His sneakers?

Nearly blind with terror, she whirled to face the window. She rushed to it and looked out onto West 107th Street. The tree-lined street was ablaze in red, yellow and golden autumn leaves all glistening in a brilliant sun, in clean blue air, under a sky of deep, crystal blue.

These were not bare, winter trees. There was no snow on the ground. But most terrifying of all was that she was not looking down from the third-floor window, but from the second-floor window, from the apartment she'd occupied in 2016.

Eve felt faint and sick to her stomach. She stumbled toward the bed and managed to sit, bouncing, before she collapsed. She took deep breaths, and they helped dispel the dancing white spots before her eyes. Bending at the waist, she inhaled and exhaled, refusing to think, refusing to feel, refusing to allow any emotion to engulf her. She couldn't bear her thoughts. Not now.

Something was terribly wrong, but she couldn't think about that right now. She had to breathe. Just breathe and not allow any gut-wrenching thought to attack and overtake her.

Minutes later, somewhat recovered, Eve pushed up, opened the bedroom door and was met by Georgy Boy, tail wagging, eyes lit up with happiness at seeing her. It was another heart-stopping moment.

Georgy Boy had changed back to the color he was before Eve had time traveled the first time, to 1885. He was back to being white with black spots and his floppy ears were completely black, not brown.

Georgy circled her legs as she blundered into the living room. She and Patrick had bought and decorated their Christmas tree the night before. It wasn't there. The white fireplace had not been stripped of paint to uncover the original mahogany finish, a project that had taken Patrick several weeks to complete.

She stared numbly at her old furniture, her old plants, two of which had long died. There was no antique mirror, no bookshelves she and Patrick had purchased six months before. The draperies were gone, replaced by her white sheer curtains and bright yellow swag. The recliner was gone; the burgundy leather chair she'd sold to Joni almost two years ago was in its place. How was that possible?

Eve's breath came out in shallow puffs. She stood trembling, no longer able to stop the stark and utterly bone-chilling reality she was now experiencing. There was no need to search her closet for the lantern. It wouldn't be there. There was no need to rush out to the bagel shop to look for Patrick. He wouldn't be there. Something unthinkable had happened.

Still, Eve fought the painful truth. Back in the bedroom, she grabbed her phone and dialed Joni. Thank God her number was there. Joni picked up on the third ring.

"Hey, there, Eve. What's up?"

Eve spoke rapidly, nearly breathless. "Joni, you know who Patrick is, right?"

"What? Patrick who?"

"Patrick Gantly," Eve said loudly, forcefully.

"Gantry?"

"Gantly, Patrick Gantly, my husband, for God's sake!"

Silence.

"Joni...?"

Joni's voice was small. "Eve, is this a joke? I mean, you sound stressed and like, I don't know, weirded out."

"Joni, what day and year is this?"

Eve had refused to look at her phone for the time and date. She wanted verbal confirmation.

"Eve...?"

"Just tell me, Joni," she demanded.

"It's Sunday, October 9th."

"The year, Joni?"

"Okay... it's 2016."

Eve shut her eyes, hoping to close off the horrible truth. Her legs went rubbery and she struggled to speak. Again, she was short of breath. "Can you come over? Now?"

Joni's voice took on an urgency. "I'll be there in fifteen, Eve. Hang on. I'm on my way."

Eve stood in the middle of the living room, eyes closed, phone still held to her ear. She couldn't move.

Georgy Boy continued brushing her legs, wanting his breakfast, sensing something was wrong.

Inside her soul, a storm raged, a stabbing pain throbbed. She felt like a trapped wild animal, and she fought the urge to stampede out of the brownstone and go screaming into the streets.

Eve sat down, staring, feeling, thinking. How could she confront the impossible truth? But there was no other explanation and no means of avoiding it. Her thoughts began to clear, as images of last night with Patrick slid in and out of her mind. When she'd dropped the lantern into the river, somehow after they'd gone to sleep, time had been reset to the time before she'd found the lantern in 2016.

As a result, her entire life as she knew it was simply gone. It never existed. It had been erased. Patrick was gone, her baby was gone—every precious moment of their lives together was gone—all had vanished when she'd thrown the lantern into the river.

Eve struggled to her feet, feeling lightheaded and lost. Sobs expanded in her chest and rose to her throat. Her legs buckled and she dropped to her knees, and the phone bounced from her hand. She wept, moaned and called out for Patrick, as Georgy Boy gently nudged her cheek with his cold nose.

CHAPTER 10

Joni left the cab, crossed the sidewalk, swung through the squeaky wrought-iron gate and climbed up the front stairs. She pressed the doorbell and, when she wasn't buzzed in, she stepped back, shading her eyes and looking up at the second-floor bay windows. The curtains were drawn against the bright sun.

Joni rifled in her purse, found her keys and let herself in. She went charging up the stairs to the second floor, rounded the oak banister, arriving at Eve's apartment door, breathless. She raised a palm and thumped on the door. She waited, then thumped again.

"Eve… Eve, let me in. It's Joni."

Joni inserted the key, pushed on the door and entered. Georgy was at the door to meet her, his tail moving. She closed the door and saw Eve curled up on the living room floor behind the couch in a fetal position, her eyes pinched shut, tears streaming down her cheeks.

Joni rushed over, crouched down on a knee and was reaching into her jacket for her phone to call 911, when Eve's swollen and bloodshot eyes opened.

"Don't call anyone. I'll be all right in a minute."

"What happened? What the hell's going on, Eve?"

Eve managed to lift her head a little. "Help me up and over to the couch."

Joni slid her hands under Eve's shoulders and heaved her up into a sitting position.

Eve sat swaying, eyes closed, feeling dizzy.

"Come on, Eve, one more time. Let's get you up and off the floor."

Joni stooped, took Eve's two hands and hauled her to her feet. She then guided Eve to the couch and eased her down.

"Can I get you anything? Water? Coffee?"

"No... Nothing."

Eve fixed her blurry, sticky eyes on her old friend. It was no surprise. By now, Eve knew what had happened, and she was resigned to the truth, if not bludgeoned by it; if not sick to heart by it; if not absolutely shattered by it.

Like everything else in her life that had reverted back to 2016, Joni, too, had reverted to the original Joni, the tall coppery redhead, who reminded many people of a young Liza Minnelli. Yes, this was the original Joni—the 2016 Joni—before she colored her hair black, cut and fashioned it into a Cleopatra style. This was the dancer, singer, actress Joni. She had no freckles and no full hips, like the Joni Eve and Patrick had returned to after their time travel in 2018.

This Joni's skin was snow white, her eyes a dark blue that looked out into the world dramatically, with wonder and suspicion. This was the Joni Eve knew, long before she had time traveled and met Patrick in 1885.

As Eve sat, gaping at her old friend in a dazed wonder, Eve couldn't allow herself to think about Patrick, nor even repeat his name. The very thought of him brought a knifing pain in her heart and in her belly, where their baby had been.

This original Joni wore skinny jeans, a black leather jacket, gold sneakers, big sunglasses perched on her head, and long hoop earrings. Yes, this was the original Joni in her full glory.

Joni stared at Eve strangely. "What the hell has happened to you, Eve?"

Eve's smile was meager, her eyes swollen and filled with grief.

"You changed back, too, didn't you, Joni?"

"Changed back to what? What are you talking about?"

"To the dancer/singer. To the woman who works in sales at that camera rental house, renting cameras and lenses to Indie filmmakers."

Joni put a hand on a hip. "Yeah? So? I've been a dancer/singer, actress since I popped out of my mother's body. Hello? Like you don't know this?"

Eve looked away in sorrow. "You don't remember any of it, do you, Joni? You don't remember anything about what happened."

Joni's face registered a severe concern. "Eve, are you sure you don't want me to call one of your doctor friends? You look terrible and you're acting like you've gone crazy or something. I mean, you sound a little bizarre."

"No... they couldn't help. Nobody can help."

Joni could see the absolute despair on her friend's pale, white face, and she didn't know what to do or say.

"I've lost everything, Joni. I've lost my life," she said, fighting back unwanted tears.

Joni squatted down, looking directly into her friend's face. "As far as I can see, you haven't lost everything. I'm still here. Your family's still here, right? Your parents didn't die, did they?"

Eve shook her head.

"You still have all your friends and colleagues. You still have a job you love, right?"

Eve shook her head again.

"Then what have you lost?"

Eve flopped over onto the couch and pulled her knees up to her chest, shutting her eyes. She'd come to the end of all thought.

"Eve, you've got to tell me what's going on. Otherwise, I will call 911 and have you sent to the ER. I will. I'm not going to stand by and watch you fall apart."

Eve opened her eyes. "No... Please, Joni. I just need time to think all this through. Don't call anybody. Just stay here with me."

"Then tell me what happened. I've never seen you like this. It's like you've OD'd on something. Have you OD'd on something?"

"No."

"Then tell me."

"I don't have the strength to tell you right now. I've got to sleep. I just need to sleep. Will you stay with me? I don't want to be alone."

"Of course I'll stay. Have you taken Georgy for a walk? He's standing by the door, looking at his leash."

"No."

"Okay. I'll take him and be right back. Can I bring you anything?"

"No."

"Okay. Sleep. I'll get the comforter from the bedroom and cover you. You're shivering."

Eve awoke a little after one in the afternoon. She sat up, the scent of a dream about Patrick swiftly receding into forgetfulness. Eve stretched, noticed a fire was going and heard a gentle stirring in the kitchen. For a split second, Eve thought it might be Patrick.

"Joni? Is that you?"

Joni took quiet steps into the living room and when she spoke, her voice was almost a whisper. "How are you, Eve? Are you feeling better?"

Eve stared with dull, lusterless eyes. "I feel drugged. I feel like I could sleep for the rest of my life."

"Hungry?"

"Not really."

"You've got to eat. I just finished eating a ham and cheese sandwich... Sorry, you're now out of ham. Want one, with grilled cheese and tomato? A BLT?"

Eve shook her head. "No. My stomach feels queasy."

"I'll scramble you up some eggs," Joni said, throwing up a hand to stop Eve from protesting. "I won't take no for an answer. While you eat, you can tell me what happened. Meanwhile, how about some coffee?"

Eve sighed audibly. "Coffee, yes."

"Then you have to tell me what happened."

Eve put a hand through her mussed and tangled hair. "What happened? You won't believe me. No one will believe me. I just lost the three best years of my life and no one will believe me. I'm not even sure I believe it."

"I'll believe you. Get up, get dressed and eat something. You'll feel better. Eating always makes people feel better."

"You sound like an Italian mother."

"Not Italian, Eve. I had my DNA thing done. Did I tell you?"

"No."

"Well, listen to this. I'm mostly Eastern European, Ashkenazi Jewish, Native American Indian, not sure which tribe and, get this, Greek. No wonder I like Greek yogurt and feta cheese. All right, girl, get up and get dressed now. Food is coming."

They sat opposite each other at the blue-wash, solid oak kitchen table. Patrick had sold this kitchen set on *eBay* over a year ago, or a year ahead, however she wanted to think about it. They'd found a beautiful mahogany table with matching chairs at a flea market on the Upper West Side.

Eve sipped the coffee, and it tasted good. The scrambled eggs had parsley and oregano, with pecorino cheese. They also were good, even though Eve couldn't finish them.

Joni sat with her right elbow propped on the table, chin cradled in her palm, waiting for Eve to tell her story. Eve fumbled with her thoughts and emotions, searching for a way to begin the telling of the impossible journey. She decided to just come out with it.

"Do you believe in time travel, Joni?"

"No," Joni said, flatly. "No way. I liked *Back to the Future*, and *The Time Traveler's Wife*, but that's about as far as I go with time travel."

Eve's eyes traveled to the open window where a breeze ruffled the curtains. "It looks like a beautiful autumn day. Maybe we should go for a walk."

"Stop stalling, Eve, and tell me. At least get started, and then we can go out. Please, just begin the damned story. What happened?"

Eve's eyes widened. She had the sudden irrational thought that she should hire scuba divers to search the area where she'd dropped the lantern. It might not have traveled far. That part of the Hudson River couldn't be that deep. Surely, if they were experts, they could find it.

She gave that a few seconds of evaluation and then quickly realized the utter foolishness of the thought. Her mind was still a muddle, her body still tethered to another time and another reality.

Of course, it was a stupid thought. Divers wouldn't find the lantern. It wasn't there. She was in a different time. What she had done in the future, in 2019, had never happened in this time. The lantern didn't exist.

"Eve?" Joni asked, waiting impatiently. "Are you going to tell me?"

Eve lifted her miserable eyes from the table. "While I was traveling in Pennsylvania, I stopped at an antique store. I found an old lantern with a letter in it. The letter was addressed to someone with my name. The time/date stamp on the letter was December 24, 1885..."

It took several hours for Eve to complete her outlandish story. By then, they were sitting on a bench in Riverside Park, in lavish golden sunlight. Eve steadied herself with an effort, the memories and emotions causing little body quakes. She swayed unsteadily for a few seconds, as if she might faint, but then she bent at the waist and took some deep breaths.

The trees were awash in color, the sun sparkling off quivering leaves. Here and there, a yellow elm leaf fell, drifted and sailed. Georgy Boy sat on his haunches, keeping his sharp eyes on two edgy squirrels, their tails flicking, their escape tree within an easy leap. When a German Shepard trotted by looking for action, one of the squirrels darted away, spiraled up the tree and fled out of sight. The other sprang away, disappearing over the stone wall.

A confused Joni stared ahead. She opened her mouth to speak, then stopped. She turned to Eve, knitted her brows and set her jaw, searching for something to say.

Eve's gaze wandered. "I knew you wouldn't believe me."

Joni opened her mouth again, but nothing came out.

"Joni... I feel like most of me has died. I can't explain it any better than that."

Joni wanted to express the weight of sympathy she felt, but she couldn't find the right words. She lifted a hand as if searching in the air for some response, failed again to find anything remotely comforting or meaningful to say, and then let her hand drop limply back to her lap.

Birds darted through the trees, kids kicked a soccer ball about, and a little blonde girl passed, gripping the string of a red balloon that danced in the air above and behind her. Her bright eyes held dreams and adventure as she marched ahead like a little soldier.

Eve smiled at the girl. She knew the world the little girl occupied. She'd lived there for a time.

Joni gave a little exasperated shake of her head. "Eve... I just don't know what to say. It sounds like some movie or some novel or some crazy dream. It sounds like some, I don't know, drug-induced hallucination or something. I have no way to relate to it.

This guy, Patrick, sounds way too good to be true. I mean, what man is like that? And then all that time travel stuff. I barely know what happened 20 years ago, let alone what went on in New York in 1885 and 1914. I'm not saying I don't believe you, but it's just that... I don't know how to believe it. I can't get a grip on it. And, anyway, you've been here in this time. It's not like you went away and I haven't seen you for, whatever, for two or three years."

Two white poodles pranced by, their heads thrown back in proud attitude.

"I'm lost, Joni," Eve said, the words choked in her throat. "Without Patrick, I'm just lost."

Joni took Eve's hand, holding it between hers, rubbing it. "What can I do? How can I help you?"

Eve puffed out her cheeks and blew the air out in a steady stream of futility. "I wish I knew. I wish I knew what to do and where to go. I wish I could get rid of all this pain and loss I feel inside."

CHAPTER 11

Eve took the following week off from work, remaining in her apartment, sleeping, reading and staring into the empty fireplace. She had no energy, no ideas and no ambition. Sleeping pills helped her erase the happy memories of Patrick, helped her forget that she'd been living the life of her dreams, married to a man she deeply loved, pregnant with their child.

She spoke to her parents once and told them everything was fine, although her perceptive FBI father said her voice sounded distant and lethargic. "Are you exercising enough? You know how important exercise is for mental health. And lay off the sugar. I know how much you love ice cream. That kind of sugar high can contribute to mood swings, you know."

Eve listened to him patiently as she settled in the chair, tucking her legs beneath her, enjoying a bowl of chocolate mint ice cream.

Friends called, she ignored them. She responded to texts only briefly and, as for her colleagues who were worried about her, she emailed that she needed personal time and that she'd be back to work the following week.

Joni came over every day after work and they had dinner together, mostly takeout from local restaurants. Eve didn't, and wouldn't, discuss the past or what her plans were for the future, and Joni didn't ask.

On Tuesday of the following week, Eve was rattled awake in the middle of the night by a dream, a face. She sat bolt upright, eyes open, staring into the darkness. In the dream, an old, wizened face appeared, and the woman was calling to her. What had she said? The dream was already receding into the deep water of her mind.

Yes, the old woman had said, "Don't you remember where I put it?"

Eve managed to hold on to the remnant of the dream long enough to recognize the woman: her name was Granny Gilbert, and she'd been the owner of *The Time Past Antique Shop*. But she'd passed away, hadn't she?

As Eve shook off her drowsy dream, a thought flashed, lighting up her brain: in this time, 2016, Granny Gilbert would still be alive and, if she was still alive, then her antique shop would still be open for business.

Eve's mind had been so cluttered, her emotions so clogged with grief and despair, that it hadn't occurred to her. It was a wild and stupendous thought. This was October 2016, the same month and nearly the same day that Eve had first journeyed to Pennsylvania and found the antique shop.

It made logical sense that if everything else around her had been reset, then why wouldn't the antique shop? More incredibly, why wouldn't the original lantern still be in that shop, sitting on the same dusty shelf, next to the old typewriter?

Heart racing, Eve leaped out of bed and glanced at the clock. It was just after 4 a.m. She'd take Georgy Boy for a walk, dress, pack a bag, rent a car and be on her way to Pennsylvania as soon as she could. She'd text Joni on the way and ask her to give Georgy Boy his afternoon walk.

Eve texted the office that she'd have to take the day off, once again, and then she broke for the shower. Inside, she presented her face to the warm spray to awaken fully, feeling high-strung and anxious. What if the antique shop and Granny Gilbert weren't there? What if the shop was there, but the lantern wasn't? What if someone else had already found the lantern and purchased it? Would the lantern hold the same letter? Would Eve have to go through every experience in 1885 and 1914 all over again? Fine, if she had to, she would. Whatever it took to find Patrick again.

Eve drove in an agony of nerves and anticipation. The early morning light was muted, the traffic heavy leaving the City. It was after 7 a.m. before she turned onto I-95 and was slowed again by light rain, high winds, traffic and construction.

She drove, nibbling on a nail; sat in traffic and pondered. Away from her apartment, where she'd been sequestered for too long feeling sorry for herself, her frozen thoughts began to thaw. New questions tumbled down in an avalanche.

Why was it that Eve could remember 2016 through 2019, and all that had occurred, but Joni couldn't, or her friends, colleagues and family?

Would Granny Gilbert remember Eve? Would their conversation be exactly the same as it had been the first time?

The day was already different. The last time she'd traveled to the antique shop it had been on a Sunday, a glorious sunny day. Eve had stopped at a roadside farm stand, bought a plain donut, an apple pie, a bag of apples and a quart jug of cider. This time, as she drove by the roadside stand, it was empty. There were no pumpkins, no apples, no donuts and no apple cider.

Okay, so what did that mean? Would the lantern, if it was even there, be a duplicate of the old lantern, or would it be different? Eve's head filled with crashing thoughts and noisy confusion. She swallowed away a bitter, dry throat, and her hands gripped the steering wheel so tightly they hurt. When she released them, they trembled.

As she turned left onto a two-lane asphalt road, rain changed to a light mist, and a gush of wind punched the trees, sending leaves scattering in a frenzy all around her. The wipers swept back and forth, smudging the windshield. She switched them off and pressed the windshield wiper fluid, but there was no spray. She flipped the wipers back on and watched them struggle across the glass, making a dull, squeaking sound.

Her heart thumped loud in her ears as she drew closer to the antique shop, as hope arose, as despair arose, as a silent prayer arose.

Eve angled onto a wooden bridge that covered a rocky, gurgling stream, listening to her tires rattle across the old beams. She remembered this bridge well. It was the same bridge she'd crossed twice before, the last time with Patrick, who was sitting in the passenger seat. She glanced left to see open farmland and a small town, shrouded in fog. All that was the same.

Minutes later, Eve spotted a green rectangle sign, with white letters:

COMBS END CITY LIMITS
POPULATION 3,510

When Eve saw *The Time Past Antique Shop*, her heart leaped to her throat. It was there! She turned into the empty parking lot, her tires popping across the gravel, and parked near the front door, just as she'd done the first time.

With a hard swallow, Eve switched off the engine and climbed out into a misty wind, gently closing her car door. She was lost in memory, examining the building with a worried gaze and excited heart. She zipped up her brown leather jacket, pocketed her hands, and stepped back, studying the place. As before, the tiled peaked roof precariously supported the battered shop sign; a good wind might send it plummeting. Yes, that was exactly the same. A weathervane swayed and creaked in the wind like a confused, drunken man, and Eve remembered Patrick had made a comment about how ancient the thing looked.

The shop appeared as a relic from the 1920s or 1930s, nestled under stately elms and maples, with quiet homes scattered about, mostly concealed in the gray, stringy fog.

It was the same quaint shop that seemed to lean to the right, as if weary, and the red paint had long faded into the old wood, which was warped around the windows. The lawn was yellow, the weeds high and rambling, and a flower garden lay wilted and neglected.

Eve allowed herself a little sigh of relief. From all appearances, it was the same shop. Yes, the very same in every aspect.

Was it open? Eve glanced at her watch. It was 9:36 a.m. She crept forward to the filmy, twelve-pane vintage farmhouse windows, pulled a breath and peered inside.

As before, she saw mantel clocks, vases, watches, a brass spittoon, and an ornate Victorian lamp, its opal, glass ball lampshade hand-painted with roses.

Eve reached for the cold doorknob and turned it gently. A little bell over the pale blue door "dinged" twice as the door creaked open. Eve ventured in, tentative, and closed the door behind her.

Inside the dimly lit room, she locked her hands behind her back and closed her eyes. Was she dreaming this? Did she even know the difference between dreams and reality anymore?

She opened her eyes, once again inhaling the scent of dust, old wood and mold, just as she had the first time. Slowly, carefully, as if she were fragile, she started forward, watchful, waiting, listening. It was so quiet, her ears rang.

Inevitably, and with renewed hope, her head lifted, her eyes narrowed, and she probed the deep shadows at the rear of the shop where she'd first found the lantern. She stood on tiptoes, but she couldn't see much of anything, just silhouettes of vases and lamps. Urgency built in her chest. She wanted to charge to the back of that little shop like a bull and find the lantern. Every cell, atom—every fiber of her being boiled with eager expectation. But she stayed rooted by fear. What if it wasn't there? She'd be devastated. Broken. Shattered.

For a quick distraction, she glanced about at the rickety-looking shelves and narrow display tables holding vintage jewelry, shoes, purses, a candlestick telephone, and some baseball cards from 1910. Eve turned in place, noticing an old rocking chair, a wood-burning stove and, hanging on the wall, a large, over-the-mantel Victorian mirror with a subtle green, ornate plaster frame. She remembered all of it. So, if they were still here, then logically, so was the lantern. Eve made a move toward the rear of the shop when a voice stopped her.

"Can I help you?" It was an old woman's thin, shaky voice.

Eve swiveled left. There she was, alive again: Granny Gilbert, a short, slender and elderly woman, with a face mapped with lines. She wore the same blue print dress as before, a long white cardigan sweater and chunky black shoes. She had the same Benjamin Franklin spectacles perched on the end of her round nose, and her snow-white hair was piled in a bun at the crown of her head. Granny adjusted her glasses and squinted a look at Eve.

As Eve stood there gawking, she felt floaty and detached. *How could this be? How could any of this be?*

"Is there something you like?" Granny Gilbert asked, a bit wary.

High on nerves, Eve spoke in an over-exaggerated, chirpy voice. "What a great shop. It's so wonderfully authentic, isn't it?"

"Well, I don't know about authentic, but it's old like me. We're both old as the hills, and maybe older than some of the hills around here."

Eve's smile was small. It was obvious that Granny Gilbert did not remember her, and Eve was relieved. To Granny, this was their very first meeting. It was also not the same conversation they'd had the first time they'd met. So everything was the same, but different. A fragment from an old college lecture suddenly flashed into her head. *There is an infinite number of choices within a confined circle.*

"Well, you just wander and look around if you want," Granny said.

Eve's attention returned to the rear of the shop, her pulse throbbing. "Yes, I think I'll just wander toward the back and take a look around. I always like to see what's lingering in the dark corners."

"There's a pull-chain light back there, on your left. Here, I can walk back and turn it on for you. I usually don't get people in here till late morning or afternoon."

"No, it's okay. I'll do it. I'll find the light," Eve said, too abruptly. "I mean, I'll just explore…"

Granny Gilbert pushed her hands into her big dress pockets, her expression suddenly cautious.

As Eve took a step to leave, Granny's voice stopped her.

"You're not from around here, are you?"

"No, New York City."

"Oh, my stars. That city is just a crowd of people going this way and that. I don't know how anyone ever knows where they're going or what their business is."

Eve smiled, distractedly, her attention still focused on the rear. "Yes… Yes, it's a busy place all right. Okay, I'll just look around then."

"I'm Granny Gilbert, if you need to call for me. I'm gonna just step away for a minute or two and finish my cream of wheat. I'm a little late getting started this morning, and that just isn't like me."

When she was gone, Eve took small steps down the aisle, hearing her footsteps creak across the old floorboards. Entering into a place of shadows, Eve's eyes darted about, her breath loud, the shop quiet.

Even in the gloomy gray light, Eve could make out the shelf and the items on it. With reluctance, she allowed her eyes to travel. They rested first on the old typewriter, paused, then slid left to the next item. When she saw it, her breath caught. There it was. The lantern!

CHAPTER 12

Gazing at the lantern in that delirious, timeless moment, Eve was frozen in place, wedged between worlds; caught in contradictions. The lantern was dull and tarnished, and yet it seemed to pulsate with incarnate possibility and power, claiming the mystery and elegance of by-gone years.

Eve took tentative steps forward, approaching the lantern with respect, with reverence, and with a mounting urgency. Was it the same lantern she had dropped into the Hudson River only days before, or was it altered, like everything else in her life had been altered; everything the same, and yet changed, like a variation on a musical theme? Everything was altered, that is, except herself. She was the same, and she recalled all that had happened, past, present and future.

Eve let out a trapped breath as she inched toward the lantern, knowing that she was about to embark on a new life that she couldn't even imagine. But the vital and profound question that hovered in the air was, if the lantern standing on the shelf before her was not an exact duplicate of the first lantern, would it, nevertheless, take her back in time to Patrick?

Gathering courage, Eve took a final step ahead, now only two feet from the shelf, from the lantern. It looked exactly the same as the first lantern. It was twelve inches high, made of iron, with a tarnished green/brown patina. There were the four glass windowpanes with wire guards, and an anchor design on each side of the roof, the exact same design as her lantern—as the lantern she'd thrown away, except for one thing: this lantern had a steel nob that opened a glass door for easy access to light the wick.

Her breath sped up as she gingerly reached for it, her hand suspended for a time as she fought the irrational feeling that the lantern might awaken from a long sleep and light up. With a shaky hand, she gently lifted the lantern by the ring handle and, again, as she'd always been, she was surprised by its weight.

As the seconds expanded and as she struggled to steady her breathing, Eve carried the lantern over to the only window, covered by red and white checkered curtains that were no doubt a style from the 1950s or early 60s. She parted the curtains and held the lantern up into the light, and a shaft of weak sunlight poured in, bathing it. With eager eyes, she peered at the sooty glass panes, straining to see inside. With anxious fingers, she tugged on the front steel nob, pulled the glass door open, and her heart jumped.

A current of cold air rushed over her and she heard the "ding" of the front doorbell. Eve didn't move. Angling the lantern to-and-fro, she inspected the interior. Just as it had happened the first time, Eve saw something inside the lantern, blocking the wick. She felt a bruising anxiety as she reached in and tugged at the corner of what appeared to be a postcard. This was not the same as before. The first time it had been a letter: the Christmas Eve letter written by John Allister Harringshaw to Evelyn Sharland.

The urgent moment drove her on. With two tweezer fingers, she gripped and wriggled the card through the open pane and out into the light.

The shop seemed devoid of air; Eve devoid of breath. It indeed was a postcard, a very old postcard, yellowed by age, glazed by dust and soot. She pulled a tissue from her purse, wiped away the soot and focused. She saw an old, black-and-white photo of the Eiffel Tower. At the lower right was printed *PARIS–La Tour Eiffel 1883*. Eve turned the card over and wiped more soot. The printing at the top read, CARET POSTALE. On the left, where a stamp should be, there was none. Under the printed letters CORRESPONDANCE was an inscription written in small, precise handwriting.

Quand le soleil brille sur moi, je pense très peu à la lune.

Celui qui trouve cela me trouve. 1884

Eve recognized it as French, but she couldn't read French. She heard footsteps shuffling toward her, and she quickly shoved the postcard into the side pocket of her purse, still holding the lantern as she turned, presenting an innocent face.

"Did you find anything?" Granny Gilbert asked. "Oh my, it's dusty back here, isn't it? I asked my grandson to clean up, but I don't believe he ever did, or, if he did, he just gave it a lick and a promise."

Eve fortified herself with a breath. "How much for this lantern?" she asked in a breezy tone.

Granny scrutinized it with her beady eyes. "Well, where did that come from? I don't remember seeing that back here before."

"How much?" Eve repeated firmly.

"Well, my stars, I don't know. It's a nice-looking lantern, isn't it? I wonder if my grandson put it back here when he was cleaning. Maybe it's his."

Eve managed a strained smile. "I'll give you four hundred dollars for it."

Granny's eyes grew big behind her glasses. "Four hundred dollars? Well, I don't believe it's worth that much."

She scratched the back of her head, indecisive. "Before I sell it, I suppose I should ask Billy, that's my grandson, if he left it here."

"Sorry, but I can't wait," Eve said, abruptly. "How about I give you five hundred for it? With that much money, your grandson can buy a bunch of lanterns."

Granny looked at Eve with a wide, watery stare. "How come you want that lantern so much, young woman?"

Eve's voice was overly loud and forceful. "I just love it and I've got to have it. Do we have a deal?"

When Eve had driven a mile or so away from the antique shop, she pulled off at the empty roadside stand, stopped, and grabbed her cellphone. She found a *Google* translation from French to English and keyed in the handwritten French inscription. The English translation jumped out at her.

*When the sun shines on me I think but little
of the moon.*

It was obviously a poem, but Eve didn't recognize it. She keyed in the second inscription and tapped ENTER. The words jolted her, scared her, a chill rippling through her body. The English translation read:

He who finds this, finds me. 1884

She shut her eyes and pinched the bridge of her nose. Had the postcard been inside the lantern since 1884? Each thought bumped into another, bouncing and tangling into a mental traffic jam. She sat cold and still, listening to rain tap the roof of her car, heard the rumble of distant thunder. When she opened her eyes, she watched streams of water wash the windshield, obscuring the world, obscuring her thoughts and feelings.

Time melted away and when she finally glanced at her watch, she was stunned to see 20 minutes had passed. She ventured a wary side glance at the lantern resting beside her on the seat. Was it a live thing? A possible threat? Was it something from another time and another world?

Finally gathering herself, she texted Joni to ask if she'd come to the apartment after work. Eve used all caps as she keyed in URGENT.

Eve shoved the car into gear and sped away. She realized she was speeding when she saw a tilting speed limit sign, and then the whirling red dome of a police car racing by in the opposite lane.

After returning her rental, she hurried home, toting the lantern in the blue plastic bag Granny Gilbert had provided. Eve walked fast, as the wind blew up and down the street, as gray rolling clouds again covered the sun, creating a gloomy mood.

She was determined to meet whatever fate the lantern dealt her. She would light the thing, there was no doubt about that, and then she'd hope and pray the light would take her to Patrick.

Inside her apartment, Georgy Boy was all bounce and happiness. She cut through the apartment with him on her heels. She sat the lantern on the hearth and backed away, studying it. How soon should she light it? How should she prepare? Where would it take her and what secrets were contained in that old lantern and its light?

CHAPTER 13

Joni and Eve stood side by side in the living room, eyes locked on the lantern. It sat on the green enameled hearth, the fireplace dark behind it.

Joni held the postcard, reading the inscription. "Okay, well, it's a postcard from 1883 and the inscription looks like it was written in 1884. Maybe it's worth something. Why somebody would stick a postcard in an old lantern I have no idea, but then, what do I know?"

Eve fought irritation. "Joni, look at the lantern. Look at the card. That lantern is almost exactly like the one I had before, except that the last time there was a letter stuck inside, and this time it's a postcard. Aren't you even a little intrigued by what the inscriptions might mean?"

"Yeah, I guess so. I mean, it's kind of weird and a little spooky. 'He who finds this, finds me?' That is like, really strange. And why didn't they write, '*She* who finds this, finds me?' Instead of *He*?"

"You're missing the point, Joni."

"No, I'm not. I get it... Look, whatever, okay? I mean, it's an old lantern with an old postcard. Okay, so it's the second model lantern. I mean, well, look at it this way, maybe it's the new and improved model."

"Come on, Joni, be serious."

Joni shrugged, went to the couch and flopped down, folding her arms. "Eve, I don't know what you want me to say. If you really want me to tell you what I think, I think you should go see somebody. Go see your therapist and work all this stuff out. I don't want to seem insensitive, and I can see that something has happened to you—something traumatic—but I don't know how to help you with this."

The fighting light went out of Eve's eyes. She stared down at the parquet floor with a sigh. "Joni... I need a friend. Right now, I just need a friend."

Joni sprang up again, went over and wrapped Eve in her arms, hugging her. "I am your friend, Eve. Come on... You know I am. I'm just no good at this kind of thing. Maybe I'm too much of a realist."

Joni drew back with a smile, hoping to lighten the mood. "I used to think you were the realist, and I was the dreamer. I mean, I'm the singer/performer and you're the scientist. We seemed to have switched. Anyway, it doesn't matter, I'm here for you whatever you decide to do."

Eve turned her eyes on the lantern. "I'm going to light it, Joni."

"Here? Now?"

"No... When I've had time to come up with a plan."

Joni's mouth tightened, and she turned away with a shake of her head.

"I'm going to need you to take care of Georgy Boy while I'm gone. I'm going to need you to come with me to Central Park and, after I'm gone, take the lantern and keep it with you until I get back."

Joni gave a lazy shrug, still not taking Eve seriously, but indulging her. "Sure, okay, Eve, if that's what you want. Fine. Whatever."

They stood in a cool silence for a time, and Eve grew circumspect. Their eyes made contact.

"I wish you remembered him, Joni. You and Patrick became good friends. He helped you install your new kitchen cabinets, and he painted your kitchen and bathroom."

Joni looked at her friend, trying to understand. "I don't have new kitchen cabinets, Eve. They're old, the shelves are warped and, just last Saturday, I had a guy from *Home Depot* come and give me an estimate."

Eve started for the coat closet. "I need to get out of here. I'm going to take Georgy for a walk. Want to come?"

Joni returned to the couch, sat, then sprawled out, enjoying a luxurious stretch and yawn. "I'm really tired. We were busy today, and I stayed up last night watching an old season of *Downton Abbey*. I'll nap till you get back, then let's go for dinner at that new Italian place on 106th and Broadway. I feel like pasta."

After Eve and Georgy were gone, Joni slid into an easy sleep, but suddenly jolted awake when an ambulance siren screamed by outside. Her eyes were only half open when they slowly settled on the lantern. They closed, reopened and refocused on the lantern fully, with a new curiosity.

It was a delicate and searching moment when Joni left the couch, self-consciously, glancing about as if she were being watched by unseen eyes. She approached the lantern as if it were a stranger and she was about to introduce herself to it. The postcard lay on the mantel, and next to it, Eve had handwritten the translation on a notepad. Joni picked it up and reread it.

When the sun shines on me I think but little
of the moon.

He who finds this, finds me. 1884

Joni returned the notepad and took a step back, viewing the lantern with renewed interest. It was odd that she suddenly recalled a phrase from an off-Broadway musical she'd performed in three years before, entitled *Dreams and Disjointed Things*.

The show opened in an old, shadowy, cluttered attic, with moonlight leaking in from an upper window, shining on a lonely young girl and on a large, red, medieval style, leather-bound book that sat on a pedestal. An eerie lilting lullaby lured the girl toward the book. As it glowed, making a whirring sound like distant fluttery wings, the girl was further entranced when glittering gold dust sprinkled down from unseen heights.

Enthralled, the girl approached the radiant book warily, unable to pull her eyes from it. She finally gathered the courage to reach for the book. As she opened the cover, a flash of light exploded out like fireworks and she jumped back in shocked wonder. Bursting out of the book came dancers, heroes, villains and pixies, all ablaze in light and music.

Joni remembered that it had been quite a spectacle. She had been one of the dancers, and that opening scene had always received enthusiastic applause.

Later in the show, when the girl's father asked why she climbed up into the attic every night, the girl's line was, "It is a marvel and a secret."

That's the line Joni recalled now as she stared at the lantern: the tarnished, solitary lantern.

Joni said, "Hey there, lantern. Are you a marvel and a secret?"

In the kitchen, Joni rummaged through the drawers until she found a book of matches. Back in the living room, she crouched down before the lantern. She had to hurry before Eve returned. She had to know for herself what Eve was talking about and if her friend had simply lost her mind.

Joni tugged on the front steel nob, pulled the glass door open and nosed forward to see the charcoal wick. She struck a match, cupped the trembling flame in her hand, and held it to the wick. It hissed, fizzled and went out. Joni made a face, glanced toward the apartment door to make sure Eve wasn't there, and struck another match. Again she touched the flame to the wick. This time, the light caught, and Joni sat back with a little smile of satisfaction.

"All right, lantern, do your thing. Let me see you dance."

Joni was soon enraptured by the lantern's soft, golden light. She closed the glass door and glanced around, observing how the light swelled the room with a purring radiance. In seconds, she was mesmerized by the light, bewitched by it, and strangely immersed in it, as though a wave had engulfed her.

Spellbound, she sat back crossed-legged, soothed by a low humming sound, as the quivering blue-fringed flame drew her deeper into a hypnotic state. When the marble fireplace began to disappear, when the walls shimmered with bluish sparkling light, Joni felt dizzy and disoriented.

The floor vibrated and began to dissolve, as the walls melted away into glistening stars and spinning, glowing moons. The world tipped and veered, and Joni began to panic. She cried out for help. Instinctively, she reached out to grab hold of something, anything, to keep from sinking, but all she got was handfuls of bubbling, fizzy air.

Now she was frightened—terrified. Everything began to spin above her: furniture, objects, light, moons. She was about to be hurled into an infinite abyss and she was helpless to do anything about it. She tried to scream, but the sound caught in her throat.

At the last desperate moment, just as she was about to be swallowed up into a vortex of spinning blue light, she heard a familiar sound. Someone was calling her name! Shouting her name.

Sturdy hands clamped down on either shoulder and yanked her about, tugging, pulling.

Minutes later, the spinning stopped, the light dimmed, the objects hovered and settled, and the humming sound of a motor faded into an uneasy silence.

Joni was heaving out breaths, her body slick with sweat. With a great struggling effort, she stumbled away from the lantern, landing on her stomach. She pushed up on hands and knees, crabbing an escape from the fireplace and the lantern, her eyes wild, searching for safety.

Twenty feet from the fireplace near the kitchen, Joni sat gulping in air, her heart pounding so hard it hurt. She held a shaking hand against it, swallowing bitter anxiety, staring soberly.

Slowly, she lifted her guilty, frantic eyes on Eve, who stood nearby, arms folded, glaring down at her.

"What's the matter with you? Are you crazy?"

Joni tried to make a sound. She couldn't.

"It's a good thing I came back when I did and blew the flame out. Who knows where you might have ended up!"

Joni blinked, fear still burning her body, her mind blazing like a raging fire. With her chest heaving, Joni pointed at the lantern. "What the hell is that thing?"

Eve tried to keep the emotion out of her voice. "I told you, Joni. I told you what it is, but you wouldn't believe me."

CHAPTER 14

Eve stood reverently in the center of the quiet, cavernous and awe-inspiring Cathedral of Saint John the Divine. At 601 feet long, it was the world's largest Gothic Cathedral, and it stood majestically only a few blocks away from where Eve lived. In the infinite silence, she gazed up at the breathtaking rose window, remembering how Patrick had once told her it was the largest rose window in the United States.

Eve had come because the Cathedral was one of Patrick's favorite places to visit whenever he had some problem to work out. He learned the Cathedral's history and had taken tours, often returning home to share, enthusiastically, facts he'd learned: that it was one of the five largest church buildings in the world; its construction began in 1892 and was never finished; it's an example of the 13th century High Gothic style of northern France, and it has the longest Gothic nave in the United States.

Eve knew that Madeleine L'Engle, most famously known for writing the Newberry Prize-winning young adult novel, *A Wrinkle in Time*, had been the Cathedral's Writer in Residence for over 30 years. She'd passed away in 2007 and was interred in the Cathedral.

Eve had come, not because she was conventionally religious, but because whenever she walked the length and breadth of the Cathedral, she felt closer to Patrick. She'd also come because someday soon, she planned to go to Central Park and light the lantern, hoping it would take her back in time, so she could find Patrick and then return to New York City with him. She'd come because she was scared, and she needed to offer a prayer to bolster her courage and ask for help.

And then there was the problem of Joni. Two days after she'd had her encounter with the lantern, she met Eve at a diner for breakfast. Eve knew Joni was about to make some dramatic announcement from the way she puckered her mouth, lowered her voice to a murmur and curved her shoulders forward as she spoke.

"I want to go with you," Joni said, averting her eyes.

Eve sat stone cold still. "What?"

"I do. I want to time travel with you."

The waiter delivered their coffee and Eve was too stunned to order. When the waiter moved to another table, Eve stared hard at her friend.

"No, Joni. No way. You know what happened to you the other day. You completely freaked out. I've never seen anyone that scared."

"Of course I was scared. Weren't you, the first time it happened to you?"

Eve blew the steam from her coffee. "Yes, I guess I was but…"

Joni cut in, "… So now I know what to expect."

"It's very dangerous. You have no idea what it's like, not only to time travel but to wake up in some strange place and realize you're on a completely different planet, where no one knows you and you have no friends or family. You are completely on your own. And that's if you don't wind up in the middle of the ocean, or on some mountain peak, or God knows where. And if we do manage to land in New York in the 1880s, it is an entirely different world."

"Okay, fine, it will be an adventure," Joni said.

"It's more than an adventure. The culture is different, the fashion is different, the language and way of talking are different, the manners, the food, the air, and the water. It's a very rough world back there. I can tell you, despite what people think about the past, it's not so romantic. The medical world is primitive; no antibiotics; women can't vote, many die in childbirth; the ones who work mostly take low-paying jobs; men are in complete control, and people work long hours for little pay. In short, it is a bare-knuckle world."

Joni's frank eyes leveled on Eve. "But you met Patrick, the love of your life, and you told me the other night over dinner that you also met some wonderful people and had experiences there you would have never had in this time."

Eve raised the cup to her lips. "Why do you want to go? Why do you want to risk your life like this? I have to. I have to find Patrick. I can't just let him go. We were in love, pure and simple, and I have to get him back. But why risk your life? For what?"

Joni settled back in the yellow upholstered booth, pondering. Joni half closed her eyes, as if projecting ahead. "I've thought a lot about it in the last few days.

At first, there was no way I was going. It seemed like an insane thing to do. Then, the more I thought about it, the more I thought, why not go? I mean, it's the adventure of a lifetime. How many people in this world would jump at the chance to time travel? I bet most people don't even believe you can do it. And, anyway, it's not like my career is going anywhere. Auditions are drying up. The last two parts I was sure I'd get went to TV and movie stars. They're taking all the theater parts these days, even though many have never acted on stage and many can't sing or dance worth a damn. Do I sound bitter? Yes, I am. Producers want the money from big money stars, and audiences want to see people they know from the movies and TV. They don't want to see a nobody like me."

"So, you're running away?"

"Yes, and no."

Joni looked at Eve pointedly. "Eve... I'm not all that noble, but you are my best friend and, yes, I'm going to say it: I love you and I would miss you like crazy. Now, having said that, if I was in your place, I would not want to do this alone. I'd want a friend. So, most of me is going because I think you're going to need me, and I don't want to be here alone, without you. No matter what happens, we'll be in it together. Anyway, I can't watch you just disappear into the unknown and stand by. If something happens—something bad—then at least we'll have each other to lean on."

Eve was touched by Joni's friendship and bravery. It lent Eve courage, and she could use all the courage she could get. And Joni had a convincing point. Having a friend along would be comforting, and very useful and practical.

Joni sat up, batting her eyes flirtatiously. "I also have to admit that if you found the perfect guy back there, maybe I will too. I certainly haven't found him here. And I want to meet this Patrick Gantly you've told me so much about."

Eve still wasn't entirely convinced. "I don't know, Joni, I have to think about it, and, anyway, you may change your mind."

"Okay, fair enough. Think about it, but I'm not going to change my mind. I'm ready to go."

The waiter returned, and they ordered. As the diner bustled, and dishes rattled and music thumped, Eve looked at Joni and said, "I just hope that if I do manage to time travel, Patrick will be there, and I hope he'll be the same guy I met and fell in love with."

CHAPTER 15

On a Monday in late October, Eve awoke at dawn and mechanically set about preparing for her time travel journey. She showered, ate, took Georgy Boy for a walk and returned home. She was ready to slip into her 1880s outfit when Joni arrived at 9 a.m. The mood was somber. Their eyes locked on each other's. It was time for them to do it: put on the corsets and layers of clothing worn by women in the 1880s. The dresses and undergarments had been designed by one of Joni's theatrical friends, a talented and skilled wardrobe designer for TV and Broadway shows, and they were similar to those Eve had worn in 1885. She was impressed by their quality and authenticity. Eve had also ordered two hats, both made of white cock feathers and elaborate ribbons. Eve's had emerald ribbon and Joni's burgundy.

Eve and Joni were in the bedroom, nearly overwhelmed by the various garments that were spread out on the bed before them. There were corsets, corset covers, petticoats, bustles, underskirts, skirts, bodices and beaded capelets. The dresses themselves were lovely. Eve's was a graceful, emerald green wool bustle dress with a velvet trim; it came with matching round-toed boots.

As Joni helped Eve dress, neither woman spoke, their eyes sharp and focused on the task before them, their minds absorbed by thoughts of the uncertain day that lay ahead.

When it was Joni's turn, Eve assisted her into a long, elegant, deep burgundy two-piece silk bustle dress, with an elaborate hem and buttons up the front. Its low waist and modest bust accentuated Joni's thin figure and perfect hips. Joni finished it off with an alluring double string of pearls, given to her by her grandmother.

The ladies went through a seesaw of emotions as they worked, neither sharing their emotions or apprehensions with the other. They worked in silence, only speaking when the work required it.

Eve's thick, shining, honey blonde hair was piled artfully on her head, with hanging tendrils. Joni had dyed her hair black, styled it into a pompadour, and added frizzy bangs, fashionable in the period of the 1880s.

Their long and tedious ordeal was concluded with a spray of rose and lilac, and then a visit to the full-length mirror to view the results. They turned left and right, adjusting their hair and corsets.

"You look absolutely beautiful, Joni. All the men will surely swoon."

"The hell with the swooning, I just want them to fall head-over-heels in love with me and put me up in one of those big houses you told me about."

Eve frowned. "Joni, like I told you, don't curse and don't use contractions. Use as much formal language as you can. Remember, you want to sound like those people on *Downton Abbey*, without the British accent. This is where your acting skills are going to come in handy, big time."

Joni's eyes moved nervously. "I've got to tell you, Eve, most of me still doesn't believe this is going to happen."

A half hour later, they paced the living room, waiting for Joni's friend, Ricky Myron, to show up.

Eve glanced up uneasily at the clock on the wall. "Where is he, Joni? He's 15 minutes late. Are you sure you can trust him with all this? It's a big responsibility."

Joni nibbled on her lower lip. "Don't worry. As you saw when you met him, Ricky's a little crazy, and not always on time, but he's cool. And he went to school to be a veterinarian. He dropped out, but he loves animals, especially dogs, so you won't have to worry about Georgy. You saw how Georgy took to him."

Eve adjusted her bulky dress, already feeling imprisoned by it. "I just wish he'd come. I mean, you really do trust this guy, right?"

"Don't worry. You can trust him. He's a painter now and lives in his head, but he'll be here, and he'll do whatever I ask."

Ricky Myron appeared at the door 20 minutes later, out of breath and disheveled, his sandy hair carelessly combed. He wore a frayed army jacket, worn, saggy jeans and sandals with no socks.

"Am I late or early?"

"Late," Joni said. "As always. Have you ever been on time, Ricky?"

He shrugged.

He took one look at Eve and Joni dressed in their 19th century dresses and exclaimed, "Wow, would I like to paint you two. Wow."

Eve seized his arm and pulled him into the apartment, closing the door behind him. Ricky was short and wiry and wore silver, wire-rimmed glasses that gave him the distracted air of a 1950s Hollywood sci-fi scientist.

Eve and Joni quickly sat him down and reviewed every detail of what was about to take place, and what he was to do after they were gone. Ricky listened blandly, calmly nodding, not showing the least surprise or concern about the fact that Eve and Joni were about to disappear before his eyes and time travel. Georgy Boy snuggled up to Ricky, licking his hand. That helped to relieve some of Eve's anxiety about Georgy.

Outside, Eve and Joni clumsily shoe-horned themselves into Ricky's 2013 gray Honda Civic, each helping the other. Ricky cranked the engine and drove away into the flow of traffic.

He found a parking space just off Fifth Avenue under autumn trees, burning red and yellow in sharp sunlight. Eve and Joni struggled out, drawing curious glances from passing tourists and New Yorkers.

They started off for East 66th Street, walking briskly toward Central Park, with Eve carrying the lantern in a canvas bag. They smiled pleasantly at the gawking people, who seemed especially fond of Eve's and Joni's lovely hats. Some even yelled out compliments.

When the trio entered Central Park, two young women hurried up to them. "Are you both performing in the Park?" one asked with excitement.

"Yes," Joni said. "Shakespeare in the Park."

Eve grabbed Joni by the elbow and yanked her along, with Ricky lagging behind.

"Why did you tell her that?" Eve asked.

"Why not? Anyway, I always wanted to be in a production of Shakespeare in the Park."

Eve had chosen Monday because she thought there wouldn't be as many people. Still, there were tourists who stared curiously as they drifted by. Eve led the way, taking the walkway leading to the lovely Bethesda Terrace and then to the Central Park Mall that runs through the middle of the Park from 66th to 72nd Streets. She marched along the broad path under a canopy of American elm trees, flashing gold in the rich afternoon light.

Minutes later, Eve arrived at their destination, The Poet's Walk, also known as The Literary Walk, at the southern end of The Mall. As she hurried by, Eve took in the statues of four renowned writers, Fitz-Greene Halleck, Robert Burns, Sir Walter Scott and William Shakespeare, and she kept walking, struggling in new shoes that pinched her toes.

Shaking off nerves, Eve searched for a quiet bench, away from the lovers and the tourists and the bicyclers, finally spotting one under a grove of trees. She motioned for Joni and Ricky to follow her as she started across the spreading lawn.

Catching her breath, Eve tugged the lantern from the canvas bag and set it down on the bench. All three stared at it.

Ricky scratched his cheek, then tugged up his pants. He pointed at the lantern.

"It looks old, doesn't it?"

Eve and Joni were silent. The time had come, and both women were fighting a mounting distress. Eve glanced at Joni and interpreted her expression.

"You don't have to do this, Joni. When I light it, just step back about ten feet and you'll be safe."

Joni inhaled a courageous breath. "Nope, I'm going. No stopping me now."

Eve reached into her purse and took out a box of kitchen matches. "All right, let's light this thing and go. Step back, Ricky. ... Back.... Back. Further back, at least ten or fifteen feet."

He did so, keeping his steady eyes on the lantern. "This is cool," he said.

A black Labrador came galloping by, his nose sniffing the grass, his alert eyes exploring the bushes. Finding nothing of interest, he tore off toward his owner, who was strolling along a dirt path.

Eve sat down and placed the lantern to her right. She patted the space next to the lantern, so that it was between them.

"Sit there, Joni. When I light it, we'll join hands. We are not going to be separated. Okay?"

Joni sat and swallowed. "Eve, who do you think the person is who wrote, '*He who finds this, finds me*'?"

"Maybe we're about to find out."

Eve slid open the glass panel, removed a match and struck it on the side of the wooden bench. The match flared. Eve cupped her hand around the fragile, dancing light, inched it toward the wick, and lit it.

The wick seized the flame, and the light blossomed and swelled. Joni stared bug-eyed as the glorious gold/blue light began to engulf them in a smoky blue, wavy fog.

Ricky was spellbound, then overtaken by shock and fear. He stumbled backwards, losing his balance and tumbling onto the grass. In an instant, they were gone. They had vanished!

He blinked, his startled eyes darting about, searching. He saw the lantern. It was still there, but the girls were not. The bench was empty. Ricky gulped in a breath and pointed at the bench with a trembling arm, his mouth open, forming an O.

Georgy Boy circled the bench, barking, yapping and whining, confused and scared.

Ricky pushed up to his knees. Eve and Joni had just disappeared, leaving behind the old dark lantern with its extinguished light, sitting alone and innocent on the park bench.

CHAPTER 16

Eve and Joni stood in a pool of buttery, yellow lamplight, shivering, dazed and staring. Suddenly, as if someone blew out the flame, the lamplight vanished, plunging the area into darkness so black they couldn't see a hand in front of their faces. Their eyes struggled to adjust, to see something, anything, in the turbulence. The moment was filled with cold terror.

Seconds later, from a short distance away, a small light flickered on and off, repeatedly, on and off, on and off. Eve's vision was blurry, Joni's eyes sensitive even to the soft light, and she shaded them with a hand.

When the light blinked on, they saw only vague, indefinite shapes. They wanted to move, to strike out, but they were disoriented and weak and didn't know which way to go. It was as though they'd landed in a dimly lighted cave where there were no clear paths or exits.

"Are you okay?" Eve asked Joni.

Joni's teeth were chattering. "… I think… so. You?"

Eve searched the darkness. "I don't know where we are. This is weird. Before, when I time traveled, I left from a bench in Central Park and landed in Central Park on a bench near the same place I left. This is new and strange. Can you walk?"

"I don't know. My legs are like rubber. I feel a little sick."

Eve worked to make her voice calm, although she was anything but. "Okay... Joni, let's just stand here for a minute longer and get oriented."

"I hope we're not trapped here," Joni said.

Eve heard the fear in her friend's voice. "It's okay. We're going to be all right. We just need to let our atoms or whatever settle. It takes time."

"But where are we?"

"I don't know. Just relax. We've got to wait until we get some strength. Then we'll explore."

They heard a staticky sound, like crossed electric wires, and they tensed up.

"What was that?" Joni said, her voice trembling, eyes straining to find the source.

They heard it again, the sound coming from their left, a short distance away, a sizzling sound. Just then, a flash of blinding light shattered the darkness and stabbed their eyes. Joni made a sound of fright as their hands flew up to cover their faces.

As the light faded to gloom, they dropped their quivering hands. In that fading light, they saw they were in a room; a wide room; a kind of laboratory.

Another flash startled them again. Hands went up again, and again as the light died away, they saw illuminated shapes around them: a rectangular table holding objects that looked like motors and generators.

A third exploding flash revealed the source of the light. On the far wall was a bank of light bulbs of all sizes, some the size of Christmas tree lights, others standard size, some larger. On a table nearby stood towering light bulbs, some over four feet high, some round, some narrow, some oval.

Eve surmised that in another room, someone must be throwing a switch that activated the buzzing, blazing lights in their room.

In another blinding flash, Eve squinted through fingers to see bales of copper wire, lead pipes and what looked to be some kind of switchboard.

"I've got to get out of here, Eve," Joni said, panic in her voice. "I can't take this anymore. I'm freaking out. My heart's going to jump out of my chest."

"Wait. Just wait a minute, Joni. Don't move."

They heard footsteps echoing in a hallway. They held their breaths, pulses racing, as the footsteps grew louder, approaching.

"Oh, God," Joni said, "Why did I do this? Why didn't I just stay home? What a fool I am."

Eve braced for what might come. An attack? She had no idea what to prepare for, because she had no idea where they were. What time? What place?

An overhead light flickered on, dimly illuminating the room. Both women blinked, their frightened, squinting eyes adjusting to the sudden light.

He stood in the doorway, looking at them with bland interest. Eve swallowed away a lump. Joni swayed and nearly fainted, just managing to stay on her feet.

The man standing fifteen feet away was thin and astonishingly tall, about six and a half feet tall, with a delicately curled mustache and slicked black hair, parted dead center. He wasn't unattractive, though not exactly handsome either. He appeared unusual and a little odd. He stared back at them with clear, piercing eyes, obviously trying to make a connection.

He was meticulously dressed in a dark suit and wearing white gloves. Eve guessed his age to be twenty-eight to thirty years old.

No one said anything for a time. They all just gaped, still and waiting.

"I don't know why... here... why you in here or something?" the man asked. "No one else here in this place because it is my place to be. My laboratory."

He had a high-pitched, thickly accented voice that to Eve sounded Slavic. His sentence construction was haphazard and difficult to follow.

Eve boosted her courage with a spasmodic smile. She decided to be blatantly bold. "Sir... forgive me but, where are we?"

"Where? And why?"

"We seem to be lost," Eve said, not knowing what else to say.

He kept his hands in his pockets as he stared into a vague and uncertain distance. He became silent again as he glanced up toward the ceiling, seemingly lost in a new, absorbing thought. Eve and Joni exchanged nervous glances.

"Lost from where?" he finally said.

Eve searched for words that might make sense, but her mind was fuzzy, and her body was feeling the exhaustion from the time travel.

"We were outside and wandered in by mistake."

"Mistake? How you make that kind of mistake like that?"

Eve offered a pleasant smile, hoping to get this strange man to communicate with them in a way they could understand.

As Eve had prepared for the journey, she'd decided to use the name she'd used the first time she had time traveled. "Sir, my name is Eve Kennedy, and this is my friend, Joan Katherine Kosarin. Would you please be so kind as to escort us out of this building?"

Joni managed a nod of satisfaction at hearing her full name. She never used it, and as it had rolled off Eve's polished, though affected tongue, Joni thought it sounded absolutely regal.

"You're then friends of my employer?"

Eve felt perspiration running down her back. "I... well, who is your employer, sir?"

"Of course you will know this man as being the Mr. Edison."

"Edison?" Joni asked, again feeling her stomach churn with anxiety.

Eve was feeling a frenzy of confusion. She needed to know where they were and what year they had time traveled to.

"Sir, would you please tell us where we are and what date and year this is?"

Joni shot Eve a glance.

The man didn't seem the least bit shocked or surprised. "I would be nice to be the one to tell you. You are in the Edison Machine Works. It rests on 104 Goerck Street, in New York City. The date you will know as Monday, October 20, 1884."

Joni's eyes registered a glassy shock, and then she folded and went down, a collapsed heap of elegant dress.

The tall, skinny man helped Eve carry Joni to a nearby wooden bench. As per Eve's instructions, they laid her lightly down on her back, with her arms at her sides. The man watched with pointed interest as Eve checked Joni's breathing. It was a little shallow, but okay. Next, Eve crouched down with as much lady-like dignity as she could muster, and gently raised Joni's legs above heart level—about 12 inches. Sure the corset was contributing to the problem, Eve loosened the front buttons and collar on Joni's dress, but not enough to seem improper in front of this man, who continued watching her with intensity.

"She has done this thing before?" the man asked.

"Not so much. She's not used to so many..." Eve stopped, realizing that what she was about to say would not be proper for 1884. She was going to say, *So many clothes and a tight corset*, but she didn't. She also couldn't mention that a person experiences considerable trauma when time traveling. Instead, Eve said, "She's not used to being in a place like this... I mean this laboratory, with all these... well, things."

The man's eyebrows arched. "But this is a good place. My best place to work. I work many things in here."

"Oh, yes, sir, it is nice. A very nice place."

"And how are you doing these things for this friend? Are you a nurse?"

Eve nodded, thinking there was no harm in telling him. "Yes, I am a nurse."

"Nurses are good for the world."

"Thank you," Eve said, still slowly lifting Joni's legs.

As she worked, some of the disorder of Eve's time travel mind dissipated, and clearer thoughts bubbled up. She tried to recall something from her past—something relevant to the moment. She lifted her eyes on the towering man, struggling to remember. And then she did, and she was stung by the impossibility of the moment.

"Sir, may I ask for your name?"

He gave her a little courtly bow. "I will be pleasured to offer my name to you. I am Nikola Tesla."

CHAPTER 17

Eve's mind and senses locked up. She gave him a dumb, meaningless grin, believing it was a joke. Then she was watchful and skeptical, as fractured thoughts, past and present, slowly knitted together to form a startling reality. She gawked, her throat tight, the hair on the back of her neck rising.

He continued. "When she wakes, I think it is comfortable for that friend there to return to her home for some rest. I can escort you both. If she can't walk over there, we will find a horse cab."

Eve's eyes stayed glued to the man, there being madness all around her. She'd had that mad feeling before when she'd time traveled. That wild, untethered feeling of being marooned and utterly lost, not knowing whether the world you found yourself in was fantasy, dream or hardcore reality. Hearing this man speak, gawking at him and suddenly recognizing him from old photos in science books in her father's library, she was shaken to her very core.

Most people in 2016 and 2019 knew the name Tesla from the Tesla Roadster produced by Elon Musk. Eve had studied Tesla, if only peripherally, but she'd learned much about the man and knew him to have been one of the greatest geniuses of all time. Even Einstein thought so. Eve recalled a quote. Once when Einstein was asked how it felt to be the smartest man alive, he'd replied, "*I don't know, you'll have to ask Nikola Tesla.*"

Tesla must have seen her wild, staring eyes. "Are you also about fainting?" he asked.

At first, Eve didn't understand his jumbled words. Then it dawned on her. She struggled to recover her wits and find her voice. "No... No, I'm not. I'm fine. I'm not going to faint."

Still, she gazed at him, studying those faraway eyes that looked at her, and through her, and beyond her.

"You are Nikola Tesla...?" Eve finally managed to force out.

He stood even taller, straightening his spine. "I am Nikola Tesla, of course, I am. Yes, I am Tesla."

Joni stirred, made a little moan of discomfort and tried to move. Eve pulled her eyes from the man and laid a soft hand on Joni's head. "Don't move just yet, Joni. I'll help you up slowly, okay?"

Joni's eyes fluttered open and blinked. "Where am I?"

"It's okay. Just take some deep breaths."

Eve noticed a window and saw it was night. "What time is it, Mr. Tesla?"

"It is somewhere near nine o'clock in the night."

Tesla turned and left the room, soon returning with a glass of water. Joni was sitting up when he handed the glass to Eve, who gave it to Joni. She sipped it gratefully.

"Thank you," she said to Tesla.

He nodded. "Ladies, may I call you Miss Kennedy and Miss Kosarin?"

They nodded. "How good of you to remember our names," Eve said.

"I have, so they say, a photographic memory. Easy for me. Now we go to your home and I escort you?"

Joni looked to Eve for an answer.

Eve rose to her feet, still craning her neck to look up at Tesla. She offered a shy smile and gathered herself so she could communicate carefully, in formal speech

"Sir, I must be rather frank with you and appeal to your kind understanding. You see, my friend and I only recently arrived in New York and we have yet to find lodgings. I am also gently embarrassed to report that we have little money... Well, actually, right at this moment, we are quite without funds, having been set upon by ruffians at the train station when we arrived."

Joni gave Eve an impressed side glance and a nod of approval.

Again, Tesla seemed neither surprised nor suspicious. "My kind and unfortunate ladies, I must share with you my story how I come to this New York. I was walking in Paris, with carrying my luggage in my hand. In this luggage is a ticket to board the ship, Saturnia, to cross the water to America. I have two nice and tailored suits, gloves and money."

Tesla patted his pants pockets. "In my pant pocket is four cents. As you say, Miss Kennedy, I was grabbed by three ruffians. They push me down and take my suitcase. A small crowd helps me to the nearest café. I brush up, I think you say. No, I clean up myself. That is right saying, no?"

Eve nodded. "Yes, Mr. Tesla. You are most correct."

Tesla narrowed his eyes as if to make an important point. "I wash up three times, then find the Ship Deck Officer. I explain to him, that I now lack my boat ticket because ruffians take it. I tell him, I have a photographic memory, and I know my ticket number, so all is as it should be."

Tesla pointed at his head. "I know the long ticket number. I have good memory for numbers. I hold them easy in my head. The Deck Officer can't believe me. Then he check that number with superiors and he learns I am right about that. So I get on Saturnia and come here to America."

Eve studied Tesla's appealing face, tall, lanky torso and kind, faraway eyes, and she decided she liked the man. She also sensed she could trust him. His distant eyes revealed no attraction to them whatsoever, and Eve knew, again from her college textbook, that Tesla never married and wasn't especially attracted to women.

"So ladies, I have only that four cents in my pocket when I land on this country. I also have some of my own poems that I write down in French. That is all I have. I was alone. You ladies will not be so alone as I was at that time, because you have Tesla to help you. So for you kind ladies, I will escort you to my hotel; it is the Gerlach Hotel on 49 West 27th Street. My room is 333 and I will pay for your room, which will be divisible by 3. It will be 336. It has been unoccupied for three days. That is good. Three is always a good number."

Joni looked to Eve for guidance.

Eve quickly considered their options and swiftly realized they had few. "Mr. Tesla, we don't know how to thank you, but we must insist that we repay you when our funds are replenished, which we hope will be in only a matter of days."

"Days, weeks or never. To Tesla, ladies, it is of no important incident. Now, shall we go?"

Eve helped Joni to her shaky feet, her face still white and damp with perspiration, but she managed to stay upright as they started out of the laboratory and entered a long hallway lit by Edison lamps on both sides. Tesla slowed his long stride so the ladies could keep up. As they passed a glass-enclosed office, a man emerged, obviously confused by what he was seeing. He wore a wrinkled suit, a black vest, and a bow tie. He was unshaven and had scruffy, dark brown hair. Tesla stopped, and the man looked first at Eve and Joni, and then to Tesla, for an explanation.

"Good evening, Mr. Edison. I am escorting these two ladies to the Gerlach Hotel. They are new in this City and, thus, are seeking lodgings."

Eve recognized the man as *the* Thomas Edison, but he was much younger than in the photographs she'd seen. This man was in his middle-to-late thirties. Again, she could only stare, hypnotized by the peculiar moment.

Edison brushed a strand of hair from his forehead. "Mr. Tesla, have you brought these young ladies into your laboratory?"

Tesla looked puzzled. "These ladies are just arriving in New York and they are lost, Mr. Edison. I, the gentleman, am escorting them to lodgings. That is all, sir."

Edison sighed, rubbing his tired eyes. "Well, all right then. You're working late again, Mr. Tesla. I take it progress is being made on DC current. You are making improvements, aren't you now?"

Tesla frowned a little. "We should talk more, Mr. Edison, about alternating current."

Edison held up a hand. "I'm not interested in further discussion on that subject, Mr. Tesla," he said, somewhat abruptly. He was about to leave, but remembered his manners, faced Eve and Joni, and offered a little gentlemanly bow.

"Have a good evening, ladies. I trust you will enjoy your time in our fair City. Mr. Tesla, please use my carriage to escort the ladies to their lodgings. I will not be needing it for at least two more hours."

Eve lowered her head in a modified bow. "That is most kind and generous of you, Mr. Edison." Joni nodded, her face showing pallid exhaustion. They started forward, with Joni walking unsteadily, looking about as if she were in a confused, cloudy atmosphere. Eve was anxious to get her into bed before she fainted again.

As they entered the lobby of the four-story factory, Eve glanced back over her shoulder. A new thought had struck, one she'd already considered, although she'd had no time to think it through. As they waited in the lobby for Mr. Tesla to return with the carriage, Eve shut her eyes, reaching deep into her still hazy memory.

Tesla traveled from Paris to New York. The postcard in the lantern was of the Eiffel Tower. The writing on the postcard was written in French and poetically mentioned the sun. The inscription below it read,

He who finds this, finds me. 1884

Tesla was a great scientist. Tesla worked with light. He was one of the greatest geniuses of all time. And there was more.

CHAPTER 18

Thomas Edison's burgundy enameled Brougham approached, pulled by two sleek black horses, each with a thin blaze, a strip of white fur running from the forehead down to the nose.

It was an enclosed carriage, comfortably seating four passengers, with doors on either side, glowing side lamps, deep leather seats and glass windows. It was designed to be elegant, trendy and private, fitting the station, wealth and prestige of one of the great inventors of the time. A stylish coachman sat perched and waiting, wearing a top hat, dark uniform and royal blue cape, reins and whip in his gloved hands.

Eve took Joni's arm and led her outside into the cool night air, streetlamps lit by dim electric lamps that the Edison company had installed. As Eve glanced about, she was surprised that the Edison Machine Works was located amongst the tenements on Manhattan's lower east side. The stain of tenement houses rose up in unfortunate dingy gray rows against the inky black sky;

they were obviously squalid and overcrowded. It was a depressing and oppressive sight.

Eve also had the immediate sense-recognition of old familiar sights, odors and sounds, left over from her journey to 1885; the smell of burning coal, burning leaves, horse manure and hay. There must have been a stable nearby.

There was no such thing as 'fresh air' in the City, in the modern sense, Eve knew. Every home and business needed energy, so they had to burn something like wood or coal, and the result was soot and smoke.

Joni seemed to sag toward the carriage as Tesla stood by the open door, waiting patiently. Joni stared in disbelief at a world she'd never imagined and knew little about. Eve knew what she was feeling, having felt it herself two separate times, in 1885 and in 1914. That sense of dizziness and floating, of not being completely locked down into your own body.

"The hotel is not so far," Tesla said, as the ladies drew up to the open carriage door. "You will have your rest soon."

He took each lady's arm separately, lending support as they stepped up on the footwell and into the plush carriage, with its facing seats. Joni sat on the soft leather with an exhausted sigh; Eve next to her. They heard Tesla call out the destination to the driver and then he entered, shutting the door behind him, sitting opposite them, offering an enigmatic smile.

"And so we will leave now."

The carriage lurched ahead, clopping along the quiet cobblestone street, and Joni shut her eyes, falling instantly asleep.

In the hazy light emanating from the outside lamps, Eve studied Tesla. Again, he seemed lost in his own stare. Eve wondered what he was pondering in that genius head of his. She also wanted to fire dozens of questions at him, but she knew this wasn't the right time or place.

And then, out of the blue, Tesla spoke up. "Do you know that Mr. Edison's favorite dessert is coconut cheesecake? We have dinner one night and I learn this. Myself, I don't take it."

Eve didn't know how to respond. "I've never had coconut cheesecake. It sounds good."

And then Tesla was quiet again, slipping away into a blank, entranced expression.

They passed row houses and taverns, a Chinese laundry and more low and dark row houses. A theater came into view, lit up in yellow and white bulbs. On the streets, single electric poles carried dozens of crooked crossbeams supporting sagging and exposed electrical wiring. It seemed unfinished and dangerous. Eve was about to point them out to Tesla, but he was lost in his own world, so she didn't.

As weary as she was, Eve's thoughts inevitably circled back to the lantern and the postcard. There was an uncomfortable coincidence regarding Nikola Tesla. Besides her science books, Eve had learned much about Tesla thanks to her FBI father. He had been obsessed by the man for years, reading nearly every book written about him, not to mention watching every documentary that was available.

Eve had learned about Tesla through osmosis. Her father had talked incessantly about him during her childhood: at dinner, by the swimming pool, or during long vacation drives. Her exasperated mother often said that Tesla was like a long-lost grandfather, an unfortunate part of the family. She once told her husband to shut up talking about Tesla, otherwise she was going to divorce them both.

Eve knew that Tesla was born in Croatia in 1856 and had moved to the United States sometime in the 1880s. He was best known for designing the alternating-current (AC) electrical system, which would quickly become the preeminent power system of the 20th century, and it has remained the worldwide standard ever since.

She also knew that the Tesla coil, which he invented in the early 1890s, was widely used in radio and television sets and other electronic equipment.

But what Eve suddenly remembered, and what kept her focused on the man seated across from her now, was the amazing historical fact that Tesla was also obsessed with time travel. Eve could easily recall her father talking excitedly about it.

"Did you know, Eve," her father once said, "that Tesla worked on a time machine?"

Eve was about twenty, home for Christmas break and studying for an up-coming anatomy exam. She was hardly listening.

Her father had just finished a new Tesla biography and he droned on, his voice high with excitement, hands cutting gestures in the air as if he were giving a lecture.

"Some say he succeeded, you know."

"Really? I didn't know that."

"Even his birth was interesting. He was born at midnight, which frightened the peasant midwife who was assisting Tesla's mother during the delivery. She predicted he would be a child of the storm. 'No,' calmly replied Tesla's mother, 'he will be a child of light!' Now, isn't that an interesting story, Eve?"

Her father galloped on. "Tesla's parents were Serbian, you know. His father was an Orthodox priest, and his mother was something, Eve. I mean, listen to this: she was known for her ability to memorize Serbian epic poetry and she was highly creative. She invented, among other things, a mechanical eggbeater."

Eve pushed her nose further into her book, but her father was oblivious. Once he got started on Tesla, you couldn't stop him.

"Tesla studied mathematics, physics and mechanics and he learned to speak six languages. He had an incredible memory and he could perform calculus equations mentally, even when he was just a student. Not only did he possess a photographic memory, he was able to use creative visualization that held practical results. He came up with a thing called 'Magnetic Flux Density.' It is officially called a 'Tesla.' And do you know what Tesla said about time travel?"

"No, Dad, I don't."

"He believed time and space could be altered by magnetic fields and he experimented with creating an artificial magnetic field. When he was in it, he claimed he could see 'the past, present and future all at the same time.' Yes, Eve, many people, including scientists, believe that Tesla actually created a working time machine."

"Good for him," Eve had said, distractedly. Time travel was one of the last things on her mind. She didn't believe in it, and it didn't interest her in the least.

A carriage wheel struck a pothole, jolting Eve back to the present.

Tesla didn't stir. His eyes were still and clear. Joni's head had settled softly on Eve's shoulder, and she was asleep.

Eve leveled her eyes on Tesla, sure he wouldn't care or notice that she was staring at him. Was this man sitting across from her responsible for the lantern that had brought her and Joni from 2016 into his laboratory in 1884? The time travel lantern? Had he been responsible for all the lanterns, including the one she'd dumped into the Hudson River in 2019?

She couldn't wait. She had to ask him. "Mr. Tesla?"

His eyes briefly cleared. "Yes, Miss Kennedy?"

She decided to come right out with it. "Do you believe in time travel?"

Tesla looked at her with an indifferent seriousness. "Miss Kennedy, if you only knew the magnificence of the 3, 6 and 9, then you would have the key to the universe."

And then he turned from her to stare out the window. Obviously, that was the end of the conversation, and Eve had no idea what he'd just said or what it meant. She'd ask him again as soon as the time was right, sure he was hiding something.

Eve followed his gaze out the window and saw a burly policeman with a waxed mustache, strolling the sidewalk, twirling his stick. He gave them a cool, level stare as they drifted by.

It was the policeman who jarred Eve's memory, and an image of Patrick flashed into her mind. But then he was always in her thoughts, even during the chaotic time travel experience she and Joni had just gone through. She felt the spirit of him, the call of him.

In this time, 1884, where was he? Had he changed? If she found him, would he know her? Remember their life together?

If everything had been reset when she'd tossed the old lantern into the river, then logically Patrick had been reset too. That's why he'd disappeared. That could mean only one thing: he wouldn't know her, and he wouldn't remember their marriage or their history together. They had first met in October of 1885. This was October 1884.

Losing Patrick had been an unsupportable loss, and now, having arrived in 1884, she ached for him, and she longed for him, and she was already itching to find him. And she would find him, one way or the other.

The carriage drew up to the Gerlach Hotel, a Queen Anne-style structure that rose ten stories to a tower. Eve awakened Joni, who complained and whined that she wanted to go home.

They entered the hotel under an iron-and-glass sidewalk canopy, stepping into a modest marble lobby with hanging gas lamps, heavy burgundy draperies with matching runners, and a royal blue circular tufted couch near the single elevator.

Tesla strolled up to the mahogany lobby desk, confident and commanding. "These tired ladies wish lodgings. Room 336. Tesla will pay for a week, now."

The very proper middle-aged desk clerk, with proper pursed lips, parted reddish blonde hair and a quarrelsome expression, looked at Tesla, then at Eve and finally at a wilting Joni.

"Mr. Tesla, this seems patently irregular."

"No need for this to be irregular as long as you give them the room 336. These ladies are new to this City. They are lost and they are weary travelers."

Tesla peeled off four dollars and placed it on the desk. "That is four-dollar notes. That is the weekly rate. Three is a better number, but I will agree to this for these ladies."

The desk clerk sniffed imperiously and took the four-dollar notes, while lowering his disapproving eyes on the ladies.

"This is a respectable hotel, ladies," he instructed.

Eve grinned at him. "Yes, as we can readily see, sir, by your fine example and by that snappy little gold and black bow tie. Thank you."

He glanced at her questioningly, uncertain if she was mocking him. He craned his neck, searching the surrounding area. "Do you not have luggage, ladies?"

Tesla spoke up, towering over the man and, as such, intimidating him.

"Like what happened to me in Paris, they were set on by ruffians. These ladies will find such things to wear that are necessary in the next days. We prefer to go to the rooms now, sir."

The elevator trip to the third floor was surprisingly smooth. When the doors opened, Tesla escorted Eve and Joni across the royal blue carpeted hallway to their hotel door and stopped some five feet away, as if to step any closer would be improper; a breach of etiquette.

He removed a five-dollar note from his wallet and handed it to Eve. "You will need money for such items necessary. This will help."

Eve and Joni stared down at it, surprised and touched. Eve nearly spoke up to protest but stopped. The truth was, they needed the money and they would pay him back later.

"If you need more of me, I am to be in room 333."

Eve and Joni gazed up at him with grateful smiles.

Eve accepted the money. "We are greatly in your debt, Mr. Tesla."

"Yes, thanks for everything, Mr. Tesla," Joni said. "What would we have done without you?"

"Not debt to me, ladies. Please rest and be good and refreshed in the morning."

"Will we see you again soon, Mr. Tesla?" Eve asked. "I would like to discuss some things with you… about science?"

Tesla brightened. "Science? Yes, we can discuss science, Miss Kennedy, but I'm afraid not soon. Tesla only sleeps two hours at night. I have much work in the morning. I leave for the laboratory early and stay late. Good evening, ladies."

Before he could step away, Eve said, "Mr. Tesla, Miss Kosarin and I would like to invite you for tea or for dinner to thank you for all you've done. Can that be arranged?"

He stared up at the ceiling and scrunched up his mouth. "We go to my favorite restaurant, Delmonico's. Yes. Next Saturday night? Will that be a pleasure for you two ladies?"

Eve would have preferred sooner. "Yes, sir. Thank you."

He walked to his room just down the hall, opened his door, entered and was gone.

Eve turned to Joni. "Do you know who that is?"

Joni shook her head.

Eve inserted their key and opened the door. The five-dollar note would allow her to begin her search for Patrick the next morning.

CHAPTER 19

Eve's and Joni's hotel room opened into a quaint parlor with a love seat, an ottoman, a lady's chair without arms (to accommodate their large dresses), and an armchair for a man. On the side tables were ornate kerosene lamps and lovely candle holders. The center table, a tea-table, had a white marble surface, and the fireplace was surprisingly ornate and impressive.

Joni swept into the bedroom, instantly taken by the canopied four poster double bed, covered by a mossy green quilt that matched the draperies. The burgundy patterned carpet looked new, the two comfortable side chairs were rococo style, and a dark wood dresser with a black marble top held a pitcher and a bowl.

The bathroom had a waffle ceiling, tile-covered walls, and a peach and white color scheme. There was a toilet, a peach and white colored tub, a shower over the tub with a small, tied-back, rose-colored curtain, a sitz bath, a sink and a mirror.

Joni and Eve took it all in with weary enthusiasm.

"It's nice," Eve said.

Joni removed her hat. "I love the parlor. That toilet looks interesting."

"You'll get used to it," Eve retorted.

Back in the bedroom, Joni stared at herself in the ornate, gilded mirror that hung on the wall opposite the bed. She placed all ten fingers on her cheeks in astonishment.

"Oh, my God. Look at me. I look tired, sick and old. I look like I've aged five years, Eve. Dammit!"

Eve flopped down on the bed, suddenly exhausted, removing her hat. "Don't curse, Joni. If you curse like that and talk like you do in the 21st century, that hotel clerk is going to think we're prostitutes and throw us out."

"But look at me, Eve. You didn't tell me that when we time traveled, I was going to look like an old hag."

"You don't look like a hag. You'll be fine once you get some sleep."

"My God, I've got wrinkles where I never had wrinkles. This whole thing is a friggin' nightmare."

"Don't use the word 'friggin,' or anything else like it, Joni. Like I told you, you've got to practice sounding like people in *Downton Abbey* or characters in Jane Austen novels."

Joni abruptly backed away as if seized by an urgent thought. Eve watched in amazement as her friend unfastened every button on her dress in light speed. She kicked away the dress, slipped out of the petticoat, the corset cover, the bustle, the underskirt, the skirt, the bodice and the beaded capelet. Finally, she peeled off the money belt and slung it onto the bed. She turned, her face contorted in distress.

"Unlace this damned corset, Eve. I can't take it anymore. I feel like I want to kill myself in this thing."

Eve pushed up and went to her friend, doing as she'd asked, unlacing the corset. Minutes later, Joni was stark naked, leaping around the room like she was dancing in a Broadway chorus, arms shooting up, hands splayed out, head snapped back with attitude, and body lost in a full-razzle-dazzle dance.

"Take it easy, Joni. I thought you were exhausted. Be quiet. You'll get the house detective up here."

After a few more gyrations around the room, Joni dropped onto the bed in a bounce, panting like a racehorse.

"I can't wait to get into that shower and wash all this time travel guck off me."

"You're lucky, Joni. This is one of the newer hotels. They have running water and a tub."

Joni sprang up and skittered across the carpet into the bathroom.

"Grab a towel and cover yourself," Eve said, with a little laugh. "You'll catch a cold."

Joni snatched a towel from the chrome rack and did so.

"While you take a shower, I'm going to check out our money belts and make sure everything traveled with us, especially the bracelet, necklace and antibiotics."

Sitting on the bed, hearing the trickling shower, Eve laid the two black money belts out next to her. She peeled hers open and drew out a diamond and turquoise necklace she'd purchased in New York for $60,000. It was still intact, although she noticed the clasp had been slightly damaged, and the diamonds seemed to have lost some of their fire. Still, it should fetch a good price—probably enough to live on for a couple years.

Next, Eve examined the Zithromax Z-Pak tablets 250mg, as well as the painkillers. She frowned. Some of the pink pills had been crushed. Not good. They would be ineffective.

Eve reached for Joni's money belt and located the silver diamond bracelet. She held it up, inspecting it. There was no damage that she could see, and the impressive diamonds glittered in the lamplight.

Eve was discouraged when she saw that the Zithromax Z-Pak tablets in Joni's money belt had also been damaged during time travel. She counted the remaining antibiotics and frowned. There was only enough for one course, and that was not a comforting thought.

During her first time travel journey to 1885, she'd had no antibiotics with her. Patrick would have died if he hadn't escaped to the future to receive modern medicine.

In 1914, Eve was able to save a young man's life with the antibiotics she'd brought with her and, because he'd survived pneumonia, he'd been able to save Patrick's life during a fight.

Eve's eyes filled with concern. Hopefully, she, Joni, and Patrick wouldn't need the antibiotics. With any luck, their stay in 1884 would be a short one.

Joni exited the bathroom, her hair turbaned. She wore a rose-colored cotton bathrobe.

"How do I look?" Joni asked, twirling about.

"Lovely. Where did you find the robe?"

"In the closet near the extra towels. There's also shampoo and soap. Rose soap, with little petals in it.

The water pressure ain't so good and it ain't so hot, but I'll take it."

Eve said, "I stayed in a boarding house in 1885. It had a makeshift tub and no shower, and you had to share a bathroom."

Joni dropped into the nearest chair. "I'll be sure to thank Mr. Tesla again. I like this place."

Joni grew thoughtful. "While I was showering, my mind was leaping from one thought to the other. I have to tell you, Eve, I didn't believe this would happen. I didn't believe we would actually go back in time. I didn't. I'm still not sure. I mean, I might be dreaming or something. In my wildest dreams, how could I have ever believed I'd be riding in Thomas Edison's private carriage, or that I'd meet Tesla, not that I really knew who he was."

"Well, you're lucky we ended up here and not in some backwater hotel or boarding house. It's not so nice out there."

"What do you mean?"

"I mean bathrooms and hygiene. I can tell you things you'll never learn from the history books, because I was a nurse at a hospital for the poor, downtown, and I saw things I couldn't believe. A woman might take a bath once or twice a month, but then again, she might not. If she did, it was a lukewarm soak, because these people believe that unnecessary hot and cold temperatures cause health problems... problems like rashes, tuberculosis and insanity."

"Insanity?" Joni asked, tilting her head sideways as if she didn't hear clearly.

"Yes, insanity. During the weeks between baths, some of the more refined ladies might wash off with a sponge soaked in cool water and vinegar. Sitz baths are also fairly common."

"And a sitz bath is…?"

"A sitz bath in this time means a woman sits in a shallow dish of water to ensure she is, well, clean."

"So that's what that thing in the bathroom is for?" Joni asked.

"Yes. I also treated women who wanted to lose weight, not that they were all that fat. Anyway, guess what they used for weight loss? Drugs that often contained life-threatening ingredients like arsenic, strychnine, cocaine and—take a deep breath—tapeworm larvae."

Joni turned away. "That's disgusting."

"Not so romantic, is it?"

Joni got up. "Okay, enough about that. So tomorrow, let's go find this guy Patrick and then get the hell out of here."

"Joni… even if I manage to find Patrick, and if by some miracle I can convince him of who I am and why I'm here, which I think will be nearly impossible, we have no means of time traveling back to 2016. We have no lantern, remember?"

Joni's face fell a little. "But… what about…?" Her voice trailed off into silence, and she slumped back down into the chair.

"We'll figure it out," Eve said, mustering confidence. "We'll take it step by step. With the five dollars Mr. Tesla gave us, we'll go out tomorrow and buy some things."

Joni tried to brighten her mood. "Maybe we can do a quick tour of the City," Joni said. "It might be fun."

134

An hour later, Eve and Joni lay side by side on the double bed in the dark room. As exhausted as they were, they couldn't sleep. They spoke in low tones.

"How much is five dollars worth in 1884?" Joni asked.

"I'd guess somewhere between $150 and $200."

"Tesla had a lot more money in his wallet. That's a lot of money to be carrying around, isn't it?"

"Yes, for this time, but Tesla's an eccentric."

"He's definitely an odd duck. He didn't flirt with us once, and we're not bad looking women. I saw a flicker of pleasure in Thomas Edison's eyes," Joni said.

Eve was silent for a moment. "I wonder if Tesla knows."

"Knows what?"

"That we time traveled. He must know."

Joni lifted on elbows and the bed shifted and squeaked. "What do you mean?"

"Joni, Nikola Tesla is a genius—probably one of the smartest people who ever lived. Remember the inscription on the postcard? He who finds this, finds me?"

Joni eased back down. "Back at the laboratory, I was too disoriented and sick to think about it. My head was spinning."

Eve said, "In the carriage when you were asleep, I asked him if he believed in time travel, and he said something that didn't make any sense."

Joni sat up. "But if he suspected we'd time traveled, why didn't he mention it? Wouldn't that be a big deal? I don't get it."

"I don't know. Maybe his mind's on other things. Maybe it's just not that important to him. Maybe there are other reasons we don't know about."

Joni eased back down, and the bed shifted and groaned. "If he created the lantern that sent us here then, surely, he can create one to send us back."

"Well, yes, one would think so."

Joni said, "We should go back to the laboratory tomorrow morning and confront him. Ask him if he created that lantern and if he can send us back."

"In this time, that would be entirely inappropriate. I'm afraid it might alienate him. Thomas Edison was already suspicious of us. I doubt if we could get in, anyway. No, I think we'll have to wait till we have dinner with him on Saturday. Then, I'll gently probe and see what Tesla says."

"That's five days, Eve. We have to get out of here."

Eve's voice held impatience. "Joni, you chose to come here. I didn't force you. I tried to stop you. All right, you're going to have to relax and stop it with the 'I've got to get out of here' every five minutes. I told you how uncertain all this would be. I told you we might never get back to our time, remember? So, stop saying 'We have to get out of here.' I've had it. Get it in your head that we may never get out of here. Now, I'm exhausted, and I've got to sleep. Tomorrow, we'll take our jewelry to a pawnshop, arrange to get some clothes and find a drugstore. After that, I'm going to search for Patrick."

The room fell into silence and, within minutes, both women were asleep.

At some point during the night, Joni awoke, feeling that Eve was awake and probably staring at the ceiling.

At a whisper, Joni said, "Eve, are you awake?"

"Yes…"

"When was the last time you were in a double bed with anybody?"

Eve whispered back. "After a tequila party in college, when three of us ended up sprawled on a double bed. It wasn't pretty. Get some sleep, Joni. We'll both feel better in the morning. Good night."

"Good night… Don't worry, we'll find Patrick. I'm sure of it."

And then Joni continued, "Eve, why don't you know where Patrick lives? Didn't he ever mention it? Did you ever visit him there?"

"I didn't visit him, and he didn't talk about where he lived. And, anyway, he told me he moved after his wife died. He was very secretive in those days for many reasons, and he didn't trust me because I wasn't sure I could trust him. It's a long story. Anyway, all I know is that when he was married to Emma, he lived downtown, probably in Chelsea."

Joni turned over, shaking the bed. "I feel like I've fallen down the rabbit hole. Good night."

CHAPTER 20

Eve had done her homework back in 2016, so she knew that the diamond and turquoise necklace which she'd purchased at a jewelry store on West 47th Street in Manhattan, for $60,000, would be worth about $2,400 in 1884. Working 60 hours a week, most laborers made about sixty dollars a month, or about $720 a year, so she and Joni should have enough to live comfortably for a few years.

But she also knew from experience that she wouldn't receive the full price for the bracelet in 1884, because it was the gritty nature of pawnshops and this historical time. Most proprietors were devious and calculating, and they would lowball a woman, knowing she was vulnerable. Eve could have tried her luck at a jewelry store, but they were more hesitant to deal directly with women, and most wouldn't offer ready cash the way pawnshops did.

Eve and Joni found a fairly reputable pawnshop, only a half block away from the Gerlach Hotel, at Sixth Avenue and Twenty-Seventh Street. The narrow shop was packed full of display tables with jewelry, trinkets, ivory, diamond cufflinks, gold inlay fountain pens, gold watches and fobs. Enclosed glass display cases offered tantalizing views of silver and gold cigarette cases, silver flasks, and diamond studs.

Hanging on the walls were violins, clarinets, guitars, a tuba and several riding saddles, displayed on saddle stands.

The man standing behind the glass-enclosed counter was a short, thick man in his early 60s, with gray, thinning hair, a carefully trimmed patriarchal beard, a curled mustache, and quick, dancing eyes that seemed to take in everything at once. Dressed in a smart black suit, white shirt and loose black bow tie, he examined the necklace with precision, care and attention. With a loupe attached to his left eye, he brought the diamonds into sharp focus, nodding and clearing his throat as he worked.

Eve and Joni waited. Eve's nerves were on edge and Joni was watchful, even while snooping at the merchandise.

The clerk removed the loupe, lifted his torso and scratched his mustache. "Well, ladies, it is a special piece. I can tell you that for certain. I saw a similar one just a month or so ago. A fine daughter of our City presented it, and let me just add that she was a kind and gentle woman, who imparted to me the rather unfortunate news that the lovely necklace had been a prized possession of her mother, who, tragically, had recently departed into that more beautiful and perfect world. I believe the woman lived on West 78th Street. Yes, I'm sure of that. And, again, if I may say so…"

Eve could see the man was going to drone on if she didn't gently interrupt.

"... How interesting, sir. And with your expertise, what value do you place on this lovely item?"

His white, bushy eyebrows lifted. "Value? Well, now, let me see. It does have some untidy scratches on the diamonds and, of course, the lobster clasp does have a tendency to be rather, shall I say, recalcitrant. Yes, that would be a test of patience for many a good woman, I dare say. But a good test of virtue. Yes, I would say that."

Joni glanced over, wondering how much he was going to offer.

"Well, I mean to say, it is still a lovely piece of jewelry, all things considered."

"Can you offer two-thousand five hundred dollars, sir?" Eve asked.

His eyes enlarged. He stood stiffly, with a tolerant smile. "Madam, that is a lot of money for any lady, and for a piece such as this; in what is, shall I say, somewhat less than perfect condition, well..."

Eve interrupted. "... I was told it is worth three thousand dollars, sir."

His eyes were round and sorrowful. "Well, again, that is quite exorbitant for such a piece that is not all that it should be. I mean to say, perhaps nineteen hundred could be managed, or perhaps less."

"That's not enough," Joni said, jumping in.

Eve gave her a cool side-glance.

The man's mouth firmed up as he thought. "Ladies, I'm going to be extra generous in this regard and give you my final offer. Nineteen hundred dollars. Now that,

I mean to say, is a good, fair and equitable offer for this somewhat tarnished piece of jewelry."

It was agreed and, as if on cue, a skinny, nervous clerk with a mop of curly brown hair appeared from behind a pulled fringed curtain. He was no more than 13 years old, if that. No doubt he'd been back there the entire time.

When the older man smiled, the corners of his eyes crinkled with satisfaction at making the sale. He reached for a piece of paper and pencil, scribbled a number on it and handed it to the kid.

"Ladies, this is my grandson, Mortimer."

Mortimer took the paper from his grandfather, avoided their eyes as he bowed, and then retreated back through the curtain.

"He will deposit your necklace and return with your money. As you can imagine, I don't keep that much money here in the shop. It is downstairs in the safe."

Outside on Sixth Avenue, Eve turned from the crowds and stuffed the money inside a hidden pocket. "Let's get back to the hotel. I have to put this money in the hotel safe."

"Why not put it in a bank?"

"Because banks won't deal with women unless a man's around. The hotel offers private safes. Get used to it, Joni, in this time, we are second-class citizens."

"Well, that really sucks," Joni said, then catching herself for her 21st century slang, she said, "I mean, wow... I mean, well, crap!"

Eve laughed. "It's not so easy, but you'll get it. Keep thinking *Downton Abbey*."

They started off.

"What are we going to do with my bracelet?" Joni asked.

"I think we should save it. It will be our emergency fund. Let's hope we're long gone back to our own time before we need it."

"How far will nineteen hundred dollars get us in 1884?"

"Let me put it this way: we can live pretty well for a couple years, if we're not too extravagant. I remember from the last time I was here that you'll pay about ten bucks a week for room and board to live in a decent neighborhood. Unskilled laborers and the poor pay about two dollars a week for a boarding house."

"Can we move to a nicer hotel? I love you like a sister, but I'm not too fond of sleeping with you in that double bed. No offense."

"I don't want to leave Tesla. Until we can find out if he is responsible for the lantern and time travel, I think we should stay where we are."

After Eve deposited the money in the safe, the women struck out to find a pharmacy and a lady's shop. As she'd done earlier that morning, Joni turned, indicating toward the City with a sweep of her arm.

"Let's take a quick tour for just an hour or so before you run off looking for Patrick. I could go alone, but it would be more fun with you. And, anyway, I feel like I'm in an episode of *The Twilight Zone*."

Eve breathed in impatience. "Aren't you tired? Neither one of us slept all that well last night."

"Yes, I'm tired, but I'm also excited, and nervous as hell, and generally freaked out. The exercise will do me good."

"Okay, but at some point, we're going down to 253 Mercer Street, just off West 3rd Street."

"Don't tell me. That's where Patrick Gantly is?"

"I hope so. It's the 15th Precinct. That's where he was working when I met him in 1885. Unless time has changed that too, he should still be there, a Detective Sergeant."

Joni saw Eve's anxious expression.

"Nervous?"

"Terrified."

"Okay, let's go then."

It was a partly cloudy day, with a cool autumn wind that kicked up dust from the streets and circulated the odors of horses and horse droppings. They started down Sixth Avenue, Joni lost in hypnotic wonder at a world she could have never imagined. It was a bustling, chaotic city with no traffic lights and few traffic rules; horse carriages zigzagged haphazardly up and down the streets in a trotting, unchoreographed dance.

On Fifth Avenue, top-hatted, wealthy men and richly dressed ladies in lavish hats strolled about as if they owned the City, and Eve told Joni that they did. They saw a horse-drawn omnibus with a driver sitting in front and a conductor helping passengers aboard, collecting fares and ringing a bell to signal the driver when to stop and go.

As they traveled further downtown, they saw horsecars that traveled on a rail instead of road, and Eve told her that the rails provided a faster, quieter, more comfortable ride. She'd ridden many the last time she'd time traveled to 1885.

A small group of the "Broadway Squad" officers were there to help pedestrians cross the major intersections and, even then, Joni thought these people were taking their lives in their hands.

Joni pointed at the church steeples, the tallest structures around. "There are no skyscrapers, no glass towers, no airplanes flying over. This is just weird."

They rode on an elevated train that spewed coal dust and, along with other passengers, they had nosey glimpses into second-floor windows.

Further downtown, the ladies saw Irish, Italian and Jewish immigrants shuffling along in frayed clothes and hunched shoulders, many with weary, weather-worn faces. Some were obviously looking for work. Others ducked into a nearby saloon.

"Many of these laborers sleep in shifts in overcrowded tenements," Eve said. "Men work as ditchdiggers for ten hours, for two dollars a day. Women roll cigars and work as seamstresses for even less."

"This is depressing," Joni said, as coal smells, body odor smells and horse smells assaulted her nose.

"Don't ever go out at night by yourself down here," Eve said. "There are armies of beggars and streetwalkers, and they're bold, clever and desperate. Patrick told me last time that it's an open secret that New York City is the vice capital of the United States. He said there are about 30,000 prostitutes working the streets, charging from 50-cents to $10 a pop, and that there are three red-light districts: the Lower East Side, the Washington Square area and the Tenderloin."

Joni walked as if in a trance. "Where was the Tenderloin?"

"Is, Joni. Remember? It still is. This is 1884. The Tenderloin is from 23rd to 42nd Street along Broadway."

As they approached Mercer Street, Eve slowed her pace, her face showing strain, her eyes filled with nervous apprehension.

"Are you okay?" Joni asked.

"What if he's not here? Then we've come a long way into the past for nothing, and we don't even know if we can get back. And if Patrick isn't here, I'll be lost."

Joni linked Eve's arm in hers, offering comfort. "You won't be lost. We're together and we'll be okay. That's why I came with you, remember? We're in this together."

Eve patted her arm. "I've got to admit it, Joni. I'm glad you're here right now."

Joni noticed a newsboy on the corner, two stacks of newspapers next to him, more papers tucked under his arm. One was clutched in his hand, raised. He stared at them curiously. Joni winked at him and he winked back flirtatiously.

"Well, that little flirt," Joni said.

"They grow up fast on these streets," Eve said, smiling at the boy, who thrust the paper toward her. He couldn't have been more than ten or eleven years old, but he had an old face and a tired, but steely gaze.

Eve walked over, handed him change she'd received from paying for the hotel breakfast that morning. She took the paper. "Thanks."

Eve remembered how Patrick had always supported the newsboys, often buying a newspaper from a boy on one corner, and then purchasing the same paper from another boy not far away. She had a bright thought as she stared at the dirty-faced boy, dressed in tight pants, worn shoes, frayed coat, and tweed newsboy cap, cocked smartly to one side.

"Do you happen to know a detective who works over there at the 15th Precinct, named Detective Sergeant Gantly?"

He gazed up at her with a predatory eye. "And if I did, what would it get me?"

Eve sniffed a little laugh. For these boys, living in this time, it was all about survival.

"How about twenty cents?"

"Then I might know him and then again, maybe I don't know him. You could spend twenty cents on a new hat, couldn't you?"

"Would you know him for fifty cents?"

He grinned, but it was a shadowy kind of grin. With the stack of papers still under his arm, he held out a palm. "Let me see the truth of it," he said. "If I don't see it, how do I know it's there?"

Eve placed two quarters into his sooty palm.

He half hooded his eyes and gave her a knowing grin. "I say the ladies like that one, that detective."

Eve straightened, now invigorated, as she scrutinized the boy. "Then do you know him?"

"Yeah, I knows him. Big guy, right? Don't smile much but he has the swagger, and when he walks by, he gives me a good day and gives me a nod. Did I tell you that the ladies have shiny eyes for him?"

Eve felt a crashing relief. She brightened, with a big smile. "Yes, you told me."

"He buys my papers every day I'm on this corner. None of the other coppers do. They gets them for nothing."

Eve took a step forward. "Have you seen him today?"

"Nah. Not seen him for some days."

"No? Why?"

The kid shoved the two quarters into his pants pocket. "How do I know? Do you think I'm a wanderin' gypsy or something?"

He was suddenly sneering and snappish. "I sells these papers. I don't do tricks with the cards or with a crystal ball, do I?"

Eve gave him a restrained smile. "No, I'm sorry. I'll just go into the police precinct and ask."

He wiped his nose with the back of his coat sleeve, glaring at her like she was an enemy.

She left the newsie standing there, and he went back to hawking the headlines of the day.

Joni had stood by, watching the encounter. "He's a little shit, isn't he?"

"He's lucky if he has a mother and a home to go to," Eve said, sympathetically. "More likely than not, he's mostly on his own. Those boys have a hard life."

Joni made a nod toward the 15th Precinct. "So, I guess we go in there now?"

Eve nodded uneasily. "Yes... we go in there."

Eve felt a jittery stomach as she lifted her worried eyes up on the narrow, red-brick, three-story building, with tall windows covered by heavy wrought-iron guards. The fence around the building was also made of wrought-iron, with spear-like bars rising to a sharp arrow point. *Not so inviting*, Eve thought.

The building sat in a middle-class neighborhood of row houses and brownstones, with swept sidewalks and a little neighborhood park on the north side of the block. It was mostly as she remembered it. There was a peddler's cart collecting rags, a barbershop across the street, a saloon further down called Sean O'Casey's Saloon, which Eve didn't recall, and a quaint-looking tobacconist shop where a man stood outside, smoking a narrow cigar, reading a newspaper.

Eve inhaled a breath for courage and walked purposively toward the precinct. Two policemen, dressed in knee-length blue coats with brass buttons and tall, felt helmets, lowered their suspicious eyes on the women as they approached. Eve knew from Patrick that cops often thought women who visited police precincts were searching for drunken or wayward husbands; or they were suffragettes with complaints about the uncontrolled vice of the City; or they were prostitutes searching for a cop for various unseemly reasons: they were pregnant, or they hadn't been paid.

Eve put on a starched face and looked at the policemen with cool, no nonsense eyes, offering no flirtation. Patrick had warned her long ago never to show cowardice to any man in the 1880s. They might not like you for it, and they might push back, but at least you'd have their grudging respect.

"Good day, officers. Would either of you happen to know where I can find Detective Sergeant Gantly?"

The taller of the two seemed to be the spokesman. He had a plump, mustached face; ruddy cheeks, probably from the love of spirits; and flat gray eyes that revealed nothing more than a bored soul.

"And who is it who wants to know?" he said, crisply, in a half-Irish, half-something-else accent that Eve didn't recognize.

The tall policeman's partner, a swarthy type, probably Italian, overtly looked Joni up and down with lusty pleasure, while she fixed him with a lazy, I've-seen-it-all-before stare.

Eve decided to lie. What truth could she tell? "I'm a friend."

The corner of his mouth lifted in a sarcastic grin. "A friend, are you?"

"Yes. I was told that he works here. Does he work here?"

"If you were a friend, you would know that he's not here, and he hasn't been here for over a week now."

Eve waited for more, but the man with the sergeant's stripes didn't offer more.

"Would you be so kind as to tell me where he is?"

"That, madam, is personal to Detective Sergeant Gantly and, I suspect, with all due respect, that if you were a true friend, you would know that he has been staying close to home because his wife is very ill."

Eve's face fell and turned white. She felt a twist of agony that nearly doubled her over.

"Now what kind of a friend could you be, madam, if you didn't know that?" he asked, with a wink of low implication.

Joni's mouth fell open as she turned to face Eve.

With his stick, he tipped the corner of his hat to let them know he was finished with the conversation.

"Good day, ladies."

CHAPTER 21

That night, Eve lay in the hotel bed, eyes shut, tears streaming. Joni sat in the chair beside the bed, lost for words. Neither had spoken for hours, not since they'd taken a hansom cab back to the hotel.

Finally, Eve grew weak and lethargic, and she fell asleep. When Joni was sure Eve was sleeping soundly, she left the hotel to find the lady's shop. She looked at fabric and dress styles, but was uncertain what to order, so she purchased only day dresses, nightgowns and underwear. At a pharmacy a few blocks away, she bought basic toiletries: egg shampoo, toothpowder, and wooden toothbrushes with boar hair bristles. She finished up at a grocery, where she bought some bread, cheese and dried fruit.

When Joni returned to their room, Eve was still fast asleep. After a few bites of food and a tepid bath, Joni slipped into a nightgown and joined Eve under the quilt, careful not to awaken her.

Later in the night, when Joni heard Eve crying, she turned up the flame on the side lamp and asked if she could help.

In the dim light, Eve's face looked swollen from tears, her hair damp, eyes wet. They talked for a while, but to Eve it was only a kind of noise. To Joni, it was a way to listen, an attempt to comfort her friend. Finally, Eve fell into the subject they both knew she would eventually return to.

"Of course it occurred to me," Eve said, "but I just conveniently pushed it away. Patrick never told me exactly when his wife died. Once we'd arrived in 2016, we just wanted to move on with our lives and we didn't talk about her and her death all that much. It had happened so long ago. Lifetimes ago. Decades ago. I assumed his wife had died in 1882 or 1883. Of course, now I remember what he said about her. He said after he lost Emma and his child, he saw the world as a cold and brutal place, as an unforgiving place. He said he grew bitter. He said after that, and before he met me, he wasn't always the best of policemen, or the best of men."

Joni straightened, and pulled her legs up and tucked them underneath herself and the gown. "Do you know how his wife died?"

"Childbirth, like so many women did in those days." Eve corrected herself. "These days."

Joni lowered her head. "Eve... what are we going to do?"

"I don't know. I have absolutely no idea. I'm just lost. Completely lost. My mind is just mush right now. I can't think. I can't think about anything. The whole thing is a disaster. Maybe tomorrow... Maybe I'll be able to come up with some plan tomorrow."

"Can I get you anything?"

"No... I'm just going to try to go back to sleep. I just need sleep more than anything else."

And then she rolled over and was asleep in minutes.

The next morning, Eve remained in bed, her mind drifting in and out of memory. Joni went for food at a café nearby and returned with boiled eggs, beans and ham. Eve ate little.

Joni paced the room. "What do you want me to do, Eve?"

Eve sat up, bunching the pillows behind her back. "I've been thinking... It should have come to me right away. I've just been thinking of myself. Feeling sorry for myself like some silly woman."

Joni stopped, waiting for more.

Eve's voice was weak, her eyes downcast. "I'm going to find Patrick."

Joni's eyes held questions.

"I'm going to see if I can help save Emma's life. I'm a nurse after all."

Joni stared as if she didn't understand. "That's really weird, Eve."

Eve leveled her eyes on Joni. "I don't know exactly what killed Emma, but when I was here in 1885, I learned a lot about how to help pregnant women."

Joni watched Eve's sudden change of spirits.

"Emma's probably in the late stages of pregnancy, when so much can go wrong. She's probably drained of energy and susceptible to infectious disease. Women in this time often have to push for days. In 1885, I saw women die of puerperal fever, so they called it; we call it postpartum sepsis, an infection usually contracted during childbirth. And then there's the possibility of hemorrhage, eclampsia or dangerously high blood pressure and organ damage. Even in our time, bearing a child is still one of the most dangerous things a woman can do. In the U.S., it's the sixth most common cause of death among women from twenty to thirty-four years old."

"Okay, Eve, that was a great science lesson, but what about Patrick? I don't think you're a silly woman for loving him... and hurting because you may have lost him. That's called suffering and loss. That's normal. Anyway, if you find her, he's going to be there. You're going to see him. Be with him. He's going to see and be with you. Won't that be just a whole lot bizarre?"

"He won't know who I am, Joni, remember? I didn't meet him until 1885."

"Okay, fine, but how are you going to feel being around him?"

Eve looked away. "I don't know. I guess I'll find out."

Joni flopped down in a chair. "This is crazy. Even if you do find him, what are you going to do? Barge in the front door and say, 'Hello, there, I'm here to save your wife and your baby'? He's not going to let you in."

"No, he won't let me in, but he'll let a respected and renowned doctor in," Eve said, the color returning to her face now that she was formulating a plan. She was always better when taking action, rather than sitting around feeling sorry for herself.

"From 1885, I know two doctors. One's a woman, Dr. Ann Long, one's a man. Knowing Patrick as I know him, and because he's a man of his time, he won't accept the woman doctor, but he'll consent to Dr. Morris Waldo Eckland. I'm sure of it."

Eve kicked off the quilt, swung her legs to the floor and stood up, revived.

"Okay, Joni, you go to that lady's shop down the street and order four upscale dresses: two for each of us. The latest style and the best fabric. You know my sizes. Tell them it's a rush order and we'll pay whatever they want."

Joni got to her feet, astonished by Eve's sudden vigor. "What are you going to do?"

"I'm going to find out where Patrick lives."

"How?"

"It's a long shot, but it's the only shot I've got right now. I know what Patrick's habits were—where he ate and some of the people he knew. But before I do that, I'm going to canvass the Chelsea neighborhood and ask the newsboys. I might get lucky. Anyway, we don't have much time. I've got to find him and then visit Dr. Eckland."

"His name sounds expensive."

"We have plenty of money, Joni. That's no problem, thank God, but we'll need those dresses before we can call on him. Okay, I'll get dressed and start off. Let's meet back here around five o'clock or so."

As Joni helped Eve with her corset, she lowered her voice. "And if Patrick's wife survives, then what will you do?"

"She will survive if we can get to her in time. After that, we'll talk to Tesla on Saturday. I'm sure he's our ticket back home."

CHAPTER 22

The air was crisp and the sunlight bright as Eve strolled the Chelsea streets, stopping to question the newsboys and bootblacks to see if they knew where Detective Sergeant Gantly lived. Most didn't know him, or they knew him only by description, a tall, serious man who always stopped to buy their papers and sometimes give them a little extra.

One smallish boy, who puffed on a clay pipe, told Eve that Patrick once asked him if he had a home to go to.

"I told him I didn't need no home. I bunk with my pals on Hester Street."

Eve tramped along brownstone neighborhoods, past old dismal warehouses, horse stables and saloons. She walked through neighborhoods with Federal-style houses, past signs that said APARTMENTS TO LENT, past a carriage house and a storefront that sold harnesses and buggy parts.

By late afternoon, the silly dress felt heavy and bulky and the corset tight and punishing. Her feet were sore, her toes pinched, and her legs were just plain tired of walking. She was also hungry, having not stopped for lunch.

She was about ready to return to the hotel when she noticed an empty hansom cab drifting by, the single horse clopping across the cobblestones, head down. The hansom was a nimble two-wheeled carriage, with a low center of gravity that was able to turn on a dime. The driver's seat was placed at the back of the carriage behind the passengers where they sat inside. It was good for two people but a tight squeeze for three.

The hansom driver turned and tipped his bowler hat to her. His lined, leathery face was friendly, his twinkling eyes bright. He wore a dusty long coat, a bandana tied about his neck in cavalry style, and his gray, bushy mustache was well over his upper lip.

It was an impulse. Eve raised a hand at him. In response, he tugged on the reins and rolled the buggy to a stop not far away. Eve approached him with a little smile, shaded her eyes and gazed up at him.

"Sir, would you happen to know where Detective Sergeant Gantly lives?"

To her surprise, the man spoke in a heavy British accent. "Would you be a friend of the detective, Miss?"

Eve perked up. "Yes... Yes, I am a friend."

"Well then, you must know that these are unfortunate times for Detective Gantly, Miss. His lovely wife, Emma, is with child and she's not in the best of health, so I hear. There has been many a prayer raised to the heavens for the good woman. She's from Manchester, England, you know, same as me. We are not what you'd say good friends, but we are good acquaintances, as folk from the same land tend to be. She gives me a hearty wave when I pass, she does, and then she calls out in a good, sweet voice, 'Hello there, Thomas Whiton. Is it a good day for you?' I'm dreadful sorry for her, Miss. But it's a small world, isn't it? A small world to find two people livin' close by and both from the same far off land."

"Yes. So the detective and his wife live around here?"

"About two blocks east. Would you like me to take you, Miss?"

Eve felt a rush of energy and started over, grateful. "Yes, thank you, sir. Thank you very much."

The driver opened the door with a lever that he controlled from his seat and Eve climbed in. She was able to talk to the driver through the hatch door.

"Thank you for your help," Eve said.

Eve smiled at her good fortune. She couldn't wait to tell Joni.

Eve and Joni had an early dinner at the Windsor Hotel on 47th and Fifth Avenue. They were seated near a window with a spectacular view of Fifth Avenue, with its extravagant carriages and ever-passing hansom cabs and horsecars. They sat in elegance at a white linen table that held fresh flowers, under a frescoed ceiling and a sumptuous chandelier. A bottle of red Bordeaux had already been decanted, their glasses poured, the menu lying beside them.

Eve glanced about the half-filled room. "What do you think?"

"I see people looking at us," Joni said, self-consciously.

Eve dropped her voice. "We're not dressed as Fifth Avenue ladies are supposed to be dressed. This is a class society where fashion, jewelry and deportment rule. To them, we're obviously tourists, and not very well-dressed ones at that, but I don't care. I'm tired and hungry and I know the food is excellent here."

Eve raised her exquisite wine glass. "And, we're celebrating. I found Patrick's house, and you ordered our dresses."

They touched glasses and sipped the wine.

Eve continued. "I also chose this place because I didn't think you were ready for mutton chops, lamb kidneys, beans, pickles, and sizzling strips of bacon, served alongside mealy baked potatoes and the ever-present tankards of ale. That's what we'd get at that chop house near our hotel. We'd also have to wave away clouds of cigar smoke."

"Definitely not mutton chops," Joni said. "The ale I could do."

After they both ordered the filet mignon, Joni leaned in. "I have to tell you, after today, I am completely freaked out. I feel like I'm walking and talking in a waking dream and I can't wake up. That lady's shop was so confusing, with so many kinds of fabric and styles and under garments and corsets. I could never live in this time. It's like women are all tied up in those things. And there are no cars. I just can't get over the fact that there are no cars. And I'm constantly having to lift the hem of this damned dress every time I cross the street, so it doesn't get dirty."

"But you ordered the dresses, right? A rush order?"

"Yes, like I told you, I just don't know if you'll like them. The lady clerk distracted me with her thinness. She was so petite, pretty and thin, like all the women in that shop. They were all two or three sizes smaller than me, and I'm in good shape. I'm a dancer. I mean, Eve, these people are really thin, have you noticed?"

"Yes, I've noticed. When can we pick up the dresses?"

"Two days. One each. The other two will take longer."

Eve sat back with a shake of her head. "I can't wait that long. Patrick's wife could be dying right now. I didn't want to visit Dr. Eckland wearing this thing, but I've got to. He's so fastidious and class conscious. I hope he'll see us."

"When do you want to go?" Joni asked.

"Tomorrow morning. If I recall, he does his hospital rounds in the afternoon."

Eve looked suddenly worried. "We should have an introduction, but again, I don't. I'm going to have to name drop and hope Dr. Eckland doesn't check out the reference."

Eve's mind whirled with electric thoughts. She took another sip of wine. "We're just going to have to charge ahead, visit Dr. Eckland in the morning and hope he lets us in."

As they were finishing their dinner, Joni said softly, "You didn't say if you saw him."

"Saw who?" And then she knew. "Oh, you mean, Patrick. I told the cab driver to wait while I climbed out and stepped up onto the sidewalk. I stood in front of his single-family row house for a couple of minutes. It's on the north side of West 22nd Street, between Seventh and Eighth Avenues. The curtains were drawn on the first and second floors. I felt lost. I felt lonely. I felt sympathy, and I felt sorry for myself. I almost climbed those stairs and rang the doorbell. I just wanted to see him again and... Okay, I wanted to see if he would recognize me."

Eve's face was suddenly tired, her eyes reflective. "God help me, I stood there remembering our first kiss. How ridiculously romantic is that? Then I snapped out of it and left. His wife, Emma, could be dying, and I'm sure he's in great emotional pain."

Joni set her fork aside and folded her hands. "I'm not sure I could have done what you did. I mean taking a chance time traveling to find Patrick. I don't think I could do what you're doing right now. I'm not so noble."

Eve met her gaze. "Have you ever really been in love?"

"I don't know... Maybe. I don't know."

"You'd do it, Joni, if you were truly in love."

CHAPTER 23

Dr. Eckland's fashionable brownstone was just off Fifth Avenue, on a quiet, tree-lined street, north of the Albemarle Hotel, where the famous actress of the day, Lily Langtry, lived.

Eve and Joni left the hansom cab and, lifting their hems, stepped onto the sidewalk and strolled the few steps to the walkway that led up the four stairs to Dr. Eckland's oak front door.

Eve passed a final look at Joni. "Let me do the talking. If anyone says anything to you, just say 'Yes' or 'No,' or just smile."

"What? You don't trust my 19th century English?" Joni said, grinning, trying to ease the tension.

Eve gave her a look. "Here we go."

Eve lifted the heavy brass knocker and let it fall. They waited, nerves heating them up.

The door slowly opened and a frosty-haired man, complete with a frosty mustache, appeared. Eve recognized the butler from 1885. He was in his sixties, dressed classily in white tie and tails. He looked at them formally, with a stiff upper lip and cool, icy-gray, appraising eyes.

"Good morning, ladies," he said, in a quivering, whispery voice.

"Good morning, sir. My name is Miss Evelyn Kennedy, and this is Miss Joan Katherine Kosarin."

He stood stiffly, not impressed, waiting for more.

"We're here to see Dr. Eckland in a matter of life and death."

"Do you have an appointment?"

"No sir, but…"

The butler's voice grew in volume. "Are either of you ladies a patient?"

"Well… No, not exactly, but I do have a reference from the Harringshaw family," Eve said, which, of course, was a lie. In 1885, Eve had had much contact with the Harringshaw family, but she had not contacted them since she'd arrived in 1884, and she didn't plan to. Eve hoped this reference would at least get them in the door. From there, she'd improvise.

The butler lifted an eyebrow, obviously recognizing the name of one of the wealthiest families in New York. "Which Harringshaw, madam, is the reference from?"

Eve forced a tight smile, lying through her teeth. "John Allister Harringshaw."

The butler's eyes blinked slowly as he considered his next action. "Do you have a letter of reference from Mr. Harringshaw?"

Joni managed to keep her pasted-on smile, struggling for composure.

"There was no time for that, sir. I can assure you, my business is of the utmost importance, and I sincerely believe that the eminent and compassionate Dr. Eckland will be both helpful and agreeable in this matter."

Joni almost rolled her eyes. *Where did Eve learn to speak like that?* She really did sound like a character from *Downton Abbey*, and Joni was impressed. The butler hesitated, still unsure.

Eve persisted. "I appeal to you, sir. Time is of the essence. A woman is gravely ill and could pass from this world at any moment."

Finally, the butler stepped aside. "Please come in, ladies, and I will inform Dr. Eckland that you are here. I cannot promise that he will see you."

They stepped into a brown marble foyer framed in cherry wood, with sunlight illuminating stained glass windows on either side.

The butler led the way to a parlor on the left, grandly opened the heavy oak door and indicated into the room.

"Please be seated, ladies, and I will see if Dr. Eckland is available."

He closed the doors, leaving Eve and Joni alone in a glorious room, softly lit by gas table lamps covered by ivory fringe Victorian shades, and a low, lustrous fire in an open grate of a fireplace. The room was decorated in gold, with gothic furniture and jade figurines on the white marble mantel top, and it smelled of wood smoke, leather and furniture polish. It was a room with burgundy draperies, dark finishes, and elaborate carvings and ornamentation.

Eve paced, while Joni sat in a French-style green armchair with bullion fringe, appraising the room.

"Now this is what I call a Victorian room," Joni said. "It looks like something out of that Queen Victoria movie I saw on *Netflix*."

Eve paced with her hands behind her back, one thought chasing another, silently repeating phrases she would use when speaking to Dr. Eckland.

The door opened, and Eve swung around to face it. To Eve's and Joni's surprise, two men entered the room. Joni shot up.

Eve recognized one of the men as Dr. Eckland. He was a gray-headed, portly man in his middle fifties, with florid cheeks, a bulbous nose and mutton chop gray whiskers. He was dressed in a black wool suit, a deep red waistcoat and a white shirt. His dark, careful eyes widened on the ladies as he fully took them in, examining them: their faces, their bearing, their hair, their clothes.

The second man was much younger, perhaps in his early thirties. He was tall, with a regal bearing and refined features; his raven hair was combed smoothly back from a proud forehead. His midnight-black suit was tailored to perfection, his white collar crisp, his black silk bowtie fixed in an exact work of art.

It was apparent that the man came from wealth, had impeccable breeding and surely had been given only the finest education. He exuded good manners and polish, and Eve was certain he could sniff out any social imposter or upstart, and she and Joni were both.

When the butler closed the doors behind the two men, leaving them and the two ladies to size each other up, Eve felt a creeping, cold dread fill her already anxious body.

Eve saw that, unfortunately, Joni's wide eyes had become stuck on the younger man. It was blatantly obvious that she'd fallen into an instant love trance, but the young gentleman observed Joni and Eve with a supreme indifference, his majestic gaze deigning to give them only a cursory glance.

Eve's hair at her neck was damp and sticky, and she swallowed away a dry throat as she tried to gather her butterfly thoughts. The moment was further stilted by the fact that she knew Dr. Eckland from 1885 and she had developed great affection for him, as he had to her. Now, of course, he didn't know her and, from his pinched expression, had no wish to.

The minutes seemed to stretch out into eternity.

"Which of you two ladies referenced John Allister Harringshaw?" Dr. Eckland asked rather brusquely.

"I did," Eve said.

"And in what capacity do you know the esteemed Mr. Harringshaw?"

Eve straightened her shoulders. "I am a nurse, Dr. Eckland. Although Miss Kosarin and I have only recently arrived in the City, I had the privilege of meeting Mr. John Harringshaw... through an acquaintance."

Dr. Eckland and the younger man exchanged dubious glances, but Eve knew Dr. Eckland couldn't take the chance of offending the Harringshaw family. He was their personal doctor.

"And who is this acquaintance, if I may ask?" Dr. Eckland said.

Eve cleared her throat, fishing the name out of thin air. "A... a Mildred Walker."

Dr. Eckland shut his eyes in finality. When he opened them, they held irritation.

"I have never heard of the lady. In any event, what can I do for you, Miss Kennedy? My butler, Ames, said it was a matter of life and death."

In this time period, protocol was such that the host or hostess always gave introductions. Eve saw that she and Joni had not even rated that common courtesy, and it annoyed her. As Patrick used to say of her tendency to take offense, "*Eve is all curves and class, and sometimes as sharp as whiskey in a broken glass.*"

Eve was not going to ignore the insult. She was going to show these men that if they, in their exalted capacity, didn't have good manners, she did.

"Gentlemen, I'm afraid we ladies have not been properly introduced. Allow me to introduce my companion, Miss Joan Katherine Kosarin. I am Miss Evelyn Kennedy."

This prompted Dr. Eckland to clear his throat, somewhat uncomfortably, realizing his faux pas. The younger gentleman lifted his proper chin and stood even more erect, not allowing himself to take the insult. Instead, he deflected it, with exalted arrogance.

"Yes, ladies," Dr. Eckland said. "Pardon me for my oversight. I have been lately consumed by business and medical matters."

The younger man spoke up. "I am Dr. Darius Compton Foster," he said, his voice deep, aloof and cultured. "And obviously, you ladies know Dr. Morris Waldo Eckland."

And then as if to speed the conversation along, Dr. Foster said, "Ladies, we were told that this was a matter of life and death. If you would be so kind, please tell us exactly why you are here and what it is that you have come for. Dr. Eckland and I have much business to address, and we have little time in which to do it."

Eve noticed Joni had finally pried her eyes away from Dr. Foster, searching for a place to put them. As Eve was about to speak, she saw Joni was flushed with attraction, her eyes eager to reattach onto the handsome egotistical doctor.

Eve carefully and concisely explained the situation, inserting some medical jargon, so they'd know she understood the medical issues and could address them articulately.

To Eve's disenchantment, Dr. Eckland made a gesture with an air of professional indifference. "Well, I am sorry for the poor woman and her detective husband, but I'm sure everything is being done that can be done."

Dr. Foster spoke up. "Miss Kennedy, you speak in educated generalities but, I fear, not in specifics. Specifically, what is the mother suffering from and in what month is she with child?"

Eve had been wrestling with this answer ever since she'd learned of Emma's serious condition. The truth was, she didn't know, because she had not seen or examined Emma. Eve would have to lie once again and then feign ignorance later, if she was wrong. She knew she would be diminished in the doctor's eyes if she was wrong, and he would feel superior, but all that mattered now was that Emma Gantly got the best care this time could offer.

Eve formed her best confident face. "Mrs. Gantly is exhausted, and she is in the midst of a difficult labor. I'm concerned about her high fever."

"Does she have a midwife?"

"Yes," Eve said, speculating.

The more Eve struggled to answer the questions, the more she felt like a fool, and all because, in this time, Patrick would not have allowed her to treat Emma Gantly.

Dr. Foster's eyes were stern. "If I decide to see the woman, the midwife must go. Is that understood? I find them a nuisance in every instance."

Eve nodded. "Of course, Doctor."

"Why isn't the woman in a hospital?"

Eve would have to speculate again. "It is the family's wish that she not be."

Dr. Foster shoved his hands into his pockets in annoyance. "Ignorance abounds."

And then to Eve's great surprise, she noticed that Dr. Foster had allowed his imperturbable and remote gaze to meet Joni's. In that moment, Eve saw a flash of attraction in his eyes before he slid them away toward the fireplace.

"Will you please see Mrs. Gantly, Dr. Foster?" Eve asked.

Dr. Eckland tugged on the ends of his coat, indicating an end to the conversation. "Dr. Foster, it sounds as if the woman has no need of us. And she should be in a hospital."

Dr. Foster glanced at Joni again, who offered him a calculated hint of a smile, suggesting a secret invitation. Eve had never seen Joni work her magic so subtly and, by all appearances, so successfully. Dr. Foster hesitated, his eyes resting on Joni longer than what was appropriate. With a sudden change of expression, he glanced up toward the ceiling and pursed his lips, lost in a new thought. When he returned his gaze to Dr. Eckland, his arrogance had melted into mild concern.

"Let us not be too hasty, my good Dr. Eckland. After all, the husband is a detective in our great City, and would it not perhaps be a kind and compassionate endeavor on our parts to at least look in on the woman? Perhaps we can be of some small help."

Eve's attention went first to Dr. Foster, then to Joni, then to Dr. Eckland. She stammered out her words. "I can pay any fee that you may require, Dr. Foster."

Dr. Foster's attention became riveted on Eve. "And how do you know these people, Miss Kennedy?"

Eve stumbled out her words. "They are... Well, they are friends."

Eve saw something pass across his face, but she couldn't read it. "I see. Friends. Do you know the Detective well?"

Joni shot Eve a glance and Dr. Foster, being very astute, noticed.

Eve looked down and away. "No, not well, Dr. Foster."

Joni astutely picked up on the subtle fact that Dr. Foster saw the lie in Eve's eyes. He deduced that she was attached to Patrick in some way.

Eve fumbled over her words. "As I said, I can pay any fee you require," she repeated, hoping to divert the conversation.

Dr. Foster turned his pleasant and coy attention to Joni. "And, Miss Kosarin, you have been silent in this matter. Do you find the conversation unsuitable?"

Joni gave a little bow. "No, Dr. Foster. I find it utterly fascinating."

Dr. Foster considered her unexpected answer, and he nodded in small appreciation. "I see. Then what is your opinion on the matter?"

Joni looked him full in the eye, with only a hint of flirtation, but it had its effect. Dr. Foster's eyes sharpened on her with new pleasure.

Joni continued, confidently. "I believe, with all my heart, that it would be the good and Christian thing to do, Dr. Foster."

Eve tossed Joni a startled glance, wondering where that line had come from. A role she'd once played? It was the perfect line at the perfect time.

With a little sniff and a square of his shoulders, Dr. Foster had made up his mind. "Well then, let us do the good and Christian thing, Miss Kosarin, and go tend to this poor, unfortunate woman."

Dr. Eckland also noticed the attraction between Joni and the doctor, and it had surprised him. He spoke up.

"Perhaps, Dr. Foster, you should go with the ladies and examine Mrs. Gantly on your own, while I meet with the hospital board. I'll be happy to inform them that you were called away on an emergency. I'm confident that they will understand."

"That will be good of you, Dr. Eckland. Yes, please do so and give them my regards."

Dr. Eckland gave Joni a final perplexed once-over. "Yes, Dr. Foster, I will be pleased to inform them of your generosity, compassion and dedication to medicine and to the community at large."

Dr. Foster stole a quick glance at Joni. His attraction was masked, but only slightly.

Eve was dumbfounded. If Joni hadn't been there, this man would have never consented to see Emma Gantly. Dr. Foster was as attracted to Joni as she was to him.

Eve had seen Joni around many men, and she'd seen her flirtation at work, but never to this degree and never with such intensity. Had Eve just witnessed love at first sight?

CHAPTER 24

The enclosed black carriage, pulled by two white horses, trotted downtown under a shockingly blue afternoon sky, past Fifth Avenue grandeur and colorful autumn leaves flashing in the sun. Further downtown, an omnibus muscled its way through the intersection as a dray shouldered into traffic, its oxen bellowing out bass tones as if calling for the right of way.

Eve saw street urchins threading through pedestrian traffic, nimble and alert, always searching for the loose pocket or hanging purse. She was not all that happy with being back in this time, with its blatant poverty, rank smells and old, worn out customs, but here she was, and Patrick was only minutes away now.

Inside the carriage, Dr. Foster, wearing his silk top hat, sat opposite Eve and Joni, his eyes trained outside the left window, watching Fifth Avenue drift by. Joni was staring out her left window, hands folded tightly in her lap. Both were making an obvious effort not to allow their eyes to meet and explore with desire, although Eve could feel the heightened attraction and sexual energy between them, hovering in the carriage.

The last thing Eve wanted or needed was for Joni to start some torrid love affair with this pompous doctor, who probably already had a wife or a fiancée, or a mistress, or two of the above. On the other hand, it had been Joni who'd somehow beguiled the man, who'd then agreed to travel downtown to examine Emma Gantly.

Now that she was on her way, Eve was second guessing her actions. Had she used poor judgement? Perhaps she shouldn't have gone to see Dr. Eckland after all. Perhaps she should have been the one to knock on Patrick's door and offer her services as a nurse? But no, knowing Patrick, he would have slammed the door in her face, not trusting or accepting the audacity of any woman who would dare do this.

Was she going to all this trouble just to keep Emma alive out of pure selflessness, or was she doing it for herself, so she could see Patrick again? So she could be with Patrick, hoping and praying that he remembered her, and still loved her, and wanted them both to return to their twenty-first century marriage? During their marriage ceremony, didn't she repeat the words "*For better, for worse, for richer, for poorer, in sickness and in health, to love and to cherish, till death do us part?*" She was not dead. Patrick was not dead.

It was impossible for Eve to be completely selfless in Emma's life and death struggle, when Eve was still so deeply in love with Patrick. Could she help it if time and fate had torn them apart so cruelly? Could Eve just snap her fingers and say some magic word that would erase all the love and passion she felt for Patrick?

Eve's insides were twisting with anticipation, guilt and anxiety, while she searched her heart and silently prayed for guidance.

Dr. Foster turned his attention to the ladies. "Are you both alone in the City?"

Unsure what to say, Joni glanced at Eve, who being lost in her thoughts and tangled emotions, had to snap out of it.

"Yes, Dr. Foster," Eve said, a bit startled. "That is to say, we traveled here from Ohio, for a brief vacation."

Joni nodded, her expression conflicted. She'd never been to Ohio.

Dr. Foster brightened. "Ohio? A fine state. And as you must know, our unfortunate ex-President, James Garfield, was from Ohio. It was such a sad business to see him felled by that assassin's bullet, and then to see his condition further aggravated by his incompetent doctor, a Dr. Willard Bliss. Forgive me, ladies, but I would call him an absolute incompetent."

Joni didn't remember much about James Garfield. Eve nodded, hoping to show interest, but she only vaguely recalled President Garfield being assassinated. She often got him confused with President William McKinley, who'd also been assassinated. She wished she'd studied more history.

"We have been in bad straits, I dare say, since his death," Dr. Foster said. "Let us hope that President Arthur will soon be out of office and return home to Vermont, where his bumbling political skills will no longer harm the American people."

Dr. Foster leaned forward, touching his hat. "Forgive me for discussing politics, ladies. I know it is of no interest to either of you or, indeed, to any ladies, who prefer gossiping about anything other than the news of the day."

Eve bristled at the backhanded insult, although she knew it was the belief of this time. But she was too preoccupied to argue and, anyway, when it came to James Garfield or President Arthur, she truly wasn't interested.

"Let me return to our previous conversation," Dr. Foster said, relaxing in his seat. "What part of Ohio do you ladies hail from?"

"A town a little north of Cincinnati. I'm sure you've never heard of it."

"I attended a medical conference in Cincinnati some three years ago. I found it a lovely and economically agreeable city. Mount Adams is charming, and the Ohio River is most impressive."

Joni spoke up. "And are you from New York City, Dr. Foster?"

Dr. Foster's eyes lit up again, and he shifted in his seat, as if his attraction to Joni had stirred him to want to act on it.

"Yes, Miss Kosarin, I am."

What Joni said next caused Eve to shift in *her* seat.

"And is your wife from New York as well, Dr. Foster?"

Dr. Foster squinted in the brightness of the sun. "I'm afraid, Miss Kosarin, that I have not had the pleasure of experiencing that most sacred and joyful partnership."

Eve found that hard to believe. The man was extraordinarily handsome and from a privileged family.

Dr. Foster continued. "I was engaged for a time but, unfortunately, events were such that the engagement has ended, and I will add, amicably."

Joni smiled her satisfaction. Eve was suspicious.

"If I may be so bold, ladies, I know it is highly unusual, since we have just been acquainted, but I feel it is my duty to offer you companionship since you are alone in this strange city. May I invite you both to dine with me and a good friend tomorrow night, Friday? I assure you that said friend, Edwin Bennett, is a fine gentleman and from a good family. I believe you will find his company both charming and entertaining. After dinner, we will be happy to show you some of the more attractive sites of our fair City."

Eve spoke up. "Dr. Foster, perhaps Mr. Bennett will have other plans on such short notice?"

"He will not, Miss Kennedy, as we are boyhood friends and I know him as a brother. He will be delighted at the prospect. Now, is dinner tomorrow night agreeable to you?"

Before Eve could decline, Joni jumped in. "We would be delighted, Dr. Foster. How generous of you."

He touched his silk top hat again, with an ingratiating smile, showing perfect white teeth. "Not at all, Miss Kosarin. I shall look forward to it with the greatest of pleasure."

Eve shrank back into her soft leather seat, already concocting an excuse for declining the invitation. But she would wait until after Dr. Foster had seen Emma Gantly, and she had seen the love of her life, Patrick Gantly.

Dr. Foster's eyes glowed with new desire as they again alighted on Joni. He was a changed man from the stodgy, condescending man who'd first stepped into Dr. Eckland's parlor.

As the carriage rolled to a stop in front of Patrick's modest, single-family row house, Eve began to tremble.

Dr. Foster noticed her unease. "Do not have a worry, Miss Kennedy. I will do everything in my power to help this poor, wretched woman."

Eve meekly lowered her eyes. "Dr. Foster… If Mr. Gantly asks who is responsible for sending you and who is paying your fee, would you please be so kind as to say that the person wishes to remain anonymous?"

There was a sudden recognition in Dr. Foster's expression and, as she looked at him, she saw he read her request the wrong way. He assumed that she and Patrick were secret lovers. Well, in a way, they were, weren't they?

Dr. Foster reached for his chocolate brown Gladstone medical bag, a tight smile on his lips. "You are quite the mystery, aren't you, Miss Kennedy?"

After a minute's contemplation, he glanced over at Joni, and then he nodded. "Do not be troubled, Miss Kennedy. Rest assured it will be done. Now, let us attend to the woman."

After Eve and Dr. Foster had stepped down to the street, Joni leaned out toward them.

"If you don't mind, I'll just stay in the carriage."

Dr. Foster tipped his hat. "Of course. I understand. As you wish, Miss Kosarin."

Outside on the sidewalk, Eve stood by the stone hitching post, gazing up at the arched ground-floor windows and columned, sheltered entrance. Eve fought a multitude of emotions as she mounted the stairs behind Dr. Foster. At the front door, he lifted the knocker and gently released it.

To Eve it was an eternity before the door swung open and Patrick Gantly appeared. Eve's emotions rocketed up into turbulent fireworks. There he was, Patrick. Her husband. He stood tall and sullen, his vivid, intelligent blue eyes red-rimmed. His broad shoulders were slumped, his shadow of beard and weary expression suggesting a lack of sleep and endless worry.

Eve hurt for him and she wanted to reach out to him, her heart aching.

Then their eyes met, and she willed him to recognize her. Yes, he was her husband, wasn't he? He was her only love. Her best friend. He'd been the father of their baby. Surely, he would remember. There would have to be some spark of recognition in his eyes.

But there was no recognition. No emotion. No expression. Just a blank stare. Her heart sank. Her shoulders sank. Her spirits sank. This Patrick didn't know her, and he had no interest in knowing her. The Patrick she'd known and loved was not standing before her. He was gone.

The knifing pain of this reality cut her deeply, and she would have to face it. This Patrick was living in another place and time, and he was married to another woman.

It took all her flagging strength to remain standing, as the ice-cold truth washed over her.

"Are you Detective Sergeant Gantly?" Dr. Foster asked in an official manner.

Patrick nodded, his tired eyes heavy and brooding. "Yes? Who are you? What do you want?"

"I am Dr. Darius Compton Foster of The New York Hospital. I understand your wife is gravely ill. I have been sent by a person of influence in this City to examine her."

177

In his fatigued state, Patrick was slow to comprehend. "Who did you say sent you?" Patrick asked, his voice hoarse with exhaustion.

"A person of influence who wishes to offer aid to your wife."

Patrick turned his frosty attention to Eve, who could not meet his eyes. She stared down at the concrete stoop.

"Who is this woman?" Patrick asked, coldly. "Why is she here?"

"She is a nurse. May we enter, sir? I understand there is no time to waste."

Patrick hesitated. "She has already had a doctor examine her. A midwife is with her now."

Dr. Foster's conceited jaw tightened. "You may have had a doctor examine her, sir, but I can assure you, I am infinitely more qualified and renowned than any other doctor who may have attended to your wife. I attend to the Vanderbilts, the Astors and the Harringshaws. Now, will you please let me examine Mrs. Gantly before we waste more precious time bantering about inconsequentials, while your wife lies gravely ill?"

Patrick stepped back to allow Dr. Foster and Eve to enter, his breathing staggered, the result of stress, grief and anxiety.

"My wife is in the back bedroom. Follow me."

CHAPTER 25

It was a clean and finely furnished Victorian, with polished wood floors, soft, dim light from oil lamps and drawn draperies. Eve noticed a slick horsehair couch, fashionable in this day, and the usual bulky, carved furniture. A thin carpeted staircase led to upper rooms, and the piano room to the left was in shadow because draperies were pulled against the light.

Eve and Dr. Foster followed Patrick through the house, past a parlor and a dining room, through a pocket door that led into the rear bedroom where Emma Gantly lay.

Weak light filtering in from a side window revealed a double bed, where a young woman lay covered to the chin by a sheet, her pretty face pallid and slick with sweat, her hair damp and careless, the room overheated. Her head whipped from side to side, her dry lips mumbling whispers, her breath labored, eyes twitching.

Patrick's sad, tortured eyes rested first on Eve, and then on Dr. Foster. "Can you help my poor wife? Can you please help my poor, suffering Emma?"

Eve felt compassion and alarm, although she didn't show it. Dr. Foster set his medical bag on a nearby chair, slipped out of his suit coat and handed it to Eve. He turned to Patrick.

"Have you been administering medicines?"

"Laudanum, as per Dr. Crane's instructions. He also administered gin. Yesterday, when she had contractions, he tried to help her out of bed to walk, but Emma was too weak."

"And where is the good Dr. Crane now?" Dr. Foster asked.

Patrick looked away.

A sturdy, broad-faced middle-aged woman standing in shadow in the corner of the room spoke up in a thick Irish brogue. "Where is he?" she asked, rhetorically. "You'll be finding him at Sean O'Casey's Saloon, you will."

Dr. Foster swallowed a disgusted breath. "Did the doctor suggest Mrs. Gantly go to a hospital?"

"Mrs. Gantly will not go to a hospital," Patrick said somberly.

Dr. Foster's lips tightened as he opened his medical bag and drew out a stethoscope.

"I can see from the look of her, Detective Gantly, that she is in grievous distress and that she belongs in a hospital, and that she must go to a hospital. While there, I can use chloroform to ease her into a comfortable sleep while the baby is delivered."

"She will not go, and I will not force her," Patrick said stubbornly.

Dr. Foster breathed out an exasperated sigh, as he indicated toward the woman across the room, who was looking on with deep anxiety.

"And who is that woman?" Dr. Foster demanded.

"That is Mrs. Connelly. She is a friend and the midwife."

Dr. Foster narrowed his eyes on her. "How long are Mrs. Gantly's contractions?"

"She began with crampy back pains late last night."

"How long did they last?"

"Around a half a minute, occurring every ten to thirty minutes or so. This morning the pains were stronger and closer together. The baby wants to come, but Mrs. Gantly is very weak and is having trouble pushing."

"You can go now," Dr. Foster said, brusquely. "I have no need of a midwife."

Patrick's left eye twitched, his gaze burning on the doctor. Grudgingly, he nodded at Mrs. Connelly and smiled. "You may go, Mrs. Connelly. Thank you."

"But Detective Gantly," she protested, taking two steps forward and wringing her hands. "Mrs. Gantly will call for me," she said, with a catch of emotion in her voice. "You know she will."

"Please go, just for a while, Mrs. Connelly," Patrick said soothingly. "Please make some tea for us all."

"Well, I will go, but I will not go far," she said with a firm jerk of her predominate, stubborn chin. She shot Dr. Foster a look of hatred, gathered up her apron, and huffed out of the room.

Dr. Foster went to work, taking Emma's pulse, lifting her fluttering eyelids and touching the stethoscope to her bulging stomach, sliding it slowly up to her heart.

Meanwhile, Eve left the foot of the bed to stand opposite the doctor as he worked. She found a basin of cold water and a cloth. She wrung out the cloth and applied it gently to Emma's burning forehead. Emma's eyes suddenly opened wide and glassy with pain.

In a hoarse whisper she said, "… Save my baby…"

Eve forced a confident smile. "We'll do all we can, Mrs. Gantly. Don't worry."

Dr. Foster finished his cursory exam and lifted his sober eyes on Eve. "She's burning up with fever. Unfortunately, it is puerperal fever—childbed fever, as you call it."

Dr. Foster turned back to Patrick, who stood stark still, his back against the wall.

"She must go to a hospital now, sir," Dr. Foster said. "She must, or she will die. Her pulse is racing, and the fever has gripped her. I will be frank, sir. The baby's heart is dangerously feeble and, in my opinion, your wife has little chance of survival if we don't remove her to a hospital without any further delay."

Patrick's face settled into lines of sorrow and he didn't move. "She is terrified of hospitals. Her sister and her baby died in one in England. She will not go, and I will not force her."

Dr. Foster became flushed with emotion. "Then she will die, sir! My God, man, is that what you want?"

Patrick fell silent, his face completely in shadow, body slumped in sorrow.

Eve had brought one course of antibiotics with her, but even if she could administer them, which was impossible with Dr. Foster standing there, at this point, she wasn't sure they would help. If Emma survived, then Eve would find some way to administer the antibiotic. But for now, Emma was about to deliver. She was as thin as a twig, her color ashen, and her cough a ragged, painful cry.

"Save my baby," she repeated, her contractions coming rapidly.

Dr. Foster threw his hands to his hips.

Eve was not a pediatric nurse, and she'd only delivered two babies in her entire career, one at a clinic with a physician present and the other in the Bronx, during an emergency, working with a midwife. Surely, Dr. Foster had delivered many. She was encouraged when she saw the sudden determination in his face, and it touched her. For all his aloof arrogance, he genuinely wanted to do his best for Emma. He wanted to deliver the baby and save Emma's life.

Eve tamped down her own emotion and spoke up, looking directly at Dr. Foster. She would have to be careful what she said to him, and yet she knew it was past the time for rushing Emma to the hospital.

"Dr. Foster, you are correct about the need to send Mrs. Gantly to the hospital, but perhaps we should try to deliver the baby now, while Mrs. Gantly still has some strength."

Emma moaned and cried out, a weak arm lifting, her hand waving through the air as if she were swatting away ghosts. "My baby... save my baby..."

The room pulsed with waiting misery. Dr. Foster fought the tense moment, considering Eve's words.

Patrick's voice was hollow, and he was on the verge of tears. "If she dies in that hospital, she will despise me for breaking my vow to her. She said that if God wants her to die with the baby, then his will be done. She said that if she must die, she will die in her own bed, with her baby and husband at her side and not in some strange, cold and dark hospital."

Patrick inhaled a sharp breath. "I will not break my vow to my dear wife. If I do, I will never be at peace in this world or in the next."

Dr. Foster removed the stethoscope from his ears and rolled up his shirt sleeves, his eyes hard with resignation. Troubled, he looked at Eve and spoke at a whisper.

"I trust Miss Kosarin will not protest too much waiting in the carriage?"

"Do not worry about her. She will be fine."

"All right, we must try to deliver this baby. Let us do all we can. There is no more time. Miss Kennedy, get us a fresh basin of warm water and plenty of clean cloths."

As she turned to leave, Dr. Foster fixed her with his eyes. "Miss Kennedy, you truly are a nurse, are you not?"

"Yes. I am a nurse."

"All right. I'll administer morphine. That will comfort her."

After Eve had returned with the water, setting it down on a table at the foot of the bed, Dr. Foster turned to her, his expression urgent.

"Now listen carefully. Let us make sure Mrs. Gantly is wearing an undervest, warm stockings and bedroom slippers."

Eve's eyes held questions.

"There isn't the time for me to explain everything to you. The supreme advantage of this method of dressing lies in the ease with which the soiled garments can be removed. Rinse and prepare the cloths. We must be prepared to stop post-birth hemorrhage. Now let us get to work."

Emma Gantly cried out in delirious pain. "Save my baby…"

Dr. Foster looked at her. "I will do all I can, Mrs. Gantly. Now you must gather all your strength and push. Now is your time of trial. To bring forth a child in sorrow will make you love your child more."

Eve prickled at the comment, but what could she say? Dr. Foster was a man of his time.

Dr. Foster went to the foot of the bed, lifted the sheets and went to work.

"Mrs. Gantly, I need you to push when I tell you and I need you to pray, so that we may bring your baby safely into this world."

CHAPTER 26

Dr. Foster and Eve made desperate and agonizing attempts to stop Emma's bleeding, but to no avail. The pretty and petite Emma Gantly passed away at 7:33 p.m. on October 23, 1884.

But she had been granted her wish: her baby girl was born a half-hour before, her breathing labored and shallow. Eve performed gentle massage on her chest and near her heart, praying as hard as she'd ever prayed for the child to live. Finally, the air caught in her lungs and she coughed, and then bellowed. Eve took her pulse, quickly calculating what her APGAR score would be if she were in a modern hospital. Appearance:1 (her hands and feet were still blue); Pulse:1 (below 100 beats); Grimace: 2 (she coughed, cried); Activity: 2 (active, spontaneous movement); Respiration: 2 (normal rate and effort, good cry). A total of eight. She appeared to be in the normal range.

Eve held the baby up for Patrick to see, but he did not move from his spot against the wall, his suffering eyes fixed on Emma's face. Finally, he dropped to his knees next to Emma's bed and took his wife's hand, kissing it gently, coaxing her, pleading with her to stay with him.

Mrs. Connelly hurried in and took the baby to clean and dress her, while Eve and Dr. Foster fought to save Emma's life. Eve wasn't sure if Emma had heard her, but several times, Eve told Emma that she had given birth to a beautiful baby girl.

Emma's last breath had been a soft, feathery whisper of a thing, leaving her body like a prayer. Patrick sobbed, his big shoulders rolling in agony. As Emma lay still and tranquil, Patrick would not release her hand, nor move from his kneeling position.

Later, while Eve was cleaning and dressing Emma's lifeless body, Mrs. Connelly and a priest entered the room in silent reverence. Mrs. Connelly insisted on taking over, and Eve didn't protest. While the priest uttered prayers, Mrs. Connelly, with tears holding in her eyes, quietly but firmly asked Eve to leave the house. Dr. Foster had left some time before, telling Eve he'd be waiting for her in the carriage.

The last Eve saw of Patrick, his head was in his hands, a broken man. Mrs. Connelly wept into an embroidered handkerchief balled at her mouth.

Eve left the room, pausing at the front door to view Patrick's daughter as she was being cradled in the arms of a young, weeping woman, who ignored Eve. It was a strange and devastating moment, and Eve absorbed a wave of grief so powerful that she nearly burst into tears.

As she left the house, she glanced once more over her shoulder, hoping to get the slightest glimpse of Patrick, but he didn't appear.

Eve had felt the catastrophic moment of Emma's death as a failure, as a needless, senseless act. She had simply come too late. Emma had received poor treatment, with none of the 21st century care and medications offered as a matter of routine. As Dr. Foster had said, if the hemorrhaging hadn't killed her, the fever most certainly would have. Had they managed to rush Emma to the hospital, she probably would have died anyway.

Eve fought the impulse to curse this backward and ignorant time and to curse the strange magic that had brought her here to witness it; to be a part of it; to experience firsthand the death of pretty, fragile Emma. And now Eve was forced to leave her husband—yes, *her* husband, Patrick Gantly, suffering alone in unspeakable torment.

As Eve descended the stairs toward Dr. Foster's carriage, she had to admit that her impression of the man was elevated. He'd done all he could to save Emma and the baby.

The carriage ride back to the hotel was mostly silent. Dr. Foster gently broke the news to Joni, while also apologizing for the interminable delay. Joni waved it off, seeing the heavy anguish in Eve's face.

Dr. Foster left them in the hotel lobby, with the promise of returning the following night at 7 p.m. with his friend, Edwin Bennett, for their agreed-upon dinner date.

In the room, Eve undressed quietly, feeling utterly exhausted and disheartened.

"I'm sorry, Eve," Joni said, softly. "I'm so sorry. Is there anything I can do?"

"No, thanks. I'm going to take a bath. These clothes are ruined. It's a good thing we're getting our new clothes tomorrow."

Eve ran a bath, hoping for hot water, but settling on tepid. She soaked for long minutes, her eyes shut against the world, her mind blunted and bruised from the day's events and from the miserable faces that kept sliding in and out of her inner vision.

She jerked awake when Joni touched her shoulder. "Eve, come to bed. It's late and you've been in here for over an hour."

Eve was shivering. "I fell asleep. The water is ice cold. Please get me a robe before I catch pneumonia."

CHAPTER 27

On Friday morning, Eve awoke alone in the bed, the sheets tangled around her. She had no idea what time it was, and she didn't care. She got up and wandered to the front window. Her fitful night's sleep had been broken by several intervals of pacing the room. Now, the soft light of morning brought the shapes of the room into focus.

Joni came from the bathroom, sleepy and concerned. "Did you sleep at all last night?"

"Not much," Eve said, looking out through the parted draperies and down onto 27th Street. It was an overcast day, with a stringy fog and needle-fine rain, puddles forming in the street. Black umbrellas slid beneath her, as did carriages and drays.

"What a fitting, gloomy morning for such an awful night."

Joni lay down on the bed. "Did you talk to him... to Patrick? You never said."

"No... I left him there. What else could I do?"

After a little pause, Joni sat up, her back braced against the ornately carved headboard. "What are you going to do?"

"I've spent most of the night and early morning thinking about that. As I see it, I have two clear options. I can talk to Tesla and hope he knows about the lantern or that he has a lantern, or he can build a lantern that will send us back home. It's either that, or I can stay here and wait, and hope that someday, when the time is right, I'll go to Patrick, put myself out there and see where it leads and hope that we can begin again."

"Didn't you tell me that when you and Patrick were together, he told you that both his wife and his baby had died?"

"Yes."

"Well, then, you've changed history. His baby survived, and it survived because you were here to save it."

"So what? I've changed history many times. You and I have changed history just by being here."

"Okay, well won't that screw everything up? I mean, what about the future? Haven't we messed everything up?"

Eve left the window and sat in the chair, pinching the neck of her nightgown, having caught a chill. "What is history anyway but a series of events? Little events, big events, personal events and impersonal events."

"Yeah, so?"

"So, do you know your neighbor next door in 2016, and their history, or the person across the hall or down the block? Do those people change history all that much as they live their little lives? We come and go like passing clouds. I don't think that by saving Patrick's daughter, history will change all that much. The First and Second World Wars will still happen. I'm sure all the presidents will still get elected, and some probably assassinated. But the world? I don't think one or two, or even three people are going to change the world all that much. In small ways, yes, but overall, big picture? Not much. No matter what happens, no matter how we might have changed the world, this whirling blue planet will still just keep right on spinning around, evolving. Evolution is constant and relentless, no matter what happens."

Eve looked at Joni. "... And speaking of evolving, what about you? What about you and the handsome Dr. Foster?"

Joni looked at Eve uneasily. "You know me and men. I'm either instantly attracted or I'm not. With him... well, the man is, as we would say in our time, hot. He just has that something that lights me up."

"And you're going to dinner with him tonight?"

"Of course I am. Aren't you?"

Eve turned away. "I'm so not in the mood for that. No mood whatsoever to meet his friend."

"I think Dr. Foster anticipated that."

"How do you mean?"

"As he escorted me into the lobby last night, and after you'd gone ahead in the elevator, he told me to tell you he would require no fee for his services last night. Instead, he said..." and then Joni did an impression of Dr. Foster that was spot on. "'Please let Miss Kennedy know that the only payment I may require will be to have the pleasure of her company as my guest tomorrow night.'"

Eve folded her arms tightly across her chest and turned to stare at the far wall. "Wonderful. Perfect. Delightful. In other words, he's saying, you owe me."

"I need you there, Eve. You know I do. I don't know how to speak or act around these people. They're like something from another planet, with all their manners and flowery words."

Eve closed her eyes, as if to shut out the thought. "I wish I'd never come here, Joni."

"You know you can't leave here without Patrick. You can't leave until you're sure your relationship with him hasn't got a chance. I know you. You'll never stop loving him."

Eve's eyes opened. "Joni... It could take months, if not years, before Patrick will be able to forget Emma and move on, if ever. I met him the first time in October 1885, a year from now, and even then, he was still grieving over her."

"Well then, maybe you should make a life here, wait for a while and..." Joni had another thought. "Eve, who knows, given enough time, maybe you'll be able to forget Patrick, meet another guy, and start a new life here."

In an outburst, Eve shouted, "No!"

Joni looked on, startled, as Eve shot to her feet.

"Never! Not here," Eve declared. "I could never live in this time for very long. It's too oppressive. Women are second-class citizens. They can't vote. They can't own property. They can't go out alone to a club or bar because they'll be called a whore or a prostitute. And God help the poor woman who can't find a man who will marry her. And if she can't find a man, then she'll be called a spinster or worse, be treated like a loser, looked down upon or gossiped about, and laughed at by smart-assed kids. If a woman does marry, she spends all her time taking care of her husband and the kids and the house. And being a woman in this godforsaken time also means you must get pregnant repeatedly because that's a woman's primary duty, isn't it? And then many women die in childbirth, like poor Emma Gantly, because the medicine in this time is abysmal, filled with ignorance and superstition and not based on solid science. And, of course, it's fine for a man to have a mistress or two, hang out in his club or the local bar and do whatever he wants while the woman is trapped alone in the house, playing the role of the good little wife. No, thank you. I could never live in this time."

Joni sighed and ran a hand through her mussed hair. "Okay. Okay... I'm sorry I brought it up."

Eve started pacing again. "I just don't know what to do. I can't think straight. I wish I'd never found that damned lantern in that antique shop."

She stopped again, breath puffing from her nose, making a whistling sound. Outside, they heard the whinny of a horse and a man shouting. Eve walked to the window and looked out. Two carriages had entangled, and a hansom cab driver was shaking his fist at a carriage driver. A portly policeman soon joined the fray, pointing his stick threateningly, bellowing at both drivers.

"Well, what do you know," Eve said. "Even in old New York, there's a good old traffic fight."

Joni's voice was still and imploring. "Please come with me tonight, Eve. Our dresses are ready. I'll pick them up a little later and we can try them on. It'll be fun. It will help to get your mind off things."

Eve didn't turn from the window. "I just want to go home and curl up in my bed with Georgy Boy, and hear Patrick come through the front door saying, 'Hey there, Mrs. Gantly, I'm home.'"

After a long silence, Eve said. "Joni... What will happen to Patrick's baby?"

CHAPTER 28

It was Joni who tried her new dress on first, demanding that Eve tighten the corset strings until she was gasping for breath.

"Tighter, Eve," Joni said, wincing, grasping the back of a chair with both hands and sucking in her stomach, as Eve tugged at the corset strings.

"I thought you hated corsets. If I pull this thing any tighter, you're going to faint."

"Have you seen all those skinny women out there, with their twenty-inch waists? I want Darius Compton Foster's eyes to pop out when he sees me, the way those character's eyes pop out in cartoons."

"They already popped out. That's why he asked you out. Obviously, he likes you just the way you are, as the song goes, even with your twenty-seven-inch waist."

"Twenty-six and a half," Joni shot back.

"Whatever. Women are smaller in this time. You've seen them. We have bigger bones and bigger waists."

"Don't care..." Joni said, sucking in her waist. "Tighter. I'm going for at least a twenty-four-inch waist."

Their new dresses had extravagant drapes and pleats, and a pronounced bustle, sitting high in the back. Joni's dress was ruby satin and velvet trimmed with gold and cream lace. It was cut with a low scooped neck; it had delicate white lace at the wrists and neckline, and foliage and tea roses at the lower hem.

Eve's dress was blue satin, trimmed with Spanish blonde lace. The sleeves were short, and the low neck was open in a V, showing modest cleavage. On the shoulders were delicate bows of blue satin and flowery lace.

After they'd dressed, the women gazed at themselves in the mirror, entranced, swaying the dresses about, hearing the whisper of the fabric. They turned left and right, and then glanced back over their shoulders, pleased and amused.

"I'll say one thing about this time," Joni said. "These people know how to make a dress. No wonder these women were so skinny. How can you eat sitting in one of these things?"

"Take it from a girl with experience and don't eat much," Eve said. "You'll feel like a stuffed turkey after a few bites."

Joni couldn't pull her eyes from the mirror. "Okay, just for clarification: you do think Darius Foster is handsome, don't you, Eve?"

"Yes, in a stiff and formal kind of way. Oh, by the way, if he asks you what it is you do back in Ohio, what are you going to tell him?"

"That I'm an actress and dancer."

"No. Never. No way. Don't ever tell any man that you're an actress/dancer in this time."

"Why? There are theaters around everywhere. Darius said he wanted to take me next week."

Eve faced her sternly. "In this time, Joni, actress/dancer means you're a prostitute."

"No way."

"Oh, yes. Very much way. Tell him you're a... I don't know. Tell him you're a teacher."

"A teacher of what?"

"I don't know. Tell him you teach children in a little red schoolhouse in Ohio. He'll love it. He'll think you're very quaint."

"You sound cynical."

"I'm feeling cynical right now."

Eve left the mirror and walked across the room to the window, staring out. "I feel trapped, and I don't know what to do. I hate it when I don't know what to do."

"Do you know what my father used to say when he didn't know what to do?" Joni asked.

Eve kept her gaze outside. "No, what?"

"Do something crazy."

Eve turned. "Joni... Look at us. We've lighted an old lantern and time traveled to 1884. Look at us in these dresses. We've already done crazy. It doesn't get crazier than what we've done, okay?"

"You know what I mean."

"No, I don't. What crazy thing could I do that I haven't done?"

Joni raised her hands in a placating manner. "Now, don't get excited."

Eve's mouth tightened, waiting.

"Go see Patrick."

"What? Joni, his wife just died. That's not only crazy, it's completely insensitive and selfish. The man is grieving. I saw him. He's devastated."

"Yes, and you were the nurse who was there when his wife died. The woman who helped to save his baby. You could comfort him. Be with him, even if it's from a distance. Okay, so it's crazy. Why did you come here? Why did you risk everything to come here? To find Patrick again. Okay, so you found him."

Eve's head dropped. "Not now, Joni. Not that way. I'll have to wait. Like I said, I may have to wait for a very long time."

"Okay, then come with me tonight and meet Mr. Edwin Bennett, a fine gentleman, or so Dr. Foster says."

Eve sighed. "I'll go, Joni, but only for you. Only because you somehow bewitched the good doctor and persuaded him to go examine Emma Gantly. I owe you for that."

Joni batted her long eyelashes flirtatiously. "I have only just begun to bewitch Dr. Darius Compton Foster. I have the feeling that he's not so uptight when you get him in the right position."

Eve laughed a little at the naughty joke. "He's not going to know what hit him. The upright and proper Dr. Foster thinks he's getting a demure 1884 woman when, in fact, he's going to get the full wattage of a 2016 wild and crazy Joni, a much more modern woman than he could have ever imagined."

They both laughed, much too hard, mostly to release nerves, exhaustion and anticipation.

CHAPTER 29

In the carriage, Dr. Foster and Edwin Bennett sat opposite the ladies, wearing tuxedos, black capes and silk top hats. Eve struggled to stay present and appear genial, wondering if her wide silk hat with bird feathers was too much. She did not like wearing a hat with bird feathers, but it was the hat that had been delivered, so she had no choice.

Joni sat still, with a fixed smile. She was all nerves and excitement, her corset cutting off air, the dress bulky and heavy, making her feel as big as a house. And then there was the long, tapered woolen coat that was hot and confining.

"How long will you two ladies be visiting our fair City?" Edwin Bennett asked.

Eve spoke up before Joni could. "We're not quite sure. Perhaps only a few days, perhaps longer."

Dr. Foster said, "Do you see, Edwin, as I told you, these charming ladies are a wondrous mystery."

Joni said, "Mystery adds attraction, does it not?"

Eve wanted to roll her eyes.

Dr. Foster grinned, showing his white teeth. "Indeed, it does, Miss Kosarin, indeed it does."

Eve needed to steer the conversation in a new direction. "And what about you, Mr. Bennett? What do you like to do in this great City?"

Dr. Foster said, "Mr. Bennett loves the glittering parties at those arrogant Gramercy Park mansions and he is quite unabashed about it, aren't you, Edwin?"

"Well, my friend, as a young attorney always seeking the best clients, I must rub elbows with a chosen few. And, anyway, my father insists upon it, since he owns one of those arrogant mansions."

Both men laughed at the thin joke.

"And where did you study law, Mr. Bennett?" Eve asked.

"Columbia Law School."

"And what kind of law do you practice?"

"Estates and wills mostly. I'm afraid my profession is not terribly exciting conversation."

"Unless one needs land, or finds herself dead," Eve said, feeling cheeky.

Edwin laughed heartily, but Dr. Foster only smiled meagerly, not so amused by Eve's rather flippant joke. There was something both curious and troubling about Eve; there was much more to her than met the eye, he was sure of that.

"And where is your law firm?" Joni tossed in, joining the conversation.

"In the financial district, at 348 Broadway. Have you two ladies been there yet on your sightseeing tours?"

"No, we haven't had the time," Eve said.

"Well, you must. You simply must," Darius said. "I believe you will find it interesting…"

Elyse Douglas

Edwin cut in, "... If not terribly exhilarating. It's all about economics, finance and law. I'm sure that does not interest you ladies and, if the truth be known, it does not much interest me either."

They heard ringing bells approach. Eve glanced out the window as three white horses appeared in the opposite lane, pulling a water truck uptown, firemen in black-buttoned uniforms hanging onto the side rails, their expressions grim and alert.

Dr. Foster peered out the window. "Too many fires these days. I fear our fair City is ill-equipped for so many fires, despite our brave firemen."

"Are you willing to pay additional taxes, my good Darius?" Edwin asked.

"It's not the taxes that disturb me, Edwin, it's the graft down at City Hall."

Benton's, a fashionable restaurant only one block from Bryant Park, was in a three-story Beaux-Arts building. It featured an ornate lobby with a grand staircase, and a main dining room richly decorated in gold and green, with less formal dining areas on the second floor.

It was a place of grace, polish and practiced attitude, where the light glistened off crystal glasses and chandeliers and diamonds; where lavish color and fashion were on majestic display; where waiters in tuxedos seemed to glide around linen-topped tables.

Fresh flowers and ivy bloomed from elaborate, standing Grecian urns. Champagne bubbled out wealth and pleasure, and women, clutching dainty hankies, fawned on tuxedo-dressed, cigar-chewing gentlemen who puffed out their chests and puffed on fat cigars, their bushy mustaches twitching with grins and salutations.

Joni was spellbound, Eve perceptive and cool, while they were escorted to their table by Dr. Foster and Edwin Bennett. The erect maître d', with the perfectly waxed mustache, the perfectly tailored tuxedo, the perfect tilt of his head and the perfect stiff smile, deposited the quartet at a private table in the rear of the room.

Eve sat stiffly next to Edwin; Joni sat happily next to Darius. The menus floated down to them with delicate care, the waiter featuring his formal face, not too tight and not too friendly.

Darius ordered a bottle of champagne, while Eve struggled to relax, and Joni glowed with a new delight.

Darius indicated at the restaurant, while looking directly at Joni. "I trust, Miss Kosarin, that Benton's meets your expectations and approval?"

Joni felt her heart purring as she smiled at him. "Oh, yes, Dr. Foster, it's an awesome room... I mean," she said, catching herself for using 2016 slang, "... It's a lovely and perfect room."

Darius lifted an amused left eyebrow. "I believe, Miss Kosarin, that 'awesome' is the perfect word for it." He swung his gaze to Eve. "Don't you think so, Miss Kennedy?"

Eve offered an approving nod. "Yes, I believe my friend has managed the perfect word. Awesome is a good choice."

Edwin Bennett spoke up, his voice resonant and playful. "I dare say that awesome is a word that has long been banished from everyday conversation and I, for one, vote to retrieve it, to bring it back into the forefront of everyday speech. I shall go even further than that and state that awesome should be used frequently in the legal and banking corridors of business. Why not tell all our clients that they are receiving awesome returns on their investments, and awesome service for their legal fees?"

Joni blushed pink. "Now you're making fun of me, Mr. Bennett."

Darius spoke. "Yes, I'm afraid he is, Miss Kosarin, and I shall apologize for his rather rakish humor."

Edwin held up a hand, serious. "Now, now, Miss Kosarin. There was no offense intended. It is all in good fun. I am having a go at you, as they say in Brooklyn, but it is only because you and..." Edwin turned to Eve, who was not looking back at him, but purposively staring at Joni. "... Yes, you, Miss Kosarin, and you, Miss Kennedy, are so charming and such pleasant company that you bring out a bit of the rascal in me."

"Well, that will be all of that rascal behavior for the evening, Edwin," Darius said. "You'll turn our charming company against us, and I simply won't have it."

While the champagne was being poured, Eve had a moment to appraise Edwin Bennett fully in the light. In the carriage, seated opposite him, the only light with which to see him were the gas lamps flickering in the city streets.

In his black tuxedo and white tie, Edwin Bennett's body was lean and athletic. He possessed an inborn, smooth confidence, and an ingratiating, if not rakish, smile. His thick auburn hair, parted in the middle, was combed back with pomade; his eyes, a gleaming hazel, were not hard to look into. He was certainly an attractive man with impeccable manners, although Eve sensed that, when it came to the ladies, Mr. Bennett was most certainly a rascal or, to put it in 21st century slang, a player.

But there was something else about him that troubled her. Within those flashing hazel eyes, she caught moments of a smoldering despair, as if dark frustration lurked just below the surface and he struggled to keep it at bay.

They started their dinner with oysters on the half shell, then had consommé Royale soup. The conversation stayed cordial and safe through the main course. Eve ate lobster tail and Joni the roast goose with currant jelly. Both men chose steak.

It was Edwin who changed the course of the conversation. "Miss Kennedy, Dr. Foster tells me that you were both commendable and skilled in your delivery of the poor, unfortunate child yesterday evening."

Eve was silent. She didn't want to discuss the incident, nor did she want to think about Patrick and the baby.

It was Joni who leaped in to fill the awkward silence. "Eve is an excellent nurse. Actually, she's a highly skilled nurse practitioner."

Eve gave her a cool glance. There was no such thing as a nurse practitioner in 1884, nor would there be until the 1970s.

Dr. Foster glanced up from his steak. "A nurse practitioner? I have never heard of the title."

Joni grimaced, realizing her mistake. "Well, it's just that…"

Eve cut in, again with a necessary lie. "It's a term used in Ohio. Its meaning is purely in title only. I'm simply in charge of other nurses."

Edwin pushed on. "I wonder, Miss Kennedy… Dr. Foster tells me you and Miss Kosarin are first-time visitors to our City. How is it that you knew the detective and his ailing wife?"

Dr. Foster's gaze brightened with interest.

Eve kept her head low as she cut into the lobster, yet another lie about to leave her lips. "They are friends of our next-door neighbor in Ohio. They suggested we look up the Gantlys when we arrived. When I did so, that's when I learned of Mrs. Gantly's critical condition."

Dr. Foster said, "... But didn't you say that the Harringshaw family had recommended you to Dr. Eckland? And yet you have stated that you have only recently come to our City."

Eve looked up, meeting Dr. Foster's inquiring gaze, her eyes steady. She saw suspicion and skepticism. Eve had never been a good liar. Patrick used to say of her, "*Eve could never win at poker. She's too honest. Her mood and thoughts are always written on her face.*"

"Forgive me, Dr. Foster," Eve said. "I learned of Dr. Eckland from a woman staying at our hotel. I was desperate. I'm afraid I name-dropped. I'm afraid I told a lie because I needed help."

Edwin lit up. "Harrah for you, Miss Kennedy! I say again, Harrah! A bold and intrepid woman you are and, I dare say, there are not many like you in all of Gotham today."

Dr. Foster touched his napkin to his lips and leaned back, resting his questioning gaze on Eve.

"Miss Kennedy, forgive me, as I do not wish to appear rude or intrusive, but at no time yesterday, in my observation, did you mention who you were to Detective Gantly. And, indeed, he seemed quite baffled that you and I were there, as if the two of you had never met before and were complete strangers."

CHAPTER 30

Eve kept her composure, deciding to go on the attack to deflect any further suspicion.

"Dr. Foster, I do not know what you are implying, but as a sensitive man and a physician, you can understand that there were many more urgent things to address than the fact that the Gantlys and I had a mutual friend in Ohio. You and I were in the desperate business of trying to save two lives."

Dr. Foster sat up and cleared his throat, gently taken back by Eve's direct tone.

Edwin grinned, brightly, his attraction and fervor for Eve growing every minute. "Quite right you are, Miss Kennedy. Well said. Hurrah again."

Eve soon regretted her chastisement of Darius. He quickly turned chilly toward her, focusing all his attention on Joni. That meant that Eve was left at the mercy of Edwin, who had slid his chair ever so slightly closer to hers.

After strawberries and cream were delivered and another bottle of champagne was displayed and poured, Edwin dropped into airy chatter.

"Do you know, Miss Kennedy," Edwin said, almost conspiratorially, "that this establishment has recruited culinary talent from the kitchens of Delmonico's?"

Eve sipped her champagne, her eyes traveling the room. "No, I did not."

"And, that the daughter of Alfred Benton, this establishment's owner, is in liaison with one of the chefs of Delmonico's? Isn't that just the most delicious of scandals? Please excuse my use of the culinary word, delicious," he said proudly.

"Yes, fascinating," Eve said flatly, wanting to leave the table, wanting to leave the restaurant and wanting to leave this time and place.

What kept her together was the prospect of meeting with Tesla the following evening. Finally, she'd get answers to her many questions and, hopefully, she'd soon have the means to travel home.

"Miss Kennedy, may I be so bold as to say, I find you deliriously mysterious. I dare say, there is something about you that perplexes me."

He put a finger to his lips. "Now let me see, what is it exactly? When I was studying at Columbia, I aspired to be a writer. Can you imagine that?"

Eve gave him an empty smile. "Yes, Mr. Bennett, I can imagine that."

Pleased by her comment, he sat up. "Can you, really? I mean, are you being honest or simply patronizing?"

"Mr. Bennett, I can see you more as a writer than as an attorney."

Edwin was elated. "Then you really think so?"

"Yes."

To Eve's further disappointment and concern, she saw Edwin's eyes go all dreamy and vacant. "You, Miss Kennedy, are a wonder. You would be the perfect romantic heroine in a novel."

She lowered her gaze. "I hardly think so."

"No, truly. There is something elusive and grand about you. A contradiction, a quality of light and shadow; an airy ghost, and yet you are a solid marble statue."

Eve's eyebrows lifted. She was startled by his words. "I can assure you, Mr. Bennett, I am not a marble statue." She wanted to say, *An airy ghost is not too far from the truth*, but she held her tongue.

"No, of course you are not, Miss Kennedy. You are flesh and blood and that is readily apparent."

Eve wanted this conversation to end. "So why not write that novel, Mr. Bennett? Or perhaps you could become a poet. What is stopping you?"

His smile fell, and he turned sullen. "My father would have none of it. My mother almost fainted when I once mentioned it to her. No, Miss Kennedy, the Bennetts are wealthy, that is true, but the family has always felt it has a duty to work and be useful to society. We are attorneys and politicians and bankers, through and through, true and true, not artisans of the pen."

Eve watched him swallow his sixth glass of champagne, his mood flitting about like a butterfly.

"Mr. Bennett, aren't you a little old to be governed by your parents? If you want to be a writer, then why don't you work at being a writer?"

His eyes flicked up at her and once again she saw darkness in them. The quick change was unnerving. Perhaps she'd been too direct and said too much.

Dr. Foster had overheard much of their conversation. He turned his stern attention to Eve. "Miss Kennedy, perhaps your opinion and your sharp tongue should be curtailed until you know more about a given situation."

The air around the table suddenly turned cold.

Joni lowered her eyes. Eve held Dr. Foster's chastising glare, struggling with her own dark mood, which was exactly why she hadn't wanted to come. Her turbulent mind had still not fully processed all that had occurred with Patrick. She should have kept her mouth shut, but the words had come tumbling out before she could stop them. Darius' condescending manner further loosened her tongue.

"Perhaps, Dr. Foster, a healthy dose of the truth is good for us all now and then, no matter where or from whom that truth comes."

Dr. Foster's jaw tightened.

Edwin slapped the table, the champagne having loosened his reserve, glazed his eyes and slackened his face. "By God, Darius, Miss Kennedy is as right as rain."

Dr. Foster's hand abruptly shot up as he searched for the waiter, who was at the table in a flash. Darius asked for the check.

"Darius," Edwin protested. "Let us all have another bottle of champagne. I have much to discuss with Miss Kennedy. By God, Darius, she is a woman to be reckoned with."

Darius reached for his wallet. "Edwin, my friend, we have all had enough champagne and enough conversation for one night."

Darius and Joni led the way out of the restaurant, with Edwin and Eve behind.

"Miss Kennedy, may I see you again, and can it be soon?"

Eve kept her eyes focused ahead. "I think not, Mr. Bennett. As I said earlier, we won't be staying in New York for very long."

"But you said it could be weeks."

"No, Mr. Bennett, I said we may stay longer than a few days, not weeks."

During the drive home, the wind picked up, and the ladies reached for the fur muffs that were available in the carriage. Dr. Foster was remote, Edwin Bennett brooding.

Joni was irritated at Eve for spoiling the party, and Eve was sorrier than ever that she'd accepted the invitation.

At the hotel, the carriage driver opened the door and helped the ladies exit. They were escorted by Darius and Edwin into the hotel lobby. To Eve, Edwin gave a little courtly bow, while Darius gently took Joni by the elbow and led her to a private area.

Eve made an effort to soften her manner. "I am sorry, Mr. Bennett, if I was too abrupt and rude. I assure you that it was not my intention. I have been out of sorts since yesterday's events. I hope you will forgive me."

"There is no need to forgive anything, Miss Kennedy. Your words were true, and they hit their mark. I have much thinking to do. Now," he said, placing his hands behind his back, "I do pray that you will give me another

Elyse Douglas

chance and agree to see me once more, at any venue and at any time you deem proper. I assure you, I will remain a perfect gentleman."

Eve just wanted to get into her bed and sleep for days. "I cannot say right now, Mr. Bennett. Perhaps in time... perhaps not."

His dispirited face turned from her. "Then I will be persistent, Miss Kennedy, for I do believe you will be my muse, and I have read that a muse, once found, cannot be cast aside or forgotten."

He stared hard at her, but she did not meet his eyes.

"Good night, Mr. Bennett."

He turned and strode away, replacing his top hat and leaving the hotel.

Eve had pressed the elevator button when Joni drew up. "Darius wants me to take a ride with him. He said he might even take me to a late show at a theater. I'm going."

Eve's tired eyes looked at her friend. "Be careful, Joni. Remember, these people live in a very different world than the one you and I come from."

"I'll be fine. Goodnight."

Eve watched the couple sweep out of the hotel, just as Nikola Tesla entered. She came alive with sudden eagerness and turned to greet him. He gave her a muted, cloudy glance as he strolled to the elevator.

"Good evening, Mr. Tesla," Eve said, following.

He removed his hat, offering a little bow. "Miss Kennedy, once again the pleasure is mine to see you."

The elevator door opened, and he allowed her to enter before stepping in. As the doors cranked shut, Eve asked, "Mr. Tesla, are we to have dinner with you tomorrow at Delmonico's?"

The elevator began to rise, shakily.

He looked at her, but his eyes were pensive and faraway. "Dinner tomorrow?"

"Yes, Mr. Tesla. You invited Miss Kosarin and me to dinner tomorrow night at Delmonico's."

"Oh, yes, Delmonico's. Yes." He made a mouth of apology. "You will please forgive me, Miss Kennedy, but I must be working tomorrow night in my laboratory. There is much work to do there. I cannot eat."

Eve's heart sank. She would go crazy unless she could talk to this man. "Mr. Tesla, may I come to your laboratory sometime tomorrow—anytime you think would be appropriate? I have something of great importance to discuss with you."

He seemed to wake up just as the elevator doors opened. Eve stepped out, followed by the towering Tesla, who was scratching his head.

"Tomorrow you want to come?"

"Yes, anytime you say."

"Are you a scientist, Miss Kennedy?" he asked, eyes probing.

Eve figured the answer was yes. "I am a scientist, Mr. Tesla, and I have something to talk to you about. I think you will find it very interesting and worth your time."

"My mother was a scientist. She was a woman of talent who created many things. She was a woman of genius, especially gifted with a sense of intuition. Whatever inventiveness I have, I give all credit to her, my dear mother. There should be more women scientists, Miss Kennedy."

Eve looked deeply into his eyes. "There will be, Mr. Tesla. In the future, there will be many women scientists."

His face changed. His eyes took on luster as he studied her. He nodded. "Tomorrow at 3 p.m. It must be at three in the afternoon and please be sure you are right with that time."

And then he was off down the hallway moving toward his room. Eve skipped a couple of steps to catch up to him.

"I will be there, Mr. Tesla. I'll be there at three in the afternoon."

"Good night, Miss Kennedy," he said as he opened his door, entered and closed it behind him.

Eve inserted the key in her door, feeling energized. She stepped into her room, closed and locked the door and turned on the gas lamp. It cast eerie, flickering shadows on the wall. She stood in the center of the room with her hands on her hips.

"What a weird day," she said aloud, feeling utterly exhausted. "What a strange and weird day."

CHAPTER 31

Joni was sitting before a round gilded mirror combing her hair. Eve was preparing for her meeting with Tesla.

"Are you sure you don't want to go?" Eve asked, standing behind her friend.

Joni looked at Eve through the mirror. "No... You're better at that kind of thing than I am."

Eve nodded. "I'm glad you had a good time with Dr. Foster last night."

Joni went into a dreamy state as she brushed her hair, her pink and gold silk robe gathered about her and tied at the waist.

"We're going out again tonight."

"So you said."

"I did?"

"Yes, when you first woke up at noon."

"Do you disapprove?"

"No. You're a big girl."

"But you disapprove."

"For what it's worth, I think you're moving a little fast."

"We're just going out."

"But you like him, and he likes you."

"Is that bad?"

"No… not bad."

Joni stopped brushing and turned around. "But what? Tell me what you're really thinking."

"We're temporary travelers here. Who knows, after I talk to Tesla today, we may be leaving, returning to our own time."

"I don't believe that."

"What?" Eve asked.

"That you're going to leave without Patrick."

Eve stared into the mirror, seeing her worried reflection, her eyes glazed with fatigue. She had aged, and her spirit lacked vitality. Last night, sleep had come with difficulty. Her dreams had all been of Patrick: Patrick in their bed in the future, about to make love to her; Patrick touching her baby tummy. And then, cruelly, the dream changed, and Patrick was running away from her, down a long, narrow alley, in harsh yellow light, his hand clasping Emma's, her free arm cradling their baby, their expressions somber and fearful.

"I don't know what I'm going to do," Eve said, turning away. "I'll know better after I talk to Tesla."

Joni swiveled back to face the mirror and returned to brushing her hair. "I feel like I've been here a month already. I'm dizzy and a little scared and kind of happy all at the same time. I feel different and new somehow. Does that make sense?"

"Yes. We're out of time and place. Each time I time travel I feel it. I can't say I like it all that much. I feel like an intruder, and I don't like lying."

Joni had a way of widening her eyes while the corner of her mouth lifted in a sexy smile. "Well, I like Darius Foster, Eve. Wouldn't it be crazy if I really did fall in love?"

Eve was silent.

"I mean, think of it. I don't think I've ever felt this kind of sudden lust and love at the same time before."

Eve laid a gentle hand on Joni's shoulder. "Just be careful. I don't want to sound like your mother, but don't get carried away. Men in this time have all the power."

Joni turned about again, smiling. "But he's not like that. He was such a gentleman last night. He was tender and kind. When I told him I was a schoolteacher at a little red schoolhouse—you know, what you told me to say—do you know what he answered? He said he would be honored and proud to send a child to me for instruction. Wasn't that a nice thing to say?"

"Yes, it was. Did he say anything about me? About what I said to Edwin?"

Joni lost her smile. "He said Edwin drinks too much, and he's sorry he hooked you two up. Well, he didn't say 'hooked you up.' Anyway, he said you came on too strong and he's afraid Edwin will go on a drunken binge like he's done in the past. He said that Edwin's mind is too busy and stormy, and he recently dissolved an engagement of almost two years."

Eve pivoted and took a few steps before stopping. "I wasn't myself last night. I should have kept my big mouth shut. Please tell Dr. Foster I'm sorry for what I said. I should have never gone to that damned restaurant. Edwin didn't look so good when he left me last night."

"It's okay. I told Darius that you have been under emotional strain. I told him you're my best friend and we're like sisters."

Eve returned to Joni. "And?"

"He said there's something mysterious about you."

Eve shook her head. "Yeah, well, duh."

"It's going to be okay, Eve. I feel like I'm in some elaborate masquerade or Broadway show, where I have to make up the lines and character. It's a wild and awesome thing. I'm just going to have some fun while we're here, so stop worrying."

"Okay, then I'll shut up. I've got to go now. I must be at Tesla's laboratory at three o'clock sharp. He has this thing about threes."

As Eve turned to leave, Joni stood, holding the brush at her side. "I'm scared, Eve."

"Scared of what?"

"What he might say. What Tesla might say."

"Such as?"

"That we can never get back. That we can never go back to our own lives in our own time."

"Well, there's only one way to find out. What time is your date with Darius?"

"Six-thirty. We're going to dinner and then to the Lyceum Theater to see Annie Russell, whoever that is, in a play called *Hazel Kirke*."

"She's a famous actress. I think she's British. I saw her name in lights the last time I was here in 1885."

They stood for a time looking at each other.

"And?" Eve asked.

Joni stared down at the carpet. "And... It's such a slower time, and a rougher time, and a more romantic time in a way."

"So what are you saying?"

"Darius Compton Foster is from a very wealthy family."

"So we supposed," Eve said, almost as a question. "What are you getting at, Joni?"

"Well... I was just thinking. I mean, I've only known him for two days but, what if we can't get back?"

"We'll get back, Joni," Eve said, firmly. "One way or the other, I'll find a way to get us back."

Joni flashed one of her exuberant smiles. "Of course we will. Of course we'll get back. You'd better go before you're late."

Eve stared at Joni in a frown of concentration, reading between the lines, knowing exactly what she was thinking. If they couldn't get back to the 21st century, Joni would allow her relationship with Dr. Foster to flower, perhaps all the way to marriage, if that would even be possible as far as his family was concerned. After all, Joni was a nobody schoolteacher from a backwater town in Ohio and not from a good, proper and wealthy New York or Boston family.

Eve knew from experience that it was more likely that Darius Compton Foster would not cross the social gulf of his time. He would marry someone "respectable," and he would keep Joni for his mistress, paying handsomely to keep her in a lovely apartment where he'd lavish jewelry and dresses on her at a dizzying pace. Eve had seen it all before in this time, and it had almost happened to her. But Eve kept her thoughts to herself. Now was not the time to discuss it.

"I should be back before you leave. If I'm not, have a good time tonight."

Joni laughed.

"What?"

"I almost said, text me after your meeting with Tesla. The one thing I do miss is my cellphone."

Eve let out a long breath and winked. "If anyone from the 21st century calls, take a message. That will be one to keep."

Joni grinned. "You got it, kid. Good luck."

CHAPTER 32

A tall, string-bean old man with sad eyes, wearing overalls and sporting white whiskers, met Eve as she was about to enter the Edison Machine Works. The bright afternoon sun was all about them, and the breeze was cool. Only yards away, workmen were in trenches, digging ditches, making little gasps of effort. Their picks were raised high, the steel head suspended for seconds, flashing in the sun, before coming down hard, thudding into the earth. Men with shovels scooped up loose rock and dirt and heaved the load above, where it lay in piles on the edge of the trench.

The old man asked, "Who are you?" in a thin tenor voice, as he stood by the glass entry door.

Eve presented a friendly smile. "I am Miss Evelyn Kennedy, sir."

"That's nice. Why are you here?"

"May I ask what business it is of yours?"

"Sure you can," he said, not offering more.

"All right sir, I am here to see Mr. Nikola Tesla."

"Are you from Westinghouse?"

"Westinghouse?"

"Yep."

"No, I'm not. I have an appointment to see Mr. Tesla and he told me to be on time. Three o'clock sharp, and unless you let me pass, I am going to be late."

He pulled a clay pipe from his top pocket and slipped the stem between his gapped, tobacco-stained teeth.

"We don't get women down here, unless they're part of the Edison clan."

Eve kept her voice low. "You must be the security guard."

"I am. I'm an old friend of Tom's, you know."

"How nice."

"I bet, young lady, that you don't know that Tom is the seventh and the very last child of Samuel and Nancy Edison."

"No, I didn't know that."

He continued, to Eve's impatience. "Tom was seven when his family moved from Ohio to Port Huron, Michigan. That's where I'm from. Port Huron, Michigan. I like to tell folks a bit about Tom. Many don't know nothing about him except he's got a head on his shoulders. ... Course I'm older than Tom, but that don't matter any. He hired me hisself to stand guard and make sure no Westinghouse people get in."

Eve let out a little sigh. "Sir, I assure you, I am not from Westinghouse. If you will contact Mr. Tesla, he will tell you that we have a three o'clock appointment."

He worked the stem of the pipe up and down with his teeth as he considered her. "Well, he might tell me, and then again, he might not. He is as bright as the noonday sun and as remote as an ornery old woman livin' in the back woods."

"Sir... if I..."

He kept on talking, cutting her off. "... Why, I bet Mr. Tesla didn't even notice how pretty you are, did he?"

"Sir, with all due respect, I really do have an appointment. Will you please let me pass?"

He looked genuinely hurt, about to lose his only audience member. "Well, if you insist on it, and if you're who you say you are, what can I do about it?"

He stepped back and opened the door for her. "Let that man behind the glass know who you are and why you're here, and he'll steer you off in the right direction. A good day to you, Miss."

At the glassed-in office was a twelve-inch hole. Eve stood waiting for a fussy-looking man to notice her. He was wearing a green visor, black vest, black suit and string tie, and he was using a ruler, obviously counting numbers in a ledger. She cleared her throat twice before he glanced up. He blinked, pursed his lips and blinked again as if to clear his head. He had a sour face, little suspicious eyes and a big mole just under his left eye.

"Yes?"

"I have an appointment to see Mr. Tesla."

"Tesla?" he said, gruffly.

"Yes, sir."

He made a face of irritation and then got up. He pointed to his right. "Down the hallway."

"Yes, I know where it is," Eve said.

That produced a surprise. "How's that?"

Eve ignored him and started off down the hallway toward Tesla's laboratory. The door was half open. Eve lightly rapped.

"Mr. Tesla?"

No response.

She knocked again, a little louder. Tesla appeared, peering through the half space, wearing a white lab coat over his dark suit and tie.

"Yes?" he asked, apparently not recognizing her.

"It's Evelyn Kennedy, Mr. Tesla. Remember, we had an appointment at three o'clock today?"

Again, Eve saw that he was deep within his own thoughts. She was getting used to it.

"I occupy Room 336 at the Gerlach Hotel."

His eyes cleared, and he gave a little shake of his head. "Yes, of course, Miss Kennedy." He opened the door fully and stepped aside. "Please come into my laboratory."

Eve did so, wanting to close the door behind her, but she didn't. What she was about to discuss with him was for his ears only.

Tesla's laboratory was just as she'd remembered it from the night when she and Joni had arrived from 2016. It was neat and clean; all objects carefully arranged. There were two long, rectangular tables holding motors and generators, electrical wire and a bank of light bulbs hanging on the wall, in a variety of sizes. There were electric coils and steel pipes and large batteries. At a side table sat apothecary jars, filled with chemicals and organic materials.

Tesla led Eve to a shorter parallel table and pointed to a transformer.

"You see here, I am working on fluorescent lighting and wireless transmission of power."

"Wireless?" Eve asked, surprised. "You're working on wireless transmission in 1884?"

"Yes, of course. I will be selling the patent rights to my system of alternating-current dynamos, transformers, and motors to Mr. George Westinghouse."

"But don't you work for Thomas Edison?"

"Edison does not believe in the alternating current, you see. His systems use direct-current (DC) electric power, not my alternating-current (AC) system."

Eve tried to take it all in, but her mind was elsewhere, on Patrick and his baby. On Joni and the lantern that had brought her back to this time.

"You said you are a scientist, Miss Kennedy?"

"Yes, Mr. Tesla, but I'm here for another reason."

"You wish to talk to me about other things than science?"

Eve glanced toward the open door. "Yes, and no. Mr. Tesla, may I close the door?"

He considered her, and then nodded.

After she'd done so, he indicated toward an old oak desk, piled with papers and files. Two high-back chairs were arranged around it. "Let us sit then, Miss Kennedy."

Ever the gentleman, he arranged a chair for her and then dragged one opposite her for himself, a good six feet away. Eve sat nervously, twisting her hands. She'd carefully composed her opening sentence that morning, but now that *the* Nikola Tesla sat down opposite her, she couldn't remember what she'd composed.

Tesla sat tall, filled with concerned interest, waiting. "Are you in need of more funds, Miss Kennedy?"

"Oh no, Mr. Tesla. No, my friend Joan and I are on a solid financial footing."

"I am happy to hear of it."

Eve's heart was beating wildly. Tesla crossed his long legs, waiting patiently. Eve decided to just come out with it.

"Mr. Tesla, are you a believer in time travel?"

A little flicker of interest danced in his eyes. "Ah, time travel. You have interest in such things, Miss Kennedy?"

"Yes... Yes, I have a lot of interest. Forgive me, Mr. Tesla, if I sound a little... well, a little strange, but I'm just going to be blunt."

He nodded, his interest sharpening. "Blunt means honest, yes?"

"Yes. Honest."

Eve swallowed hard. "Mr. Tesla, did you somehow, or someway, create a lantern... you know, a regular old lantern, whose light allows one to time travel?"

Eve trembled, waiting for his answer. So much was riding on his answer.

His eyes were at first vague and then large. Then to her utter surprise, he smiled, and it was the enigmatic smile of a child who was hiding something behind his back, not quite ready to reveal what he held in his hands.

Eve pressed on, quoting the back of the French postcard she'd found in the lantern in 2016. *"When the sun shines on me I think but little of the moon."*

Tesla kept his inscrutable smile.

Eve continued with the final quote that was on the back of the postcard. *"He who finds this, finds me. 1884."*

Eve's voice hung in the quiet air. Outside, she heard the picks and shovels. She heard a dog barking. She heard hammering from somewhere in the building. All these sounds made the moment fragile with possibilities. If Tesla denied knowing about the lantern, she was lost, with no other options.

Tesla opened his mouth to speak, his eyes lifting toward the ceiling, and Eve held her breath.

CHAPTER 33

Tesla stood up, and Eve watched him stalk back and forth between the tables, his hands laced behind his back, his head down. He was terrifyingly restrained. His silence nearly unbearable.

He finally stopped, made a little clicking sound with his tongue, and then he began talking to himself, or to something, or to someone, or perhaps he was lost in prayer. Tesla's father was an Eastern Orthodox priest.

He approached Eve, stopping a few feet away, pulling himself to his full, towering height.

"Miss Kennedy, when I was in Paris, I found a postcard in a bookshop on Rue de L'Odeon. I was much interested by this postcard, because of a graphic drawing of The Statue of Liberty, with light rays shooting out from its lamp into six directions. I had not been to New York but learned that the statue had not yet been fully erected. I was told that the statue's arm was being displayed in Madison Square Park, while it was waiting for a pedestal to be built to hold the complete structure. What I want to tell you, Miss Kennedy, is that the statue of freedom's light in that drawing made the impression on me. How do you say it? I was captured with intuitive ideas that came in flashes of equations and images. I was trained in Europe in the fields of physics, mathematics and mechanics, but many there called me a dreamer."

His soft eyes rested on Eve. "I purchased that postcard and I purchased one of the Eiffel Tower too. They were grand structures and filled with meaning, both practical and intuitive. Both were inspirations to me. Miss Kennedy, when I see things of wonder, I see, perhaps, more than just what meets the eye. I see other worlds and many more possibilities. Do you understand this, Miss Kennedy? All of this I am trying to get out to you?"

Their eyes made contact.

"I think so, Mr. Tesla."

He nodded. "The longer I looked at the drawing and the rays shooting out from Lady Liberty's lamp, the more I felt things shifting and flowing inside me. I felt the quick and the sharp energy of ideas. I must let it be known to you that I was as excited as a child who wants to build a new toy. And what was that toy? Well... it concerned time, and the bending of time, and the appearance and disappearance of time."

He paused, as if some other thought interrupted his flow of words. When his attention returned, his expression had changed. His enthusiasm swelled.

Eve noticed that Tesla's English improved when he was enthusiastic or when he was discussing science.

"You see, Miss Kennedy, what I am talking about? I am talking here about the mystical motors of time, and the mystical appearance of light and dark. But it is not so mystical when it reveals itself to you."

He made a grand gesture with his arm. "You see, it is all in the air around us... numbers and light, and space and time."

Eve had no idea what the man was talking about. She wanted to get straight to the point. "Mr. Tesla... did you build, or did you create, a time travel lantern?"

Again, he became evasive. "Where are you from, Miss Kennedy? I sense you are not from this world."

Eve rose to her feet, feeling frustration build in her chest. "No, Mr. Tesla. I am not from this world or from this time, and I think you knew that the first time you saw me and my friend."

That pleased him, and his eyes grew round and eager. "What time then do you come from?"

"I'm from the twenty-first century. I traveled here from 2016."

Tesla stared beyond her, at nothing, but his eyes danced in splendor. He absently pinched his lower lip with two fingers. And then to Eve's disappointment, he turned and walked away toward a row of windows that looked out onto the street below.

Eve was growing irritated by the man's remote manner and by his obviously infinite, inner, secret world. She followed him to the windows and, for a time, they both watched the ditch diggers work.

"I worked as a ditch digger for a time when I first came here. I made two dollars a day for long hours. It is hard work, but good work. Those men are preparing the way to install electricity throughout the City. In order to run electric current underground, they have to tear up the streets."

"Mr. Tesla. I need to tell you everything that has happened. I need to tell you what has happened to me, and how it all began, and how I came to be here in this time. After I'm finished, I would appreciate it if you could tell me about the lantern, and if you created it, and why you created it. I would like to know how it all began."

He gave her a transient grin. "How it all began, Miss Kennedy? Do you mean, you want to know my secret?"

Eve grew excited. "Yes, Mr. Tesla. I would like to know your secret."

"Very well. First, let us go and sit. I will find us some tea and you will then please to tell me your story."

Soon after Eve began telling Tesla about how she found the first lantern in *The Time Past Antique Shop* in Pennsylvania in 2016, he sipped his tea with a transcendent expression, as if he were actually there with her, living the events and feeling the emotions.

Eve detailed the events of 1885 and how she met Detective Sergeant Patrick Gantly, and how they barely escaped the clutches of the infamous Inspector Byrnes. When she described how Patrick had been shot and was close to death, Tesla leaned forward, folding his hands, engrossed. Eve explained how antibiotics had saved Patrick's life, and how she and Patrick had married a short time later, after he'd fully recovered.

Tesla was fascinated by Eve's explanation of what antibiotics were and how they worked, and he asked her many questions.

Tesla gazed sightlessly while Eve described her loving relationship with Patrick, and how she was three months pregnant when the lantern was stolen in 2019, by a man from 1925. Tesla smiled when Eve described the details of how they had paid the man's girlfriend to get the lantern back.

Eve hesitated before concluding her story. The memories and emotions were still close to the surface, and hard for her to form into words. She stammered out how she and Patrick destroyed the lantern by tossing it into the Hudson River, because they were afraid the lantern would draw more bad people from the past.

Tesla rose, standing in place, evaluating, judging and measuring her every word as she revealed how, the morning after they'd disposed of the lantern, her life had been completely reset to 2016.

"Mr. Tesla, my husband, Patrick was gone. Vanished, as if he'd never existed. And I was no longer pregnant. The entire life I had built with Patrick since 2016 had simply been erased."

Eve finished the story, explaining how she'd returned to *The Time Past Antique Shop* in 2016, where she found another similar lantern, with Tesla's postcard inside.

"So, Mr. Tesla, when I lit the lantern, my friend Joni and I found ourselves here, in your laboratory, on Monday evening."

Tesla returned to his chair, sitting quietly, his mind blazing with thoughts, ideas and wonder. Eve waited, her stomach in knots.

Finally, he heaved himself out of the chair and wandered back toward the windows. By now, heavy gray clouds appeared, blocking the sun.

Eve stretched and yawned, her voice hoarse from speaking. She had no idea what time it was. She picked up her half-drunk cold tea and drained the cup. Again, Tesla seemed off in another world.

"Mr. Tesla... I want to return home. I would like to return to 2019 and to my life there, with my husband and with a baby on the way."

From across the room, he turned about and shoved his hands into his lab coat pockets.

"You cannot return to that world, Miss Kennedy."

His words were shattering, and she felt some of the life go out of her.

"Miss Kennedy, I created the lanterns and sent them out into the world like messages in a bottle. But instead of the sea carrying them to distant shores, I let the ocean of time and chance and light be the currents."

Eve stared at him through misty eyes. "But why? Why did you do it? For what purpose?"

He seemed surprised by the question, as if his reason were self-evident. "For science's sake, Miss Kennedy, don't you see? Didn't you tell me you are a scientist? In science, one must experiment and test. My passion is light, and all the wonders of light and the movement of light, and light through time itself. Do you see? It came to me on Christmas Eve, Miss Kennedy."

Eve tried to understand. "Christmas Eve?"

"Yes, it was the lights—all the lights at Christmas: the candles, the lamps, the lanterns. That's when the equations came crashing into my head. That's when I heard the mystical motors of time, and I knew I had my Christmas toy, the lanterns. I sent the lanterns out into the world to learn what those gifts of light might do. Do you see it all now? They were my Christmas toys. All of it was my very own Christmas Eve secret, Miss Kennedy."

CHAPTER 34

Eve was speechless. His incredible explanation floated between them, and she could only stare into those eyes that seemed filled with visions.

He gave the barest whisper of a smile. "I, myself, have seen the future, Miss Kennedy."

Her eyes narrowed. "You've seen the future? You have time traveled?"

"Not as you have done, but yes, in another way."

Eve took a step toward him. "Has anyone else returned, like me?"

"No, Miss Kennedy."

"How many lanterns did you... set afloat, so to speak?"

"How many?"

"Yes. How many lanterns are out there?"

He smiled again, that boyish, impish smile. "Shall I tell you all my secrets, Miss Kennedy?"

"I don't care about all your secrets, Mr. Tesla, but I would like to know how I can get back to my own time and to my own world. I would like to know how I can resume my life with the man I love and deliver the baby I was carrying."

Tesla shrugged sadly. "When you destroyed the lantern, Miss Kennedy, you took all that life away. It has been erased. It is gone. That time is over, and it cannot be returned to."

Angered, Eve marched toward him. "How can it be gone, just like that? I won't accept it. I won't."

Tesla wasn't disturbed by her outburst. "Time is quicksilver, Miss Kennedy. Time ebbs and flows. It comes and it goes. When great storms or fire destroy a home or town, one must rebuild. It is the way of life and the way of time. You must, how do I say it... You must get a bigger picture of the universe and the world and how it all truly works. Right now, Miss Kennedy, you see reality in only one way, going in only one direction. But your own experience tells you that reality is often strange and works in secretive ways. Is that not true?"

Eve's eyes were turbulent. "I don't have your kind of mind, Mr. Tesla. There is much I just don't understand and probably never will. All right, fine, but then tell me this: Do you have another lantern that has the power to send me back home?"

He slowly shook his head, keeping his flat eyes on her. A sick, hollow feeling came over her, and then a cold fear.

"Miss Kennedy, I have sent all the lanterns off onto the currents of time. I have no others, and now I have much work to do here and now. My toys are all gone."

Eve struck the table loudly with a fist. "Then build another toy, Mr. Tesla. Build another!"

Tesla stepped back, away from the onslaught of her indignation. Eve's breath came fast, the only sound in the stunned silence. It was a minute or more before Eve regained control of herself, folding her hands at her waist and staring down at the table.

"I apologize for my outburst, sir. Please forgive me. I'm too emotional."

And then in a more even voice, Eve said, "Mr. Tesla, the lanterns, once used, do not travel with the time traveler. They stay in the same time and age, naturally, through normal time. Isn't that correct? At least that has been my experience."

Tesla was quiet, observing her cautiously.

Eve said, "When I was here the first time, in 1885, I found a lantern that returned me to my own time. If that is true, then might there be a lantern around somewhere? One that will take me back home?"

"All my lanterns did not succeed, Miss Kennedy. It is normal in science, is it not, often to fail? Some experiments fail, some succeed. Some people light the lantern, and nothing happens to them. Others, like you, travel to new times and places. That was all part of the experiment. You, Miss Kennedy, must have been particularly receptive to the light, perhaps because you, too, are a scientist."

Eve put a hand to her hot forehead and turned away. She inhaled two deep breaths and turned back to face him, struggling to keep her face under full control.

"Mr. Tesla, can you help me, in some way, return to my time? Please…"

He stared at her with compassion as his mind went to work. "My last lantern was set adrift onto the ocean of chance only two days ago. It was my last message in a bottle."

Eve straightened, suddenly alert. "Where is it?"

Tesla's smile was mischievous. "I hooked the lantern onto the rear axle of a Morton's Bakery delivery wagon. You should be able to find it easily, Miss Kennedy. I doubt whether it has been noticed. After all, it is just a lantern, like any other lantern, except we both now know the secret: that if a person is receptive, it has time-travel power. I must tell you that I am never entirely certain if the lanterns will work. There is always an uncertainty principle involved."

"You said you put it on the rear axle of a Morton's Bakery delivery wagon?"

"Yes."

Eve glared at him, wanting to curse him for everything that had happened to her. She wanted to expose him, and his damned secret, to the entire world. But she wouldn't, of course. And anyway, who would believe her?

"Mr. Tesla... Does it bother you that you have changed the world?"

"Bother me?" he said, producing a proud grin. "No, not at all. It gives me the best of pleasure to view all my experiments, to see how they perform and do their reaction. It gives life great happiness and purpose. This is a world of shadows and light, Miss Kennedy. We are born, and grow, and then vanish, just like your life in 2019 did. Tell me, Miss Kennedy, in this experience called life, where did we come from and where will we go at death?"

Eve had had enough. She couldn't think anymore. Even though she was deeply shaken and feeling exhausted, it was time to act. She would have to find that lantern. It was her only hope. And if it was gone, stolen by a street urchin, or taken by a baker or by the owner, or by anyone else, how would she find it?

She looked up at Tesla and, in his eyes, she saw a drowsy peace. The man was truly from another world, or maybe another planet. She'd never met anyone like him, and it was unlikely that she ever would again. He was, no doubt, a genius, not to be understood by an ordinary person.

"Mr. Tesla, what does the lantern look like? In case someone has taken it. In case I must go searching for it. Is there some particular marking or emblem or engraving?"

His crafty eyes lit up. "Oh, yes, Miss Kennedy. It is twelve inches high and made of iron, with a dark green and brown patina. It has four glass windowpanes with wire guards, and there is an anchor design on each side of the roof. One anchor is painted red and one is painted blue."

"That sounds very similar to the one I discovered in *The Time Past Antique Shop*."

Tesla nodded. "Then think of it this way, Miss Kennedy. Perhaps you have already found the lantern."

Eve's gaze was direct for a moment and then it drifted away. "I don't understand."

Tesla held up two fingers, a tiny space apart. "Your world in the future, and this world here and now, are very close, Miss Kennedy. Tesla hopes you find my lantern. Will you come and tell me if you do?"

Eve's face clouded over. "I don't know, Mr. Tesla. I really don't know."

CHAPTER 35

A little over a week later, Eve had located the lantern, but the woman who possessed it was out of town. Meanwhile, Eve was fighting panic.

She had started her lantern search at Morton's Bakery, located between Eldredge and Orchard Streets. Only one apple-cheeked delivery boy remembered seeing the lantern. He confirmed that he had seen it on the back axle of a wagon, unlit, describing the red and blue anchors accurately. He told Eve that it wasn't on the delivery wagon the following day, but then mentioned that a blacksmith and farrier, named Moses Poe, who fashioned horseshoes for the Bakery's horses, may have taken it. As Eve was leaving, the boy said, "Lanterns and such often disappear around here."

It took Eve almost two days to locate Moses Poe because he was never in his shop; he was either frequenting some pub or working at carriage houses around lower Manhattan.

When she finally did catch up with him, he told her a delivery driver from Morton's had given him the lantern. He'd then given it to the daughter of a woman who ran a boarding house on West 16th Street.

Moses Poe was a brawny man, with massive arms and an earthy manner.

"Did you light the lantern?" Eve asked.

"Of course I lit it," he said curtly. "What good is a lantern that isn't lit? I then gave it to Miss Abagail Tannin because the night was dark, and it was raining. It was the gentlemanly thing to do, wasn't it?"

"Yes, of course, Mr. Poe."

"How did I know it was your lantern, Miss? I thought it was Morton's. Now when you go visit Mrs. Tannin, don't you go saying that her daughter was given that lantern by Moses Poe. The mother would be none too pleased hearing about the likes of me, if you get my meaning, Miss."

Eve did get his meaning. No doubt, Moses Poe and Miss Tannin were a secret item.

Eve located the boarding house and met Mrs. Emma Tannin, a tightly-strung woman with tight lips, a tight bun, and a tight bustle dress revealing a very tight, thin waist.

Eve introduced herself cordially. "I'm Evelyn Kennedy," Eve said, pleasantly, and then mentioned the lantern.

"I don't know anything about a lantern. I have not seen Abagail with any lantern. What do you want with the lantern?" Mrs. Tannin asked, with small, suspicious eyes.

"It was a gift. It has sentimental value and I will pay handsomely for it."

Mrs. Tannin's distrustful eyes grew in size, as lively avarice gleamed in them.

"Handsomely?"

"Yes."

Mrs. Tannin considered it.

"Mrs. Tannin, may I enter and perhaps search your daughter's room for it?"

"Absolutely not. This is a respectable boarding house and I only let boarders in. If you'll wait in the parlor, I will examine my daughter's room for the lantern. If it is there, then we will discuss the price."

As she turned to enter the house, Eve followed. Mrs. Tannin whirled about. Eve stopped abruptly, almost bumping into the woman.

"This is highly unusual, young woman, and mind you, I am only consenting to this because of my daughter."

Eve was fidgety as she stood in the Victorian furnished parlor near the heavy, upright piano and a roll-top desk, piled with invoices. A tall grandfather clock ticked and chimed on the hour.

Mrs. Tannin returned in a cloud of disappointment. "I do not see a lantern. If it was ever in Abagail's room, then it has been removed."

"Might it be somewhere else? Perhaps it's in the carriage house?"

"After not finding it in Abagail's room, I promptly searched the carriage house. I did not see a lantern."

Disappointed and growing desperate, Eve licked her lips. "Mrs. Tannin, could you perhaps write to your daughter and ask if she is in possession of it?"

The stern woman crossed her arms tightly, her eyes narrowing, almost squeezing shut.

"How much will you pay for the lantern?"

"I will be generous, Mrs. Tannin. It is of vital importance that I have it."

"Well, it seems strange to me that a lantern can have such value, but I will write to my daughter. Please come to the desk and write down your address, and I will contact you as soon as I hear from Abagail."

Two days later, Eve lay in her bed on a rainy Sunday morning, listening to Joni gently snore away in the next bed. They had finally persuaded the hotel to take out the double bed and install two single beds, with the condition that the two ladies agreed to stay for a least another month.

Joni had been out with Dr. Foster the night before, the fifth time the two had been together since meeting at Dr. Eckland's over a week ago.

Edwin Bennett had called for Eve on Thursday evening but, fortunately, she'd been out searching for the lantern. He left her a note.

Miss Kennedy:

I am sorry to have found you absent. I have written some verses inspired by our first meeting and I would love to share them with you at your earliest convenience. Enclosed within this note, please find my card. I will deem it a kindness, and indeed a distinct honor, if you would contact me at your pleasure to let me know when and where we may meet. Until then, I am,

Your Obedient Servant,
Edwin Lancaster Bennett, Esq.

Eve lifted an eyebrow at Edwin's middle name, Lancaster. *Where did they come up with those names?* But she had to admit that it was a nice name, and a nice note. She was flattered that he had written verses to her.

No man had ever written verses to her before. Patrick had left her some witty notes, if he was up first and out of the house, especially on weekends. She recalled one, with a little secret smile.

Good Morning, Eve:
Roses are red, violets are blue. I sniffed your pillow and went Achoo! I like scented pillows, my dear lover, but that one attacked me. Is that the perfume I bought you for your birthday? Well, there's no accounting for good taste, is there? Except that you tasted so sweet last night. All right, you have my permission to pour the rest of the bottle down the toilet.

Oh, by the way, Georgy Boy almost caught a squirrel this morning! Almost is the word here. Another eight feet and he would have had that tail-flicking rascal. He's put on weight.

Sending you kisses,
Patrick

A light knock on the door jolted Eve from her daydream. Joni groaned, lifted a hand, waved and moaned again.

"Tell them we don't want any," Joni said, covering her head with the sheet.

Eve gave the blankets a toss and swung her feet to the floor, snatched her robe, slipped it on and belted it. At the door, she said, "Yes?"

"It's the hotel clerk. There is a gentleman downstairs who wishes to see Miss Kennedy."

Eve dropped her chin to her chest, letting out a sigh. That would be Edwin Bennett. It was only ten o'clock in the morning—a Sunday morning. She was in no mood to see him. Her hair was a mess, her face was a mess, and she was, overall, a mess, again having slept little the night before. Her eyes were bloodshot and puffy, and her face was puffy.

"Who is it?" Eve asked.

"Detective Sergeant Gantly."

Eve jerked up straight as if struck by lightning. "Who?"

"Detective Sergeant Gantly. He said he will wait for your response."

Eve stood frozen in place, unable to think or move.

"Is this Miss Kennedy?" the clerk asked.

Eve snapped out of it. "Yes... Yes."

"Should I tell the detective to wait for you?"

Eve's head was spinning.

Joni yanked the sheet from her face and lifted up. "Did he say Patrick's downstairs?"

Eve waved her down and then whispered at the door. "Yes."

"Miss Kennedy."

Eve turned back to the door. "Yes. Tell the Detective to wait. Tell him I'll be down in about twenty minutes."

Eve boiled about the room, grabbing her hairbrush, searching for undergarments, kicking off her house slippers.

"Get up, Joni, and help me. What the hell is Patrick doing downstairs? What does he want?"

Joni flew out of bed and went to work, helping Eve with hair, makeup and dress.

"I don't feel good about this," Eve said. "And then again, maybe I do. I feel like I'm about to shake apart and fall into little quivering pieces."

"What are you talking about? Why are you so freaked out? It's Patrick, for God's sake. *Your* Patrick."

"I know. I know. But why is he here?"

"You'll find out."

"I'm a nervous wreck. I hope I don't say something stupid."

"You probably will," Joni said, with a little laugh, "… and then I will feel so much better about myself, because I won't be the only dumb broad who can't talk right."

"Thanks. You know what I'm thinking?"

"What?"

"Maybe he remembers. It's possible, isn't it? Maybe he had some kind of breakthrough and he remembers everything. Maybe that's why he's come."

"How could he remember, Eve? It wouldn't make sense. You didn't meet him until next year, 1885."

"I don't know, but wouldn't it be a perfect miracle if he did remember?

CHAPTER 36

Twenty-five minutes later, the elevator door opened and Eve stepped out, wearing a plum-colored bustle dress with cream-colored sleeves, black trim, and a matching coat and broad hat. She felt half put together, and her heart seemed to be bouncing around in her chest.

Patrick, who had been seated, stood up, looking somber and grave. As his eyes took Eve fully in, his expression softened, but his eyes were uneasy. He held his bowler before him, gripping it with both hands. He tried a smile, but it failed.

Eve felt the familiar flood of love, as she always had whenever she'd seen him. It was as if nothing had changed and no time had passed. Her eyes fell on him with guarded and subdued pleasure. He had a haggard look, with a shadow of beard. The sensual mouth she'd kissed so many times drooped in sadness, and his intelligent, vivid blue eyes held a deep sorrow.

The reunion was silent, as Eve pushed down emotion and desire, and Patrick, feeling awkward and confused,

246

having gathered the courage to appear, now couldn't find any words.

Eve started toward him, clearing her throat. "Hello, again, Detective Gantly. I hope you are well."

He only nodded. Silence stretched out until the quiet began to hurt. Eve glanced about, timidly, waiting for him. The front desk clerk fought the urge to stare, and Eve knew the little man was concerned that Patrick was there on business, and that an arrest might be underway. That would be bad for the hotel's reputation.

Patrick gave her a quick, nervous smile. "I hope I didn't frighten you, Miss Kennedy, by my message, and I hope you're not uncomfortable at my being here. These are not my intentions."

"And what are your intentions?" Eve gently asked. She wanted to keep any flirtation out of her voice. But did he read it as flirtation, nonetheless? She hoped not.

Patrick glanced about, seeing the wandering eyes of the hotel clerk. "Miss Kennedy, would you be so kind as to accompany me to a nearby café? It's not far, just off Madison Square Park."

Eve felt a lift she hadn't felt since the last time she'd seen Patrick all those days ago.

"Yes, Detective Gantly. I will accompany you."

Outside, the rain had stopped, but a fine mist fell and the wind was wet and snappy. Eve bundled her coat against the wind, and both clamped hands on their hats to keep them from flying away. They said nothing as they strolled, Eve fighting nerves and Patrick appearing distant and troubled.

Kelsey's Coffee Café was printed in gilded letters on the plate-glass window that was still beaded with raindrops. As Patrick opened and held the door for Eve, the overhead bell "dinged."

He removed his hat, hanging it on a silver standing hat stand along with others, and then helped Eve out of her coat, hanging it on a coatrack nearby.

Kelsey was a florid-faced man, about 50 years old, with an ample belly, stubby arms and a low, gravelly voice. When he saw Patrick, his bored eyes came to life, and he left his place behind his ornate, gold cash register to greet him, first wiping his hands on his white apron.

"Well, Detective Gantly, where have you been, mate?"

They shook hands cordially and then, to Eve's surprise, Patrick introduced her as the nurse who had tended his wife on her sickbed.

Kelsey nodded politely at Eve, and then his smile dropped into a frown and his shoulders slumped.

"Condolences to you, my good friend. I heard the dreadful news and I am heartily sorry for you. Please come in and sit at your old table in the back with a good view of the garden."

The café was half filled, with couples in conversation and two men seated near the front window, puffing cigars, lost in their newspapers.

Eve and Patrick sat near a window across from each other at a white marble tabletop, on chairs with red, padded cushions. A gaslight chandelier hung above them, adding subdued light to gray light coming in from the window. Kelsey brought menus and a silver pot of freshly brewed coffee, as well as freshly baked bread and muffins in a wicker basket.

"You sit and relax now, Patrick, and call Mary Ellen when you're ready," Kelsey said, with a little pat on Patrick's shoulder.

"Thank you, Kelsey," Patrick said.

Kelsey gave Eve a demure smile. "A pleasure to meet you, Miss Kennedy."

When Kelsey was gone, Patrick slid the basket toward Eve. "A good man, Kelsey is. He's from Australia. He used to sail the clippers around Cape Horn. His route ran from England down the east Atlantic Ocean to the equator. He was shipwrecked three years ago going around the Horn and nearly perished. Most of the crew were lost. Only he and another mate survived. After that, he never went back to it. Shall I pour your coffee?"

Eve nodded. "Thank you."

She shook out her white napkin and placed it on her lap, and then helped herself to a warm raisin muffin, first smelling its sweetness. She placed it on the white plate provided and waited for Patrick to pour his own cup full.

Eve would have to take everything slow. She was rattled by nerves and emotion and an easy desire. It was another surreal moment. There he was, her husband, her lover, her best friend, and yet he knew none of it. To him, this was only the second time they'd met.

Patrick blew steam from his coffee and sipped at it. "Kelsey has the best coffee. I haven't been here for months."

Without being aware of it, Eve stretched forward to listen to him, to be closer to his scent, his breath and his wide, welcoming chest that she'd snuggled up to so many times in the future. His Irish accent was more pronounced than she'd recalled, much of it being softened in the New York of the future.

"Did you used to come here with your wife?"

Patrick shook his head. "No, this place was a little far for us. We stayed close to home. Emma liked to cook and bake, and she knew her kitchen well, and all that was in it. Most who tasted her food said she had a gift. I suppose people are good at what they love."

"Yes, I suppose that is true," Eve said, trying to keep the conversation moving.

"I hope, Miss Kennedy, that this meeting is not awkward for you. I know I should not be seen with you, so soon after my wife's death... but..." His voice fell away.

"It is quite all right. I understand, and I believe most people would understand. After all, I did help deliver your child. And how is your baby daughter, Detective Gantly?"

Patrick avoided her eyes. "I suppose she is well."

"Suppose? Is anything wrong?"

"No, nothing is wrong. Truth be told, I haven't seen much of her. My work has occupied much of my time and will continue to do so."

"Who is taking care of the baby?"

"Mrs. Connelly and her daughter, Megan O'Brien. They live two doors down. You met Mrs. Connelly, isn't that right?"

"Yes. She seems like a good woman and a strong one."

"A good woman she is, Miss Kennedy. My Emma thought quite highly of her. You know, Emma's own mother passed, so I suppose Mrs. Connelly became a kind of mother to Emma."

Eve watched a hansom cab drift by, its wheels striking a pothole, splashing water onto the sidewalk. Two women darted away from the spray, glaring up at the driver as he trotted away.

Patrick shifted in his chair and then ran a shaky hand across his cheek.

"Is there a reason you asked me here, Detective Gantly?" Eve asked softly.

He cleared his throat and squirmed before settling himself and reaching for his coffee cup.

"Yes, Miss Kennedy. I hope you will not be offended by what I am about to ask. It has weighed heavily on my mind for some days."

Eve replaced her coffee cup on the porcelain saucer. "Please continue, Detective."

His eyes came up and met hers. For a brief second, Eve believed that he recognized her; that he knew her and remembered their life together in the future. But then she saw a sudden blankness, replaced by curiosity and nothing more. It had all just been her hopeful imagination. He didn't recognize her as anything more than the woman she was pretending to be.

"Miss Kennedy, I spoke to Dr. Foster two days ago."

Eve's chin lifted an inch. "Dr. Foster? Why?"

"He told me you were from Ohio and had friends there who knew me and Emma. Is this true, Miss Kennedy?"

Eve glanced away toward a couple nearby, who were engaged in a private argument. Their irate, whispering voices were filled with explosive Ss and Ps. Eve needed time to consider her answer.

Patrick continued. "A few days after Emma was gone, I had a bit of memory return to me after that dreadful night, and I recalled you and the doctor with a clearer sight. And then I began asking questions. How was it that you and Dr. Foster came to the house? I wanted to know who had sent you to us at such a crucial time. When I asked Dr. Foster, he confessed that it was you, Miss Kennedy, who had first contacted a Dr. Eckland and pleaded on my behalf to come to try to save my Emma's life. But, in fact, it was Dr. Foster who came. Dr. Foster said you were entirely responsible for him coming to our aid. He said that if it hadn't been for your entreaty, my daughter would have surely died, along with my wife."

Eve couldn't meet Patrick's imploring eyes.

"Miss Kennedy, I do not know who you are or why you came, but I thank you just the same for your kindness. If I may ask, who is it in Ohio who is acquainted with me? I know of no one there, nor have I ever been there, nor has Emma, as far as I know. Who then are these people, Miss Kennedy?"

Eve was not prepared for this. Again, she'd have to lie, and she hated that. But just as she was about to speak, a new thought intruded. She decided to bend the truth, but only slightly.

Her eyes met Patrick's. "Detective Gantly, I heard about you and your wife from a hansom taxi driver. He told me your wife was deathly ill."

Patrick stared, confused. "I'm afraid I don't understand, Miss Kennedy."

"Forgive me, but as a nurse, I felt it was my duty to try to help, so I told Dr. Foster and Dr. Eckland an untruth, so I could solicit their urgent help. I knew there was no time to waste."

Patrick was still perplexed. "A hansom driver? Who is this driver?"

"He knew your wife. He told me he was from the same town in England as she, Manchester. His name is Thomas Whiton."

A light went on in Patrick's eyes, but it was quickly replaced by suspicion, as if he felt Eve's explanation didn't quite ring true. Eve knew Patrick, and she knew the detective in him would never settle for an explanation like that. But for the moment, it would have to do.

"Would you like something else to eat, Miss Kennedy? Perhaps some eggs and beans?"

"No, thank you. The coffee and muffins will do nicely."

"Do you expect to stay in New York long?"

Eve hesitated. "At this time, I'm not sure."

"And if it was not to visit me and my wife, then why did you travel here?"

Patrick was into his detective mode. "For pleasure. My friend, Miss Kosarin, and I have come to see the City sights."

"What town in Ohio are you from, Miss Kennedy?"

Eve went into her deflect mode. "I can see that you truly are a detective. I don't remember when I've been asked so many questions."

Patrick lowered his head in false humility. "Forgive me, Miss Kennedy. I didn't wish to intrude."

Yes, you did, Patrick Gantly. Eve thought to herself. *You'll intrude on anyone and anything once your curiosity has been aroused.*

"May I ask you a question?" Eve countered.

"Yes, please do."

"What are your plans for you and your daughter?"

He drained his cup, reached for the coffee pot, refilled Eve's cup and then his own.

"I will be moving soon. I do not wish to stay in that house. As for my daughter, having no wife to care for her troubles me. I have been thinking that perhaps Mrs. Connelly's daughter, Megan, and her husband, Colin, might make good parents for her."

Eve sat up, flabbergasted. "What? Are you saying you would give up your own daughter?"

"I believe it might be best for her, so she has a mother."

"But Pat…" Eve swiftly caught herself, almost using his familiar Christian name, a complete taboo in this time.

Patrick was alert to her mistake. He sat dead still, drilling into her with his cool, penetrating eyes.

Eve drank coffee, hoping she wasn't blushing, although she could feel the red spreading from her neck to the top of her head. What a stupid mistake. A moment later, she tried again.

"Detective Gantly, what is your daughter's name?"

He turned his head away. "I have not named her yet."

"But it has been over a week since her birth, Detective Gantly, and…"

Patrick cut her off. "I know how long it's been," he said, sharply. "I will name her when I am ready to name her. At her christening. It is my affair and my business. You are too bold, Miss Kennedy."

Eve drew back, chastised, feeling his anger and his pain. They both let the quiet fill the space between them, while they heard the shuffle of footsteps, the rattle of dishes and the low hum of conversation nearby. The arguing couple arose hastily, the man ruffled, the woman fuming. They left the café, leaving behind an invisible and unsettled cloud of sorrow.

Patrick adjusted his coat, his face softening. "I apologize for my harsh words. The subject is a sensitive one for me. And my work is demanding. I will confess that I am seeking clarity on many fronts."

Eve wanted to reach for his hand, she wanted to hold and comfort him. Could he see the love in her eyes? Could he feel her full heart pulsing, aching for him?

"Detective Gantly, may I see the child? Whenever it is convenient, of course."

His forehead wrinkled into thought. "Mrs. Connelly does not take kindly to outsiders, Miss Kennedy."

"Could you speak to her on my behalf? I would love to see her."

He pondered Eve's expression, looking deeply into her beautiful, clear eyes. There was a strange mystery about the woman that raised his interest. She had an alluring manner, and she was a very attractive woman, that was certain, but there was more to her than that, although in his still blurred and aching mind he could not grasp what that was.

"Yes, Miss Kennedy. You are entitled to see her, as you helped to bring her into this world. I will talk to Mrs. Connelly about it."

And then to Eve's surprise, Patrick stood abruptly. "I hope you will forgive me, but I must be on my way. May I escort you back to your hotel?"

Disappointed, Eve lowered her gaze. "No, thank you. I will remain here for a time."

"Please order whatever you wish. I will cover the bill."

"When may I see your daughter, Detective Gantly? May I come at a time when you will be there?"

Patrick was conflicted by her request. "Yes, well, how about next Sunday afternoon, say around two o'clock? Will that be convenient?"

"Yes. I will be there. Thank you."

"A good day to you, Miss Kennedy. Thank you for joining me."

After he was gone, Eve sat in a gloomy mood. There was a dark remoteness in Patrick that she'd never seen before. He was swimming in the deep waters of hurt and anger.

Still, it was hard to believe that he had not named his child, and that he was willing to give the girl up to his neighbors. She knew Patrick well enough to know that if he did give the child away, he'd regret it for the rest of his life.

Patrick had a good and generous heart, and she knew those qualities would eventually return when all the grieving was done. Right now, his heart was covered by grief, pain and exhaustion.

She couldn't let him give his baby away. But if he was determined to, how could she stop him?

CHAPTER 37

Sean O'Casey's Saloon was a place of shadows, muffled voices and foggy cigar smoke. It was frequented by laborers, gossipy old men, a few actors from the nearby theaters, and oily, shadowy characters who lurked in the corners, plotting mischief.

Patrick sat at the bar on a wooden barstool, hunched over a pint of porter, his choice of alcoholic beverage. It was a strong, dark beer made from heavily roasted barley, highly hopped and strong in alcohol. The dark color came from a batch of malt that had once been accidently over-roasted, resulting in a beer that proved popular in England and America. It provided intoxication, refreshment and a boost of calories.

To Patrick, the room was a dark, anonymous place, although he knew some of the regular patrons, such as Brodie Grant, a washed-up old actor with crinkly white hair and a drinking problem who, after one, or two, or three porters, would stand unsteadily on his thin twigs of legs and quote Shakespeare.

Whenever he did, his voice boomed off the walls and his countenance took on an ancient glory. Most patrons paused to listen, either out of respect for the old thespian, or simply for art's sake.

Brodie was seated on the stool next to Patrick, his colorless gaze focused on his beer.

"She was a fine woman, Patrick," Brodie said. "Light on her feet with the jig, she was, and she played the piano with gifted, nimble fingers. And she had the voice of an angel. Remember that pretty dinner she gave, Patrick? After you placed her on your chair, being the wee lass she was, she broke into the verses of *Red is the Rose* till it brought the tears to us both. Let the truth be told that I never heard it sung as well, Patrick."

Patrick turned his benevolent gaze onto the old man. "Emma was fond of you, Brodie."

"Not so fond of my drink, if the truth be told, Patrick, but she was a good, God-fearing woman, she was, and I say it with a heavy heart, that she is missed by all who knew her."

When a man pounded the bar with his fist, Patrick and Brodie glanced over. He was a well-dressed gentleman in his late twenties or early thirties, with bulging, agitated eyes. The man snatched up his shot glass of rye whiskey and took it down in a gulp. He slammed the glass down on the bar and ordered another from Sean, the tall, red-headed bartender, whose disapproving eyes settled on the man.

"You will want to be going a bit slower on that whiskey, sir. I don't want to be having to toss you and your tailored suit out into the street."

The man glared up at Sean. He reached into his leather wallet, drew out some dollar bills and slapped them on the bar.

The man raised his voice. "I'm a paying customer, my good man, and I can take as many as you can pour. Do not worry about me or my tailored suit. I have more and they are just as tailored."

Reluctantly, Sean reached for the bottle of whiskey and refilled the shot glass. The man took that one down in a swallow and expectantly replaced his glass.

Brodie swung his gaze toward Patrick. "As the Bard once said, 'The empty vessel makes the loudest sound.'"

Patrick turned away and reached for his beer.

And then to Brodie's surprise, the man launched into a Shakespearian quote.

"Oh, had I but followed the arts!"

A few heads turned, Sean the bartender shook his head, and Patrick ignored him.

Surprised, Brodie gently elbowed Patrick. "By heaven, Patrick, the man just quoted from *Twelfth Night*."

The man pushed his stool back, turned to the bloated room and lifted a dramatic hand as he continued with his recitation of Shakespeare.

This love that thou hast shown
Doth add more grief to too much of mine own.
Love is a smoke raised with the fume of sighs;
Being purged, a fire sparkling in lovers' eyes;
Being vexed, a sea nourished with loving tears.
What is it else? A madness most discreet,
A choking gall, and a preserving sweet.

Brodie was the only patron to applaud, overtaken by the man's emotion, if not his rather poor vocal technique and lack of rhythm. Still, it was Shakespeare, and Shakespeare among the saloon's rabble.

Brodie left his stool next to Patrick and approached the young man, hand outstretched.

"My dear man, allow me to offer you a hearty shake for your most worthy *Romeo and Juliet* recitation. May I introduce myself? I am the once, and perhaps the once again future actor, Brodie Grant."

The young man's eyes looked Brodie up and down with dazed suspicion. "I am Edwin Lancaster Bennett, sir," he said, taking the old man's bony hand and shaking it.

The rest of the room went back to drinking, smoking and plotting. Sean remained wary and watchful, nodding to Patrick, as if to say, *I'll have to watch this one.*

Brodie said, "I detect a man who has come to this noble place to wash away, as it were, the scent and the song of a woman. Am I correct, sir?"

Edwin's eyes clouded up. "How perceptive you are, wise old man. One loves me with a burden no man can bear, and I have discontinued our engagement. The other, my muse and a woman of mystery, spurns my requests and ignores my letters."

"Allow me, sir, to offer you a libation to help ease your pains. Please join me and my friend in a toast to the worthiest of all writers, William Shakespeare."

Patrick saw them coming, and he lowered his head. That was the one problem with Brodie, he never knew a drinking stranger.

Patrick half turned to meet Edwin and, when he did, he quickly sized him up. He was a gentleman from sole to crown, meaning he was from a wealthy family, he was well educated, he had fine clothes, and he was overindulgent in his lifestyle, manner and emotions.

Patrick nodded to him and then went back to his porter, while Brodie ordered another rye for Edwin and a porter for Patrick and himself.

"Are you an actor, Mr. Bennett?" Brodie asked.

"Oh, no, sir, although it had been my wish to be one when I was just a lad. More so than an actor, I had felt destined to be a writer of the stage, of the verse and of the novel."

"You don't say, sir? Well, then, what has happened to those noble aspirations?"

Turbulence darkened Edwin's eyes. "I have a father and a mother who set my course to the law, and they would have none of my literary aspirations. Sadly, I did not want to risk losing my inheritance, so even though I am a man of means, in the truth of the heart, I am a bankrupt."

Patrick rolled his eyes, but only Sean saw him, and he winked with a sarcastic shake of his head.

Brodie lay a hand of sympathy on Edwin's shoulder. "Poor lad. But as our most noble bard hath said, '*But the comfort is, you shall be called to no more payments, fear no more tavern-bills.*'"

It was meant as a little joke, but Edwin did not crack a smile.

Brodie held his tankard of beer close to his lips, then paused as a thought struck. He narrowed one eye on Edwin. "Did you say, Mr. Bennett, that you have a muse?"

Edwin straightened his back, proud and solemn. "I do, sir. She is both noble and fair, both lovely and mysterious as the golden moon in dark, wispy clouds. She captured my heart from the first, but as I have previously stated, she rebuffs my advances and ignores my verse and letters. Why is it, sir, that a man can possess the woman he doesn't love, but can't possess the woman he loves? What a wretched fate have I," Edwin whined.

Brodie was quick with encouragement. "Women speak many languages, my good Mr. Bennett. Perhaps in time you will find the correct verse with which to woo her."

"But time is fast running out, Mr. Grant. She is not from New York, and she will be leaving town soon."

"And is the fair maid called Juliet, Mr. Bennett?" he asked, and then immediately launched into verse from *Romeo and Juliet*, basking in the sound of his own voice. "*'Forswear it, sight, For I ne'er saw true beauty till this night.'*"

"Juliet? No her name is not Juliet, sir. Her name is Miss Evelyn Kennedy, and she is from the State of Ohio."

Patrick spun around, the recognition of Eve's name sharpening his gaze. "What did you say her name is?" Patrick asked.

Edwin was perturbed by Patrick's sudden intrusion. "I was not speaking to you, sir. My words are for Mr. Grant."

"Well, you are speaking to me now," Patrick said, pointedly. "Did you say the woman's name is Miss Evelyn Kennedy?"

Brodie was surprised by Patrick's sudden, forceful interest. "That is the name, Patrick."

Patrick left his stool, pulling himself to his full height, a good four inches taller than Brodie or Edwin. "What do you know about Miss Kennedy?" Patrick demanded.

Edwin looked up at Patrick slowly, tilting his head to bring one eye to bear, the whiskey having emboldened him.

"And I say, sir, this is not your business."

Patrick was in no mood to converse with a drunk. He leaned over, his face immediate to Edwin's, and he spoke in a low, clear voice. "Do not play with me, Mr. Bennett, for I am not in the mood for it. Do you know Miss Kennedy well?"

Patrick was a big man, and there was no humor in his eyes. Edwin took a nervous step back, losing some of his courage.

"No, sir. I do not know her well."

"Do you know her family?"

"No. We have only met twice."

"Where?"

"Once at Benton's Restaurant. Once we took a carriage ride."

"When?"

Edwin's fuzzy head went to work. "Now, let me see... This is Saturday evening. It was yesterday. Yes, Friday."

"Did she say why she has come to New York?"

"I don't know, sir. I'm not sure. She says to see the City. She is a nurse, and she helped to save a baby almost two weeks ago, I think. As I said, she is a noble woman. That is all I know about her. Do you know Miss Kennedy?"

Patrick ignored the question. "How did you meet her?"

"Through my good friend, Dr. Darius Foster."

Patrick massaged his forehead. He knew something wasn't right. There were too many coincidences; too many loose ends, but he was too stressed and too tired to put anything together.

Edwin continued. "Miss Kennedy is a mystery. A lovely mystery who, I think, is perhaps from the world of the lofty fairy lands."

Patrick edged even closer to Edwin's face, his eyes burning. "Don't be a romantic fool, sir, she is a woman, like any other woman."

"Go easy, Patrick," Brodie said stepping between the two men. "Go easy, now."

Brodie saw a sleeplessness in Patrick's eyes, a sudden vacant, weary look.

"Go home, Patrick, my good and wounded friend," Brodie said. "Go home and rest."

Patrick pulled coins from his pocket and placed them on the bar. He gave Sean a friendly glance and Brodie a nod. He ignored Edwin.

He buttoned his coat, placed his bowler firmly on his head and strode out of the saloon into the cold November night.

Patrick walked most of the night, ducking into saloons for warmth and a beer, and then, toward dawn, he hailed a cab, telling the driver to take him anywhere.

At gray dawn, as the world turned a misty pale and the East River glassy, Patrick left the cab and wandered to the Brooklyn Bridge. He started across, pausing halfway to view the horizon, as the rim of the sun peeked up through moving, clay-heavy clouds.

The bridge was a towering wonder, with its gothic arches and massive cables, having only been completed the year before, in 1883. He watched the formidable dance of the river, heard the cry of seagulls, and watched their wings dip and pivot in an airy ballet.

He inhaled a fresh morning breath, taking in the spires and the jagged skyline of Manhattan, ghostlike in the morning mist. Patrick longed to thrust a hand out and reach up into that mystic cloud and draw down some truth. In his hand he wanted to hold some shiny bit of wisdom, something revealed, some sharp understanding of life and death and love.

Eve Kennedy lay heavily on his mind. Where had she come from and why was she in New York? Why did she appear at his doorstep, from out of the blue, on the day of Emma's death? He hadn't believed a word she'd said about Thomas, the hansom driver. He'd been a detective long enough to know she was lying. But why? What was she hiding? What did she want? She was a mystery to be solved, and he would solve it. He had no doubt about that.

Perhaps he would solve it on this dawning day, Sunday. She'd be coming to see his daughter at two o'clock. Patrick was sure he'd be able to get some answers and learn why it was that she had mysteriously and suddenly appeared in his life.

CHAPTER 38

Eve waited alone in Patrick's parlor, seated stiffly on the slick, horsehair sofa. Patrick had let her in but had then retreated, explaining that the baby was still with Mrs. Connelly and her daughter, Megan.

"I'm afraid that Mrs. Connelly does not approve of your seeing the child," Patrick said candidly. "She says it isn't proper, especially in Emma's house."

"Should I leave then?" Eve had asked.

"No, Miss Kennedy. I granted your request to see my daughter and see her you shall. Mrs. Connelly is a good woman, if a stubborn one. Excuse me. I will return shortly."

Eve had pulled her eyes from him with difficulty, although she was sure he hadn't noticed.

The house was quiet, the fire in the fireplace crackling and warm, the flowers wilting in a corner vase. How sad the house seemed, how lost and forlorn Patrick seemed. She could easily see he hadn't slept much, and he had lost weight. His body was lean, his jawline sharp, his stomach tight, his blue eyes sunken and dark.

Eve wondered if Emma's spirit roamed the house, watching, listening for her name to be repeated, a household name still hovering in the silence.

Inevitably, Eve's thoughts turned to the lantern. She had still not heard from Mrs. Tannin or from her daughter, Abagail. Something was wrong, and Eve intended to march to the boarding house first thing Monday morning to inquire about the status of the lantern, hoping she could take possession of it.

And then the dreaded question arose. If Eve could, finally, get the lantern, could she leave this time without Patrick? And if she couldn't leave, was there any possibility that he would fall in love with her again, or would he drift away from her and never remarry?

When Eve heard footsteps on the porch, she stood up to see Patrick and Mrs. Megan O'Brien enter the parlor. Megan cradled the baby in both arms, the child protected from the cold and light by a pink cotton baby blanket.

Patrick shut the door and he and Megan approached Eve, who struggled for calm.

Eve smiled warmly at Megan. "Hello."

Megan's smile was kind and welcoming. "Hello, Miss Kennedy. My name is Megan O'Brien. I've brought the little beauty with me."

Patrick glanced away from the child. "Can a baby be a beauty?"

Megan was a thin redhead in her early 20s, with friendly, green eyes and a swirl of freckles on her girlish face. "Yes, Mr. Gantly, this one is a beauty," Megan said looking tenderly at the child, peeling back the soft blanket from her forehead. "Just look at her lovely eyes, and the button of a mouth. You fall into those eyes, and she holds you with them. And when she grows up, she'll be a heartbreaker, she will, make no mistake about that, sir. I fear you'll be fighting off the lads."

There was a mildness about Megan and a natural refinement and charm. Eve was grateful for her convivial spirit. Megan's mother, Mrs. Connelly, had not been so pleasant.

"May I see the baby, Mrs. O'Brien?"

Eve didn't dare ask if she'd been named.

Still cradling the child, Megan tilted her up so Eve could glimpse her. Eve's face lit up with glowing happiness. "Oh, look at her. How pretty she is with her reddish-blonde hair. Yes, she *is* a little beauty."

Megan gently rocked the child, smiling down at her. "She has grace all about her and she's no trouble," Megan offered. "She hardly cries at all."

Eve glanced at Patrick, and his face was impassive. Knowing him as she did, she sensed his churning emotions.

Megan said, "I told the little tyke that when she is old enough, I am going to take her upstate. There is a beautiful swimming hole there, where we will jump from the rocks down into the clean, cool, mountain water. She'll love that."

Megan hummed a little lullaby. "Her mother would have been so proud."

Megan's words hung in the fragile air as she continued the lullaby, a sweet smile on her lips, her eyes lost in the baby's sleepy magic.

"Thank you, Mrs. O'Brien, for letting me see her, and please send my regards to your mother."

Megan ceased the lullaby, as her eyes flickered up to meet Eve's. "If I may say so, Miss Kennedy, although my mother would never say it, she was grateful that you came to help. She said she watched you from the doorway as you helped deliver this little angel. She said you were a good nurse. She said you were patient and skilled. She said it was you who saved this little one from the jaws of death."

Megan winked. "But don't tell her I told you so; she'd never forgive me. She is a good and God-fearing woman, Miss Kennedy, and the loss of Emma Gantly affected her deeply. She is of the old ways, where her bark is much worse than her bite."

Touched by Megan's words, Eve felt the sting of tears, but she stopped them. "Thank you for sharing that with me."

Megan turned to Patrick. "I should get her fed and put her to bed now, before she fusses at me."

To Eve, Megan said, "A pleasure to see you again, Miss Kennedy. You are welcome to visit the little child whenever you wish."

After Megan and the baby had gone, the parlor became loud with silence, as Eve and Patrick sought words that didn't come. Whatever words or questions arose in Eve's mind, they were too intrusive or too bold for the strained moment.

It was difficult for Eve to accept that this Patrick was not the same man she'd known in 1885 or 2019. This was the man before she'd met him in 1885, and before they had grown and been changed by their relationship and 21st century culture.

It was Eve who spoke first, her eyes avoiding Patrick. "Mrs. O'Brien is a lovely young woman."

"Yes... I learned only yesterday that she is in the family way. Her husband, Colin, is more than happy. He's a good and hard-working lad."

Eve felt compelled to speak about the baby. She wanted to confront his seeming lack of affection for her, if for no other reason than to try to open him up emotionally.

"In this difficult time, Detective Gantly, I trust your baby girl offers you some tender comfort."

There was a blank emptiness in his expression. "Tender comfort? Emma died so the baby could live. Perhaps, Miss Kennedy, I should feel tenderness toward the child, but I'm finding that emotion to be somewhat elusive. And, anyway, a girl needs a mother more than she needs a father."

"A baby needs love," Eve added. "That is the most important thing. Most women say that having a loving and caring father can make all the difference in their lives. That trust, that love, is a bond that is treasured and can never be broken."

Patrick gave her a severe look. "Have you been married, Miss Kennedy?"

The question pushed her off-balance, and she hesitated.

"Miss Kennedy, that is not a difficult question. Marriage is something that either is or is not. Why do you so often hesitate when questions are put to you? Such as, where are you truly from?"

Eve met his eyes fully, ready to confront him. She had recently read in a New York paper that the former general and President of the United States, Ulysses S. Grant, was from Ohio. She'd focused on the town's name, in case she needed to use it. Now, she did.

"If you must know where I am from, I come from the same town as Ulysses S. Grant. I am from Point Pleasant, Ohio. As to marriage, my life has not been so simple."

"And so I surmised, Miss Kennedy. Forgive me my analysis, but you seem to have been blown in by the wind from some unknown, far-off place. I suppose Point Pleasant, Ohio is one such far-off place?"

Eve wanted to say, *You have no idea, Patrick Gantly,* but of course she didn't. She remained silent.

Patrick glanced about awkwardly. "We should leave the house. It will not do for my neighbors, who are no doubt watching, to further speculate as to our business here. I will hail a cab and escort you back to your hotel, or to wherever it is that you wish to go."

Eve accepted his offer, excited to spend as much time with him as possible.

In the hansom, they sat next to each other in silence, as snow flurries flitted by and the cab adroitly cut in and out of traffic, past the commotion, the bustle and the smells. The drafty cab provided a woolen blanket during fall and winter, and Eve used it to cover her knees and legs.

Patrick had crossed his arms, and he was staring out the window, drifting back into himself as he tried to calm his rambling thoughts and sparring emotions. Eve Kennedy bothered him, and he didn't want to be bothered. He didn't have the time to be bothered, and his loss and his grief could not tolerate being bothered.

Miss Kennedy had grace and style; she had an independent, intelligent nature; she had initiative, and she was resourceful. He liked the easy swing of her waist and the ride of her bosom. And there was a kind of inner glow about the woman that bothered him, and her eyes were full of light. Her purposeful mouth, often pursed ever so slightly as if expecting a kiss, also bothered him. Was he imagining that?

Patrick wished he'd never met her—wished she'd never come to the house to begin with. What business was it of hers, anyway? It was an audacious thing to do, and he should have never let her and Dr. Foster in. What had made him do it? What had he been thinking about? Well, of course, he wasn't thinking clearly. He was lost in a morass of anguish. He naturally believed that if a well-known doctor had come to help Emma, then it was his duty to allow him and the nurse in, to allow Miss Kennedy in.

But she bothered him with her mystery and her warm, attractive smile. It was a good smile and a caring smile, but it bothered him, and it wasn't right that he was bothered. It wasn't the time to be bothered, and it wasn't respectable.

Patrick faced ahead, tired of his thoughts, upset by his thoughts and, yes, bothered by his thoughts.

"I have considered three names for my daughter," he said casually.

Eve snapped him a glance. "And... What are they?"

"Perhaps you will be so kind as to tell me your preference."

"Yes, I will."

Patrick still didn't look at her, keeping his eyes focused outside, as New York blurred by.

"Colleen is the first. Moira next and finally, Caitlin."

"All good Italian names," Eve said, soberly, hiding a cheeky grin.

Patrick turned his head. "Italian? I can assure you they are all good Irish names."

Eve gave him a modest smile. "Are they really?"

Patrick saw the glint of humor in her eyes and he nearly smiled, but it quickly vanished.

"You have humor. I have not seen it before."

"We have not spent so much time together for you to have seen it before."

Once again, Eve hadn't intended it to sound flirtatious, but that's how it came out and how it lingered in the chilly cab air.

Patrick turned his attention back to the window. "I met a friend of yours last evening."

"Oh... I don't have many friends in the City. Who is it?"

"He said his name is Edwin Lancaster Bennett."

Eve stared at the back of Patrick's head in utter shock. It took her a few moments to find her voice. "Have you been following me, Detective Gantly?"

"No, Miss Kennedy. Mr. Bennett and I met at a drinking establishment called Sean O'Casey's Saloon. I admit I was surprised that he knew you, and then maybe I wasn't so surprised, aware that you seem to thrive on mystery. Anyway, according to his rather dramatic discourse, I believe he considers you to be his muse."

Eve blew out an exasperated sigh. "His muse?" she asked with annoyance. "I hardly know the man. He seems to have some idealized image of me. I'm also afraid that Mr. Bennett is quite fond of, well, shall I say, stimulants."

Patrick faced her, his eyes exploring. The questions were bursting inside of him.

273

"Miss Kennedy, you never did answer whether or not you have been married."

"I am currently not married."

Patrick let that settle. "When will you be leaving town? Mr. Bennett seems to think it will be soon."

"Mr. Bennett is of no concern to me, sir, and neither am I concerned about when he thinks I will be leaving New York. I will leave when it is time to leave."

To Eve's surprise, this brought the slightest of smiles to Patrick's lips. Yes, Patrick had always smiled at her whenever she showed her independence. Eve was encouraged by his meager smile. She had reached him.

At the hotel entrance, Patrick paid the driver, climbed down, took her gloved hand and helped her from the cab to the sidewalk. He ushered her into the hotel lobby, pausing at the closed doors. His eyes came to hers.

"I trust, Miss Kennedy, that I have not offended you in any way?"

"You have not, and I thank you for allowing me to see your daughter."

"And now that you have seen my daughter, may I ask again, which of the three names do you prefer?"

"I have been thinking about that, Detective Gantly, and I have made my decision."

The couple stepped aside to let two men, who had left the elevator, pass them and exit the hotel.

Eve stared into Patrick's vivid blue eyes, as he waited for her answer. She did not want him to leave, and she sensed that he felt the same. That old, and now new, passion they'd always felt for each other crackled in the air, and there was no ignoring it.

"Colleen," Eve said. "I like the name Colleen."

Patrick brightened. "Colleen... Yes, that was my choice as well. How remarkable."

And so they stood there, each waiting for the other to speak, as time seemed to stall.

His faint smile was shy. "May I say, Miss Kennedy, that you have a way of distracting me from my recent troubled thoughts. Perhaps it is your mystery, or perhaps it is because you come from a different state, with different manners and cultural ways. Forgive me if that sounds too forward or inappropriate."

Eve worked to keep the love from showing in her eyes, but she was sure he must have seen it. The simple truth was, she loved Patrick with all her heart and soul, and to see him hurting and lost was an agony to her. In his pretended casualness, she saw a spark of attraction for her in his eyes, but she was all too aware that he'd never act on it, at least not so soon after his wife's death. It might take months, and they didn't have months. They were about to part.

"Your daughter looks like you, you know," Eve said.

A heavy curtain seemed to fall over his eyes, and he turned away. She'd said the wrong thing, and she swiftly tried to recover.

"It is a great gift to have a child, Detective."

But he had once again closed off.

He gave her a pained expression. "I must be going. I trust you will enjoy the rest of your stay in our City. I thank you again for all of your good efforts and kind wishes."

Eve couldn't let him go without reinforcing her concerns about the baby. "Detective Gantly, again, forgive my boldness, but I implore you to reconsider your relationship with your daughter. Please think long and hard before you agree to give her up to be raised by others. I fear that if you do, you will be sorry for it for the rest of your life."

His eyes hardened as he replaced his bowler on his head and touched it with two fingers. "Yes, Miss Kennedy, you do have a way of insinuating yourself into other people's business and I, for one, find it an offensive personality trait. Good day to you."

Eve watched him go with slumped shoulders and sad eyes. *Was that it? Would she never see him again?*

CHAPTER 39

Monday morning was cold and overcast, with a blustery wind that whipped the last of the stubborn leaves from elms and oaks. Eve felt the pressure of the moment, just as she felt gusting winds nudging her toward Mrs. Tannin's boarding house. Had she lost the lantern? Had she lost Joni to Dr. Foster? Had she lost Patrick?

Would Patrick really give up his daughter to the O'Briens? Eve had tried to push the heavy feeling away, but it remained. She didn't believe that her love for Patrick could sustain such a callous decision. If his heart was truly so frigid with anger, and his emotions so eclipsed by loss, that he'd relinquish his own daughter, a child that Emma had given her life for, then he wasn't capable of loving anything or anyone with any real depth, and that included her.

She strolled by a little park enclosed by a white picket fence, where boys were crouched playing marbles, and girls jumped rope while chanting nursery rhymes.

As she walked past a white Presbyterian church with an enclosed cemetery to its right, she had the odd feeling that she was being followed, and she glanced over her shoulder several times but saw no one, nor anything out of the ordinary.

Two Catholic nuns across the street walked prayerfully, their heads down, their hands folded. An elderly man, with a white Santa Claus beard and a cane, plodded along with grim determination, while a scruffy brown and white dog sniffed the ground, looking for scraps. Eve thought of Georgy Boy, and she wished she had some food to give the poor, streetwise dog. But his eyes were bleak and hostile, and he moved like a hungry predator.

Eve noticed a canary-colored carriage pass, being pulled by two lovely white horses, but she saw no passenger inside. Further up the street, two ladies were involved in animated conversation, their long, tailored coats flapping in the wind, their hands pressed to their elaborate feathered hats to keep them from flying away.

Eve did not focus on the black and burgundy square-fronted Brougham, parked under a row of elms, its driver perched above, wearing a top hat, a black wool, fitted jacket with silver buttons, and a black and yellow striped vest. Two horses, black as a raven's wings, stood by stoically.

Inside the carriage, hiding from view, was a moody and inebriated Edwin Bennett, still wearing his formal dinner clothes from the night before. His face held fatigue and disintegration, and he talked to himself in a booze-blurred voice.

"She has the form of a goddess, Mr. Bennett, yes I do believe it is so," he said to himself. "She has a most curious mystery that draws my heart toward hers. Shall I quote my latest verse to her as she glides by, like a lover to the dance?" Edwin cleared his throat, softly launching into his own created verse, as Eve drifted by, unaware.

Oh mystery of sight, both day and night,
She is a whispering breath of sleep.
Through a window, across the street,
A shade draws up and I see her lovely sight.
A lamp embraces the night, and how I wish
I was that light, that shimmer of hungry light.
There! Her shadow stretches through sight
And she, my love, doth share my night.
A winter wheeze of wind, like death,
Doth chill my heart and take my breath.
It shakes the silence of night, as
She awakens to my sight.
A kiss, I pray, a kiss of light,
Then up to heaven and regal height.

Edwin slumped down as Eve turned right onto a side street, where row houses and brownstones sat sequestered from the main street. Edwin had instructed his driver to follow Eve from a discreet distance, and Edwin had extinguished the side lanterns and kept to the shadows, avoiding the windows.

He mumbled out some inaudible words and then sat up, clumsily alert, as Eve, still in good sight, started up the stairs of a brownstone. Edwin squinted, just able to read a boldly printed sign that was visible in a first-floor window.

ROOM AND BOARD 1 VACANCY

"Why are you here, Miss Kennedy?" Edwin asked himself. "Are you about to move away from the hotel and leave behind Miss Kosarin, so she and Darius can enjoy a dalliance? How interesting. Perhaps, Miss Kennedy, it is you who have another secret admirer, one beside myself, and you wish for your own private rooms for a clandestine rendezvous? You must know, Miss Kennedy, that I am your only true and faithful admirer, and I will never allow another to touch your glowing cheek or kiss your rose lips. You must know that if you are unfaithful to me, it can only end in the death of us both. Yes, we will leave this most troubled world, united, and thrive for all time in Beulah Land, that more perfect and shining world."

Eve used the brass knocker to rap softly on Mrs. Tannin's front door. It opened as if it had been yanked, startling Eve. Mrs. Tannin stood as straight as a post; her unfriendly eyes narrowed on Eve.

"I am sorry to bother you again, Mrs. Tannin," Eve said mildly, "but I have not heard from you. I stopped by in the hope that you have some news from your daughter regarding the lantern's whereabouts."

Mrs. Tannin sighed through her nose. "I did not contact you, Miss... Miss..."

"Miss Kennedy..."

"I did not contact you because my daughter has not replied to my letter, which I sent promptly after you were last here. That does not surprise me. Abagail is lazy, negligent and thoughtlessly rebellious, and she wallows in recklessness and irresponsibility like a dog in a mud puddle, just like her father did. I know nothing more about the lantern, and I doubt that I shall until Abagail returns."

Eve was about to speak, but Mrs. Tannin's hand went up to stop her. "Now, Miss Kennedy, do not ask me when Abagail might return because I do not know. Perhaps she will stay until Christmas, perhaps indefinitely. If I know anything about it, and I do because my sister has informed me, Abagail has a gentleman admirer, and she is in no hurry to return home. Frankly, I fear the worst for her and must wash my hands of it."

Eve offered Mrs. Tannin an indulgent smile. "Mrs. Tannin, would you be inclined to give me your sister's address in Albany where your daughter is staying? I could travel by train and…"

Mrs. Tannin's expression took on insult. "… I will certainly not give you, a perfect stranger, my sister's address. Neither my sister nor Abagail would ever speak to me again. Frankly, Miss Kennedy, I find your behavior over this silly lantern to be eccentric and tiresome. I suggest you find some other more normal interest to occupy your time. Good day."

The door closed and Eve heard the metallic click of the lock. The heat of anger gushed up to her face. *What a bitch*, Eve thought. *No wonder Abagail is rebellious and wants to be out of the house. The woman's a witch.*

Eve descended the stairs and started back toward the hotel, her stride fast and sure. She had to get that lantern one way or the other, and she couldn't wait until Christmas. But how? And she had no idea where it was. She had to find a way to contact Abagail Tannin.

As she crossed Sixth Avenue, her attention was diverted to a food cart. The sign on its side read:

SEAFOOD
Oysters and Clams 1 Cent Each

Patrick loved clams, and she knew he often stopped at food carts. Suddenly, an idea arose, and Eve stopped in her tracks by the curb as an omnibus went by. Patrick once told her that he could find anyone, that is, if their body hadn't already been tossed into the East River.

He was a detective, after all, and he was a good one. Maybe he would know how to find Mrs. Tannin's sister and thus also find Abagail Tannin? Eve had to get her hands on that lantern. Without it, she was trapped, and she hated feeling trapped.

And anyway, it would give her the opportunity to see Patrick again, wouldn't it?

CHAPTER 40

It was the middle of November, and Eve and Joni had been in 1884 for over four weeks; a very eventful, stressful and long four weeks. After her encounter with Mrs. Tannin, Eve had gone to the precinct several times, hoping to speak with Patrick. He hadn't been there, and the cops and detectives on duty were closed-mouthed and frosty towards her.

Eve also stopped by Mrs. Connelly's, but the tight-lipped woman claimed she hadn't seen Patrick, adding that he seldom visited them or his daughter. Eve was sure the woman was lying, but what could she do? She hadn't invited Eve in to see the child, nor to visit with Megan O'Brien.

And then Joni caught a bad cold and Eve stayed in, nursing her until she improved. The last thing Eve wanted was for Joni to catch pneumonia. Darius Foster had sent roses twice that week, along with warm wishes for a speedy recovery and the promise to escort her to dinner and to the latest shows as soon as she had recovered.

"He keeps asking how long we're going to stay in New York," Joni said thoughtfully, sitting up in bed, sipping the hot tea that Eve had just handed her.

Eve lowered herself in a tufted burgundy chair with a black velvet fringe, a recent addition to their room. It was deep, soft and luxurious.

"And what do you tell him?"

Joni avoided Eve's eyes. "I tell him I don't want to leave."

"And what does he say?"

"The last time... just before I got sick, he said he didn't want me to go. He said if I stayed, I wouldn't have to worry about a thing."

Eve turned away with a frown. "Yeah, I just bet."

"Why are you so negative about this?" Joni asked. "And don't start in with the whole mistress thing. You've already told me at least ten times."

Eve gave Joni a frank, female appraisal. "You don't care, do you?"

"Maybe I do and maybe I don't. He has a lot of money, and we really care for each other. So maybe I'll ask him. The next time he brings up that he wants me to stay, I'll say, okay fine, why don't we get married?"

Eve rolled her eyes. "Oh, yeah, that will be cool. You'll completely freak him out. Way too forward, Joni. A woman in this time can't bring up marriage to a man."

"Well, I can. What's the worst he can do?"

"He can walk away from you and find another hot-looking chick, with a snap of his fingers."

"That's bullshit, Eve. That's a shitty thing to say."

"I'm only saying it so you won't get hurt."

"It's none of your business if I get hurt. It's *my* business. Not your business, okay? It has nothing to do with you. You're just so damn bossy sometimes, Eve, and conservative and controlling. Let go a little bit, for God's sake. You're all tied up in knots and you're making me all tied up. I care about Darius, okay? Is that a bad thing? I care more about him—no—I feel more for him than I have ever felt for any other man. I can't help that. It's just there. I'm falling in love with him and it surprises me, and it scares me, and it is also one of the most exciting things that has ever happened to me."

Eve lowered her chin, softening her voice. "Your dancing and acting days will be over, Joni. You must know that."

"So I'll do other things. I was getting tired of auditioning for lousy shows, anyway. It's not like I was getting anywhere in my career."

Eve groped for words. "It's just that I feel responsible for you. You came here to help me, and I feel protective of you."

"Don't, Eve. I'm a big girl and I can make my own decisions."

Eve cast about for a change of subject, but she couldn't find one. "Well, maybe I've been mothering you because things haven't gone so well, and I'm frustrated and lost. Meanwhile, you're having the time of your life."

Joni reached for a lace hanky and blew her stuffy nose. "Eve... maybe it's time we both faced it: we probably won't be able to get back to our time, so we'd better start looking around here and figuring out what we're going to do for the rest of our lives."

Eve leaned back and shut her eyes. "How did everything go so wrong, Joni? I was so happy. My life was so good."

"And it can be again. Edwin really likes you, Eve. He's hot for you. Darius says he's more attracted to you than he has been to any other woman."

"Edwin Bennett is a loose cannon. Sometimes when I look into his eyes, I see a little crazy in there."

Joni wiped her nose. "Darius wants the four of us to double date again."

Eve got up. "No thanks."

Joni looked at Eve doubtfully. "Eve... I think your Patrick is gone. The Patrick you knew... Well, you've said it. He's just not the same."

Eve circled the chair, arms folded, staring down at the carpet. "I haven't given up on him yet. I know his heart and it's a good one. He just needs more time to work through his grief. It's only been a month. It takes time. It's not like he can get psychotherapy or read a self-help book or take some antidepressant. All he's got to soothe his sadness is booze and that horrible poison, Laudanum, which I doubt he'd drink."

Joni looked at her friend with compassion, but she didn't speak. She wanted to say, *You should just move on with your life*, but she didn't.

Eve made a sudden turn and marched toward the closet. "Now that you're better, I'm going to get dressed, go back to Patrick's neighborhood, and camp out on his or Mrs. Connelly's doorstep until Patrick appears, or somebody tells me where he is. I'll wait all night if I have to."

Eve took a cab downtown, hoping against hope to find Patrick home or at Mrs. Connelly's. Once again, Eve didn't realize that Edwin was following her. Although he wasn't drunk, he'd been drinking, and his manner had coarsened. In the past few weeks, his coworkers had noticed a disturbing change in him. He mumbled to himself at the office and often drank from a silver hip flask. He brooded over his work; he was distracted and curt with his coworkers, especially his subordinates.

His father had called him into his office and spoken sternly to him about his absences and frequent tardiness, but Edwin offered a charming smile, insisting that he'd been ill and needed rest.

Once again that day, he hadn't shown up for work. He'd planted himself in a café across from Eve's hotel, scribbling love poems and drinking brandy. When he saw her leave, he quickly grabbed a cab and followed her, sure she was off to meet a lover.

By the time Eve arrived at Patrick's row house, it was early afternoon. She left the cab, hesitated at the curb, then climbed the stairs to his porch. She knew she was being forward, but she no longer cared.

She knocked and waited. When there was no answer, she descended the stairs to the sidewalk and started for Mrs. Connelly's row house, a building similar in style to Patrick's. There was no surprise when Mrs. Connelly appeared, her broad face expressionless, eyes chilly.

Eve smiled pleasantly. "Good afternoon, Mrs. Connelly. I apologize for disturbing you again, but I've been searching for Detective Gantly and…"

Before she could finish, Patrick arrived at the door with his daughter nestled comfortably in his left arm, the baby's brand-new face filled with innocence and surprise.

Patrick's curious eyes rested on her, as Mrs. Connelly stood stubbornly next to him.

"Oh, Detective Gantly," Eve said, startled. "There you are."

"Good afternoon, Miss Kennedy. What can I do for you?"

"Well, actually..." Eve hesitated, her attention turning to Mrs. Connelly.

Patrick handed his daughter to Mrs. Connelly. "Thank you, Mrs. Connelly, and could you please leave us alone for a few moments?"

Mrs. Connelly was displeased, but she obeyed, turning about and taking the baby away into the parlor.

Patrick stepped out onto the porch, closing the door behind him. He hunched his shoulders against the chilly day, looking skyward.

"What brings you out on this cold day, Miss Kennedy?"

Eve thought he seemed pleased to see her, but she wasn't certain.

"I'll come right to the point. I want to hire you."

"Hire me? Hire me for what?"

"To find someone."

He perked up, energized by the possibility of gaining some knowledge of her mystery. "And who are you looking for?"

"A young woman who is currently living somewhere in Albany."

Patrick made a little face of confusion. "Albany? That's a bit out of my territory, Miss Kennedy."

Eve looked away and Patrick studied her thoughtful profile. Again, he was bothered by her convincing elegance.

"I can pay well."

"Paying me well may not help, Miss Kennedy. Albany is a long way off."

Eve faced him again. "I'm sure you are a good detective. I don't think it will be that difficult for you, and I wouldn't be surprised if you know people in Albany. Perhaps you even have relatives there."

Patrick grinned. "You are a confident woman, aren't you, Miss Kennedy?"

"Will you help me?"

He didn't hesitate. "I will. Write down the woman's full name, and as much as you know about her, any small detail."

Eve reached into her purse, drew out a folded piece of paper and handed it to him.

He looked at it, amused. "Yes, Miss Kennedy, it seems you are a very confident woman. Let me just say that I will look into it, but I do not promise anything."

"What is your fee, Detective Gantly?"

"There will be no fee, Miss Kennedy."

"But I insist."

"Did you charge me for helping to deliver Colleen?" Patrick asked.

Eve was pleased he called his daughter by name. She must have been christened.

"And that still is a mystery to me, Miss Kennedy. Perhaps you'll tell me the entire truth someday?"

Eve let that go by. "How shall we be in touch, Detective?"

"I will find you, Miss Kennedy. Please have patience. It might take a few days. Shall I assist you in finding a cab?"

Any time she could spend with Patrick was welcomed. "That would be kind of you."

At the sidewalk, a hansom approached and Patrick waved it down. The door opened and Patrick took Eve's hand, holding it longer than he needed to, and helped her inside. When the door closed, Eve waved.

Patrick gave her a quick smile and a little bow of his head.

After Patrick returned inside, Edwin Bennett's carriage slipped behind Eve's cab at the end of the block and began following her uptown. Edwin's eyes darkened; his face filled with a jealous rage.

CHAPTER 41

Eve leaned her head back and shut her eyes as the hansom lurched adroitly uptown through a tangle of traffic. She wanted to savor the time she'd just spent with Patrick and bask in the glow of desire and memory.

She had detected a small change in him; she was sure of that. The fact that he cradled Colleen and called her by her name was encouraging. It also had not gone unnoticed that, when he'd helped her into the cab, Patrick had held her hand longer than was necessary.

That strange magic of attraction between them was still there, oblivious to time and place, whether it was 1884, 1885 or 2019. But Eve was not naïve. Their relationship had a long way to go. It could take months before Patrick confessed his attraction.

So as uncomfortable as it was to see him and not be able to touch him, she'd have to hope that he'd find Abagail Tannin and thus the lantern. Eve would have to remain in this time until Patrick could heal his broken heart; until they were both free and ready to expand their relationship. Then, when the time was right, they could return to the 21st century.

Outside, as the cab trotted by the Pantheon Theatre, Eve did not see two delivery men at the curb on her right, struggling with a heavy trunk filled with props and costumes. They had wrapped it with heavy rope, and the stronger of the two had stooped, preparing to tug it from the flatbed wagon onto his broad back, and then haul it into the theater.

Just then, three boys darted up to the bay horse that was hitched to the wagon. One boy struck the horse in the neck with a sturdy limb, and then the three boys gleefully fled into an alley. Spooked, the horse whinnied, reared up on its hind legs and bolted, just as Eve's cab jogged by.

The big man hefting the trunk lost his grip, and the trunk crashed to the ground, props, wigs and dresses spilling out onto the sidewalk. He turned in a rage, cursing at the retreating boys.

In the street, the collision was nearly instant. The alarmed bay horse galloped away, just missing Eve's cab, but it yanked the flatbed wagon away from the curb. It swung out left, slamming into the hansom's rear wheels. The hansom jerked left, just missing a horsecar bloated with passengers, many hanging on the front and rear platforms and on the sides of the car.

Inside, Eve was slammed to the right, her head striking the cab's interior wall, as it lurched left and then toppled.

Edwin had seen it from his carriage window only 20 feet away. He saw Eve's cab take the hit and overturn. He watched in horror as the driver leaped from his perch, striking the ground in a roll as the horse screamed out in terror, dragging the cab slowly along the street.

Edwin burst out of his carriage door, hit the cobbles and raced up the street toward the cab. A young man, alert to the accident, darted toward the horse. Unaware that he was within range of one of the horse's flying hoofs, one hammered him in the jaw, sending him tumbling to the ground, unconscious.

Two other agile men managed to grab the horse's reins and restrain him, while two women hurried to aid the young man lying still in the street. The street became agitated and choked with traffic and startled crowds, circling and pointing.

Edwin bounded up on the body of the cab, reached in and yanked the door open. Eve was sprawled inside, staring wildly. She squinted, looking at the man who was blocking out a sizable piece of the gray-quilted sky.

"Miss Kennedy... Are you quite all right? Do you need assistance?"

Eve touched her sore head, then pushed up on elbows. "No, I don't think so. What happened?"

"There was a carriage accident."

Eve examined and moved her legs and arms to ensure nothing was broken and, when she was certain nothing was, she peered ahead.

Edwin outstretched his hand to her. "Let me help you out."

Eve worked her way toward him and for the first time, she focused, dazed and surprised. "Edwin? What are you doing here?"

"Please take my hand, Miss Kennedy. I need to get you out of here."

She took his hand, and he carefully drew her up and out the open door into daylight.

On the street, Eve stood on wobbly legs, blinking at the gathered crowds and at a stocky policeman who bellowed orders.

"How is the driver?" Eve asked.

"I believe he is fine. He jumped free. Yes, he's standing over there, speaking with the policeman."

"Is everyone else all right?"

"Yes, I'm fairly certain. It all started because three young ruffians spooked a horse. They should be caught and horsewhipped."

A second policeman, with a large gut and jowls, lumbered over, his handlebar mustache waxed to perfection. "Are you injured in any way, Miss? We have an ambulance wagon on the way."

"No, I don't believe so. I guess I was lucky."

He touched his hand to his hat. "That you were, Miss. Very good then. You'll have to remain for a time while we complete the report. It shouldn't take long."

Edwin made a face. "It's damned nonsense, these reports. This woman was nearly injured and needs looking after. Waiting is an inconvenience and a nuisance. I say we leave, and we leave right now."

The policeman strafed him with his eyes. "You will want to watch that kind of talk, sir. I could haul you in for obstructing police business, if I had a mind to."

Edwin turned away, pocketing his hands, mumbling.

When the report was completed, Edwin pointed to his carriage. "My carriage is just over there. Let us leave this place. Shall we go to a hospital and have you thoroughly examined, Miss Kennedy?"

Eve was still shaken, but she knew she wasn't physically hurt except for the bump on her head. She was certain there was no concussion.

"No, Mr. Bennett. Perhaps you could just take me to my hotel."

"Miss Kennedy, I insist on taking you some place where you can be calm and refresh yourself, and perhaps get something to eat."

She wasn't interested, but she could see it was futile. Edwin had made up his mind and, anyway, she was still light-headed and wanted to get out of the chilly air.

It was an enclosed carriage, with a hard-top roof, glowing side lamps and glass windows. Eve sat opposite Edwin on a soft leather seat, scented with the smell of rum and lavender.

He wore a well-made suit of brown tweed, the coat being a cutaway, a white starched shirt with a standing collar, and a small, chocolate-brown scarf tied in a bow knot.

"How was it that your carriage was so close to my cab, Mr. Bennett?" Eve asked.

"Purely coincidental, I assure you. Imagine my surprise when I mounted that overturned cab, opened the door and found you inside. You gave me quite a shock, Miss Kennedy."

Eve was wary.

"Do you doubt me?" Edwin asked.

"Aren't you supposed to be working today?"

"Of course. I was out on business."

"Well then, shouldn't you be attending to that business?"

He gave her a boyish grin. "Right now, I can think of no more important business than to be here with you."

"Where are you taking me?"

"Near Union Square, to one of the clubs I frequent. It is the Salmagundi Club. It took its title and literary inspiration from a collection of Washington Irving stories. Have you read Washington Irving?"

Eve's dazed mind went to work. "I believe so…" she said, hoping he didn't ask her which stories.

"I must admit that my favorite is *Rip Van Winkle,*" Edwin said with some pride.

Eve certainly recalled that story, but not the details. She'd read it in high school. "Yes, it's a charming story."

"I have read it numerous times, amazed at its originality. There he is, Rip Van Winkle, who falls asleep in the Catskill Mountains and wakes up twenty years later, having missed the entire American Revolution."

Edwin leaned forward, energized. "If you could travel back and forth in time, Miss Kennedy, what time would you wish to travel to?"

Eve gave him a long look of wonder. *If he only knew*, she thought.

"I would travel to the future, to 2019."

He stared, puzzled. "What an odd answer, Miss Kennedy. What a perfectly curious and strange answer."

Eve shrugged a smile.

They sat in a graceful, square room at a linen-topped table, under a chandelier cluster of electric lights made by Edison's company. A generous, roaring fireplace and a bar were close by, and along the walls were several pedestals, displaying busts of Washington Irving, Edgar Allan Poe and Herman Melville. The room was a little over half full, inhabited mostly by businessmen and politicians, and perhaps a mistress or two.

Edwin ordered champagne, oysters and clams, and again, Eve thought of Patrick and his seafood street carts.

"I am still concerned that you did not have a physician examine you, Miss Kennedy. You took a nasty spill."

"I am fine, Mr. Bennett. I was napping when the accident happened, and I must have been greatly relaxed so as to cushion the impact."

After the champagne was poured and they toasted her health, Edwin leaned back, working on a thought. "Miss Kennedy, there is something I wish to say. Please do not respond until I have concluded."

Eve dreaded what was about to come. She sampled the champagne, hoping a gentle buzz would lighten the effect of his words.

"I have grown quite fond of you... That is to say, you've captured my heart in passionate, inexplicable ways. There is a certain mystery that surrounds you that I find utterly fascinating. But more than that, I wish you to know that I am a wealthy man, Miss Kennedy."

Eve sipped the champagne, feeling the bubbles tickle her nose and throat. She wanted to stop him, but she also wanted him to finish his declaration and business proposal, so she could end his dreamy and lusty infatuation once and for all.

Edwin sat up straight and cleared his throat:

Here comes the pitch, Eve thought, still smiling with girlish innocence.

"Miss Kennedy, I can offer you whatever you wish: the latest fashion, jewelry and hats; dinners at the finest restaurants and, of course, I am in the position to offer you a fine residence with a carriage and driver at your beck and call day and night. I can introduce you to the right society, where we'll attend lavish parties, which will benefit you in a constellation of ways. If I may be so romantic, I will write you verses, and I will treat you like the goddess you are."

Before she knew it, Eve had drained her glass, and the stiff, tuxedoed waiter with a bushy white mustache promptly refilled it. Ironically, Edwin's glass had hardly been touched.

For a moment, the champagne glass claimed Eve's interest as she watched the shimmering bubbles dance.

"What I am saying, Miss Kennedy, is that if you are agreeable, I wish to keep you here in the City, living a life of luxury."

The champagne made Eve feel naughty. Her eyes opened fully. "Mr. Bennett, are you proposing marriage?"

Her question startled him and he swiftly reached for his glass, taking a generous drink. He recovered with a tight smile and tried again.

"Miss Kennedy, I must tell you that, as a young man, I once had the glorious and sterling ambition for the pen. Indeed, it was my one true passion. I spent hours writing poems. And now, here you are, my muse, the one woman who has reawakened that dormant ambition in me, and I am ready to rise and roar. I tell you true, Miss Kennedy, that with you at my side, this time I will not be stopped. I must realize my dream and take possession of my ambition to be a poet, but only if you agree to be my one and only. If you say no, then I will never have the courage to break away from my father and my family."

He opened his hands. "So you see, Miss Kennedy, it is up to you whether I succeed in my artistic effort or utterly fail."

Eve's eyes were clear and kind. "Mr. Bennett, you must have the courage and the fortitude to forge your own path, with me or without me. It is time that you explain to your father who you are, and what you want to do with your life."

Edwin didn't seem to hear her. "Will you be my own muse, Miss Kennedy? Will you be my one and only?"

Eve decided to try another way. "Forgive me, Mr. Bennett, but I'm not sure of your meaning with regard to marriage."

Edwin sat back. His laugh was small and nervous. "I cannot offer you marriage at this time, Miss Kennedy, but, on the other hand and more important for us, I can offer you comfort, entertainment and luxury."

Eve dropped her act and grew serious. She didn't want to antagonize or hurt the man, sensing his ego bruised easily and deeply.

"Mr. Bennett, it is a kind and generous proposal and I am, of course, flattered that a man of your character would even consider me, a simple woman from Ohio, to be your well, shall I say, partner in this venture. However, I must decline, with humble gratitude."

The change in him was immediate. Edwin's entire face tightened with offense and anger. Eve could feel darts of rage being thrown at her.

Edwin shot up and tossed his napkin down. He pushed his hands into his pockets, licked his lips and stared hotly at her.

"Miss Kennedy, I don't believe you understand. Perhaps that is because you are from a lowly, ignorant town or because you are a woman of no real experience in the world. I am offering you what no man you have ever known before could offer you."

Eve wanted to attack, but she didn't. She did not want to make an enemy. It was obvious that Edwin was emotionally unbalanced and perhaps even dangerous. She maintained an easy smile.

"And I am grateful to you, Mr. Bennett, but currently, I have other plans."

"And who is your other plan, Miss Kennedy?" Edwin spat out. "That tall man I saw you talking with earlier in that poor and pathetic neighborhood?"

Edwin drew stares from nearby tables, but he was too livid to notice or to care.

Eve felt a jump of anger and fear. So it was true. He *had* been following her. Well, of course he had. Eve looked into his eyes and saw a desperate intensity. She saw detachment and she saw fury.

Eve arose, maintaining her cool. "Mr. Bennett, I will be leaving now. I will find my own way home. Thank you again for your help. It is most appreciated. Good day."

With that, she pivoted and started out of the room, hearing Edwin shout at her.

"You are a damnable and thankless woman, Miss Kennedy! I will not forget this affront. Never!"

CHAPTER 42

Eve spent the next few days reading novels, taking walks and looking over her shoulder for Edwin. Thankfully, she didn't see him, and so she was relatively sure that he'd stopped following her. With everything else that was going on, the last thing she needed was a 19th century stalker.

When Eve told Joni what had happened, Joni said she'd tell Darius. Eve told her not to.

"I don't want Edwin any crazier than he is. If Darius gets into Edwin's face about this, I'm afraid he'll wind up threatening us all. He's a bad drunk, Joni, and he's also a little crazy. I saw it the first time I met him. He needs to be on medication."

On the Tuesday before Thanksgiving, November 25, Eve was strolling through Madison Square Park. There was a powdering of dry snow on the ground from an early morning snow, but the sun was out and the breeze pleasantly cool.

When she saw Patrick seated on a bench, reading a newspaper, his long legs crossed, she stopped in her tracks, making a little sound of surprise.

She approached, pausing before him. He glanced up casually over his newspaper, in mock surprise. He folded the paper, laid it aside and stood, tipping his bowler to her.

"Good day to you, Miss Kennedy."

Her eyes shifted furtively. "How did you know I'd be here?"

"I was having a coffee over at Kelsey's and I saw you walk by. I was about to call on you at your hotel, but I thought I'd first take in the late morning air and catch up on the news of the day."

Eve weighed his words.

"You look doubtful, Miss Kennedy."

"If you were coming to call, then you must have some news for me."

"I do. Will you sit then?"

She did and Patrick joined her. "I have located your friend, Miss Abagail Tannin." And then he paused.

"And?"

"She is indeed in Albany, but she is not currently lodging at the sister of Mrs. Tannin."

"Okay... So?"

"She has taken up with a rather unfortunate man by the name of Warren Combs. He's a petty thief, a gambler and a saloon owner, who is also known to live off the, shall I say, good and generous graces of older widows. My source, a friend named Joseph, who works for the Albany Police Department, visited the saloon and learned that Mr. Combs is quite the ladies' man, a real charmer, and a man of low character."

Eve allowed it all to sink in.

"In his final telegrams, Joseph stated that he did not believe Miss Tannin will be returning to New York any time soon, if ever. He learned that Miss Tannin has a bitter hatred of her controlling mother, and she has refused to write or contact her."

Eve twisted up her lips in disappointment. "Did you get an address?"

He reached into his inside coat pocket and drew out a folded piece of paper. He handed it to her.

Eve took it, unfolded it, and studied the address.

"Do you plan to travel to Albany, Miss Kennedy?"

"Yes... I have to."

"Alone?"

"Yes, alone."

Patrick stared at her. "Miss Kennedy, Joseph said that your man, Combs, is a dangerous and desperate man who seeks any ready opportunity to pad his pockets. Joseph added that the man is a cad of the worst sort, a jumped-up member of the lower classes."

"I don't need to talk to him, just Abagail."

"Joseph said the young woman is reckless."

Eve met his eyes. "I have to go."

Patrick turned away, crossed his legs and nodded.

Eve swiftly changed the subject. "How is Colleen?"

"She's well, and she remains a quiet and pleasant child."

Eve took a breath and took a chance. "Have you thought any more about giving her up for..."

Patrick cut in. "That is not an easy subject, Miss Kennedy, and I do not wish to discuss it."

He turned his body from her, tugging his hat down more securely on his head. When he spoke, his voice was low, barely audible. "Had Emma not been with child, she would have survived."

Eve angled her body toward him. "That is not Colleen's fault. She is just a little child in a troubled world, and she will want and need her father for love and guidance."

Patrick refused to look at her and so they sat, neither budging. Eve had a sudden inspiration. She recalled one of Patrick's old sayings that he'd learned from his father and had often quoted.

"A friend used to quote an old Irish proverb to me that he'd heard from his father."

Patrick turned, meeting her waiting eyes.

Eve softened her voice and spoke the verse as if it were a prayer. *"Having somewhere to go is home; having someone to love is family; having both is a blessing."*

Patrick searched her eyes, probing their secret depths; those calm but determined eyes that drew him into a private intimacy. Suddenly shaken, he broke the stare, got up and distracted himself by gazing up into the shining day.

Eve sat still, embracing the power of that moment; the electric passion, the miracle of attraction that she and Patrick had always felt for each other.

He faced her with a worried expression. "Miss Kennedy, you have a way of turning and twisting a thing."

Eve left the bench and took small steps to him, wanting to remain close, wanting the moment to lengthen.

"Detective Gantly, thank you for finding Abagail Tannin. Please allow me to pay you for your services."

"That will not be necessary. It was a small thing."

"Not to me."

"We have already discussed this. Keep your money. When do you plan to travel to Albany?"

"After Thanksgiving. Friday, I suppose. The sooner the better."

Patrick tapped the crown of his hat. "I have not seen Joseph and his good wife and baby daughter in many months. He was a detective here but moved because his brother was ill. He's helping to support two families. I should go for a visit, and this will be a good time for it."

Eve stamped her feet to induce a little warmth. "Are you saying that you will accompany me, Detective Gantly?"

He faced her squarely. "Yes, Miss Kennedy. You should not be alone with these people. I believe they are quite unsavory types."

"Then I will not say no. I'll take an early train to Albany on Friday morning. Shall we meet at the gate at 7:30?"

Patrick jerked a nod. "Very good. I will be there, Miss Kennedy."

CHAPTER 43

As Patrick had promised, he met Eve at The New York Central and Hudson River Railroad ticket counter at 7:30 a.m. Her heart leapt when she saw tall, serious and dignified Patrick, wearing a wide brim hat, a knee-length dark woolen coat, and tall boots with his pant legs tucked inside. He puffed on a corn-cob pipe and stared at her out of cool, watchful eyes. Eve thought him quite fetching, reminding her of a young Clint Eastwood in his old westerns.

They smiled cordially.

"Joseph offered you a room in his house if you are planning on staying the night."

"I don't plan to stay. I'm hoping this will be a quick trip, and I'll return on the evening train. But please thank him for me."

They purchased their tickets and waited quietly on the bustling platform until they heard the "ALL ABOARD" call from the stout, blue-uniformed conductor.

It was just after 8:00 a.m. when the steam locomotive hissed out of the station. Eve sat alone in the forward car, with Patrick seated two rows behind at a window seat. The view along the Hudson River was breathtaking, the rising hills lovely. She saw steamboat ports, a stately mansion with a grand view of the river, quaint villages, and white church spires.

She nodded off several times, finally drifting into a deep sleep, awakening, with a start, when Patrick gently touched her shoulder.

"We're coming into the station, Miss Kennedy."

Outside in the crisp air, Patrick found a taxi and helped her in. Patrick had been told about a boarding house that, for a small fee, would accommodate them for the day.

"Would you like to freshen up, Miss Kennedy, or drive straight to your destination?"

"I want to get this over with, so let's go see Miss Tannin and hope she has the information I came for."

Patrick opened the roof hatch and told the driver the address. Eve sat back, gazing out the window at Victorian style buildings with their turrets and wrought-iron balconies, at Queen Anne homes with dramatic gables, and at Greek revival government buildings looking imposing and formidable.

It took nearly a half hour to arrive at the address. They stopped and Eve peered out guardedly, grateful now that Patrick was with her.

It was an unprosperous neighborhood, with dreary-looking row houses and a cemetery with broken, gothic headstones, enclosed by a heavy, wrought-iron fence. Across the street was a vacant lot littered with an old upturned buggy, some broken wagon wheels, discarded trash and coal ash piles. In summer, the lot was surely a thicket of weeds and skittering rats. There was a rickety old wooden fence surrounding it all, and a weather-faded sign nailed to a fence post that said,

PRIVATE PROPERTY- KEEP OUT!

A black cat darted out from behind a barrel and stalked off into the lot, disappearing behind the buggy. Across the street was a luckless-looking Saloon called YELLOWSTONE, with a buggy and two horses tied to a hitching post. Next door was a snug and sooty three-story brick house with faded gray shutters and a warped porch with a staircase that needed repairs.

"That's the house, Miss Kennedy."

Eve's expression said it all: a rising anxiety filled her eyes. "It's pretty bleak-looking, isn't it?"

"That it is."

Eve looked at him. "Thank you for coming, Detective Gantly."

"From now on, please call me Mr. Gates. I use the name often as an alias."

"Should I have an alias?" Eve said nervously.

"I'll call you Miss Blakely."

Eve lifted an impressed eyebrow. "I like it."

"Shall we go, Miss Blakely?"

Eve nibbled on her lower lip. "Yes, Mr. Gates. Let's get this over with. The sooner the better."

She made a motion to the door, but Patrick stopped her with his voice. "Miss Kennedy... are you going to tell me what this is about? It might come in handy in there."

Eve looked down, and then up. "This is going to sound rather silly and frivolous to you, Mr. Gates, but here it is. I am seeking a lantern, and Miss Tannin knows where that lantern is."

He waited for more, and when she didn't offer more, he exhaled a breath. "Are you telling me that you have had me find this woman, then travel all this way, just to retrieve a lantern? A simple lantern? I don't understand."

"Detective Gant..." She stopped. "Mr. Gates, it is a very special lantern, I assure you, and I must have it."

He pulled his corn-cob pipe from his coat pocket and slipped it between his teeth. "All right then, Miss Ken... Miss Blakely, let us go and get your lantern. Shall we try the house first?"

"Yes... I don't like the looks of that saloon. As my grandfather used to say about most bars, it looks like the Devil's hideout."

"Well said, Miss Blakely."

Outside, Patrick instructed the driver to wait. The weather-worn man, with his rounded shoulders and dusty derby, nodded affably as he chewed on his cigar.

Eve climbed the steep wooden stairs to the house, her hand gripped tightly on the wobbly railing, with Patrick behind, keeping a sharp eye out for anything suspicious. He saw two men stroll by, but they were locked in conversation, passing below with no interest.

Eve balanced herself on the uneven porch, noticing that the dingy curtains were drawn and there was no light on inside.

Patrick stood tall behind her; his eyes half-hooded. "I don't feel good about this, Miss Blakely."

Eve swallowed back her trepidation and knocked on the paint-chipped door. When there was no response, she tried again. No one answered.

Eve turned to Patrick with an uneasy shrug. "Well it looks like it's on to the Devil's hideout."

"And all for a lantern, Miss Blakely?"

She nodded. "Yes, Mr. Gates. If there were any other way, believe me I would take it."

They gingerly descended the stairs and sauntered along a little dirt path, mounting a wooden walkway that led to the saloon's entrance. They traded uneasy glances as they approached the saloon's door.

"Miss Blakely, I'll enter first. You stay close behind."

Patrick wrapped his hand around the tarnished brown knob and nudged the door open. He stepped inside with Eve on his heels.

Patrick's eyes slowly adjusted to the dim light, and he instantly knew, from much experience, what kind of malevolent establishment this one was. Some bars were fun, with a kind of chummy energy and a feeling of spontaneous celebration. Some were simple watering holes for folks who needed a break from the daily slog, and then there were the bars for those who had lost their way, having been spirit-killed. The Yellowstone Saloon was one of those.

It was dim and smoky and smelled of old beer, sweat and cigars. The floor was covered with old, damp sawdust. The atmosphere reeked of despair.

Eve stood at the door, letting in light from the outside. Patrick told her to close it, and she did, with renewed reluctance.

The strangers instantly drew attention. A man seated at the bar on a wooden stool turned, revealing a slouching, slack-faced man with a sad mustache and dead eyes.

A short, fat man, with a pug hat, pug nose and damp face, sat next to him, sipping his pint of beer lazily, as if in slow motion. He stirred at the sight of Eve, an attractive woman in their midst, a rare delight.

An old, drunk-slurred woman, in a drab print dress and a tired, wrinkled face, grasped a bottle of beer and babbled something to the burly bartender, who had long since turned off the sounds hitting his big, arching ears.

Two quarrelsome men sat at a low, wooden table, hovering over flat beers. Their expressions and bowed shoulders suggested that they were well-practiced in the art of misery and gloom.

It was the man seated in the far corner of the room that drew Patrick's eyes. He sat alone; a deck of cards spread out before him. He was playing with a rubber band: twisting it. Knotting it. Springing it.

He was handsome, in a dangerous way, with a lean and sinister manner, slicked-back raven hair, heavy eyes and heavy dark brows. His ominous, twinkling-quick eyes expanded on the room, not missing a mouse's fidget. He had no whiskers, but was cleanly shaved, his chin sharp, his body looking taut and fit under a stylish dark suit, white shirt and burgundy tie.

His and Patrick's eyes met, and there was an immediate challenge. Patrick knew, from Joseph's description, that this was the infamous Warren Combs. Patrick did not want to confront Mr. Combs. He was certain he had a pistol and a knife. In the deep pocket of his coat, Patrick had his Police .32 caliber, with $3^{1/2}$-inch barrel. He would use it only in an emergency.

Eve glanced about fearfully. She'd never seen a place so forlorn and tattered.

Patrick ignored Mr. Combs and stepped over to the bar, with Eve just behind him on his right.

The beefy bartender wore a soiled white apron. He had no smile, no neck, and no spirit of good will on his very intimidating face. His burning eyes were aimed at Patrick, with a menacing threat. Patrick was taller than the bartender, but the man had the wide shoulders, broad chest, mashed nose and thick, muscular arms of a boxer.

Patrick looked somberly at the bartender. "This lady here is looking for a Miss Abagail Tannin. Would you have any knowledge of her whereabouts?"

The bartender's flat, gray-cold eyes looked at Patrick with immediate hatred.

"No, I don't."

"Have you ever heard of the lady?"

"No, I haven't."

"Do you think anyone else in the room would know of her?"

Out of the corner of Patrick's eye, he saw Warren Combs rise and start over.

Patrick continued. "I was told that she might be living next door in that brick house."

"And who would have told you that?" Warren said, elbowing his way to the bar, nudging away the little fat man and his half-drunk pint.

Patrick turned to Warren, who looked back at him with a toxic grin and frosty eyes. Patrick stood two inches taller than Warren, but Patrick swiftly sized him up, certain the man was cat-quick, a practiced street fighter, experienced in the art of the surprise attack.

"Good day, sir," Patrick said, genially, touching the brim of his wide hat. "Would you know where we might find Miss Abagail Tannin?"

Warren turned, leaning back, his elbows resting on the bar, his grin calculated to offend. "Is that your playgirl?" he asked, nodding toward Eve.

Patrick didn't take the belligerent bait. "Miss Blakely? Oh no, sir, she is the good daughter of our Reverend. We hail from the great state of Ohio, sir."

Warren tossed a disbelieving glance toward the bartender, who joined him in a crooked, nasty grin.

Warren's eyes lowered, and his baritone voice dropped an octave. "Go back to Ohio, Big Man, but leave the reverend's daughter behind. She'll be good for my business, in a variety of ways. She has the pretty looks for it, don't she?"

Again, Patrick didn't take the bait. He wanted to punch this man in the face, but the consequences wouldn't be worth it. Eve was too close, and Patrick was sure the bartender had ready access to a gun. And if Patrick managed to beat the man and the bartender in a fight, wherever Miss Tannin was, Warren would surely take out his rage on her.

Patrick kept his voice calm and measured as he turned to Eve. "Miss Blakely, would you kindly wait for me outside?"

Eve swallowed, lowered her head and left.

Warren called after her, in a taunting voice. "Please don't leave, Miss Blakely. I want to read the Bible with you. We can pray together, just you and me. Who knows, you may even save my black soul."

Most in the room chuckled as Eve left the room. Some didn't laugh, smelling a fight about to start.

Patrick grinned darkly at Warren, raising himself up to his full height. He lowered his voice into a gritty whisper, deciding to go for a bluff. "Miss Blakely's brother is a detective working for the Albany Police Department. I am certain he would not appreciate your humor, sir."

"Oh, Big Man, are you threatening me?" Warren asked, not the least bit shaken.

Patrick knew how to get him. This type was always impressed by violence and by money. Patrick leaned in toward Warren. "I'm sure you have paid off all the right people. I mean, a man of your status knows the good of it, don't you?"

Warren's grin was sardonic. "Right, Big Man. I pay off the right and the wrong, pal."

"Miss Blakely's brother is not a religious man, sir, like his father. He is a worldly and materialistic man, who loves his sister with all his heart. He doesn't know you or your lovely establishment. But rest easy, sir. I will be talking to him about you when I leave here. Believe me when I tell you that he has many good lads you have not yet had the privilege to meet. You understand me, don't you, sir?"

Warren's nasty smile fell.

Patrick's smile held a threat. "You know how we Irish are, sir? We know all the right people in all the low places. It helps us get ahead in life. And, as you must know, our lads are always ready to get into a good old donnybrook. I'm sure you can relate to that."

Warren pushed away from the bar, his eyes flashing with wrath. "Who are you?"

Patrick shoved a hand into his pocket, feeling for his gun. A side-glance revealed that the bartender was snaking a hand under the bar.

"Tell your bartender that if he reaches for his gun, I'll gut shoot you."

Warren's face drained of color and, for the first time, he showed fear. He gave a sharp shake of his head to the bartender, and the bartender froze, helpless, eyes watchful.

Patrick's voice was harsh and direct. "Just tell me where Miss Tannin is, and after we visit her, you will never see or hear from us again. I will have no need to trouble you further, nor mention your rude insults to Miss Blakely's brother and his Irish lads."

Warren's lips tightened. Every facial feature was in conflict.

"Where is she, Mr. Warren Combs? Where is Miss Tannin?"

It was the first time Patrick had spoken Warren Combs' name. It startled him. He flinched and cursed.

CHAPTER 44

Patrick stood with Warren on the street below, while Eve ascended the stairs to the front door of the red brick house. Warren fidgeted tensely, his eyes smoldering. He glanced up at the house to see Eve knock on the door three times.

"Miss Tannin didn't answer the door the last time we knocked," Patrick said, his eyes burning into Warren, who'd lost most of his fight.

"She's there. I told her not to let anyone in. I just waved at her. She'll open the door."

Eve knocked once more before the door swung partially open, and a pale, frightened face peered out of the three-inch space, eyes squinting into the sudden light.

"Miss Abagail Tannin?" Eve asked. "Your friend, Warren Combs, said I could talk to you."

Her voice was tentative. "Talk to me about what?"

"May I come in, Miss Tannin? I won't stay long, I promise."

"No... He doesn't want anyone to come in here."

Eve turned, pointing down to the two men. "He said it's okay. He said you can let me in."

Abagail coughed, a deep, hacking cough that was startling. "Are you ill?"

"I am fine," she said, a hand covering her mouth as she barked out a series of agonizing coughs.

"You *are* ill," Eve said with concern.

Abagail struggled to recover. "I'm fine... What do you want?"

"Please, will you let me in? I'll only be a moment."

The door opened just wide enough to allow Eve to turn sideways and enter. When the door was closed behind her, Eve's eyes slowly adjusted to the shadowy room. It was a gloomy place, with shabby furniture and the smell of sickness.

Abagail wore a long, gray gown that was much too large for her. Her lovely long, reddish/auburn hair was piled on her head in a tangle, her face was ashen, her eyes bloodshot and vague.

Abagail turned her face aside, as if to hide it, but Eve had seen something that alarmed her. She reached, gently lifting the girl's chin to see a yellow/purple bruise clearly visible around her left eye.

Abagail jerked her face away. "Don't do that. Don't you touch me."

"Has he struck you?"

"It don't mean anything. He loves me. He has a lot on his mind, like most men."

Abagail fell into another deep-throated cough, bending over, her entire body in spasm.

"How long have you had that cough?"

"That's none of your business. What do you want? Why are you here?"

"Miss Tannin, you are sick. Perhaps very sick. Have you seen a doctor?"

"I don't need a doctor. What do you want?"

Eve gave a little shake of her head. It had been a trying, emotional day, and it wasn't getting any better.

"Miss Tannin, why don't you return home to New York with us?"

Abagail took a step back, scowling. "Did my mother send you here? Is that why you're here?"

"No, she didn't."

"You're lying."

"I'm not."

Abagail's hand flew to her mouth again, as the racking cough took her over. She staggered, coughing up phlegm. Eve moved toward her, but Abagail stopped her with an outstretched arm.

"Don't touch me."

Abagail stumbled over to the tattered, frayed couch and dropped, teetering over sideways, her face pinched in pain.

Eve went to her, reached and tugged an old woolen blanket over the sick girl, who was too ill to complain.

"Miss Tannin, can I please take you to see a doctor? Is there a hospital nearby? You are suffering."

Abagail's feeble body lacked the strength for resistance. She looked up at Eve, her gaze flat and cloudy. "He doesn't want me to be sick."

"I don't give a damn what he wants. We need to call a doctor. Do you know of one?"

"Mr. Combs doesn't like doctors."

"Okay, fine, then I'm going to help you dress and take you to a hospital."

Abagail's eyes swelled with terror. "No, no. He'll leave me if you do that."

Eve fought her rising temper. "Fine. Good. Let him leave you. When you're healthy, I'll return and take you back to New York."

The fight in Abagail returned. "I'm not going back there. Never. I'm never going back to mother. Never!"

Eve heaved out an exasperated sigh and lowered her voice. "All right, Miss Tannin. All right. Just lay quiet."

Abagail's eyes shuddered as exhaustion took over, and Eve felt compassion and a helpless despair in the bleak moment. How did this young girl let herself get trapped like this, without having any sense of self-protection or self-worth; without the innate awareness and strength to fight for her dignity?

Eve had seen the same behavior in the 21st century, in clinics and hospitals; that perverted desire in a woman to give herself over entirely to some low-life son of a bitch like Warren Combs.

Eve kneeled beside the couch and laid a soft hand on Abagail's forehead. It was burning, her face damp with sweat. Eve scanned the area and spotted a green bottle on a side table. She arose and went over, picked it up and examined it in the light. It was cough syrup; the ingredients were alcohol, chloroform and cocaine. Frowning, Eve replaced the bottle and returned to the couch, where Abagail lay breathing with difficulty, a wheezing sound coming from her lungs. Eve kneeled again.

"Miss Tannin, will you please let me take you to a hospital?"

Abagail twisted up her lips in aversion, her eyes twitching. "No hospital. Can't go there. He'll leave me. Mr. Combs will leave me."

Eve considered her options. She could ask Patrick to come in, gather the woman up and carry her out to the taxi. Surely, a hospital wasn't far. But then what? If Mr. Combs abandoned her, what would she do? After recovering, she would no doubt run back to him, begging for another chance.

And it was certainly possible that Abagail could die in the hospital from what was surely pneumonia. Although she was young and probably strong, who knew what physical and mental traumas she'd undergone from Warren Combs' abuse? Abagail was a grown woman, if a very sick one. Wasn't she old enough to make her own decisions?

Conflicted, Eve reached into the side of her dress where she'd instructed the seamstress to sew a hidden pocket. She released two buttons and took out a small velvet bag with a tie string that held her only course of antibiotics, six pink Zithromax Z-Pak tablets.

Would Abagail survive? And, if so, what would she do with her life? That was not up to Eve. Eve's job was to try to keep her alive.

Each pink pill was 250mg. Eve needed a loading dose of 500mg in Abagail's system immediately, and then one 250mg pill for the next four days.

There was a half-drunk glass of water on the floor nearby, and Eve reached for it. Whispering, Eve stroked Abagail's damp hair.

"Miss Tannin, please open your eyes and look at me."

Slowly, and with difficulty, her eyes flickered open.

"Miss Tannin, I'm a nurse. I have six pills," she said, holding them up for Abagail to see. "You're going to take two now and then one for the next four days. Do you understand?"

"You're a nurse?" Abagail said weakly.

"Yes. Now here are two pills. Swallow them down with water."

Eve helped Abagail to sit up. She swallowed the pills one at a time, with some difficulty. Eve repeated the instructions, handing Abagail the velvet pouch that contained the four remaining pills.

"Promise me you'll take them," Eve said.

Abagail nodded, sniffing back tears. "I don't want to die."

"You're not going to die, Abagail," Eve said pointedly, using the woman's first name for impact. "If you take those pills, you will live. Remember, take one pill each day for the next four days."

Abagail took the velvet bag, staring at it with interest. "Is this why you came to see me? To give me these pills?"

"No. I came to ask you an important question. It may not seem all that important to you, but it is very important to me. Now, think very hard. Do you recall a man named Moses Poe?"

Abagail's crystal mint eyes held recognition and mischief. She grinned, a little secret grin. "Yes, Mr. Poe, the blacksmith?"

"Yes, that's right. Do you remember the night you dropped by to see him, not long before you left town?"

"Yes, of course. While I was there at his shop, he shoed my horse, and then he trimmed and balanced Pepper's hooves."

"It was raining that night, wasn't it?"

"Yes, it was raining."

"Did Mr. Poe give you a lantern?"

Abagail coughed deeply, snatched a hanky from the pocket of her gown. She nodded. "Yes. He gave me a lantern for the buggy. It was dark."

Eve grew hopeful. "Miss Tannin, when you arrived home, what did you do with the lantern?"

"Do with it?"

"Yes. Where did you put it? Where is it now?"

Abagail's face sagged with a new fatigue, her eyes dull and staring. "I was dizzy."

"Dizzy? What do you mean? When were you dizzy?" Eve asked.

"I don't know… When I got home, I felt dizzy and strange."

"Where was the lantern? Was it hanging near you?"

"Mr. Poe attached it to a nail near the seat. The light made me feel a little drunk and sleepy. I blew the lantern out before I got home, because I thought I was going to faint."

Eve leaned in. "Where did you put the lantern, Miss Tannin?"

"I unhooked it and took it to the toolshed where Henry Hancock keeps his tools. He likes me, and he gave me a key to the lock. I put things in there I don't want my mother to find. If she saw me with the lantern, she'd ask me where I got it."

"Who is Henry Hancock? What does he do?"

"He's the handyman for my mother's boardinghouse. He works for other businesses around the neighborhood as well."

Eve breathed in, feeling her heart thumping high in her chest. Would it still be there, or would Mr. Hancock have taken it to who knows where?

"Why do you want the lantern?" Abagail asked.

Eve's eyes slid away. "I need it to get back home."

"I don't understand…"

Eve stood up and brushed off her dress. "Miss Tannin, don't forget to take those pills."

"I won't. I'll take them. What is your name?"

"Evelyn Kennedy. Please take care of yourself."

At the front door, Eve turned once more to the young woman, who had flounced back down on the couch, her eyes closed, her breathing heavy. Eve whispered a silent prayer for Abagail's health and happiness. There was something about the girl that had touched Eve. She was so pretty, and so girlish, and so very lost.

CHAPTER 45

In the cab, returning to the train station, Eve was silent, and Patrick didn't press her for information. Finally, as they arrived, Eve broke the silence.

"I'm sorry you didn't get the time to see your friend Joseph."

"He'll understand."

"Will you thank him for me?"

"Yes, I will."

While they waited for their train, they stopped for an early dinner at a nearby café, a pleasant place, filled mostly with travelers.

As they were eating dessert, thick pieces of warm apple pie, Eve finally shared the details of her encounter with Abagail. She didn't mention the antibiotics but said, instead, that she'd given Abagail some miracle pills she hoped would help. Eve tried not to sound too depressed while she mentioned the bruise on Abagail's face.

"I'm sure there were more on her body," Eve said. "In my experience with men like Warren Combs, where there's one, there are always more."

Patrick had listened passively, although Eve saw a rising sadness in his eyes.

On the train back to New York, Patrick sat next to Eve, his arms folded, his hat pulled low over his forehead, his head bobbing forward as he napped. Eve was glad he had decided to sit next to her. It felt familiar and intimate. It felt right.

Eve stared out the window into darkness, feeling the gentle sway of the train, hearing the haunting moan of the whistle. She longed to erase the tawdry images of the day: the ugly, hellish Yellowstone Saloon, and the shabby rooms where Abagail lay bruised and sick, her thin body covered by a skimpy, damp woolen blanket

When the train came to a whistle stop to load passengers, Patrick awoke, glancing about. "Where are we?"

"Some small town," Eve said. "This is a local train. Did you have a good nap?"

He sat up and stretched. "Yes. Lately, I find that catnaps are the best. Did you nap, Miss Kennedy?"

"No... I keep seeing images of the poor girl lying there. I wish I could have done more for her. I should have insisted that she go to the hospital. I should have had you come and get her."

"That could have provoked a very ugly fight. Mr. Combs had friends in that saloon, and they were watching; just aching to come for me. I doubt we could have succeeded in stealing Miss Tannin out of that house and getting away with it."

Eve watched passengers embark and find seats. Patrick reached for his unlit corncob pipe and bit down on it.

"That girl needed help," Eve said, not able to let it go. "And I'm afraid she's not going to get it."

Patrick looked at her pointedly. "Are you out to save the world, Miss Kennedy?"

Eve turned her attention outside, watching a conductor wave a lighted lantern back and forth, signaling the engineer. The train lurched forward, hissed and gathered speed.

Patrick continued. "If you try to save the world, you will become very disappointed. The world has its own play, both tragic and comic. Sometimes it's best to let people be as they are, and trust that they'll find their own way."

"That's very philosophical for a New York City detective, isn't it? Is that what you and fellow detectives discuss when you're on a stake-out?"

Patrick grinned. "Oh my, no, Miss Kennedy. They'd club me on my hard head and bundle me off to Ward's Island Insane Asylum. These are my private thoughts."

He stared into the soft blue of her eyes, and for a brief time he was lost there, allowing himself the fantasy of taking her into his arms and kissing her. Eve did not avert her eyes. She wanted to pull him into her, to explore his mouth with her tongue and lips.

A moment later, it was he who averted his eyes, slightly embarrassed by his boldness. Eve was warmed by his obvious desire, and when he angled his body away from her, she smiled inwardly.

"Detective Gantly, when you're letting people be as they are, do you include criminals, thieves, murderers and con men? Do you just leave them the way they are and hope they will find their way back to being good, peaceful and moral citizens?"

Patrick pulled the pipe from his mouth and grinned. "I'm afraid you have me there, Miss Kennedy. I suppose, having seen much of the bad side of life, part of me holds fast to the hope that, like on a stormy day, life can suddenly turn sunny. Sometimes a lost soul can turn about and become surprisingly decent. I have seen devils in preachers, and angels in streetwalkers."

Patrick turned reflective. "Emma used to say I was a 'daft man, with too much of the Irish blarney in me.'"

Eve softened, feeling awkward and a little jealous. "And I'm sure she loved you for it."

He paused, feeling the back of his throat tighten. "I confess, Miss Kennedy, that during our short marriage, there were times when my wife was not a happy woman."

Eve stared down at her lap, but she was gently startled by his confession.

"Emma did not like New York, with its noise, tenements, filth and low characters. She missed England and her childhood friends. She missed the green, rolling hills, the scattered meadows and the refined manners. She told me several times that she wanted to return. But how could I return? My life and my work are in New York."

He lowered his voice in an apologetic tone. "I was away from home much of the time, as is the nature of my work. And detective work is hard and black, filled with the low and the corrupt. It made me a brooding man, and a man who locked himself up inside. Emma was a lonely, sad woman in ways I didn't see, until it was too late."

Patrick pushed his hat up off his forehead. "Forgive my ramblings, Miss Kennedy. I suppose that old adage is true: you'll talk to a perfect stranger, but you won't bare your soul to a good and trusted friend. Anyway, these last few weeks have turned me into a man who thinks too much."

Eve looked at him, seeing his furrowed brow and gloomy, distant eyes. "We are not strangers, Detective Gantly."

He didn't acknowledge her words. "So, what I'm saying is that sometimes life has to deal a blow before one wakes up to see the true man or woman standing before the mirror. I'll wager that Miss Tannin will wake up someday and see the folly of her ways. Let us hope that it will not be too late for her."

Eve could feel love for Patrick blossom in her chest, and she wanted to kiss him. Instead, she folded her hands in her lap and watched a kid in the aisle ahead, bouncing and making pretend worlds with his hands; his frantic little face animated; his busy little bottom strutting; his arms raised as if wanting to fly.

"How old do you think he is?" Patrick asked.

"Three. Maybe four."

"So *are* you out to save the world, Miss Kennedy? You never said one way or the other."

Eve watched the playful child. "I'll save as much of it as I can, one person at a time. That's one reason I went into nursing. I wanted to help. I wanted to heal. I've seen people's lives changed in an hour—in a day—by a doctor's skill or by a nurse's patience, ability and compassion. Maybe all that sounds idealistic or naïve to you, but there it is. I love what I do and, to answer your question, yes, I want to save the world. Why not?"

Patrick looked at her with new admiration. "I do not believe it is idealistic, Miss Kennedy. As my old Da used to say, 'No one ever becomes poor in heart who gives freely to the sick and to the needy.'"

After a few minutes, Patrick turned to Eve. "You never said if you learned the location of your lantern."

"Yes, I believe I did. I'll know for sure when we arrive back in the City."

"And will this lantern help you save the world?"

"I don't know. Perhaps."

They both grew silent and dozed off. Eve awakened some time later, lost in thought. The train went thundering across the quiet countryside, the horn blaring, the chimney belching clouds of black smoke.

She was dreading their arrival in New York. After they parted, how could she arrange to see Patrick again?

CHAPTER 46

Eve awoke early the next morning to see that Joni was already sitting up in bed, leafing through a catalog.

"Good morning. Can you look at this and tell me if I should order one?"

"One what?"

"A corset."

Joni tossed back the white quilt and, catalog in hand, crossed to Eve's bed and plopped down on the edge, holding the page up for Eve to see. What do you think? I think the style is fascinating and fun. And this one will tuck in my tummy even more."

Eve wiped her sleepy, sticky eyes and focused.

WHY ARE

THE MADAME MORA'S CORSETS

A MARVEL OF COMFORT AND ELEGANCE?

Try them and you will find out!

WHY they **need no breaking in but** feel easy at once.

WHY they are liked by Ladies of **full figure**.

WHY they do **not break down over the hips,** and

WHY the celebrated **French curved band** prevents wrinkling or stretching at the sides.

WHY dressmakers delight in fitting dresses over them.

WHY merchants say they give better satisfaction than any others.

WHY they take pains to recommend them.

Eve shook her head. "You and your corsets. The woman who hated corsets and said she'd never wear one—now is completely obsessed."

Suddenly, Eve was distracted by the sketch of the woman modeling the corset. "Hey, doesn't that woman in the ad look like she's staring into a cellphone? That's weird."

Joni shook her head, pointing. "She's looking at her nails. You're seeing things. Anyway, corsets aren't so bad once you get used to them, and they definitely tighten my stomach. And I think Madam Mora is like the *Victoria Secret* of her day. So what do you think?"

Eve sat up, finger-combing her hair. "Go for it. What the heck, buy one for me, too."

Eve handed the catalog back to Joni. Engrossed in the pages, Joni returned to her bed, flopped down, braced her back against the headboard and pulled up the sheets. She distractedly thumbed through the catalog.

"Do you want me to come with you to get the lantern?"

Eve swung her feet out of bed and put a hand to a yawn. "No. The fewer people the better. If it hadn't been for that old barking dog, I would have found a way to get into that shed last night. I was so close."

"You should have asked Patrick to go with you."

"No way. He's already done enough. Anyway, we parted awkwardly. He didn't know what to say, and neither did I."

Eve blew out a sigh as she stretched. "Joni, yesterday was one of the weirdest days of my life, and let me tell you, I have had some weird days in the last few years."

Joni looked up over the catalog. "What happens if the lantern isn't there?"

Eve stood up. "It will be there. It's got to be there. I just have to find a way to stay clear of that witch of a woman, Abagail's mother. I wouldn't put it past her to call the police on me. Okay, I've got to get going."

At a little after 8 a.m., Eve crept along the sidewalk toward Mrs. Tannin's boarding house, anxiety rising in her throat. The area seemed quiet, with light street traffic, and as she approached the house, she noticed the white lace parlor curtains were drawn. The overcast silver sky threatened rain, and Eve gently swung a black umbrella, hoping to appear relaxed and carefree. In the corner park, two boys chased a puppy around the bronze statue of some historical, proud and austere politician.

Eve edged ahead, strolling beyond the house and then cutting back through a side path that led down to a creek. From there, she could see the shed. She was hoping she'd soon see the handyman, Henry Hancock, as well.

She brightened when she saw that the shed door was open. Continuing on under a large oak, skirting a pile of lumber and broken bricks, Eve approached the shed, throwing darting glances, hoping to see Mr. Hancock before she saw Mrs. Tannin. She neither saw nor heard anything, except the gurgling creek and a violin lilting out a waltz from a house nearby.

Eve's expression was tense as she stalked forward, only 20 feet from the narrow, six-foot tall, gray shed, with its peaked tile roof and rusty hinged doors. She saw the heavy padlock, its shackle in the hinge loop. Was Henry inside? Eve strained her ears but heard nothing.

It was now or never. She straightened her shoulders, pulled a breath and started forward, just as the violin broke into a bouncy tune, perfect for an Irish jig.

At the entrance, she stopped short, shading her eyes with her hand, peering into the shadowy interior. Advancing, she saw four shelves immediately in front and three shelves to her left. They held tools, wire, boxes of nails and screws. Her eyes traveled up and down, scanning and searching.

A male voice jolted her erect, and she made a little scream of fear.

"What are you doing?" the scratchy male voice asked.

Eve pivoted, heart jumping. She saw a thin man, about 50 years old, wearing a sweat-stained, striped denim train cap, blue overalls, and round frameless glasses. His glowering, bold eyes narrowed on her with suspicion.

"You scared me," Eve said, a hand over her heart, catching her breath.

"Well what are you doing nosing around my shed? I don't let nobody near my shed. This here's private property, young lady. And anyway, what is the like of you doing in a man's tool shed?"

Eve's mind went to work. "Sir, please forgive me. I looked around for somebody and when I didn't see anyone, I came over."

Henry was a nervous, jittery man, with a pockmarked face and a line of a mouth that didn't seem inclined to smile. "Well, what do you want?"

Eve decided to come out with it. The last thing she needed was for Henry to call Mrs. Tannin.

"Well, sir, I am looking for a lost lantern."

"A lantern?"

"Yes. A lantern. Is there a lantern in your shed? I can describe it in detail."

He was holding a hammer in his right hand. Naturally, Eve's eyes went to it.

"Now what would your lantern be doing in my toolshed?"

Eve was distracted by screeching birds overhead. She glanced up to see sparrows dropping out of trees and circling the area. The violin, now accompanied by a piano, played another jumpy tune. In that moment, Eve decided to go for broke.

"May I ask your name, sir?"

"You may, but that does not mean I am going to tell you," he responded defiantly. "Now, tell me, young lady, what your lantern would be doing in my toolshed?"

Eve fortified her courage with a breath. She glanced up at the boardinghouse, her expression turning from victim to aggressor. "I was told that your name is Mr. Henry Hancock."

"And who would have told you that?"

Eve threw a pointing finger toward the house. "Miss Abagail Tannin. She said she has the lantern. She took it from me, and now I want it back. She said she put it in your toolshed. You know how she is. She is a wild and rebellious young woman, and she took my lantern."

Mr. Hancock scratched his cheek. "Why didn't you ask Mrs. Tannin for it instead of coming out here to look in my shed? This is my own personal property and I do not like strangers poking around."

"Would you please look in your shed for the lantern, Mr. Hancock? I would be extremely grateful."

Mr. Hancock grew even more petulant. "All right then. Step away from that door and let me look inside. For crying out loud, I don't remember seeing any lantern in there and Miss Abagail Tannin hasn't been around for days now."

Eve stepped away, praying that the lantern was inside. Henry Hancock walked with a mild limp, and he observed that Eve noticed. "I got this old limp in the war, at the Battle of the Wilderness. A Johnny Reb shot me, and I shot him. He died and I lived, and we won the war. So let there be no more story about it."

Henry struck a match and lit an oil lamp hanging inside. Eve calmed her breathing as she listened to Mr. Hancock mumble out annoyance.

Just then Eve heard Mrs. Tannin's snide voice, and Eve turned to ice. She whirled about to see the woman standing only ten feet away, holding the lantern chest high, her face an ugly picture of smug triumph.

"Mr. Hancock will not find the lantern in there. I have a key to that old, smelly shed. I found the lantern early this morning after I finally realized where it must be. I thought you'd come looking for it."

Mrs. Tannin called out. "Mr. Hancock. Come out!"

He emerged, squinting into the weak sun that had broken through thin, gray clouds. He saw Mrs. Tannin, and he saw the lantern. "You see, young lady?" he said, gruffly. "You should have gone to see Mrs. Tannin. You're wasting my time."

With that, he grabbed a wooden toolbox and trudged off toward the house.

Eve and Mrs. Tannin faced off, the hostile air circling them.

"I do not trust you, young woman," Miss Tannin said, biting off her words.

Eve held out her hand. "May I please have the lantern?"

"No, you may not, because it does not belong to you."

Eve lowered her hand, clenching her fists. She was weary of this woman, and weary of trying to get her hands on that lantern. "As I said before, Mrs. Tannin, I will pay you handsomely for the lantern. How much do you want for it?"

"I'll tell you what I want for it. I know that you have seen my daughter. I want to know how you found her and why you left her."

Eve felt a bewildering chill shoot up her spine. How did this woman know? Did Abagail send her a telegram? Eve considered her next words carefully.

"And if that were true, how do you know it?" Eve said, worried that perhaps something had happened to Abagail.

"I know it, that's all you need to know about it."

Eve feared the moment. She lowered her voice. "Is Abagail all right?"

To Eve's utter astonishment, she watched as Mrs. Tannin's face slowly fell apart. The lantern dropped from her hand. It bounced once, then toppled over in the low, thinning grass. The woman began to cry, pumping out tears, her hands covering her face, her body a spasm of anguish.

On impulse, Eve hurried toward her, but just as she arrived, Miss Tannin threw up both hands to stop her.

She screamed, "Don't you touch me!"

Eve stared at the woman, trying to understand. Mrs. Tannin's face was an angry storm; her eyes wild with agony. She wiped her wet face with a hanky, struggling to recover, her entire body trembling.

When she spoke, her voice cracked with emotion. "She is dead. Do you hear me? My daughter is dead."

Eve couldn't take it in. She'd only left Abagail yesterday afternoon. Eve tried to speak, but Mrs. Tannin cut her off in a low, accusing tone.

"She was beaten to death. She was beaten to death by that animal and you could have stopped it. You were there! Detective Moran said you were there with your detective gentleman friend. My dear loving daughter told the detective your name, Evelyn Kennedy, only minutes before she died."

Eve staggered backward, hand on her hot forehead. "Detective?"

Mrs. Tannin jerked a telegram from her apron pocket and held it up, shaking it. "Would you like to read the three telegrams sent by Detective Joseph Moran of the Albany Police Department, delivered last night and this morning? Yes, your name is in there, Evelyn Kennedy!"

Eve's eyes lit up with alarm. Patrick's detective friend, Joseph? But how? So fast? Eve felt the rise of nausea.

"He must have thought we knew each other, Miss Kennedy, because he mentioned you. He said he'd been the one to give your detective friend Abagail's true address, an address I was not even aware of."

Eve fought the urge to vomit, as the horrible realization struck. It must have happened just after she and Patrick left. Warren Combs must have charged into the house and taken out his rage and humiliation on Abagail, beating her to death, as she lay sick and bruised.

Eve's body sagged as her mind throbbed with rage, guilt and hopelessness. What could she possibly say to this woman? She should have taken Abagail out of that house and to a hospital. Why didn't she? Why had she walked away like that? How would she ever forgive herself?

Mrs. Tannin fell back into tears, her eyes searching sky, wind and moving trees for help. Eve crept toward her, but Mrs. Tannin turned away, her head held high, revealing her tight, severe hair and perfectly arranged bun. But the woman was broken, and Eve knew it.

Eve waited, unable to move, wanting to help, wanting to say the right words, but she knew there were no words, and there was absolutely nothing she could say or do. This time—this time of 1884—was a low time, a punishing time, a bare-knuckle and ugly time and Eve wanted to run from this place.

Finally, in the painful space between them, Mrs. Tannin turned, her burning eyes staring at the lantern and then up at Eve.

"Take that cursed thing. Take it, and take yourself away from me."

With a hanky balled in her hand, Mrs. Tannin meandered off in no clear direction, as heavy clouds lowered, and a light rain began to fall.

There it lay in the grass, still and seemingly innocent, Tesla's "message in a bottle." Eve wanted to grab the thing and smash it to bits, but isn't that how she got here in the first place? Destroying one of Tesla's lanterns?

Eve hovered over it for a time, as rain tapped her elaborate hat and the shoulders of her long, tapered winter coat. No, she wouldn't destroy it. She would snatch it up and use it one more time to escape, to return to her own time, to her own reality and to her own life.

CHAPTER 47

When Eve returned from Emma Tannin's boarding house, her black umbrella open, the lantern conspicuous in her other hand, Patrick was standing by the hotel entrance, looking distant and grave. He wore a long coat, boots and bowler hat, the brim turned down against the misty rain.

Eve drew up to him and stopped, her eyes detached.

Patrick said, "And so I see that you have found your lantern. I can also see by your expression that you have heard the news about Miss Tannin."

Eve stayed silent.

"Do not reproach yourself. You had nothing to do with what happened to Miss Tannin. Warren Combs was the culprit, and he is in custody and he will be hanged for his crime."

Eve tipped back the umbrella to show him her face. "I could have taken her away from there."

"We would have been stopped, and in a violent way. And, anyway, sooner or later, the shrewd and evil Mr.

Combs would have found her, and he would have killed her."

Eve felt low and mean, her eyes flaming. "Detective Gantly, if I had not traveled to Albany, looking for this…" She nearly spit the word out, "… *lantern*, Mr. Combs would have had no reason to beat her to death. He wouldn't have been angry and humiliated. So tell me again, Detective Gantly, how the world has its own play, both tragic and comic? Is it best to let people be as they are, and trust that they'll find their own way? Isn't that what you said on the train coming home last night?"

Patrick shoved his hands into his coat pockets, rain beading up on his hat and shoulders. He narrowed his eyes on her. "Miss Tannin doomed herself when she took up with Warren Combs, and when she wouldn't leave him. Those were her choices. Not yours."

"Miss Tannin will not have the choice to find her own way now, will she, Detective Gantly?"

"You are suffering. Give yourself some time. Time heals many things."

"Time is fickle, and time is often an enemy," Eve said harshly. "I have a lot of experience with the volatile alteration of time and what it can do to people."

Patrick stared directly into her anguished face. "I do not know the meaning of what you just said, but I can tell you that a day, a month and a year are both long and short. As we have just witnessed, much can happen in just twenty-four hours."

Eve looked down and away. "I'm going to be leaving town," she said flatly.

Patrick withdrew his hands from his pockets, eyeing her carefully. "Well then, may I say that it has been a pleasure knowing you, Miss Kennedy? If I may be so bold…"

She interrupted. "… Yes, please be bold. I think this is the time to be honest and bold."

Patrick looked at her frankly. "I have observed you to be a mysterious shadow, as if you are seeking the light of your true self. You fill a busy space and you seem to move and grope after some elusive thing. In short, Miss Kennedy, I cannot find you. You seem both out of place and out of time. You seem like a woman who is trying to fit in where you can never fit in. I have rationalized this by the fact that you come from a small town, but I am not even sure of that. You do not seem like a woman from any small town. You seem to be a wanderer who has lost her way."

There was an intimate pause as Eve pursued that thought. "So you are perceptive, aren't you, Detective? Is that what police work has given you?"

Patrick ignored the question. "When will you leave, then?"

"Maybe tomorrow. Maybe the next day. I'm not sure."

"Will your friend, Miss Kosarin, go with you?"

"I don't know. I really don't know."

Eve folded her umbrella and made a move toward the door. Patrick stepped aside, opening the door for her. Before entering, she glanced at him.

"Detective Gantly, may I be bold?"

"I suspect you will always be bold, Miss Kennedy."

In that brief moment, she was naked and unguarded in her loving glance. She loved him with her eyes, and she loved him with her body, and with her heart and her soul. "I don't have the strength to pretend any longer.

Please don't give your daughter away for adoption. Find another wife and raise her together. You won't regret it."

Eve cleared her throat, opened her mouth, but was silent for a few seconds. "I will miss you. I will miss you like crazy, Patrick. I love you and I will always love you in whatever time I'm in... Goodbye."

She left him there, blinking, stunned and haunted by her declaration. He stared strangely, unable to move from the door.

In the elevator, climbing to the third floor, tears streamed down Eve's cheeks. When the doors parted, there he was, the towering Nikola Tesla, dressed immaculately in a dark suit, crisp white shirt and bow tie, hair gleaming, parted to perfection.

Both were startled. Tesla offered a little bow.

"A good morning to you, Miss Kennedy."

And then he saw the lantern and his eyes brightened. "So you have found it. You have found my last message in a bottle?"

Eve stepped out of the elevator and onto the royal blue carpeted hallway. She tilted her head back and looked up at him.

"Yes, Mr. Tesla, I found it. Do you know something? I hope you don't make any more of these. I think that would be wrong."

"Wrong?" Tesla said, not comprehending. "What does it mean here, when you say wrong?"

"It means, this lantern and others like it have really screwed up my life. Do you know what screwed up means?"

He thought about it. "You are unhappy, Miss Kennedy, as I see tears in your eyes. My apologies if my little time experiment makes you unhappy."

"Unhappy? You have no idea."

"You will return to your time now?"

Eve stood limply, staring at the rosebud wallpaper. "Yes, Mr. Tesla, I will return to my own time and to my own life. But everything has been changed, and it will never be the same again."

"No, and that is the way of life, is it not?" Tesla said. "Always changing. If there is no change, I fear there is no understanding and growth."

Eve turned from him, irritated at his pontifications.

"Do you plan to leave the lantern with me, Miss Kennedy?"

"No, Mr. Tesla," Eve said with vigor. "I will not leave the lantern with you. You'll just send it off again to who-knows-where."

He frowned. "I think, Miss Kennedy, that you are not so much of a scientist. You have fears that stop you from exploring all the worlds, both seen and unseen."

"Are you afraid of dying, Mr. Tesla?"

He was not startled by her question. He laughed, a kind of jerky laugh that suggested real amusement. "Afraid of dying? Never. In the future, I have seen my death, and I have seen the place of my funeral. No, Miss Kennedy, death is just, as you might say, another good journey, another experiment for me."

He bowed, abruptly, his smile gone. "I must leave you now for my laboratory. I have much of the working and things waiting for me. A good day to you, Miss Kennedy. I wish you a pleasant and happy journey back to your home."

CHAPTER 48

Eve entered her hotel room to find Joni seated in a chair, perusing yet another catalogue, her legs crossed, a blue velvet shoe dangling from her right foot as if it might fall at any moment. Eve closed the door and Joni glanced up.

"Hey there. I'm looking at these silk bloomers. They are sexier than the stuff we have in the 21st century. They have layered ruffles, lace trim and cute little blue ribbons."

Joni saw Eve's sad, fatigued face, and then noticed the lantern hanging from Eve's hand. Joni sat up, flinging the catalogue onto her bed.

"Oh my God, you found it!"

Joni shot up and hurried over, stopping when she saw the tears glistening in Eve's eyes.

"What's wrong? What happened?"

Eve dropped the wet umbrella. "I'm leaving. I'm getting the hell away from this time and place."

Joni stepped back. "Eve... tell me what's going on."

"Not now. Now, I'm going to sleep. God, how I wish I had some Ambien so I could sleep for twenty-four hours."

Eve walked past Joni, placed the lantern on the parlor table and pulled off her damp hat. She tossed it onto the couch and went to work unbuttoning her dress.

"Help me out of this thing. I'm sweaty, cold and tired."

Joni did so, and they didn't speak until Eve, now wearing only pantaloons and a camisole, wilted into bed and crawled under the covers.

Joni stood with her hands on her hips, staring at her friend. "So, what's the story, Eve?"

"I'm leaving. Tomorrow. Are you coming with me?"

Joni studied her nails. They were a polished mother-of-pearl and perfectly manicured, thanks to her recent visit to a hair salon only a block away. She shifted her weight from her left foot to her right.

"Okay, Eve, you have to tell me what happened."

Eve shut her eyes and gave Joni a condensed description of everything that had occurred, concluding with her declaration of love to Patrick and her encounter with Tesla.

While Eve talked, Joni lowered herself onto the chair, not pulling her eyes from Eve, who lay still, her voice often taking on emotion.

The room was quiet. Outside they heard the clop of horses' hooves as cabs and carriages drifted by below.

"Eve… You won't leave Patrick. I know you. How can you?"

"I can, and I will. I can't take it anymore, and I want to be home for Christmas. You don't understand. He's the same, and yet he's not the same. I know he's still

346

grieving. I mean, Emma only died a little over a month ago. It's just too painful to see him, or not to see him. And what if he finds another woman? Which he will, because he is smart, sexy, brooding and handsome. I've seen the way women look at him. He'll find another wife, just like that, and then I'll be devastated. I can't take it. I remember how it was with us. I remember our love and how perfect it was. I remember everything, but he doesn't remember anything, because to him it never happened. No, it's better to get out of here now and get back to my own time and my own life. I've got to begin again. I've got to start my own life again. And anyway, I don't like this time. I miss home."

Joni pushed up, standing firmly. "Well, I *do* like it."

Eve stared. "You like it?"

"Yes, and Darius has asked me to stay with him."

"What do you mean, stay with him?"

"He doesn't want me to go back to Ohio."

"You have never lived in Ohio."

"I know that, but he doesn't. Now before you get all crazy and judgmental, I'm just going to come out and say it: Darius has offered to put me up in a new and gorgeous brownstone and take care of me."

Eve's face flushed scarlet. "Take care of you? Joni, this is just what I warned you about."

Joni's expression took on conviction. "Yeah, so tell me something I don't know. Just because it's not right for you, doesn't mean it's not right for me."

"Do you hear yourself?"

"Yes. And I have more courage than you because I'm willing to do whatever it takes to be with Darius."

"What does that mean?"

"It means, you're walking away from Patrick. Well, I'm not going. I'm staying right here because I love Darius. He loves me too."

"Has he told you that?"

"Not in so many words, but he will."

"Oh, bullshit, Joni. How many times have I heard that one? You've known the man for what? About a month? Has he asked you to marry him?"

"No."

"And he won't, because in this time..."

Joni cut her off, her eyes flashing with emotion. "... I know, I know, Eve. You've already told me. I don't need to hear it again. I know that 1884 is all about social class, and I'll never fit into Darius' social class. Okay, fine, then I'm okay being his mistress. Now before you start with the motherly speech and moral outrage, I'm just going to come out and say it. I don't mind being his mistress. He treats me well. He's kind and generous and he's always the perfect gentleman."

Eve dropped her eyes. "So you've slept with him?"

Joni turned and marched toward the window. She stood there for a time, looking out into the rainy day. "He's a good lover, Eve. He's sensitive, and he's good. We have fun together, and we like being together. We laugh. We like the same things. We like to touch and explore our bodies. I have never had that with a man. I wake up in the morning and I can't believe how happy I am."

Joni turned to face Eve, who remained sitting up in bed with her arms crossed, her face turned aside.

"I love him, Eve, and I don't care if I've only known him for a month. People who say there's no such thing as love at first sight, simply don't know what the hell they're talking about. Just because they haven't experienced it doesn't mean that it doesn't happen. It just means that they've never experienced it."

The words seemed to echo off the walls and then hover in the unstable air for a time, finally settling into a quiet, chilly hush.

Eve started to speak then stopped, the first two words trailing away. Joni waited, expecting another ethical speech.

Eve slumped a little and tried again, all the energy drained from her body. "Do you remember the time we were out at that bar down in the Village? I don't remember the name of it. Something like The Crafty Dog…"

"The Crafty Cat," Joni said.

"Yes, that was it, the Crafty Cat. Anyway, these two guys came up to us and asked if they could buy us a drink. I said, 'No, we just want to be left alone.' But you smiled at the blond guy who looked like a surfer who'd just flown in from some Southern California beach, and you said, 'I'd love another Cosmo and a burger, if you're buying.'"

Joni's voice was soft with memory. "Yeah, I remember. We dated for a couple of months. He was good looking, but he was an airhead who was more into his body and his blond curly locks than he was with me."

Eve looked at her friend tenderly. "You were always more open to life than I was. Always ready for a new adventure. You're the one who should have found that first lantern in Granny Gilbert's shop."

Joni returned to her chair. "But you were always my anchor, Eve. I always knew you'd be there for me, and you always have been. Remember the promise you made to me a few years back, on Christmas Eve? You said if I ever needed anything from you—if I was ever in trouble—to call you, and just like in the song, *You've Got a Friend*, you'd be there…"

Eve peeled back the covers and got up. She went to Joni and sat on the broad arm of the chair. The ladies' eyes met with warmth.

"I'm happy you're happy, Joni. I am, really. My problem is, I'm ready to be a mother and I don't have a kid. So, I guess you've been my kid."

Joni took Eve's hand, and gently squeezed it. "Girlfriend, I love you. You've been my sister for a long time, and I will miss you when you're gone."

Eve said, "Well, I never thought you'd want to stay here. It never occurred to me that you'd fall in love, so I guess it's a bit of a shock."

"It's a surprise to me, too. How weird is it that I had to time travel back to 1884 before I could meet the love of my life?"

Eve smiled. "Well, look at it this way. If things don't work out, after I'm gone, you'll have the lantern. You can always use it to return home."

"Eve… are you really going to leave Patrick?"

Eve turned her attention toward the window, hearing rain strike the glass, sounding like little pebbles.

"I don't know. I'll give it a few more days and see how I feel. Meanwhile, what are we going to do today?"

"Darius is coming by in about an hour. We're going to have lunch and then go to a museum or two. I can cancel if you need me to stay."

Eve pushed up. "No, no, you go ahead. I'll be fine. I'm not good company anyway. I've got a lot of thinking to do, and I've got to stop feeling sorry for myself, although right now, it feels good."

After Joni left, Eve lay in bed drifting in and out of sleep. She awoke once, remembering Abagail's pretty face and lusterless eyes. She thought of Joni and Darius Foster, and she tried to feel good about Joni's decision.

When her mind turned to Patrick, she suppressed frustration and confusion. Finally, her eyes settled on the lantern which still sat on the parlor table. It seemed to stare back at her, with a challenge. Her brain, which had been on high alert for so long, began to let go and soften. It would be so easy to leave the bed, walk to the lantern and light it.

Could she leave Patrick?

CHAPTER 49

Early afternoon on Monday, December 1, Patrick was in a hansom cab hurrying uptown to see Eve. Thirty minutes earlier, Dr. Darius Foster had stopped by the precinct to see him. Patrick was at his desk when he looked up to see the Doctor striding toward him, his body moving with urgency, his expression solemn.

Patrick stood to meet him. "Good afternoon, Dr. Foster."

"Good day, Detective Gantly. I have come with some rather disturbing news and I thought you were the man to speak to about it."

Patrick indicated toward a wooden straight-back chair. Dr. Foster sat, placing his hat in his lap, quickly scanning the square room to see high windows, wooden filing cabinets along the left wall and six tarnished walnut desks, three of which were occupied by detectives in various states of activity: some picking through files, one interviewing a troubled woman who was weeping in her hand, and another smoking a cigar, staring out a window as if deep in thought.

"How can I help you, Doctor?"

"Detective, I have a good friend, Edwin Lancaster Bennett. We have known each other since boyhood and our families are friendly and connected. I am afraid that in these last few weeks he seems to have become rather strangely absent and, when seen by myself and others, he has appeared to be intoxicated and dissipated. His father, the head of a prominent and prestigious law firm, contacted me, quite alarmed and concerned about his son's absences and his overall mental condition. Frankly, Detective Gantly, I fear for his sanity, especially when he consumes spirits copiously, which he has been doing with increased regularity."

Patrick leaned forward, placing his folded hands on his desk. "Has he committed any crime, Dr. Foster?"

"No… at least not yet. Tipped off by a reliable friend, I saw Edwin last night. I found him in a pub called Sean O'Casey's Saloon."

"Yes, I know of it," Patrick said. "And I know your friend, Edwin Bennett."

Dr. Foster stiffened. "You know him? I don't understand, sir."

"I was in Sean O'Casey's Saloon one night, and I met Edwin Bennett, quite by accident. He was tossing back the rye with relish, and he was inebriated. I learned that he was quite taken by Miss Evelyn Kennedy."

The two men locked eyes.

Dr. Foster inclined forward. "Yes, Detective Gantly, and that is why I am here."

Patrick's interest sharpened.

Dr. Foster continued. "When I found Edwin last night, he was in a low state and he was rambling and troubled. He would not come with me when I endeavored to extricate him from that gloomy saloon. Of course, Edwin frequented that rather tawdry establishment because he was well aware that he would not encounter anyone who knew him, or his family. In any event, it was only by the intervention of the bartender that I was finally successful in removing Edwin from the place. However, once outside, Edwin became belligerent and threatened me with violence if I ever came near him again. He uttered invectives at me and made mean and hurtful threats."

"Did he say anything about Miss Kennedy?"

Dr. Foster's jaw tightened. "When I tried to lay a friendly hand on his shoulder, he brushed me off and shoved me away. He shouted at me and told me I was no longer his friend but an enemy. He said I had poisoned his relationship with Miss Kennedy. He said, if he couldn't have Miss Kennedy for his own, then no man should have her. He said he would kill her first, and then he would kill himself. He seemed like a man who had lost all control over his faculties, and I actually feared for my life and for the life of Miss Kennedy."

Patrick pushed up; his eyes hard. "Why didn't you come to me right away with this information, Dr. Foster? Why have you waited?"

"You must understand that I have known Edwin for most of my life, and this is not the man I knew. I thought it was the whiskey talking. I thought his words absurd. I didn't believe he was serious."

"Well obviously, Dr. Foster, your mind has been changed."

354

Dr. Foster stood up, his hands shaking. "Yes, Detective Gantly. After my rounds this morning I went to Edwin's residence and learned that he has not returned home since yesterday afternoon. I have had much agitation while pondering this."

"Have you contacted Miss Kennedy?"

"No, I didn't want to alarm her, or Miss Kosarin."

"Then Miss Kennedy has not left the City?"

"No... She said she was staying in New York for as long as it takes. She did not explain what she meant by that statement. In any event, I offered her volunteer work at The New York Hospital, and she readily accepted. In just a few days, she has shown great professionalism, dedication and skill."

"Is that the hospital between Fifth and Sixth Avenues?"

"Yes."

"Is that where she is now?"

"No. She is working only Wednesdays, Thursdays and Fridays. I was going to travel to her hotel after I met with you."

Patrick rounded his desk, moving aggressively to the hat stand. He snatched his hat and greatcoat and was out of the room, and out of the building, before Dr. Foster could catch up with him.

In the cab, Dr. Foster was fretful. Patrick was still, but worried. He punched the roof of the cab and shouted at the driver to hurry. The cab raced ahead, the midnight black horse responding to the snap of the reins. It went from a cantor to a driving trot, its hooves loud on the cobblestones, jets of vapor puffing from its nostrils in the cold December air.

As the cab drew up to the curb at the Gerlach Hotel, Patrick had already paid and was up and ready to leap down to the sidewalk. With Dr. Foster behind, Patrick entered the hotel and stepped up to the lobby desk. He asked the desk clerk if Miss Kennedy was in her room.

"No, sir," he said, icy and polite. "She left over an hour ago."

"Do you know where she went?"

"No, sir."

Dr. Foster spoke up. "Is Miss Kosarin with her?"

"No. Miss Kennedy was alone."

"Please send the bellhop to their room and tell Miss Kosarin that I am here in the lobby," Dr. Foster said.

Patrick turned to Dr. Foster. "I'm going to look for her."

"Be cautious, Detective. I fear Edwin is not in his right mind."

Outside, Patrick threw glances up and down the street, but he saw nothing. He set off in the direction of Madison Square Park. Only a moment later, to his surprise and relief, he saw Eve approaching him from 30 feet away.

When Eve saw him coming toward her, she stopped, a pleased smile forming on her face. In reflex, without thinking, she raised a hand and waved at him. She felt the same lift of mood and fountain of happiness she'd always felt whenever she saw him.

Patrick moved ahead toward her, sighing out a breath of relief, when his attention was swiftly diverted by a sudden movement to his right. Instinctively, Patrick reached for his pistol, holstered at his right hip.

Edwin Bennett, wild-eyed and disheveled, jutted out from behind the rear of a carriage, a Smith & Wesson .38 short barrel gun aimed directly at Patrick's chest.

Everything seemed to happen in slow motion. Eve saw Edwin, saw his gun, and she saw Patrick throw back the flap of his greatcoat, his hand sweeping down for what she knew was his weapon.

Eve threw herself forward toward Patrick, screaming out for Edwin to stop. Edwin turned to her as she closed the distance on Patrick.

"You have betrayed me, Miss Kennedy," he shouted.

While Patrick was drawing his pistol, Edwin aimed and fired. The first bullet whispered by Patrick's head. He ducked away, his pistol now drawn, but not aimed. Before he could take a sure aim, Eve darted out in front of him, her arms up, waving at Edwin.

"No, Edwin. Stop! Don't shoot!"

Edwin squeezed the trigger, and Patrick heard the POP of the firing gun. In horror, Patrick saw the bullet impact Eve, whipping her right. She screamed, stumbled, then collapsed onto the sidewalk. There were more screams; horses whinnying; people scrambling and diving for cover.

Edwin marched forward, firing wildly at Patrick, his face set in a fierce determination. "I'll kill you, you scoundrel! I will finish you once and for all."

Patrick felt a bullet graze his coat's right shoulder, then he heard another sing past his ear. He forced his eyes from Eve's still body and, in one swift motion, he brought the pistol to bear on Edwin's chest and squeezed off two shots. The explosions shattered the air.

Edwin's forward motion was stopped by a bullet to the chest. The other missed him. Stunned, he cried out. "I'm shot! God save me, I'm shot!"

Patrick squeezed off another shot that slammed into Edwin's stomach. He staggered back, his face went sick, eyes wide. Stumbling, he toppled over onto the street, his chest heaving, the pistol still loose in his hand.

Patrick hurried over, his pistol poised, aimed at Edwin's head. Edwin struggled to speak, but he could only manage a hollow, wheezing sound. The only word Patrick understood was, "Heartless…"

Patrick kicked Edwin's pistol from his hand and watched as the wounded man's round, pained eyes glazed over. They slowly emptied of life and went blank, gazing up into the heavy, gunmetal sky.

Patrick holstered his pistol, pivoted and rushed over to Eve, where a curious, mumbling crowd had gathered around her.

"Move away from her!" Patrick shouted. "For God's sake, move away."

He shoved men and women alike, dropped to a knee and gently swept the hair from her face. She stared up at him with a weak smile and fluttering eyes. In a feeble voice she said, "There you are, my darling. You've found me again."

With an effort, she lifted a gloved hand to touch his face, but she lost strength and it fell, with Patrick catching it. He held it firmly, without thinking, and it was cold.

"Miss Kennedy, take heart. You're going to be all right. Lie still while I go for the doctor."

At that moment Dr. Foster appeared, and when he saw her and realized what had happened, his face went white with shock. Joni fought her way through the crowd, and when Eve's fallen body came into view, she screamed out in an agony of pain.

Dr. Foster crouched beside Eve, searching for the wound. When he found it, he grimaced. "Let's get her inside the hotel lobby. I must stop the bleeding, or she will not survive."

Patrick gently lifted her up into his arms and carried her into the lobby. Someone had found a blanket and Patrick eased her down onto it, while Dr. Foster shouted out commands for water and clean towels.

Patrick stood by, circling a space, watching Dr. Foster intently as he worked.

"Will she be all right, Doctor?" he asked.

Dr. Foster glanced up soberly. "We must get her to the hospital, and we must do it now or she will surely perish."

CHAPTER 50

Patrick sat hunched in the hospital corridor, his face in his hands. Joni was pacing the hallway, caught in a thicket of emotion, her eyes red, face splotchy from persistent tears.

Two stalwart uniformed policemen stood near the second story stairwell to keep back the press and the curious. Two press wagons had followed the carriage carrying an unconscious Eve, Patrick, Dr. Foster and Joni to the hospital.

Eve had been in the operating room for over four hours, with Drs. Foster and Eckland operating. None of the medical staff had briefed Patrick or Joni, nor updated them as to Eve's condition. When Patrick and Joni had twice approached the nurses' station and inquired about Eve, they were stiffly told that they would have to wait until one of the doctors emerged from the operation.

Mentally and emotionally exhausted, Joni finally sat down in a chair near Patrick, who lowered his hands, his face taut, his eyes filled with torment. Their nerves were frayed; neither spoke for long minutes. As the time dragged, they shifted in their chairs, often turning their wary eyes down the corridor toward the operating rooms.

Joni folded her hands and stared up at the ceiling. "Dr. Eckland is supposed to be one of the best surgeons in the City," she said, her voice hoarse and low. "That's what Dr. Foster told me. He said Dr. Eckland operated on soldiers on battle fields in the Civil War."

Patrick nodded distractedly. "Why did she do it? I just don't understand why she stepped in front of me like that."

Joni wanted to tell him the truth, but how could she? And anyway, it wasn't her business to tell him. Eve would have to do that.

A half hour later, Dr. Foster stepped out into the hallway, with Dr. Eckland soon behind. Patrick was on his feet first, followed by Joni, who looked at the men with trepidation and hope.

The two doctors appeared fatigued and concerned as they whispered comments.

Patrick went striding down the corridor toward them, with Joni behind.

Dr. Foster turned to meet him, his expression remote and guarded.

"How is Miss Kennedy?" Patrick asked, his voice trembling. "Is she conscious?"

Dr. Eckland didn't meet Patrick's eyes.

"I believe the operation went well," Dr. Foster said.

"What does *well* mean?" Patrick demanded.

"As you know, Detective Gantly, Miss Kennedy took the bullet in the shoulder and, fortunately, it passed through her body and did not pierce a vital organ or major blood vessel, namely, the brachial artery which is the main artery of the arm. Yes, that is very good news. Miss Kennedy did lose a large amount of blood, despite my efforts to apply pressure to the wound both in the hotel and in the carriage as we traveled to the hospital. I wish we could have arrived earlier."

Patrick waited tensely for more, and Dr. Foster continued, working to keep his voice low and steady.

"It was Dr. Eckland's vast experience and skill that I believe helped to stabilize Miss Kennedy. He quickly located the injury and deduced both the size and speed of the bullet. From there, he…"

"… Is she in pain?" Joni asked, interrupting.

Dr. Foster spoke affectionately to Joni. "Do not worry about that, Miss Kosarin. We applied numbing powder and used chloroform. Miss Kennedy did not feel any pain during the operation. Afterwards, I injected a one-half grain of morphine subcutaneously, and she is resting very easily.

"Can I see her?" Joni asked.

"Not at this time. She must rest. Rest and more rest are what she needs most."

"Will she have a full recovery?" Patrick asked.

Dr. Foster blinked rapidly. "We must keep the dressing and the area around the wound clean and dry. Dr. Eckland was most concerned about material and debris being pulled into the wound with the bullet, thus causing infection."

"Infection?" Patrick asked, looking first at Dr. Foster, then to Dr. Eckland for further explanation.

Dr. Eckland said, "Be comforted, Detective. I did my level best to clean the wound thoroughly of all such foreign debris. Unlike many of my colleagues who still laugh at germ theory, I am not one of them. We surgeons and the nurses thoroughly washed our hands and instruments in anti-septic chemicals, before we operated. My paramount concern for this young woman is an infection and septic blood poisoning. Our enemy is infection, and we must be vigilant."

"She will recover fully, then?" Patrick repeated.

Dr. Foster looked to Dr. Eckland, who stepped to Patrick, searching his eyes, seeing the pain in them and something more; he saw deep affection. "Take courage, sir. She is a young woman and a strong one. There is no reason why she should not recover fully."

As a woman of 1884, Joni could not remain in the hospital overnight. Dr. Foster took her to dinner, although she was quiet and ate little. When they arrived at the Gerlach Hotel, they remained inside the carriage, each lost in private thought. Realizing that Eve had been close to death terrified Joni to the core. She felt alone, marooned and edgy. Eve was her anchor, her protector, her good and trusted friend.

Dr. Foster broke the sad silence. "Have you contacted Miss Kennedy's family?"

Joni was startled by the question. No, of course she hadn't. Neither had any family in this time, at least none they knew about.

"No... Not yet."

"Perhaps you should."

Joni turned abruptly. "I don't like the way you said that. Do you think Eve will die?"

Dr. Foster spoke calmly. "No, Joan... Miss Kosarin. I only meant that they should know, should they not? Perhaps they will want to travel here and take her back home while she recovers."

Joni turned away, miserable. "Yes... Well. I don't know. I don't know about anything right now. I'm just so tired, and I'm just so scared."

Darius reached for Joni's gloved hand, moving closer, his voice at a mild whisper.

"Do not be afraid, Miss Kosarin. I am here and I will help you and protect you."

Joni stared frankly into his eyes, and her voice took on a frightened edge. "Will you, Darius?"

He was gently startled by her tone. "Yes... Of course."

"Do you love me?" she asked with a challenge.

He drew back, unsure how to respond to her change of mood. "Miss Kosarin, have we not spoken about these delicate issues before?"

"Not in so many words. Not directly. Not so I know how you feel. You said you'd put me up in some awesome brownstone and give me anything I wanted. I'm sure most women in this time would jump at that. Hell, I jumped at it. But you know what? Everything changed tonight. Everything changed when Eve was nearly killed by your friend, who wanted her to be his mistress. What the hell is the matter with you men in this time? Did you ever ask me if I wanted to meet your parents or your friends? Oh, excuse me, I did meet Edwin Bennett, didn't I? The good and trusted Edwin Bennett, who shot my best friend. Oh, yes, I was good enough to meet him."

Darius was struck dumb. He lifted his chin to speak in his defense, but Joni charged on, galvanized by fatigue, fear and anger.

"Well you know what, Darius Compton Foster? I'm not falling for your bullshit."

Darius was flabbergasted by her blistering attack and coarse slang. "Miss Kosarin, you go too far."

"Oh, I'm just beginning, pal. Now, let me get this: as I understand it, you want to lock me away in some goddamned house, oh excuse my friggin' French, where you can have me all to yourself, whenever you want me, right? Well, isn't that just so convenient for you? A little doll baby all to yourself, who'll swing her ass about at your beck and call."

Darius was stricken, mouth open.

"Look, Darius, I'm not some punk-stupid bitch from Ohio, okay? I grew up in Chicago, and I live in New York City, *the* New York City; a real city that dwarfs this little old town. I'm not naïve. I realized that I was going to be the chick on the side, so to speak. Well, I've checked you out, and I've learned that you have a more suitable and proper woman also waiting on the side. That's two sides. How friggin' cozy! You will soon be engaged and then you will marry her. Her name is Elizabeth Atkins Worthing, and she comes from a *muy, muy* wealthy family. Don't you think I read the papers? Oh, that's right, men in this time don't think women read newspapers, or shouldn't read papers; they shouldn't work, they shouldn't go to bars by themselves, they shouldn't discuss politics and they shouldn't breathe, which is why I'm wearing this damned corset. Well, my dear doctor friend, I've decided that I am *not* going to be the little mistress on the side. Go find some other dumb broad. I'm sure there are many in this god-forsaken time."

Darius' face was granite hard, his wounded eyes fixed on Joni with contempt and loathing.

"You brazen, low woman. You have cut me to the quick! Thank the gods I have seen your true colors and your true vulgar character. All I ever did was to offer you my protection and companionship. If that is too much for you to bear, then so be it. I will be rid of you, here and now, and be the better for it. Now, leave my carriage, Miss Kosarin, before I slap you, which is what you deserve."

Darius shouted for the coachman.

Indignant, Joni shoved the carriage door open and was met by the stoic coachman. He ushered her out of the carriage to the sidewalk. Without looking back, Joni stormed off into the hotel.

CHAPTER 51

Patrick refused to leave the hospital. He remained outside Eve's room all night, pacing the halls or briefly napping in a chair that a kind nurse had brought him. Before she left him alone, she paused, her eyes filled with sympathy.

"Is she your betrothed?" the young nurse innocently asked.

Patrick stared up at her as if in a trance. "No... She is not."

Early the next morning, December 2nd, Patrick pleaded with a stout, middle-aged nurse to let him in to see Eve. She refused, citing Dr. Foster's orders.

"You must understand. It is for the best. Miss Kennedy is in no condition to see anyone. She must rest. You should return home and get some rest yourself. You look exhausted."

She gave him an approving smile. "You are quite the hero, Detective Gantly. The newspapers are full of how you saved Miss Kennedy's life."

Patrick's eyes were direct and intense. "I did not save her life, Nurse. It was she who saved mine. Did the reporters not write that? Can they never write the truth of a story?"

The nurse ducked her head and walked away.

Dr. Foster arrived moments later, striding down the corridor, looking haggard and low. The two men's eyes met, Patrick's hopeful, Dr. Foster's despairing.

"I need to see Miss Kennedy, Dr. Foster, if only for a few minutes."

The Doctor looked Patrick up and down. "Have you been here all night?"

Patrick stroked his unshaved face, self-consciously, and then ran a hand through his curly hair, aware that he must look a mess. "May I see her? Just for a few minutes?"

Patrick and Dr. Foster entered Eve's private room. Privacy curtains enclosed her, and a nurse standing by rose from a chair, her eyes expectant. The one window was covered by cream-colored curtains, and a vase of flowers rested on a table near the bed. Patrick had ordered them the night before from a local florist, and they were delivered just after Eve was wheeled into her room.

"How is Miss Kennedy this morning?" Dr. Foster asked the nurse.

"Resting quietly. She awoke twice and asked for water."

"Very good. No other complications?"

"No, Doctor."

Patrick stepped to the foot of the bed and waited, head down, swallowing back nerves, while Dr. Foster drew back the privacy curtains just enough to examine Eve.

When Dr. Foster waved him over, Patrick felt his pulse rise as he approached. When he rested his sleepy, sandy eyes on her, he felt the flame of a crisis brewing in his chest, near his heart.

Eve lay on her back, silent and still, a sheet pulled up to her chin, hiding most of her right bandaged shoulder. Her breathing was feathery soft, her eyes closed and gently twitching; perhaps she was in the midst of a dream. Eve's lush, honey-blonde hair was neatly combed back from her forehead, framing her heart-shaped face, revealing strong cheekbones and a small chin. He denied himself the impulse to reach and stroke her cheek. He couldn't pull his eyes from her. She appeared as both tangible and real, as an apparition and a paradox; someone who seemed so familiar and yet so far away.

And then there was a twisting of emotion and memory and, for fleeing minutes, Patrick lost all sense of time and place, as if he'd been shattered, his pieces tossed into the air and scattered into a restless wind.

Dr. Foster noticed Patrick's faraway stare.

"Are you quite all right, Detective Gantly?"

Patrick shook his head, returning to the present, certain that his strange feelings had occurred because of lack of sleep. "Yes... I'm fine."

"I gave Miss Kennedy another shot of morphine. She needs much rest. I will examine the bandage later this afternoon. We should leave her now."

Outside, Patrick glanced up and down the hallway. "I suppose the papers reported the events of yesterday with their usual drama and creativity?"

Dr. Foster nodded. "Yes, you are correct about that. The headline in *The New York World* is **SCANDAL,** in bold letters.

"You don't look as though you managed much sleep either, Dr. Foster," Patrick said.

"No. I fear it was a disquieting night, in many aspects. I spent many distressing hours with Edwin's family."

"What happened to the man?" Patrick asked.

Darius pursed his lips in thought. "He was always rather tightly coiled, I'm afraid, being more the sensitive and precarious poet than a man of the rational arts. Although, I must say, I never envisioned this violent and devastating business. God forgive me for not taking the appropriate action of insisting he be sent to a sanatorium. I was too close to him, you see. We were the best of childhood friends, and I was blinded by that. Even yesterday morning, I fear I procrastinated, and it is absolutely unforgiveable. Of course, I should have visited you much earlier, Detective Gantly. If I had, Miss Kennedy would not be lying in that bed wounded, and fighting for her life."

Patrick didn't like the sound of Dr. Foster's last statement. "But Miss Kennedy is improving, is she not?"

Dr. Foster stared down at the floor. When he spoke, his voice was weak and rusty. "She must survive. If she does not, I will never forgive myself for my unmitigated negligence."

Patrick looked away. "I will cover all Miss Kennedy's expenses."

Darius lifted his steely eyes. "All will be covered by me, and by me alone, sir. Miss Kennedy will want for nothing."

The silence expanded between them. Patrick turned to leave and then stopped, glancing back at the forlorn, melancholy doctor.

"Did I tell you that Miss Kennedy darted out in front of me to take the bullet?"

Dr. Foster slowly turned toward Patrick. "Yes, Detective, you did."

"She said things to me... Familiar words... Intimate words. I have no answers for these things and they trouble me, and they haunt me."

Darius stared at him with understanding. "Let's face it, Detective Gantly, Miss Kennedy and Miss Kosarin are mysteriously unique and uncharacteristically disconcerting. I noticed it from the beginning, and I have no answers either. Simply put, they are not ordinary women, are they? Perhaps that is why you find Miss Kennedy most attractive, despite your recent loss, and why I am equally at a loss to know why I find Miss Kosarin utterly disturbing and alluring."

Patrick was expressionless, but he felt the impact of Dr. Foster's words.

"By the way, Detective, leave by the side door. Reporters are swarming the front and rear entrances. I have had a sign placed at the side door exit that says Smallpox, Quarantine."

Patrick went striding off, head down, hands in his pockets. Dr. Foster watched him leave through the exit door, hearing the echo of his footsteps descending the white marble stairs. Darius turned back to Eve's room, sighed heavily, and stepped back inside.

CHAPTER 52

Joni sat in the hospital hallway outside Eve's room. Her eyes moved; her mind raced. Eve had been in the hospital for three days, and although there had been an improvement at first, Dr. Eckland was now concerned that some debris had remained in the wound and that infection was setting in.

The morphine affected Eve strangely. She was lucid one minute and dreamy and disconnected the next. Joni had to make decisions, and she had to make them soon. The only course of antibiotics that had survived the time travel from 2016 had been given to Abagail Tannin, and who knows what had happened to them. If serious infection set in, Eve's body would have to fight it off. If it failed, she would die.

Joni had spent her days and nights alone, suffering with indecision and guilt. Indecision about Eve, and guilt over the sharp words she'd fired at Darius. When she'd visited the hospital, she and Dr. Foster had managed to avoid each other, although a few times, Joni had been aware of Darius watching her.

When Dr. Eckland exited Eve's room, Joni shot up, hands twisting. "How is she, Dr. Eckland?"

His heavy brows lifted as he considered his words. "There is some infection, I'm sorry to say."

Joni's face fell. "Oh, God."

"Take heart, Miss Kosarin. Miss Kennedy is young and strong, and I believe that with rest and additional wound cleaning, we can eradicate the infection."

"Can I see her?"

"Yes, but please limit your visit to only a few minutes."

Inside Eve's room, Joni stepped softly toward the bed, noticing the heavenly scent of two flower arrangements. Joni knew that Patrick had brought one; Dr. Foster had sent the other.

The privacy curtains were open, and Eve lay quietly, her eyes closed. Joni eased down in the chair next to her bed. Eve sensed a presence and her eyes opened, cloudy and vague. She gently turned her head, saw Joni, and smiled faintly.

"Hey there, Joni... What's up?"

Joni shook her head. "What's up? What a crazy thing to say."

"So tell me what's happened since yesterday, not that I know when yesterday was, since all of time is melted together."

Joni glanced about conspiratorially to ensure no one was at the door.

"Dr. Eckland says you have some infection."

"I'm not surprised," Eve said, matter-of-factly. "But I'll fight it off."

373

"And if you don't?"

Eve held her smile. "Then away I go, either to the great beyond or back home to the future."

Joni whispered. "To the future, and the sooner the better. I think we have to get you out of here, now, while you still have the strength. We'll catch a cab to Central Park, find an isolated bench and light the lantern."

Eve turned her head away. "Yeah... That may be best. If the infection takes hold, it might take me out pretty fast."

"Don't say that."

Eve looked up at Joni, studying her friend's conflicted face. "I have a vague memory of your telling me that you blasted Darius. Did you make up?"

"No."

"Don't you think you should?"

"No... What's the use? Anyway, when we get back home it won't matter, will it? He'll have been dead for decades."

"Joni... Let's get real. We're almost out of time. Do you love him?"

Joni frowned. "God help me, I do love him, or whatever. I mean, is it love, or just lust? It's all new to me, so I don't know what the hell it is. All I know is that he makes me happy and I want to be with him. I've never felt this way about a guy... Listen to me. I've said all this before, haven't I? I just keep repeating myself."

"I can return home alone, Joni. All you have to do is prop me up on a bench. Nikola Tesla's lantern will do the rest."

"No, I'm going with you, and make sure you get back safely, and then rush you to a hospital."

Eve closed her eyes. "Think about it. Think long and hard about it. You like living in this time, and you love Darius. You know you do. Will you regret leaving?"

"Darius has written me off. I told you what I said to him. I was awful. All this angry shit just came pouring out of me. I was like a crazy woman. No, it's over between us."

"I doubt that. Every day he asks me how you are."

Joni lit up. "Does he really?"

"Yes..."

"Well, I'm going with you anyway."

"I don't want you to."

"What do you mean, you don't want me to?"

Eve winced in pain.

Joni stood up. "Are you okay? Are you in pain? Should I call for Dr. Eckland?"

"No... I'll be all right. I don't want any more morphine. That stuff is so addictive, and I feel loopy and weird."

"Can I get you anything?"

Eve's gaze was earnest. "Yes. Think about how you'll feel if you leave without making up with Darius. At least talk to him, apologize or whatever. Just talk to him and then see how you feel about staying."

Joni eased back down in the chair, her mind working.

Eve said, "You'll have the lantern. You can always use it if things don't work out."

"And what if the lantern doesn't work for me?"

"It will work. If it doesn't, go see Tesla. You know where he is."

Joni arose again, removing her hat and fingering a loose strand of hair back in place. "I don't know. I'm not going to be Darius' mistress, and I know he's not going to marry me, so that's it."

Eve gently closed her eyes.

"I should leave," Joni said. "I'm tiring you out."

"No, stay a little longer."

"Has Patrick been to see you?"

"Yes. He comes every day. Once I was so underwater from the morphine, I couldn't get my mouth to work. He sat next to me, still as a statue. Yesterday, he asked me when I was going home, and because I was so out of it, I told him that I missed Georgy Boy, and why didn't he bring him to see me?"

Joni winced. "Oh, wow. What did he say?"

"He asked me who Georgy Boy was. I think I said, he's our dog, silly. Have you been taking him for walks?"

"Patrick must be really confused," Joni said.

Eve smiled lovingly. "I really thought we were back home on West 107th Street. But you know what he said? He said, 'I'll take you home.' He said he'd do whatever he could to help. Anything."

Joni sat again. "Okay, so the big question is: can you leave him?"

Eve's eyes struggled open. "Do you know what he asked me? He said, 'Miss Kennedy, why did you take a bullet meant for me?'"

Joni leaned in close.

"You should have seen him, Joni. He looked exactly like the first time I saw him, with that wide chest, muscular neck and broad shoulders. He gave me a small, shy smile, and I stared up at him like a goofy teenager. I looked into his blue eyes and said..." Eve paused, changing the tone of her voice. "Now, you've got to understand that I was under the influence of morphine and mostly out of my mind. Anyway, I said, because I love you, Patrick, and I have loved you for a long time."

"Oh, my God," Joni exclaimed. "What did he say?"

As I recall, and I could be all wrong about this in my drug-induced state, but as I recall, he didn't say anything for a while. Then he said, 'When you recover, would you consider staying in New York? Dr. Foster said he could get you a nursing job here in the hospital.'"

"And what did you say?" Joni asked, sitting on the edge of her seat.

"I said, 'As long as you're here, Detective Patrick Lott Gantly, I'll be here.'"

"You said his middle name!? That must have shocked him, if he wasn't already shocked out of his mind. Didn't you say he didn't tell you about his middle name until a year or so after you were married?"

"Yep."

"What did he do?"

"He just stared at me, as if I were the greatest mystery of all time. And then he gave me the faintest little grin. And then I passed out."

Joni turned serious. "Well, sister friend, I can tell you that I am not going to sit here and let you die. If you don't get better soon, you and me are out of here."

Eve made a little sound of pain and she grimaced. Joni was distressed to see that all the color had drained from Eve's face.

Eve struggled to get the words out. "I'm so tired, Joni. So tired. I can't leave Patrick. I just can't do it."

CHAPTER 53

On Friday morning, December 5, Joni was in her hotel room, seated at the desk, finishing up a four-page letter to Patrick. She'd already written a letter to Darius. A knock on the door startled her. She was worried and on edge. The night before, Eve had taken a turn for the worst, and Joni knew she had to take action.

She left her chair and went to answer the door. A bellhop handed her a folded note and stood by, waiting for her answer. Joni opened the note, seeing it was from Darius.

Miss Kosarin:

I am in the lobby. Would you please grant me a few minutes of your time to discuss a delicate matter? I would be grateful. I will await your answer.

Joni lifted her eyes from the page and nodded to the bellhop. She tipped him, closed the door and quickly began to change clothes.

Twenty minutes later, she exited the elevator to find Darius waiting. He looked subdued and cheerless as he approached.

"Good morning, Miss Kosarin. Thank you for seeing me."

Joni stood awkwardly, shyly meeting his gaze. "Of course, Dr. Foster. I have written you a letter." She looked toward the elevator. "I forgot to bring it."

"Can we talk?" Darius asked.

"Is it about Eve? Has she improved?"

Darius indicated toward a burgundy couch at the far end of the lobby, near a potted plant. "We can speak in privacy over there."

After they were seated, Darius adjusted himself twice before he spoke. "I'm going to be frank, Miss Kosarin. I fear Miss Kennedy's condition has not improved since last night. She has been unresponsive to our treatments."

Joni's face firmed up. "Okay, that's it then. I need to get her out of the hospital."

Dr. Foster reacted in disbelief. "Out of the hospital? My dear Miss Kosarin, I don't understand. Miss Kennedy must be carefully monitored and administered to."

Joni was skittishly aware of the impact of her words. She stared directly into Darius' eyes, knowing that what she was about to say would sound crazy. "Eve is dying, and I have a way to save her."

He looked at her with confusion. "I do not understand."

Joni arose. "Dr. Foster, Eve and I must leave, and we must leave now. Today."

Dr. Foster stared, bewildered. He stood up, his eyes filled with pleading. "Miss Kosarin, please understand

Elyse Douglas

that Miss Kennedy is in no condition, whatsoever, to travel."

"I can't explain it, but you must help me get her out of that hospital and into a cab."

Darius turned indignantly stubborn. "I will not, Miss Kosarin. You are speaking like a mad woman."

Joni sighed heavily. He was right, she did sound like a mad woman. Of course Darius wouldn't help her bundle Eve up and take her to Central Park, to sit on a park bench, to be hurled off into the future, 2016.

Joni softened. She was prepared for Plan B. "Of course you're right, Dr. Foster. I'm just a bit overwrought right now."

Darius relaxed a little. "Of course you are, and it is understandable, but we must keep our heads. We must not lose faith and hope. Dr. Eckland is with Miss Kennedy now and he is doing everything he can for her."

"Is Detective Gantly at the hospital?" Joni asked.

Dr. Foster nodded. "Yes, he is. I am on my way to the hospital now. Shall I take you in my carriage?"

Joni turned to see Nikola Tesla leave the elevator. He spotted her, stopped, offered a little bow, and then strolled across the lobby, placing his hat squarely on his head and exiting the hotel.

"I have to get something first. Can you wait? I'll be right back."

Upstairs, Joni quickly snatched up both letters, folded them and stuffed them into envelopes. When she turned to view the lantern, she felt a flutter in her chest. Would her plan work? It had to. She had to make it work.

She grabbed the lantern and lowered it into a brown canvas bag that Eve had purchased days ago. Before leaving the room, she gave the place one last passing

380

glance. The next few hours would determine whether she would ever return.

In the carriage trotting toward the hospital, Joni sat opposite Darius, whose face was lost in heavy fatigue. She reached into her coat pocket and handed him the sealed envelope with the letter inside.

"When you have time, please read the letter. It will explain what I can't explain in words."

Darius took the letter, holding Joni in his eyes. "Very well," he said, slipping it into his inside coat pocket.

Joni was running out of time, and she had to make a decision. It was now or never with their relationship. She lowered her voice, her eyes showing a vulnerable affection.

"Darius... I'm sorry for what I said to you. I was upset and out of control. I should have found another way. I should have found better words. Please forgive me."

Darius looked at her for a time, betraying no thought or reaction to her apology. With his chin, he pointed outside, as snowflakes flew by the window.

"Look, it is snowing. How lovely it is. When I was a boy, I played in the snow for hours. My governess could not pull me away from it. She often had to call my mother and, even then, I resisted, and so I often received an awful scolding from my father."

Darius smiled at the thought. "But I do love the miracle of falling snow. How gently and completely it covers every space, seemingly with so little effort. I love the way the City looks just after a snowfall: so pure, so clean, like a world of make-believe. At night, the lamplight makes the soft, white blanket glitter, and the world becomes magic."

He turned his full attention on Joni and smiled into her eyes. "Miss Kosarin, when I am with you, I once again become something of that boy who believed in magic. All my good traits expand, all my hopes and wishes seem possible, and all the hard edges of my practical and often gloomy nature are softened. Also, mirth swells in my chest and I feel like a better man."

Joni's chin began to quiver, and she was moved to tears.

"Although you are not an easy woman to understand, Miss Kosarin, you are a woman who brings out the better angels of my nature. What I am about to say, I say with the tenderest of hope and with a sincere, full heart. Will you please stay in New York? I have no further plans to continue my engagement with Miss Worthing. I ask that you please allow time for me to work out the political and social aspects of our relationship with my family. These are rather delicate issues."

Joni reached for her lace handkerchief and blotted away tears. Expectation hung in the air.

She gave him a slow, flirtatious smile, and she saw the immediate effect. He smiled, his eyes filling with warmth and tenderness.

CHAPTER 54

When Joni and Dr. Foster started down the hospital corridor, they saw Patrick pacing, tense and agitated. He started for them.

"Miss Kennedy has taken a bad turn, Dr. Foster," Patrick said. "Dr. Eckland is in there now. He will not let me in. Can you please go to the woman and see what you can do?"

Joni and Darius traded anxious glances. He left her and entered Eve's room.

Left alone, Joni and Patrick avoided each other's eyes. Joni stared at Eve's closed door with cold speculation, and then she decided to act.

Patrick made a tight fist and pounded it into the palm of his other hand. "If I could just fight the thing. If I could just do something instead of standing out here helpless and useless."

Joni pulled the letter from her hidden dress pocket and handed it to him. He looked down at it enquiringly.

Joni swallowed. "Detective Gantly, when you read this, you're going to think that I am out of my mind. You're not going to believe it. Do me a favor. Read the entire letter without stopping, without thinking."

He hesitated. "What is in it?"

"The truth. The truth about Eve, and how and why we came here. It also explains how you can save Eve's life."

He narrowed his doubtful eyes on her. "How I can save her?"

"Didn't you tell her you'd do whatever you could to help? Anything?"

With reluctance, Patrick took the letter, turned and walked away down the hallway to a window where light streamed in; where snowflakes blurred the world, scattering in a gusty wind.

Joni massaged her forehead and sat, drawing the canvas bag next to her ankles and patting it, just to make sure the hidden lantern was still there.

The minutes ticked by, each seeming like an eternity, while she waited for word about Eve, and while she waited for Patrick to return from reading the letter. In it, she had described everything that Eve had shared with her, from the first time Eve found the lantern in *The Time Past Antique Shop* in Pennsylvania.

Joni described Eve's first time travel journey to 1885, where she'd first met Patrick. Joni concisely retold all that had transpired, including when he'd been shot protecting the wealthy Albert Harringshaw, and how Eve had used the lantern to time travel back to 2016 with him, so his life could be saved using "miracle drugs." Joni told him he and Eve were married a short time later.

The words had tumbled out of her, as she described Eve's and Patrick's time travel trip to 1914, and how they had saved Patrick's daughter Maggie from an early, violent death.

Near the end of the letter, Joni documented the incident in 2019, when Eve, pregnant with Patrick's child, had dropped the time travel lantern into the Hudson River, hoping to put an end to any possible future time travel adventures.

Joni finished the letter by writing, *"Eve's life with you was entirely erased. She lost you and the baby. She was determined to find you again, and she did. Patrick, Eve will never leave this time without you. She loves you that much. If you don't help her now, she will die."*

The waiting was punishing. Patrick was still at the end of the hall, reading, and both doctors remained in Eve's room. Joni closed her eyes, having slept little, and whispered a silent prayer for Eve as she dozed off.

Minutes later, she was jarred awake by the sound of heavy footsteps. She wiped her eyes to see Patrick approach, his eyes cold, his face rigid. He stopped a few feet before her, looking down at her with an odd, indignant contempt. He held up the pages and shook them.

"What is this nonsensical fantasy? What madness has possessed you, woman? Why have you composed these pages of lies at such an urgent and dreadful time? I do not understand you."

Joni summoned strength as she stood up, facing him squarely. "Detective Gantly, there is no time to try to convince you about the letter. But it is the truth. Why do you think Eve went searching for the lantern? Why was a silly lantern so important to her? Didn't you ask her that same question? Back in October, weren't you surprised when she appeared right out of the blue with Dr. Foster, and tried to save your wife, and did save your baby? Why did she say those loving things to you? Why did she stay here in 1884, when she could have returned to her own time, and not been shot protecting you? Because she loves you, and she has loved you for a long time. Think about it."

Patrick peered into Joni's eyes, searching for some reality in them. "You are mad," he said, his voice low with anger. "You are utterly stark, raving mad."

Joni folded her arms, obstinate. "Okay, fine. If you don't believe me, then go visit Nikola Tesla at the Edison Machine Works. It's on Goerck Street. Tesla will tell you all about his invention. He created the time travel lanterns."

Patrick stood like a block of granite, breathing, his eyes staring but not seeing.

Joni shook her head in frustration, dropped her arms and stooped over the canvas bag. Reaching in, she retrieved the lantern, holding it up in plain sight.

"You said you want to fight something. Okay, this is how you fight. You take Eve and the lantern, and you travel to the future to a time when the medicine of 2016 can save her life. You and I can save her life now, the same way she saved yours when you were shot in 1885."

Patrick stood in a stupor of discontent and doubt; his mind in turmoil.

Joni continued. "But if you can't do this—if you don't believe me—then can you at least help me carry her out of the hospital into a cab, so I can get her to Central Park? Will you at least do that much?"

He squinted at her. "Central Park?"

"Yes. There are common areas that haven't changed that much during the past hundred and thirty-odd years. We can't take a chance on lighting the lantern here; we could end up stuck in the concrete of a skyscraper or trapped in the floor of some deli or bank. Will you please help me, before it's too late?"

He didn't budge.

"Please. You can save Eve's life, Patrick, but you can't wait until she dies. You've got to help me get her out of here now."

Overloaded and bewildered, Patrick flung the pages away. Joni watched helplessly as they sailed and drifted to the floor. Up the hallway, two nurses' heads popped out from the nurses' station. They looked on, concerned.

Patrick grabbed his greatcoat and hat, pivoted and stormed off down the hallway.

Outside, he strode aggressively down Fifth Avenue, the smoke of confusion, worry and anger hanging over his head like a cloud. His hat and shoulders were soon dusted with snow, and white clouds of vapor puffed from his mouth. He felt as though his head were about to explode.

He walked aimlessly, hollow-eyed, hands deep in his pockets, face stinging from the onslaught of snow and bitter wind. Crowds of people flowed around him as he trudged ahead, finally finding himself at Sean O'Casey's Saloon. In the half-full, dimly lit room, Patrick planted himself on a barstool, removed his hat and stared at himself in the tarnished mirror behind the bar.

"You fool," he said, tearing both hands through his damp, curly hair. "You daft fool. You know you will not be able to live with yourself if she dies."

Sean, polishing a pint glass, lifted an eye and went over. "Are you all right, Patrick?"

"Whiskey, Sean."

"You don't drink whiskey this early."

"Well, today I do. Whiskey," he demanded.

Sean shrugged, grabbed a bottle of whiskey and a shot glass and splashed some in. He slid it over, and Patrick took it down in a gulp, and then ordered another. Sean poured, and Patrick tossed it back.

"I could use a pint," Patrick said.

Sean drew one, head foaming. He plopped it down before Patrick, who was staring ahead with unfocused eyes.

"You should shed that coat, Patrick," Sean said. "The snow has soaked it through. You'll catch your death."

Patrick shot him a glance. "Death?"

"Yeah. Your coat is wet from the snow, Patrick. You've been through enough, haven't you? Do you need more of the devil coming after you?"

Patrick pushed off his stool and obeyed, hanging the heavy, damp thing on a coat stand to the right of the bar. When Patrick returned to his seat and took a long draft from the pint, Brodie Grant, the rail-thin, washed-up old actor with frosty white hair, drifted over, a half-drunk pint in his hand.

"Well, if it isn't Detective Patrick Gantly, the savior of women and the destroyer of all scoundrels and evil men. I salute you, sir," he said, lifting his glass in a toast. "To the hero of the hour, I propose a toast to the health of Detective Sergeant Patrick Gantly."

The bar shouted "Hear, hear!" as they clinked glasses and drank. Some twirled handkerchiefs, and others pounded fists on the table.

Patrick regarded Brody with a disapproving stare. "I didn't save anybody. Miss Kennedy took the bullet meant for me. If there is to be toasting, it should be for Miss Kennedy and Miss Kennedy alone."

Brody was hurt. "My deepest apologies, Patrick. There was no intention to offend in any way, I assure you. I was greatly surprised to read about Mr. Edwin Bennett's unhinged and violent actions. It is quite evident that the man wrestled with many demons and he lost the fight. But Patrick, my good friend, the newspapers are full of your heroics."

"The papers are wrong, Brody! *I* should be lying in that hospital, not Miss Evelyn Kennedy."

Brody lowered his head as if to pray. "I am truly sorry for her, Patrick. Truly, I am. *The New York Herald,* did write of Miss Kennedy's feminine bravery, and I was moved by her courageous act."

Brody made a broad sweep of his hand as he quoted a verse. "As the great Bard wrote in his superlative play, *Coriolanus, 'It is held that valor is the chiefest virtue, and most dignifies the haver.'*"

The bar applauded, and Patrick turned back to his pint, swallowing half.

Brody laid a kindly hand on Patrick's shoulder. "In these dark days, my friend, you are navigating troubled waters and I can see that your burden is most heavy. How is Miss Kennedy, the courageous woman? The papers say she is making a valiant recovery."

Patrick stared blankly. "She is not. I fear she is dying."

"Then I am sorry for it, old friend. No man should be tested as you have been, and my heart is heavy for you."

389

Patrick twisted around; his eyes filled with grief. "Brody, what does your friend Shakespeare have to say about time and the future?"

Brody's brow contracted thoughtfully. "Well now, let me see." He tapped his nose with a crooked finger as his mind went to work. Seconds later, his eyes brightened. "Ah yes, friend Patrick. Perhaps this will soothe your troubled soul."

Again, he lifted his arm, and then his chin, as if he were on stage speaking to a packed audience. *"Oh heaven! that one might read the book of fate and see the revolution of the times."*

Patrick sat still and thoughtful. "In other words, Brody, if we could read the book of destiny, we would see how time changes everything?"

Brody smiled his satisfaction. "You are a discerning man, Detective Gantly."

Patrick drained the last of his beer, stood and reached for his wallet. Sean threw up a hand to stop him.

"The drinks are on me, Patrick. May the good Lord be with you and Miss Kennedy."

Patrick shrugged into his still damp coat, said his goodbyes and left.

Outside, snow flurries danced, and there were already three inches of snow on the ground. Patrick turned up his collar and started for home.

They stood in Megan's parlor in late afternoon, the smell of ham and boiled cabbage wafting through the house. Megan O'Brien held Colleen up for Patrick to see, and to her surprise, Patrick leaned and kissed his daughter on the forehead.

"What's the matter?" Megan asked, seeing the strain on Patrick's face.

"I have to go away for a while," he said, keeping his eyes on Colleen. "At least, I believe I will go away."

"Away? Where to?"

"I don't quite know. I can't explain it, even to myself."

"You're being mysterious, Mr. Gantly."

"There is a wildness in the air, Megan, and it seems that, against my will and my reason, I am caught up in it and I must respond. I see no other way. No other recourse. Will you please wrap Colleen in warm blankets and prepare her for travel?"

Megan questioned him with her nervous eyes. "Travel? Where are you taking her?"

"She is my daughter, and I will not leave her. She should be with her father. Megan, Colleen and I are about to become pilgrims, come what may. We will read the book of destiny and see how time changes everything."

"Mr. Gantly, you are frightening me. What do you know about taking care of a baby?"

Patrick gave a little shake of his head. "I wager that I am about to learn, Megan. Please prepare Colleen for her journey. We must leave immediately. It is a matter of life and death."

Patrick took his daughter's little hand and held it in his own big hand, looking at her with quiet joy. "Let us be off, Colleen. Let us see where destiny takes us."

Megan stood at the front door, watching Patrick descend the front stairs, with Colleen cradled in the crook of his strong arm. Patrick turned and waved to her, then climbed aboard the waiting hansom, the driver being Thomas Whiton, the man who hailed from Manchester England, the same town Emma was from.

He was the same friendly driver who had first brought Eve to Patrick's door.

Troubled and holding back tears, Megan watched the cab lurch and canter ahead, soon disappearing into a haze of falling snow.

CHAPTER 55

Patrick arrived at the hospital as darkness was settling in. He found Joni sitting despondent outside Eve's room. When she saw Patrick coming toward her, cradling a baby, she shot up, surprised.

"How is Miss Kennedy?" Patrick asked.

Joni stared first at the sleeping, bundled baby and then at Patrick. She breathed in anxiety. "She's dying. The infection is spreading."

"Are her doctors inside?"

"No, they're upstairs in Dr. Foster's office in conference."

Patrick stared down at the canvas bag. "I do not believe in your so-called time lantern, Miss Kosarin, and I do not believe it will help Miss Kennedy survive her ordeal, but I will help take her wherever you wish. I owe her that for saving my daughter, and for saving me. But when this madness and folly are finished, I will return Miss Kennedy to this hospital and pray to God that she can be saved. Now let us begin."

Inside Eve's room, Patrick was startled by Eve's labored breathing. Her face was the color of paper and damp with perspiration. She moaned out inaudible words, her lips dry, her eyes twitching.

"We must wrap her in several blankets, Miss Kosarin. It is cold and lightly snowing. She must be kept warm."

Joni covered Eve with two heavy woolen blankets, while Patrick, cradling Colleen with ease, tucked her feet and wrapped her head.

Patrick's eyes met Joni's. "Please take Colleen, while I carry Eve out to the cab."

With a smile, Joni accepted Colleen, who was wrapped so completely she could see only a bit of her chin.

"She's a quiet child," Joni said.

"That she is and let's hope she stays that way."

With gentle care, Patrick stooped, slid one arm under Eve's head and shoulders, and the other under her hips. As he lifted her, he uttered a silent prayer. Joni scanned the hallway left and right, then waved that all was clear. Patrick angled out of the room, turned left and started down the hallway.

With Colleen secured, Joni tugged the lantern from the bag, clumsily reached for her coat and hurried off, leaving her elaborate feather hat and the canvas bag behind.

Outside, the breath of cold wind bit into their faces. Still Colleen didn't cry. Joni held her in one arm, her coat draped over the other, the lantern's wire handle gripped in her fingers, swinging like a pendulum. Joni walked briskly, the cab's forward lantern giving off an amber glow, glittering the snow all around them.

"Do you need some help, Mr. Gantly?" Thomas called down from his driver's seat.

"No, thank you, Thomas. Just get ready to speed us along smartly once we're inside."

Inside the cab, Patrick placed Eve in a sitting position. Her head teetered to one side as she groaned and complained.

"Cold... I'm cold. Where am I? Take me home. I want to go home."

Patrick tugged the blankets more securely around her, turned toward the door, reached and took the lantern from Joni, storing it at his feet. He clasped Joni's hand and hauled her and Colleen up and into the cab.

"Let's go, Thomas." Patrick called, pounding the roof with his fist.

Patrick scooted close to Eve, and she leaned easily against him, her head resting on his shoulder.

The cab door closed, Thomas shook the reins, and they were off. Just then, Joni turned to see Darius Foster burst through the side hospital entrance and race after the cab, hands waving, shouting for them to stop.

Patrick stared ahead in fixed determination. He'd made up his mind to see this thing through and nothing was going to stop him.

"Faster, Thomas. Faster!" The horse trotted ahead, across the snow-covered street toward Central Park.

Joni glanced at Patrick and, in the dim light, she was surprised to see a far-sighted shrewdness in his eyes, as if he had a plan for what was about to unfold.

Joni twisted around. "I think Dr. Foster is following us."

"Fine, let him follow. We are going to finish this thing, come what may."

Patrick looked at his daughter, who made gurgling sounds. "Are you awake now, Colleen?"

"Did you feed her before you left?" Joni asked.

"Don't you worry about my Colleen. She's had her supper, and now she's ready for wherever Providence leads us. This little lass has fire in her skin."

Joni believed Patrick was speaking more about himself than about his daughter. Joni heard the crack of Thomas' whip as they entered Central Park at 59th Street and headed north.

"Does the driver know where he's going?"

"Yes, Miss Kosarin. I know of a secluded spot. When we arrive, you tell me if it is appropriate."

Joni rocked Colleen gently as she made little ooh, ooh sounds. "Mr. Gantly... I wrote you another letter, just in case something happens, and we get separated."

"God save us," Patrick said. "Not another cursed letter..."

"Yes. It's in my pocket. I'll give it to you when we stop. Anyway, it tells you what to do once you reach 2016. It includes the name of the hospital where Eve should go; doctors who will know her; where her apartment is with the keys, and how to contact her parents for help. Everything you'll need in the future is in that letter, like I said, just in case. I also have other things you'll need: credit cards, insurance cards and money."

Patrick sighed. "You do believe in this... lantern, don't you, Miss Kosarin?"

"Why are you here with your daughter if you don't believe it, Mr. Gantly? Anyway, you'll want to brace yourself for what is about to come. The world that you are about to see and live in, will seem like a wild storm to you and there is nothing I can say that will prepare you for it."

Patrick's eyes filled with steely determination. "Colleen and I will manage, Miss Kosarin. Don't you have a worry about that."

Eve's eyes opened. "Where am I?"

Joni spoke up. "It's okay, Eve. We're going home."

"I'm so cold…"

Patrick lifted his arm and wrapped her shoulders. "I will try to warm you, Miss Kennedy."

Eve's wide eyes stared up at him. "Patrick?"

"Yes, Miss Kennedy."

"Is that you, Patrick?"

"Yes, I am here."

"Going home? Are we finally going home?"

Patrick cleared his throat. "Yes, Miss Kennedy. We are… We are going home."

Eve nestled her head into his chest. "I am so cold and so happy, Patrick. So hap…" Her voice trailed off and, again, she was out.

The cab bumped and ramped along the snowy carriage path as it climbed a slight hill toward a grove of trees and park benches. Patrick glanced out, squinting.

"There's no one out in this weather, thank God. Yes, we're almost here. Prepare, Miss Kosarin."

Joni faced him. "Patrick, you'll have to get rid of your gun. Where you're going, you won't need it and it will complicate things."

Patrick glowered, grumbling under his breath. "Where I'm going, I no doubt *will* need it," he said, removing it, and leaving it beside him.

The cab bounced to a stop. Eve mumbled out pain, and Colleen oohed.

Thomas dropped down to help Joni exit with Colleen, and then he circled around to help Patrick gingerly ease Eve out of the cab, holding her upright.

"There's the bite of winter in this wind, Detective Gantly," Thomas said, puzzled by the entire adventure. "And the woman looks poorly."

Patrick nodded as he gathered Eve up into his arms and trudged to a lone park bench blanketed with snow. Thomas was ready with a cloth, and he efficiently cleared away the snow. As Joni approached with Colleen and the lantern, Thomas surveyed the scene and then scratched his head. He hurried back to the cab, removed a woolen lap blanket from the backseat and tramped over to Patrick. Thomas placed the blanket on the bench, smoothed it out and assisted Patrick, lowering Eve to the bench.

"Very good, sir," Thomas said, blowing on his cold hands and looking skyward. "I don't believe the snow will be stopping soon, Detective Gantly. I'm sure you have your own good reasons for being out here."

Patrick slipped a hand into his coat and drew out his wallet. He removed several bills and handed them to Thomas. "Thank you, Thomas. You're a good man. Someday, you and I are going to laugh about all this over a pint at Sean's."

Thomas gave a little bow. "Yes, sir. I suppose you'll be wanting me to stay around?"

Patrick looked at Joni, carefully. "Yes, Thomas. Just for a few more minutes."

Joni suddenly grew alarmed. She pointed at the road. Coming toward them were two lighted lanterns and the silhouette of a carriage, growing in size.

"It's Darius!" Joni exclaimed, stress crinkling her eyes. "Dammit!" Joni quickly put on her coat, the first time she'd had the chance.

"Give me Colleen," Patrick said.

Joni did so, while her attention remained on the approaching carriage. "I knew he would follow."

"Get that lantern," Patrick demanded. "Let us end this and be done with this folly."

Thomas watched, in perplexed wonder, as Joni took the lantern to the park bench and set it down next to Eve. Shivering, Joni slipped a hand into her coat pocket and took out a 5"x7" cream-colored envelope. She handed it to Patrick.

"Everything I told you about is in there," Joni said, her voice tight with tension.

From her opposite pocket, Joni retrieved a cardboard box holding wooden matches. Her teeth chattered as she slid the box open.

"Sit next to Eve, Patrick, and wrap your arm around her. Once I light the lantern, it won't take long."

Darius' carriage was nearly on them when Patrick sat down next to Eve, self-consciously, as little flecks of snow pricked his face and dusted Eve's woolen blanket.

"Strike the match and light the damnable lantern," Patrick snapped. "It is bitterly cold, and I fear for Miss Kennedy and Colleen."

Joni fumbled in the box and withdrew a match and struck it. It flared, but before she could cup her hand over the flame, a gust of wind puffed it out.

"Hurry!" Patrick barked.

Eve's lips were a pale blue, and she called out, incoherent. With her breath smoking, Joni reached, struck another match and watched in distress as it burst into flame, then fizzled in the sharp wind.

"Take Colleen and give the matches to me," Patrick said, his hand jutting out.

Joni gathered Colleen into her arms and handed Patrick the matchbox as she glanced up nervously to see Darius emerge from the coach and start for them, his face stretched into a frantic disbelief.

Patrick reached for the lantern, carefully placing it between Eve and himself. He slid the matchbox lid open and plucked out a match. With aggression, he swiped the match against the striker. A spark ignited, and the match blazed. Patrick cupped a hand to shield the flame, while guiding the flickering light through the open glass lantern door toward the wick.

He held his breath as the flame trembled, nearly going out. Patrick touched the wick and watched with relief as the flame caught and danced.

Joni was on her feet, rocking Colleen, when Darius Foster drew up and stopped short, his breath panting smoke, his bold eyes and startled face taking in the scene in utter disbelief.

"What is this madness?" he asked, spreading his hands. "My God, what lunacy has made you all take leave of your senses? Miss Kennedy is dying, and you bring her out in such a night as this?"

From the lantern, a glorious buttery glow grew and expanded, and the light spilled out into the frenzied night, circling the bench, illuminating Patrick's and Eve's faces.

Joni turned, and Darius' eyes widened, the lantern light drawing him in, captivating him.

A cocoon of shimmering light encircled the area, and it warmed and soothed them. The scream of wind and the biting cold of it diminished, and all became quiet and still.

Eve's eyes gently opened, finding Patrick's handsome and astonished face. "Almost home, my love," she said, with a dim smile. "We're almost home, Patrick."

Joni stood on the edge of the light, Colleen still in her arms. To Darius, she said, "Did you read my letter? I'm leaving."

Darius's expression was urgent. "Your letter made no sense, Miss Kosarin."

"I'm going back to my own time. I'm leaving."

Darius shook his head. "I don't understand this; any of this. Where will you go? What are you doing out here? Nothing is making any sense."

Joni leaned, offering Colleen back to Patrick, who welcomed her into his arms, the light bathing the child, her face aglow, her little eyes gleaming and searching.

"I told you everything in the letter. I don't have time to explain it all now."

Darius took a step forward, careful not to step fully into the light. He stretched out his hand. "Don't go, Miss Kosarin, Joan. Please don't go. Stay with me. I will be lost without you. We will be married. I promise you."

There was a whirring sound, like a small motor, and all present glanced about, searching for the source. The golden light swelled into a cone of brilliance, and Patrick, Thomas and Darius all stared in wonder. Thomas back-stepped, stumbled, found his balance and, in a panic, he scurried off into the darkness toward his cab.

Joni went to Eve, crouching down, her face close to her friend. She explored Eve's distant eyes; her expression conflicted. "Eve, should I go or stay? What should I do?"

Eve's voice was feeble. She tried to raise her arm to touch Joni's cheek, but she failed. "I have Patrick and the baby. You have Darius... and the lantern."

Patrick became tensely aware that the air felt unstable and fragile, as if it could shatter. Ready to face the unknown with ready eyes and a fixed chin, he clutched Colleen protectively at his chest, and curved an arm around Eve's shoulders, drawing her in close.

The bench, the ground, all began to dissolve beneath him, swallowing them up. The world around him glittered with dazzling, bluish light, and he grew dizzy and disoriented, feeling the hair on the back of his neck stand up.

Joni and Dr. Foster began to fade, like images on the face of a stream, disappearing into its depths. They drifted and trembled, finally dwindling into a bottomless golden light.

Patrick held fast to his daughter and to Eve. When a brilliant flash of white light blinded him, he felt himself flung away like a piece of straw into a sailing, scattering whirlwind.

CHAPTER 56

"Hey there, man, are you cool?" a voice said.

Patrick was sure he was floating, alone and detached in some infinite void. His body felt in pieces, stretched and scattered, his thoughts circling. He tried to speak but his tongue clogged his mouth, and he couldn't form any words.

"Hey... are you cool, man?"

Patrick forced his sticky eyes open, straining to focus on the figure standing before him. His eyes slowly cleared. He saw a heavy-set young woman in her 20s, wearing an orange coat with big black round buttons, a white ski cap, and a thing swung on her back that looked like a pack.

"Cool?" Patrick forced out. "Yes, cool. Yes, it is cool but not as cold as it was."

"No, man, I mean are you all right? That woman next to you doesn't look so good. And it's cold out for a baby, isn't it?"

Patrick inhaled a gust of a breath and it awakened him, invigorated him. He sat up, suddenly aware that Colleen was still clutched in his arms. He whipped his aching head left and saw Eve, wilted and white, eyes closed.

Patrick shot up and then was swiftly engulfed by a wave of dizzy turbulence. He staggered back down onto the bench, struggling to stay conscious.

"Can I call somebody for you?" the girl said. "Are you homeless?"

Patrick's breath came fast. What had Joni said to him? She'd mentioned a number. As soon as he arrived, he was to have someone call a number. Colleen began to cry, just a little whimpering cry that shook Patrick's memory loose.

"Can you call nine... Call nine and something...?"

His head was throbbing.

"Do you mean call 911?"

Patrick nodded, relieved. "Yes, call 911. Miss Kennedy is very ill. Please call that number. An ambulance... Yes, she needs an ambulance."

In the racing ambulance, Patrick sat terrified with Colleen clutched in his arms, the siren wailing, dome light flashing, and the bright lights of the City blurring by. His heart was pounding, he was sweating, and every sound jarred and spooked him.

He stared numbly at the two paramedics as they prepared Eve for the Emergency Room, their wary eyes occasionally finding him, but not lingering there. They were busy efficiency.

"Will Miss Kennedy be all right?" Patrick asked, his voice shaky.

Eve was on oxygen, and they'd begun IV therapy. Upon their examination in Central Park, they'd promptly called Mt. Sinai Hospital to prepare a room in the ER. As per Patrick's request, they'd also called Dr. Simon Wallister. Later, the doctor had returned their call to say he'd meet them in the ER as soon as possible.

"For now, she's stabilized. What the hell were you all doing in the Park this time of night?" the older of the paramedics asked, yet again. "I just don't get it. I've called the police. Where did she get this gunshot wound?"

Patrick stared blankly outside as the dome light swept the night. He stared at a passing world that seemed a nightmare to him. The fast cars, the endless streams of traffic, the glaring lights, the cellphones and the medical equipment that beeped and pulsed.

"Please save her life," Patrick said, at a near whisper.

"We'll have a pediatrician examine the baby," the younger paramedic said, whose neck and left arm crawled with tattoos. He looked at Patrick doubtfully. "Do you have insurance?"

Patrick nodded. "I have cards," he said, patting his pocket. "Are they used for insurance?"

In the hospital, Eve was whisked away to the ER, and Patrick was instructed where to check her in. He blundered his way to the front desk, disoriented and exhausted. He managed to hand over Eve's insurance and credit cards, allowing an admitting nurse to fill out the appropriate forms while he stared bleary-eyed, Colleen sleeping in his arms.

Soon after, Patrick was approached by a kind, middle-aged woman with gray and white hair, Dr. Blair, a pediatrician. She knew Eve, but she hadn't seen her in a few years. She told Patrick that she'd take Colleen two floors up to be examined and cared for. Patrick released her reluctantly, and only after the doctor assured him that he could visit her whenever he wished.

Patrick's body felt bruised and his mind blunted. As he moved and listened and watched, it was as though he were sleepwalking. He was aware that he was in a kind of shock, unable to absorb this strange, bright and fast world.

In a waiting lounge with orange and blue plastic chairs, Patrick sat, eyes closed, thoughts scrambled. An African American nurse brought him a sandwich and coffee and introduced herself as Nurse Hodges.

Patrick thanked her. "Has there been any word about Miss Kennedy?"

The nurse was confused. "Miss Kennedy?"

"Yes, Miss Evelyn Kennedy, the woman who was in the ambulance with me."

The nurse blinked. "You mean Eve Sharland?"

"No, Miss Evelyn Kennedy. Her name should be on those cards."

The nurse tried to understand. "Sir, I saw her name on the credit card. The name is Sharland. I've known Eve for a long time, although I haven't seen her in over three years. Is Kennedy her married name?"

Patrick stared down. "No…"

"Well then I can definitely tell you that her name is Eve Sharland, not Kennedy."

Patrick closed his eyes and massaged them. He opened them on the nurse and gave her a thin smile. "It seems I am confused. I don't know much about this world," he said, lifelessly. "Nurse, may I ask you a rather unusual question?"

"Of course."

"What day and year is this?"

The nurse scrutinized him: his unfashionable and retro suit of clothes, the shadow of beard and haunted eyes. There was something about him that seemed oddly out of sync and out of place, but she had no idea what that was. "It's December 6, 2019."

"Not 2016?"

"No…" She looked at him strangely, then left the room.

Patrick let the nurse's answer settle, feeling the weight of it on his already flagging spirit. It was an impossible moment, and yet he was obviously anchored in another time, out-of-place and lost.

He drank the coffee and ate the sandwich mechanically, grateful for them, since he couldn't recall the last time he'd eaten. But the food in his stomach made him sleepy and, against his will, his eyes closed and he drifted off.

He was awakened by Nurse Hodges. Two police officers, dressed in uniforms he'd never seen, stood over him with stern expressions. Patrick rubbed his stubble of beard, gazed at his hand and then stood up, feeling sluggish, not sure he had a center of gravity. His body was so heavy with weariness that it felt as though his weight would drop him through the floor. He struggled to be present and appear deferential and eager to please.

"Are you Patrick Gantly?" the heavy-faced cop asked, his tummy sagging over his belt.

"… Yes."

"Do you have identification?"

"No. It was lost in the park."

The two cops exchanged a glance.

"Where do you live?"

Patrick had memorized Eve's New York address on West 107th Street, and he gave it to them.

"What is your relationship to Miss Sharland?"

"Relationship?" Patrick asked, feeling as though his head were stuffed with cotton.

The cops waited.

"Miss Kenne... I mean to say, Miss Sharland and I are traveling companions."

"Traveling to, and from where?"

"My memory is currently unclear about that, I'm afraid."

The heavy cop said, "Are you and Miss Sharland married?"

"No, sir."

"Are you the parents of the baby?"

"I am the father," Patrick answered politely.

"Is Miss Sharland the mother?"

Patrick thought ahead. If he told them that Eve wasn't the mother, then they'd want to know who the mother was, and when and where she died. Patrick decided to keep it simple and lie.

"... Yes."

Nurse Hodges' brown eyes twinkled with questions. She knew Eve, and this surprised her.

"Why were you in Central Park at ten o'clock at night with your baby and Miss Sharland, who is suffering from a gunshot wound? And how did she receive the gunshot wound?"

Patrick saw suspicion and doubt swelling in the cops' eyes, and he knew he'd have to strike the right tone. "It has been a day of confusion."

The cops waited for more. Nurse Hodges stood by, engrossed. Patrick knew he sounded strange and evasive, but he had no other choice.

"Officers, quite honestly, my memory is impaired. I can only say that about four days ago, Miss Sharland was cleaning my .32 revolver when it went off, the bullet passing through her shoulder. She, not wanting to create suspicion and cause unnecessary alarm for her family and colleagues, decided, as a nurse, to treat the wound herself. She did so, and I assisted her. As we know now, she and I collectively made a wrong decision, and that is why she is here."

"Is the handgun registered?" the heavy cop asked.

"In anger, I threw it into the Hudson River."

The thinner cop, who had a very straight nose and large ears, was taking notes. He glanced up from his pad and stared directly into Patrick's face. "What has caused your confusion, Mr. Gantly?"

Patrick decided to play the part of the confused man, glancing around the room as though something had been misplaced. "Since the pistol accident, and Miss Sharland's ultimate decline in health, I have not been myself. Frankly put, I have been greatly distressed. I'm afraid I have not slept well, and my usual clear and focused mind has fallen into forgetfulness and disorder. I find I am often confused. I can only say that I was on my way to the hospital when we stopped to rest on a bench in the park."

The cops and Nurse Hodges noticed Patrick's rumpled suit, his choice of words, and his arcane use of formal language. They were puzzled by it, but it helped to bolster his case that he was confused.

The thin cop asked, "Were you born in the United States, Mr. Gantly?"

"Yes, I was."

At that moment, a salt-and-pepper-haired middle-aged man entered the room, wearing a white coat over his scrubs. He was ramrod straight, alert, with quick intelligent eyes, and he wore black-rimmed glasses. He assessed the gathering, his eyes swiftly resting on Patrick. "Are you Patrick Gantly?"

Patrick nodded. "Yes…"

The doctor pardoned himself to the policemen and stepped over to Patrick. "I'm Dr. Simon Wallister, Eve's friend."

The men shook hands.

"How is Miss Sharland, Doctor?" Patrick asked, with urgent concern. "Has she improved?"

Dr. Wallister was surprised by Patrick's use of Eve's surname. "I believe she is out of danger. The wound was thoroughly cleaned, and she is on antibiotics. She is stable and resting in the ICU. I want to keep her there overnight for observation, but tomorrow we should be able to move her to a private room and, if all goes well, I will discharge her home in two or three days."

"And what of my daughter, Colleen? Do you know how she is? I seem to be confused as to where she is."

"Colleen is doing just fine. She's been fed, and she's sleeping."

Patrick let out a little sigh. "Well, that is good then. Very good."

Dr. Wallister said something else, but Patrick didn't hear him. He had a moment of sudden bafflement and deep uncertainty. If Eve was discharged home in two days, where would he and Colleen go? Would they have to stay with her? Patrick knew nothing about this electric, pulsing and rushing time. He had no means, nor employment, and he knew no one living in this time, and he knew absolutely nothing about the ways of this world.

As Patrick stood pondering, Dr. Wallister turned to speak to the cops, asking them if they had any further questions, mentioning that it was obvious Patrick was exhausted and needed rest.

At first reluctant, they finally relented after Dr. Wallister mentioned that he'd known Eve for years, and that she was one of the most skilled and professional nurses he'd ever worked with. The doctor said, "I'll vouch for both of them, Patrick and Eve, and there are other doctors and nurses who will do the same." He concluded by stating that it was obvious no crime had been committed and that Eve was improving.

After the cops and Nurse Hodges had gone, Patrick and Dr. Wallister were alone, neither speaking for a time. Finally, Simon placed his hands on his hips and stared candidly and soberly at Patrick.

"All right. No more bullshit. Who the hell are you and what happened to Eve? I haven't seen her in over three years."

CHAPTER 57

Patrick awoke in darkness, heart pounding, eyes wide and staring, his body drenched in sweat. His loud voice echoed back at him. He'd called out for Colleen. Where was she?

It took frantic seconds before Patrick recognized the room. He was in the guest bedroom of Dr. Wallister's condo on the Upper West Side of Manhattan, in the year 2019!

Colleen was in a spare bedroom next door, where Dr. Wallister's wife, Edith, had put her the night before. She was also a nurse, who'd raised two kids. She'd been kind and gracious when Dr. Wallister showed up with Patrick, Colleen cradled in his arms.

The night before, when Dr. Wallister had confronted Patrick in the hospital lounge, Patrick had remained calm and stoic.

"Dr. Wallister… When Miss Sharland is able, she will tell you everything you want to know. Right now, I am simply too spent and exhausted to explain anything. If you will please tell me where I may find lodgings for the night, I will take my daughter and leave you in peace."

Dr. Wallister relented, and then he invited Patrick to stay with him and his wife. Patrick lacked the strength to resist.

In the bedroom, Patrick saw a digital clock, its amber light glowing 4:24 a.m. He sat up, cushioning his back with a pillow and, in the confidential night, he fought back tears.

He had always been in control of himself, shouldering trials and misfortunes with rigid acceptance and bull-headed obstinance, except of course, when Emma died. But now, in this time of the future, in this distant, strange and foreign land, he felt utterly lost and at sea, like a tall ship with broken masts and flapping sails.

Fatigue soon overtook him, and he slumped left, falling back to sleep. Toward dawn, floating, wispy images and faces appeared in his inner mind. They hovered on the edge of his memory as he lingered in a half-dream state.

Before he could fully awaken, an inner movie began to play on the screen of his mind, projecting images that triggered memories from another time and place.

Incredibly, he saw himself in the past being shot, and Eve saving his life by using a lantern to transport him into the future. He saw himself in that future with Eve and a dog, strolling in a park on a bright summer day. Suddenly, he knew, without any doubt, that he and Eve had met before, and they had been lovers! He was stunned to witness their marriage ceremony. Yes, they had been married, and in the year 2019, she had become pregnant with his child! He remembered the awe and joy and excitement they'd shared, anticipating the child's birth.

And then, in moments of rapt wonder, Patrick watched another movie being presented in his head.

Eve held a lantern out over the churning Hudson River. She released it and it dropped, plunging into the water in a white splash. As it disappeared under a curling wave, a flash of golden light rocketed up like a Roman candle, shooting past Eve's and Patrick's faces into the infinite dark sky, briefly piercing the clouds in an explosion of bluish white light and then fading into dark, moving clouds.

They stood cold and shivering, gazing up, speechless and worried. The night was a fury of chaotic snow and biting wind.

"Let's get out of here," Patrick said. "Let's get that Christmas tree and go home. We're finished here."

"Did we do the right thing, Patrick?" Eve said, staring down into the water.

He wrapped his arm about her shoulders. "Don't worry, my love, everything will be all right."

Patrick was fully awake now, as more scenes and images came crashing in. Somewhere in his mind, doors opened, bells rang, and curtains were flung back, allowing gleaming sun to stream in, banishing shadows, revealing memories that had been buried and forgotten.

He was still in a kind of trance, caught in two worlds, mentally struggling to merge his two halves, past and present, into a recognizable whole.

He'd left the world of 1884, and now it was a fading dream, receding into the depths of his mind. The world he awoke to today seemed both strange and familiar, both frightening and thrilling. How would he ever be able to put all the jumbled pieces of his jigsaw life back together?

Patrick stood up slowly, feeling oddly reborn. He opened the blinds, walked to the mirror and studied his face. Even the light was different in this time, and yet there he was, Patrick. Those were his eyes, his cheeks, his forehead. He pressed his hands against the sides of his face, as if to force the various parts of himself to unite, to solidify into this new version of himself. He walked to the window and looked out onto the street, to the dark tree limbs, to the parked cars, to the sparrows hovering against the cold. A woman dressed in a red jacket was walking her dog on the sidewalk. The woman reminded him of Eve. Eve! Laughter and joy suddenly bubbled up inside him. Eve! His heart was alive with love for Eve. Incredibly, he understood now what she had done: she had risked everything to time travel and bring them back together. Because of her courage and persistence, he had found her again, and once again, he was wildly in love with Eve.

Early afternoon of the following day, Dr. Wallister gave Eve the all-clear sign. She had had made a remarkable recovery and could go home.

Patrick arrived at the hospital, cradling Colleen, and went striding down the hospital corridor toward Eve's room. As the blood coursed through him, it brought lucidity, excitement, desire, and a light pounding rhythm of new life.

Dr. Wallister met him outside Eve's room. "I'll leave you here, Patrick," Dr. Wallister said. "She's anxious to see you both."

"Thank you for all your help and hospitality, Dr. Wallister."

The Doctor twisted up his lips, inspecting Patrick once again with suspicion. "I can't wait to hear from Eve who the hell you really are and what happened to you both. Go on now, she's waiting."

Inside, Eve was sitting up in bed, her right arm wrapped in a sling and the other swiping through an E-tablet. A small tabletop Christmas tree sat on the table next to her bed, blinking colored lights. On the opposite side was a flowering poinsettia and 24 red roses.

When her eyes lifted and she saw Patrick, they expanded in joy and longing; her face yielding to love. She folded her hands, took in a breath and sighed it out, audibly, with a little smile, feeling an intense, unmatchable pleasure.

"Well now, there you are. There's my family. I've been waiting for you both."

Patrick approached the bed, tentative. Eve looked him over. "I like your new clothes. Where did you get them?"

"Marshall's. On sale. Not bad, huh?"

"I like the red and green flannel shirt. Very festive."

Patrick placed the sleeping Colleen on the bed near Eve. She was dressed in a pink and white snowsuit. Eve cradled the baby as Patrick unzipped the snowsuit and removed the hood. "She's beautiful," Eve whispered.

"And you look lovely," Patrick said to Eve. "How do you feel?"

"Like I want to go home… like today. Like now."

They stared; their eyes tender. Eve said, "On the phone, Detective Sergeant Gantly, you said that you remember everything. Is that true? Do you remember everything, including falling in love with me?"

Patrick nodded. "Yes. Thank you for saving us."

416

"Thank you for bringing us home. You were not so easy back there, Patrick."

"Thank God you were persistent, but you must have known that even the 1884 Patrick had fallen in love with you."

Eve batted her eyes playfully. "Flattery heals all pain, sir, and it will get you quite far in our marital bed."

"You can still make me blush, madam."

"Detective Gantly, we'll have to get married again, you know."

Patrick shifted his weight, thinking about it. His eyes twinkled, and he gave her one of his sexy little grins. "That might be fun, especially the part about the honeymoon. I liked our last honeymoon."

Eve gave him an extravagant smile. "And I like your attitude, Patrick Gantly."

"Well, I guess we have a lot to talk about," he said.

"Indeed we do."

Just then, Colleen stirred. She opened her eyes and began to squirm. "And how is our little Colleen?" Eve asked.

Patrick scooped the child up. "She's as good as gold, and she is very happy to see you," he said, taking one of the baby's pudgy little hands and waving it at Eve. "See, she's waving at you."

Eve waved back with a shiny grin. "Hey, there, Colleen." And then to Patrick, she said, "By the way, thanks for sending the little Christmas tree and flowers."

"Since Dr. Wallister wouldn't let us see you yesterday, Colleen and I went Christmas shopping."

"You two are my best Christmas presents. Come here and give me a kiss, darling."

Patrick went to her, stooped and kissed her warm lips. After they broke the kiss, Eve reached up with her free hand and touched his lips with a finger. "Yes, I'm home."

Patrick gently stroked her face and she sighed, welcoming the feel of his hand once more. She stared happily into his loving eyes and grinned flirtatiously.

"Finally. I have been waiting for that kiss for a hundred and thirty-five years."

EPILOGUE

Patrick stood on a stepladder, leaning over the eight-foot Christmas tree, angel tree topper in hand. With grunting effort, he reached to place the white, flowing angel dead center on the vertical limb. After completion, he leaned back, appraising it with some pride.

"I like it. Perfect."

In the background, Nat King Cole sang *The Christmas Song,* and outside the bay windows, snow flurries drifted.

"It's not centered," Eve said from below, with Colleen couched in her healthy arm. Her right arm was in a blue support arm sling, and remained stiff and sore, but she loved holding Colleen for short periods in her good arm.

Eve took two steps back, looking up. "Yeah… It's definitely not centered."

"Well, it looks centered to me," Patrick said with some defiance.

"Well, you're up there, and I'm down here, and I'm telling you that the angel is not centered. She's leaning to the left. Just nudge her a little and you've got it. We can't have a crooked angel on Christmas Eve."

Patrick screwed up his lips with some irritation, stretched out his hand and readjusted the angel.

"Too much," Eve said. "Just a little. Now you've shoved her too far right."

Colleen made a spitting sound, her hand reaching up to grab a loose strand of Eve's hair. She'd pinned it back so loosely that parts fell across her face. She kissed Colleen's nose.

"See, even Colleen says it's crooked."

"Okay, okay. I've got both of you ganging up on me. How is it now?"

Eve took another step back. "Perfect. You've got it. Oh, wow, it's such a beautiful tree, and I love the colored lights and Victorian ornaments."

Patrick climbed down, moved the ladder and evaluated his work. "It's a bigger tree than last year's."

"It smells heavenly," Eve said, smiling. "It reminds me of when I was a girl. My father insisted on heading off to the woods and cutting down his own tree. It always smelled so fresh."

Patrick made a face. "What time are your parents coming tomorrow?"

"Don't play dumb with me, Patrick Gantly. I've told you at least five times."

"And I have conveniently forgotten five times. Ten in the morning?"

"Yes, sir. We have to face this. They haven't seen me in three years, at least in their time."

"I'm glad you didn't tell them you were back until yesterday. They would have descended on us like a charging army."

"They are very freaked out. Dad had his FBI friends and a private detective looking all over for me. I mean, I just disappeared in 2016."

Patrick sighed. "I just wish you hadn't told them you got lost in the Amazon. Of course they didn't believe that."

"Well, I had to tell them something. I'm going to get the third degree, especially when it comes to you and Colleen. Thank God Dad is a rank capitalist, and he kept this place, renting it as an Airbnb."

"I dread having to start that relationship all over again. I wish *they* remembered everything that happened in the past like I do."

"Don't worry about it. They'll love you, just like they did the last time."

"Your father did not love me the last time. He tolerated me and he never trusted me."

"He doesn't trust anybody. He's in the FBI, Patrick, and he'll be able to get you an identity like he did the last time. And, anyway, they're my family and I love them."

Patrick shook his head with another sigh, pocketing his hands in his jeans. "Are you going to tell them you twisted your arm when you tripped and fell while jogging?"

"Yeah. Why not? I certainly can't tell them the truth. My father won't believe it, of course, but what can he do? He'll rant and rave, while my mother will cry and say I've put her through hell."

Patrick closed the ladder, shaking his head. "I can hardly wait," he said sarcastically. He carried the ladder to the closet and stored it.

When he returned to the living room, Eve had shifted her gaze from the dazzling Christmas tree to the window where she watched the play of snow in the agitated wind. She hummed along with Nat King Cole as he sang *Away in a Manger*.

"What are you thinking?" Patrick asked, sensing the sudden change of mood.

"It looks like we're going to have a white Christmas."

"And?"

"And I miss Joni and Georgy Boy, especially now, at Christmas. And, of course, I'm still wondering what happened to the lantern."

"What lantern, Eve? There is no lantern. For once in our lives, there is no lantern to worry about."

Eve turned to face him. She had a look of both contentment and agitation. "Yes, I know."

"I know you, Eve, and there's something else going on behind those eyes."

"Colleen's getting heavy and my shoulder's starting to hurt. Can you take her?"

Eve handed the baby off to Patrick, then she rounded the couch and sat down before the gleaming fire, gazing reflectively into the orange glow.

Patrick stared into Colleen's brand-new sparkling eyes. "Colleen, my daughter, when you grow up, I hope you will have a more normal life than your parents have had."

Eve twisted around to Patrick. "I just can't stop thinking about everything. I have dreams about Joni and Georgy Boy... And dreams about the lantern."

"I know, I know. I keep running the whole time travel thing in my head too. Even after two weeks, I still can't come up with anything. I always end up at the same spot. In 2016, you and Joni left Georgy Boy with this Ricky Myron, who was also going to keep the lantern. You time traveled back to 1884 and then assumed we'd arrive back here in 2016. But we didn't return to 2016. We are here in 2019."

Eve cut in. "... But it's not the same 2019 we were living in before we destroyed the lantern, because Joni and Georgy Boy and Ricky are not here."

Patrick said, "And if Ricky Myron can't be found anywhere, in this social media world, it means he doesn't exist, which logically means that Georgy Boy doesn't exist, which means that neither does the lantern. The lantern is gone, which means we finally don't have to think about it or worry about it anymore. I'm sorry about Georgy Boy. He was a great dog, but let's look on the bright side: we are finished with the lantern forever. We can finally have the normal life we wanted the last time we were in 2019."

Eve sat wrapped in thought. "Patrick... I haven't mentioned something else to you because I didn't want to think about it. I don't even want the thought in my head, but it is in my head and I can't get rid of it."

Patrick drifted over and eased down beside her. Colleen's eyes fluttered closed, and she was soon asleep. Eve looked at Patrick with apprehension while she gently stroked Colleen's soft head.

"I'm willing to bet that if we drive to Pennsylvania to *The Time Past Antique Shop*, we'll find the lantern sitting on that back shelf."

"Then we won't go to *The Time Past Antique Shop*," Patrick said firmly. "We will never go there again. We don't need the lantern. And, anyway, the old shop surely doesn't exist anymore."

When the doorbell buzzed, Eve jumped, and Patrick turned toward the door.

"Oh God, who is that?" Eve said, suddenly frightened. "I hope it's not my parents, or somebody from the past."

Patrick arose, still cradling Colleen. "Relax. It's okay."

He stepped over to the speaker button and pressed it. "Who is it?"

There was some static on the other end. "I'm looking for Patrick and Eve Gantly." a light female voice said.

"Yes… who are you, and what do you want?"

"I'm Gabrielle Pinton. I'm an attorney at Miles, Freedman and Pinton. I have a letter and package for you."

Eve stood at Patrick's shoulder. "Attorney?"

Patrick shrugged a shoulder, handed Colleen back to Eve and buzzed the woman in. He stood waiting in the hallway as the elevator door opened. A tall, slim, attractive woman in her late 40s exited the elevator, her one-inch heels clicking across the marble floor as she approached Patrick. Her wavy, black hair was styled in a short bob, and she wore a long, cashmere winter coat and stylish, clear-rimmed glasses. A gold strapped purse was swung over one shoulder, and she gripped a brown leather briefcase. In her free arm, she hugged an elaborately wrapped gift.

She met Patrick with a formal smile. "Mr. Patrick Gantly?" she asked.

"I am."

"I'm Gabrielle Pinton."

"Please come in."

Eve was waiting nervously in the living room, having already placed Colleen in her baby crib near the couch. She'd covered her tummy and legs with a light blue blanket.

After introductions, Eve hung Gabrielle's coat in the hall closet while Patrick accepted the gift. Eve joined the other two in the living room as they politely offered each other a "Merry Christmas."

Gabrielle declined tea, stating that the business at hand wouldn't take long. Eve and Patrick sat on the couch and Gabrielle in the comfy leather chair to their right. Her gray business suit was fashionable, and it had a tailored fit.

She inhaled a breath and smiled it out. "Well, I am very pleased to be the bearer of good news. But first, a little history. My law firm represents the fourth such law firm in this matter, since the items at hand were first willed to you in 1900."

Eve and Patrick traded glances, anticipating what was to come.

"In 1900, the item in that lovely Christmas wrapping was included in a trust fund drawn up in Evelyn Aleta Sharland's name. It also consists of bonds and cash."

Gabrielle opened her briefcase and removed a 9"x12" manila envelope. She stood and handed it to Eve.

"Inside, Ms. Sharland, you will find recent financial statements of your holdings, as well as a letter written to you in 1900 by Mrs. Joan Katherine Kosarin Foster."

Eve's attentive eyes fell on the envelope. "Joni?"

Ms. Pinton returned to the chair. "As part of my instructions, as per Mrs. Foster's will, the letter should be opened and read in my presence. Afterwards, I'll answer any questions you might have. Going forward, I will be happy to represent you in any and all financial and legal transactions which may arise as a result of this matter."

Eve looked at Patrick then pinched back the copper pins, opened the flap on the envelope and reached in. She retrieved a letter-sized envelope, yellowed with age, and she held it up, studying the clear handwriting on its face. It was addressed to Eve at her current address. The letter was sealed. Eve slipped her thumb under the flap and opened it.

Swallowing away nerves, Eve drew out the folded pages, gently smoothed them out, and began to read.

Dear Eve and Patrick:

Well, who would have ever believed that I'd get old? Not me. In case you haven't seen the date and year on the upper right of this letter, it is Christmas Eve,1943, and I am eighty-nine years old. Okay, I just saw your jaw drop.

I'm writing this letter to you from my son-in-law's family's Georgian-style mansion in Tarrytown, New York. It has nine bedrooms and eleven bathrooms. Are you impressed?

Eve, what a life I have had. I have missed you terribly, but we both had to take our own separate paths and do what we had to do. There were times when I really missed the modern world. But overall, I had a full and delightful life, and I don't regret living my life as I did.

It didn't start out so good. After you and Patrick left, Darius had second thoughts about marrying me, and I lived as his mistress, more or less, for three years, until 1887. Don't judge me, Eve. I was very much in love with him, and I knew that he was in love with me. He said our marriage had to wait until he could reconcile various family financial, legal, real estate, political and social issues. To his credit, he did not get engaged to Elizabeth Atkins Worthing, although he faced a lot of family pressure and push-back over it.

Finally, one evening, we were having dinner at Delmonico's, where, by the way, I had a clear view of Nikola Tesla having dinner alone at a table nearby. Anyway, during our dinner, I told Darius that either he would consent to marry me then and there, or I was going to use the lantern to return home to the future.

After you and Patrick vanished, I took the lantern and hid it. That lantern scared Darius to death, and he wanted no part of it.

Anyway, we were married six months later and, sure enough, his father worked against his only son to cut Darius out of the family money and property. I met them only once, and it was not very pleasant. His father was a tall, fierce man, who mostly ignored me. His mother was stout, cold and condescending. Fortunately, Darius had been raised by a governess who was the sweetest woman. We hit it off.

In the three-year interval, as we waited to get married, Darius managed to secure a good-sized fortune for himself, and his father couldn't do anything about it.

*After all that drama, Darius and I married, and we were very happy. We had two wonderful children: a son, William H. Foster, born in 1889, now 54 years old, and a daughter, Lavinia Joan Foster, born in 1891. William is a successful banker here in New York, and Lavinia is a smart, elegant woman, married to Benedict Vanderbilt, yes one of **the** Vanderbilts! You would not believe the mansion she lives in. The Gilded Age has come and gone, but Lavinia still lives in luxury, like a queen.*

Sadly, the world is in the midst of World War II, and even though I know what the outcome will be, it is not easy to see all the loss and suffering that is going on.

My son, William, is very much involved in Washington politics, and he knows President Franklin Roosevelt quite well and, yes, I have met the President too. Eve, I was tempted to tell him a few things that could have shortened the war but, thank God, I didn't. I have never uttered one word about future events or anything about the lantern, even to my kids. To tell you the truth, as I got a little older, I locked that lantern up and never wanted to see it or touch it again. Darius and I both knew the power of it. Tesla knew the power of it.

Eve, I attended Nikola Tesla's funeral on January of this year, 1943. Did you know that it was a state funeral held at the Cathedral of St. John the Divine? Of course the Cathedral is located only a few blocks from where you live. How weird is that? I never went back to see him, but I read about him. He became a sad man, I think, or maybe he was just too far ahead of the rest of us.

I thought of you and Patrick after Tesla's funeral, and I had my chauffeur drive to West 107th Street, so I could see your brownstone. Of course I knew you wouldn't be there. Anyway, it really freaked me out. I got out of the car, and since my knees are weak (there's no knee replacement surgery in this time) Lavinia helped me up the first two steps, and I gazed up at your bay windows and, being the crazy old woman that I am, I waved at you and called out your names. Lavinia thought I was completely out of my mind.

Well, I'm going to wrap this up now, Eve and Patrick. Darius passed away in 1930 from a heart attack. He was at the hospital examining a patient when he keeled over and died. That was it. We had no time to say goodbye, and I hated that. I was sad for a long time, but I finally moved on. Darius and I had a lot of good years together, and he was always good and kind and generous to me. I am a wealthy old woman, and I have my children, whom I love more than my own life.

Eve, I think of you every day and, yes, I miss you every day. We had so much fun together, didn't we? I have good friends, but none like you, a person I could say anything to. You were my sister, Eve, and I still love you. My old eyes are misting up as I write this.

I am not well. It's my heart and blood pressure. I don't believe I'll live much longer, so I'm writing this letter to tie up loose ends.

Do you remember the necklace and bracelet we time traveled with? Remember we pawned the necklace, but we never did pawn the bracelet? Well, guess what? Years ago, Darius had it appraised. We sold it for a good price, and I told him I wanted the money to go into a trust fund for you. You should have seen his eyes. Anyway, he said he had a friend, a broker who could invest the money, and I agreed. Years later, my son, William, took over management of the money. He is quite gifted at making money.

In 1943, the financial statement says your money is now worth a little over six thousand dollars. I don't know how much that will be in your time, but it doesn't matter. It was all for fun anyway. By the time this letter reaches you, the money will have been continually invested. Maybe you will get a couple hundred thousand. Not bad, huh?

I'm getting tired, Eve, so I'll end this letter. I'm sure you know by now that the beautifully wrapped Christmas present holds something from the past. I hope it's wrapped beautifully. I put that clearly in the will.

Anyway, I have willed the lantern to you. It is the same lantern that sent you back home in December 1884. Now I'd love to see your faces.

Okay, here's the thing, Eve. I'm not taking any chances. I have instructed the law firm I have entrusted all this business with to visit you and Patrick on Christmas Eve, 2016. I know how volatile that lantern is, so I stipulated that if you are not there in 2016, they are to return on

Christmas Eve 2017, 2018 and 2019, or until they make definite contact with you. As I said, I'm not taking any chances, girlfriend.

I hate to say goodbye, Eve. I hope you, and Patrick, and the baby have the best of lives, just as I have had. It could have been improved only if you had been here with me.

And now, your old friend, who is very old and very tired, is signing off, but maybe not for good. We may see each other again, in some future time and place. Who knows? After all, you now have the lantern, the last Nikola Tesla lantern, the last message in a bottle. Oh, yes, and don't forget to read the message I have placed in the lantern. You know where I put it, don't you?

All my love to you, Eve and Patrick,
Joni

Tarrytown, New York,
December 24, 1943

With damp eyes, Eve handed the letter to Patrick, and waited in silence until he'd read it and handed it back to her.

Gabrielle Pinton opened her briefcase and removed a financial statement. "Shall I read the current financial statement from Mrs. Foster's will?"

Eve nodded. "Yes, please."

"As of last month, the total amount, including equities, bonds and treasuries, is worth one million, eight-hundred and forty-one thousand, nine-hundred and fourteen dollars and seventy-three cents."

Eve and Patrick stared ahead, astounded.

After Ms. Pinton had gone, Patrick brought the wrapped lantern to Eve. Neither spoke as Eve slowly tugged off the red bow and anxiously removed the paper, revealing an old cardboard box. Patrick retrieved his pocketknife and sliced through the brown tape, opened the flaps, and let Eve remove the old newspaper used as packing paper.

Eve hesitated, passing a final glance at Patrick, who was resigned.

"Let's do it, Eve."

Eve reached in, gripped the wire handle and lifted the lantern up and out. They stared, absorbed, as Eve sat it down on the carpet between them. There it was, 12 inches high and made of iron, with a tarnished green/brown patina. It had four glass windowpanes, with wire guards and a painted anchor design on each side of the roof, one anchor painted a faded red and the other a faded blue.

Eve opened the glass panel door and peered inside, seeing a small envelope wedged behind the pane. She reached in, and with two fingers wriggled it free. The envelope, yellowed with age, was sealed. Eve thumbed it open and removed a photograph and a slip of yellowed paper that had writing on it.

Eve held it up for Patrick to see. "Look, it's a photo of Joni and her family!"

The vintage black-and-white photo showed the family posing in a photography studio. Darius and Joni wore stylish clothes of the period, Darius standing straight and somber in a dark suit and waistcoat, with a perfectly appointed tie. Joni was seated beside him in an elegant Victorian chair, wearing a sumptuous dress and an elaborate silk and feather hat.

To Joni's left were two children, dressed formally. The serious, studious boy, about 11 years old, wore glasses, and he stared into the camera with a challenge. The pretty, nine-year-old girl had bouncing curls and bewitching eyes, with a faraway dreamy stare, her features very much like Joni's.

Eve turned the photo over and read the inscription: *June 1900, New York.* Eve handed the photo to Patrick and read the note aloud:

Eve and Patrick: This is my wonderful family in 1900. Aren't they the best? I could never think about using the lantern to return home once my kids were born.

Eve… notice my dress in the photo. It's in La Belle Époque style: big bust, tiny waist and rounded backside, all achieved with the help of a thing called a swan-bill corset. Yes, I'm still wearing those damned corsets! Lol. Can you see

Elyse Douglas

I've gained weight?   Miss you and love you, always!

Joni

An hour later, Eve, and Patrick were wandering the carriage path of Riverside Park. It was snowing, and the night air was still and crisp. Patrick carried Colleen in a baby carrier baby sling, wrapped in a warm blanket, her head covered by a red cap.

"By the way," Patrick said, wrapping a strong arm around Eve. "We have to be back at the house in an hour."

"Why?"

"One of your Christmas presents will be delivered."

Eve stopped and turned toward him. "Okay... And you're telling me this because?"

Patrick grinned. "I can't keep the secret any longer. Because, Ms. Evelyn Aleta Gantly, I found a new Georgy Boy. He's younger, and he has black spots, not brown, but the moment I saw him, I knew he belonged to us."

Eve leaped straight up in a yelp of happiness, dancing about, kicking up clouds of snow. She reached for Patrick's neck and pulled him down to her lips. She kissed him, giving him quick pecks on the lips and cheeks.

"I love you, Patrick Gantly."

"As I do you. Merry Christmas, my darling."

436

"I am so happy," Eve said, beaming. "Let's sing a Christmas carol."

"You know I can't carry a tune to save my life."

"It's okay. It's quiet. Nobody will hear you. Let's sing *White Christmas*. Come on, you can do it."

Patrick gave her a doubtful look. "You start, I'll follow."

Eve took his hand, tugged at it, and they sauntered off, Eve singing in a low contralto and Patrick stumbling over the words, his voice searching high and low for the elusive notes.

Colleen awoke and started to cry, but Eve lifted her head and sang on.

Snow gently covered the streets and was not deep; flecks of it danced in the amber streetlights and sailed like happiness, sugar-coating the trees, turning the world into romance.

Thank You!

Thank you for taking the time to read *The Christmas Eve Secret*. If you enjoyed it, please consider telling your friends or posting a short review. Word of mouth is an author's best friend, and it is much appreciated.

Thank you,
Elyse Douglas

Other novels by Elyse Douglas that you might enjoy:

The Christmas Diary
The Summer Diary
The Other Side of Summer
The Christmas Women
The Christmas Eve Letter (A Time Travel Novel) Book 1
The Christmas Eve Daughter (A Time Travel Novel) Book 2
The Lost Mata Hari Ring (A Time Travel Novel)
The Christmas Town (A Time Travel Novel)
The Summer Letters
Time Change (A Time Travel Novel)
Daring Summer (Romantic Suspense)
The Date Before Christmas
Christmas Ever After
Christmas for Juliet
The Christmas Bridge
Wanting Rita

www.elysedouglas.com

Editorial Reviews

THE LOST MATA HARI RING – A Time Travel Novel
by Elyse Douglas

This book is hard to put down! It is pitch-perfect and hits all the right notes. It is the best book I have read in a while!
5 Stars!
--Bound4Escape Blog and Reviews

The characters are well defined, and the scenes easily visualized. It is a poignant, bitter-sweet emotionally charged read.
5-Stars!
--Rockin' Book Reviews

This book captivated me to the end!
--StoryBook Reviews

A captivating adventure...
--Community Bookstop

...Putting *The Lost Mata Hari Ring* down for any length of time proved to be impossible.
--Lisa's Writopia

I found myself drawn into the story and holding my breath to see what would happen next...
--Blog: A Room Without Books is Empty

Editorial Reviews

THE CHRISTMAS TOWN – A Time Travel Novel
by Elyse Douglas

The Christmas Town is a beautifully written story. It draws
you in from the first page, and fully engages you up until the
very last. The story is funny, happy, and magical. The
characters are all likable and very well-rounded. This is a
great book to read during the holiday season, and a
delightful read during any time of the year.
--Bauman Book Reviews

I would love to see this book become another one of those
beloved Christmas film traditions, to be treasured over the
years! The characters are loveable; the settings vivid.
Period details are believable. A delightful read at any time of
year! Don't miss this novel!
--A Night's Dream of Books

Made in the USA
Middletown, DE
21 January 2020